Mars on the Rise
TOP SHELF
An imprint of Torquere Press Publishers
PO Box 2545
Round Rock, TX 78680
Copyright 2012 by Rae Gee
Cover illustration by Alessia Brio
Published with permission
ISBN: 978-1-61040-305-4

www.torquerepress.com

First Torquere Press Printing: April 2012
Printed in the USA

**If you liked Mars on the Rise,
you might enjoy:**

A Private Hunger by Sean Michael

Alphabet Soup CB Conwy

The Deviations Series by Chris Owen and Jodi Payne

Drawing Closer by Jane Davitt

Mars on the Rise

Mars on the Rise
by Rae Gee

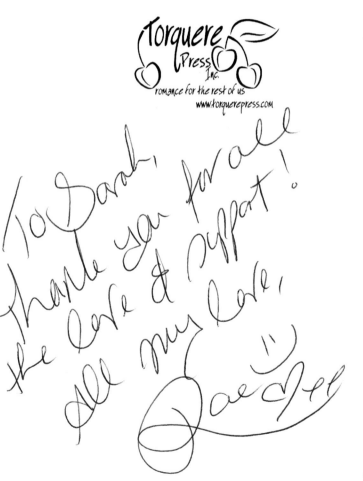

Mars on the Rise

DEDICATION

For Mum, Dad, Andy and Joe. Thank you for all your love, encouragement, help and patience. And Alex, for answering odd questions at inane hours of the day.

Mars on the Rise

PROLOGUE

The body was laid out on the hard wooden floor, naked, limbs and torso delicately curling as they tried to reach each other in some far off dreamland. Fingers, splayed and broken, spread over the varnished floor, bloody trails left in their wake as the body's occupant tried to pull itself into a different, less awkward position. Across one hand swirled the unmistakable image of a mouse crouched in a claw.

But that would not happen. Never would the lithe creature on the floor walk tall and proud again. Never would its face twist into the smile that had dazzled a million people. Never would its eyes gleam with the innocent charm of the forever young. And never would its childlike laughter fill a room. Instead, it would remain the discarded toy, only picked up when its owner needed something to shake and break.

The fingers slowly inched through the pooled blood, making grotesque curls and swirls as they spidered closer to the leather bound book. What was written upon its crisp, white pages had once been a secret between it and the person on the floor.

But no longer. Once the snarling menace that ruled the secluded house had found it, the special bond between writer and written had been snapped like a twig. Pages, as pale and as bloodstained as the whimpering human's skin, were scattered about the empty room. Some lay in piles while others, jagged tears separating words from their partners, had been thrown to the wind, escaping through the room's one broken window. The window that now hid its healing light behind heavy, bolted shutters.

A tiny, kitten-like whimper left the child-man's mouth as his fingers swept over the supple leather, imprinting and marking it with his fingerprints. It was the only thing that linked him to a life long forgotten.

CHAPTER 1

Once upon a time, before this life, Cedo had been a darling. An artisan, a storyteller, a weaver of dreams, forever spinning yarns with the tendrils of past ideas left dangling by their disenchanted owners. People had traveled to listen to Cedo, to watch his hazel eyes sparkle as he lost himself in whatever tale he was winding that evening. Beneath the stars he would stand, lips twisted into a happy smile, thick, honey-blond hair lifting in the wind as he raised his hands high into the night sky.

The end of the pier was where he took these flights of fancy. A monument to steel and engineering, it rose from the tumultuous sea like a creaking, snarling whale. Propped on the winding railings, Cedo would turn his eyes heavenward, his lips would curl into his trademark smile, and the story would begin. What fell from his lips in the following hours mesmerized those who found him.

On one such night, Cedo sat on the railings, one leg on either side as he dared the curling waves fifty feet below him to claim him. Forever filled with the mischief of a child, he turned back to his growing audience. Men, women and a smattering of children stared back at him. Cedo watched them with glee, taking in their wide-eyed, slack-jawed looks of disbelief. They were so taken by the story he was weaving that they had regressed deep into their minds, imagining things that their world would not let them.

Letting his patched frock coat flutter in the wind, Cedo tossed his head back, long hair caught up in the breeze. Maybe it was the lure of the open sea, the possibility of what was beyond the coast that had caused him to keep it long. He had not seen anyone, bar the shore-bound mariners, with hair anything like his. But while theirs was neatly tied into pigtails, Cedo allowed his to be wild and free.

"And," his soft voice began once more, carrying on the gentle wind to even the outermost watcher, "at night, sometime around the witching hour, they leave the kingdoms of the deep and swim. Higher and higher they swim," dramatically, he waved his hands above his head, linking his thumbs and making his fingers flutter like wings, "until they can see the stars through the waves. Just before they break the surface, their fins change, twisting and tugging until they become huge wings. Then, beneath the gentle light of the stars and the smile of the moon, they spread the magnificent wings and break free of the sea. Higher and higher they fly, spiraling upward, wanting to catch the moon and bring it to light the darkness of the sea."

Cedo stood on the railings, feet clamped firmly around the wrought iron as he spread his arms wide, his long coat billowing behind him. Tossing his head back, he cried to the moon that clung to the velvet black sky.

"Moon man, moon man, thee of the purest light! Come with us and fly tonight, lighting depths of blackest night!"

Coins clattered into the well-worn cap he had placed upon the deck of the pier. A satisfied smile stayed on Cedo's lips as he watched the throng depart. He did not tell the stories for the money, but it certainly helped. He kept a room in a beautiful town house and it was thanks to his stories that he had it. Cedo was blessed and he knew it, knew he could not take what he had for granted because what was given could certainly be taken away. He gave nods and small waves to those who acknowledged him, those who were not still lost in their minds. They were the ones who would be back the following evening. Perhaps they would bring friends and lovers so that all become part of something magical. But they would come, alone if need be, wrapped in heavy clothes, trying to hide from the biting, salty wind. He was their little secret, better than any of the penny dreadfuls that cluttered the news sellers' rickety stands.

Cedo pocketed the heavy coins deep in his pockets. It weighed him down, but he was floating somewhere above the pier so he could not feel it. He was, as his mother had told him, away with the fairies. Cedo joined the last of the stragglers as they headed back toward the bright lights of the sea front. Back toward the public houses and homes, to speak of what they had heard and to dream the dreams they should not be allowed.

Eyes on the candlelight-dappled pier, Cedo slowed. He left his spot regretfully. It was where he belonged, not in the stuffy room of the boarding house.

Where there had once been a run of railings, the symmetry was broken by a tall figure. A top hat was pressed down onto its head, face clothed in shadow. The rest of it was hidden in a suit of the blackest night, hand wrapped around the head of a cane. The only thing that did not absorb the light from the dance hall was the shadow's hair. Thick waves of fiery red hair lay on the shoulders, the blazing candlelight making it shimmer as the shadow moved to look out to sea.

The gaslight whispered awake and Cedo sank to the small bed, relieved to be home. He never wanted to come in from the night but, once wrapped in the thick blankets, he found himself grateful for the time away from his ever chattering brain. The flock-wallpapered room with its small, squeaking iron bed frame was his one luxury. Rumbling purrs filled the room and Misty, his large, white cat, lazily leapt into his lap.

Silent for the first time that evening, Cedo smiled as she turned, claws and paws kneading his lap before settling down. Cedo gently scratched her head, purrs quieting his mind, a smile curling his lips. Yet the smile faded a second later as he remembered the shadow. There was something sinister about how the faceless figure had watched him, its eyes—if it had eyes—tracking his movements before nonchalantly looking out to sea. Cedo tried to rid his mind of the image, yet it stayed, black against the night, fire hair blowing in the wind.

The following evening was as dark and chilly as the previous one. His heart pattered with the excitement of returning to the life-filled city. Cedo chattered quietly to Misty as she wrapped herself around his legs.

"I can feel it," he said, sliding his coat onto his shoulders. "Tonight is going to be a good night."

He smiled down at her watching her twist and turn in her little attention-seeking dance. Pulling the coat around himself, Cedo gave her a wink. "Do not wait up, will you? You get your beauty sleep and do not worry about me. I shall make enough money to keep you in salmon."

As with every evening, the pier was awash with life. Fairground rides and penny viewing booths were favorites among the courting couples. Women dressed in heavy woolen clothes and shawls, fingers decorated with rings, asked people to cross their palms with coins in exchange for a cheap fortune. The stalls, food carts and brightly lit rides were broken apart by the music halls. Their gilded interiors were filled with the sounds of brass bands, dinner dances, and speeches by the latest mystics and inventors.

Cedo walked by them, gazing enviously through the big windows. He wanted to stand on the stage of those vast halls, face lit with the ever-changing color of the gas jets at his feet. He wanted to tell his tales, not to a handful of passers-by, but to a theater full of people. Despite his love of the pier, there were things away from it he craved. His life was not as stable as he wished, his income forever in doubt. There had been more than one occasion where he had been unable to pay his rent. Yet, more than the steady income, he craved the companionship and acceptance of another. With someone by his side, he could achieve anything.

"One day, men shall come from Mars," Cedo announced, the wide, childish grin back on his lips as he watched the assembled crowd. There were not as many as previous nights but then, he mused, it was the end of the week and most people, the hard pressed workers of the city anyway, would be in the gin houses of the gas-lit streets. The tourists, those who had chanced upon his fairy tales, would be returning to far off homes, left only with the memories of their time beside the sea.

"These men," he continued, "will be lords of war, bringing fighting machines made of no metal we will ever have witnessed. They will fly without the aid of feathers and walk upon the earth on spindly metal legs. These machines will breathe poisonous fire and lay waste to our feeble planet. But wait!" His voice raised an octave. "We shall fight it with all that we have! It will rule neither us, nor our world! We will conquer this nemesis!"

Excitement seemed to tremble through the crowd, hushed whispers and muted comments chasing to his ears.

"But sir!" a voice called from the crowd. "How will we defeat these monsters?"

Cedo smiled and lifted a rogue wave of hair from his eyes as he turned to reply. "These vicious machines will be defeated far easier than we can ever imagine. While the metal will survive a Martian atmosphere, our atmosphere, our very air will eat away at it, thus killing whomever is driving it. And it will not erode in months or years, but days and hours. They will not be able to survive here for long. They will wither and die, their fragile bodies sucked dry by the very air that gives us life!"

They listened, spellbound, for nigh on an hour before a joyous cry rose from the crowd. Drinking it in, Cedo smiled heartily and inclined his head, appreciating the cries and applause more than the assembled people could possibly imagine. Chin against his chest and hair hiding his suddenly weary eyes, Cedo listened as the coins tumbled into the cap. How much longer could he keep on telling tales before the ideas died just like the monsters he spoke of? Maybe it was time to move on, to find another seaside town where he could tell his tales. His only hope was that he would never find himself in some dark and stinking alley.

As the crowd seeped from the darkness of the end of the pier and back into the light, Cedo turned, eyes on the crashing waves far below him. He had heard many tales of the people who had jumped from the pier to an untimely death below. Would he join them one day?

"Cedo Reilly, I believe." The voice made him jump, his grasp on the railings slipping.

Eyes wide, he turned and looked in the direction of the voice, heart faltering as he saw the shadow from the previous evening. Slowly it stepped closer, heavy, handmade shoes and walking cane thudding on the boards.

"Y-Yes, sir?" he managed to stammer, knuckles white as his hands tightened around the steel.

The shadow chuckled and pushed the brim of the top hat away from its face.

"A good start."

The shadow turned to look out to sea, one hand on the railings. Cedo was able to get a good look at the other's features as the moon bathed them in soft light. He had a strong nose and pursed lips, skin paled by the moon, all framed by the waves of hair that settled around his shoulders.

Cedo stepped closer but as he did, the man swung around, coat fluttering like a sail as he retraced his steps toward the beach. Confusion swept over Cedo and he paused, wondering whether he should follow. Why would the man seek him out only to disappear like a thief in the night? Eyes still fixed on the departing back of the man, Cedo knelt down, picking up his hat before quickly following. Taking a deep breath to settle his jittering nerves, he stepped up beside the suited man. Yet there was no acknowledgement as the man kept walking, eyes focused on the lights of the promenade.

Finally, he worked up the courage to speak." What is your business, Sir? Why did you seek me out?"

"That will become clear, Mr. Reilly," he said, voice strong and sending shivers down Cedo's spine. There was something about the man, about the way he spoke and held himself, that made Cedo feel as insignificant as an insect. It was a voice that seemed to have the ability to build people and fortresses from nothing. Yet it was also the voice of someone who could snap and break things like a mere twig. It was a voice that rattled Cedo to his core.

The man said no more. He never turned to look at Cedo, yet did not dismiss him either. The man had not invited him to walk with him but the storyteller felt he should; after all, the man had known his name in a city where very few did.

There were so many questions he wanted answered, yet he dared not ask them. *Who is he? What is his name? Where did he come from? What is his purpose?*

Stepping from the pier and into the crowded street, Cedo obediently trotted alongside his new companion. People jostled around them, most elegantly side-stepping, others looking more flustered as the top-hatted man strode toward them. High above them, on tall poles and buildings, gaslights flickered, giving Cedo a better look at his companion.

The man had skin that was nearly as white as the moon, pale freckles whispering across his cheekbones. Turning back toward the street, Cedo carried on. Around them, people from all classes walked, courting couples arm in arm, and large groups made for the pier. Momentarily, his heart swelled as he watched one couple stand beside the railings, looking out over the waves.

Contraptions of all kinds wheeled past them, wheels and legs clunking and clicking on the cobbled street. A few were horse-drawn, high-backed carriages that hid their occupants in padded velvet seats. Others were big brass and metal steam powered perambulators, hissing and puffing great clouds of white into the black sky. High upon them sat their drivers and passengers, smugly watching those unfortunates walking. There were a few that looked like great, metal, headless horses. Smartly dressed men sat astride leather seats, hands clasped to controls on the pommel, swaying back and forth as they glared down at all who stepped into their path.

A flick of radiantly-colored hair caught his eye and Cedo turned to see the man step out into the busy street. Gathering himself together, Cedo raced after him, dodging screaming people and omnibuses. He dared not call out as he chased after the man's coat tails, his own midnight blue frock coat flapping wildly in the wind. Stepping onto the opposite pavement, he threw a glare in the direction of the man.

"You could have been killed!" he exclaimed. "Those machines stop for no one!"

The man just gave him a slow, withering look, one that indicated that he already knew about the machines and that Cedo should keep his opinions to himself. He did just that, as they ducked through a low door and into a low-rent gin joint.

The smoke prickled Cedo's eyes and he blinked as he walked between the closely set tables. As they approached the bar, the redhead turned and looked at him, eyes stern.

He pointed to a table in a corner. "Go sit down."

Nodding, Cedo silently walked toward it, grimacing as his feet caught on the sticky wooden floor. He slithered between tables and people, quietly apologizing before dropping onto a rickety chair. His eyes turned and watched the man collect a bottle of gut-rotting whisky and walk toward him. The dark bottle was slammed into the table, followed by two heavy glasses. The man sat and Cedo found himself trembling as he watched as the bottle was uncorked and a shot thrown down the other man's throat.

With a fascination bordering on the morbid, Cedo watched the man knock back shot after shot of fiery alcohol. Finally, with eyes that blazed with the same passion as his hair, the man filled the glass that sat before Cedo.

"Drink," he commanded, face contorting into a snarl.

Hands shaking, Cedo did so, tossing the liquor into his mouth, flinching as the lava-hot liquid slid down into his belly. With watering eyes, Cedo looked to the man, watching as he took another shot of whisky.

"Sir," he quietly begged. "You must tell me of yourself and your business. Who are you, and why have you sought me out?"

Green eyes as wild and as bright as the hills that surrounded the city bore into him.

"That is of no concern to you right now. All you need to know is that you are now my business," the man said, voice harsh and laden with liquor. "Mr. Reilly, how much do you charge for one of your tales?"

Caught off guard by the abruptness of the first comment and the almost curious calm of the question, Cedo trembled and looked at his salt-softened fingernails. They were rough and picked, hardly becoming of a man who laced together dreams for a living.

He gave a little shrug of his shoulders. "As much as people are willing to pay, Sir."

The top hat was placed on the table. For the first time Cedo saw the softer, more delicate curves of his features. Eyes that were harshened with time looked at him, thick waves of hair framing a chiseled face. Lips pursed as Cedo studied him, as if the man wasn't used to being so intently looked at.

For a moment, their gazes locked, each sizing the other up before the man snapped his head away, almost seeming to be irritated.

"Sir," Cedo began. "I still do not know your name. Nor do I know your business, other than that it somehow involves me."

He felt, for the first time in his life, fear, a prickling sensation beneath his skin. He had never been commanded to do the bidding of another, nor had he ever been under the control of another. The sensation made him feel both hopeless and deathly alone.

"For now," the man began, eyes lost in the murky

depths of the whisky bottle, "neither is of any interest to you. What is of interest to you is that you come to my house. I wish to hear you speak, as you do every night at the end of the pier. I would like you to—" The flame-haired man paused, toying with the heavy glass, "entertain me."

Cedo flicked his tongue out, wetting his dried lips. He wanted to believe it was from the alcohol but he knew, deep down, that it was from the force of the final statement. Two words, so heavy and so powerful.

"Wh—Whatever you desire, Sir."

In that instant, the other's face changed, a smile fleetingly crossing the lips.

"Good boy," the man said before sweeping up his hat and the rapidly emptying bottle of liquor. "Now come. We have a way to travel."

CHAPTER 2

The smart, brougham carriage, while dark, was the most comfortable Cedo had ever found himself in. He sat quietly in the deep padded seats, lulled by the motion and the sound of hooves rattling over the roads. Outside the scenery slowly changed, city to suburbs to outskirts to rolling countryside. Top hat back on his head and face returned to shadow, the man said nothing except to offer him a drink from a flask. Despite imbibing most of the bottle of whisky, the man appeared not to be intoxicated, at least not in the way that Cedo assumed he should be. Taking the flask, Cedo drank. A liquor, far smoother than the rough booze from the tavern, slid down and settled in his belly, relaxing and silencing him. He had no desire to talk, rather to watch as scenery, lit by the light of the moon, rolled by.

As they left the city, the air cooled and Cedo found the threadbare frock coat was past its best. Shivering a little, he pulled the thinning velvet closer to him and slid farther down the seat. It had been many years since he had last left the boundaries of the city. The streets and boarding houses were his familiar home, the place his mother had brought him to after his father had run off with a harlot.

Cedo had been too young to remember, but had learned about the shame of being cast from such an upstanding family. The spite and poison his mother had spat, her ravings about how her one child would never grow to be like his father. Before her mysterious disappearance a year before, she had instilled her dreamer of a son with every moral she could think of. And Cedo was determined to live up to her expectations.

Which is probably why I am in this carriage.

He smiled a little as he recalled his mother's words:

"Not everyone in this world is as nice as you, Cedo, nor has everyone had the privilege of a good upbringing. Do not argue with me; just because you live in a boarding house does not mean you have to view yourself as a peasant. But at the same time, you must not look down on people who are less fortunate than yourself. Cedo, you must remember that everyone in this world, no matter who they are or where they have come from, deserves a chance."

"There is a blanket on the opposite seat," said the husky voice.

Looking up, Cedo caught the man turning his head back toward the window. Giving a small nod, he reached out, fingers finding the heavy wool blanket and pulling it to himself.

He counted eight windows at the front of the house, each gently lit by a small lamp, illuminating leaves and vines, darkened to black, winding around the frames. High above him, a gas light hissed and flickered. For a moment, Cedo stood watching, fascinated. In the middle of the city where the prevailing sounds were drunken baying and clattering wheels no one could hear the gentle whisper of the lamps: gentle whispers that, if you listened hard enough, sounded like voices from other places, voices that came to calm and to warn. This one, Cedo concluded, was screaming something at him.

"Come." The magic was broken, whisked away into the branches of nearby trees, and Cedo looked to the man who stood beside the door of the house.

It was a modest house for a man who appeared to be wealthy. From the little Cedo had seen, the man lived well out of the city, in a village that appeared to be just one long, winding road. Stepping between the two old and twisted trees, Cedo silently walked the dark, cobbled path. The light from the whispering gas light refused to touch the path, as if some unseen boundary stopped it passing.

Silently, he stood behind the man as a large key was thrust into the door. Surprise flickered through Cedo. Somewhere in the door, there was the sound of not just the key turning but also the grating noise of a mechanism. That was followed by the *thunk* of something heavy pulling back. Three times the dull noise filled the air and then the man stretched out his hand, fingers barely brushing over the smooth surface. The heavy door swung effortlessly open.

With trepidation in his heart, Cedo obediently followed the man into the hallway. Gas jets jutted from the walls that were hung with rich red and gold wall hangings. Directly before him a steep staircase arched upward, while more heavy doors, each firmly closed, lined the hallway. A strange smell, like that of carbolic acid, curled through the air. The fear in Cedo's heart grew as he followed in the man's wake. There was something oppressive about the building, something that unsettled his light and airy disposition. The house appeared to be empty yet, at the same time, it did not.

The hallway did not end at the stairs, instead separating and carrying on beyond them. To what, Cedo did not know. He was not sure if he wanted to know, either. The man shrugged the coat from his shoulders before pulling the hat from his head, thick hair even more vibrant beneath the glowing lamps. Both garments were thrown over the banister of the stairs before the man pushed open a door to his right, never offering to take anything from Cedo. An arm was extended, gesturing for Cedo to enter the room, the man's face not showing a flicker of emotion as he slipped past.

Standing just within the room, Cedo looked around in awe. A large window occupied one wall, heavy curtains covering it. Another wall was covered with books, and before a richly carved fireplace sat an ornate desk, a beautifully upholstered chair standing behind it. A fire had already been laid, and more gas lamps hung from the walls. Two brass lamps, their necks carved to look like dragons, arched from the corners of the desk, their flames hungrily eating the precious air. Air that Cedo couldn't seem to reach as he watched the man seat himself behind the desk.

The man leaned forward, fingertips touching in an arch and green eyes intensely watching Cedo. Shrinking back, Cedo withered beneath the glare, heat racing to his cheeks. One hand lifted, motioning Cedo to the open space before the gargantuan desk. Breathing in short gasps, he followed the fingers, body automatically straightening as he stared at the man. The man's silence, mixed with his obvious position of authority, further unnerved him. He could not guess at the other's age; he could have been mere weeks younger than Cedo or entire millennia older. The man had given nothing of himself away. Even the blatant drunkenness from earlier seemed to have faded back into the man's body. Once more, he was poised, elegant even, as he looked straight into Cedo's nervous hazel eyes.

"Please." It was the first time Cedo had heard the man use the word.

Mouth agape, Cedo looked at him, trying to translate what was meant by the single word. Finally, he asked,

"Sir, what you know of the future?"

For a moment, the man sagged. "Nothing, Mr. Reilly. What do *you* know of the future?" A slow smile crept over the man's lips although his eyes remained as cool as glass. "Do you have some new-fangled machinery up your sleeve that will transport us there?"

The uneasiness remained and the statement caught him off guard. Pulling the hat from his head, Cedo ran a hand through his hair, desperately trying to calm himself. Cedo focused on the bare wall above the man's head. He had yet to see any pictures hanging in the house, which made him wonder about the man's standing within the community. If he did not have children, he should at least have a wife, no?

"In the future, people like you and I will not live on this planet. Earth will be ruined, ravaged by monsters from other worlds, intent on destroying and taking over this small world. They will come to take all that is good, to take the air, water, and nouris—"

"Mr. Reilly!" the man's voice caught him off guard and Cedo found himself shaking as he looked to the man. The green eyes peered over towered fingers. "I would appreciate it if you looked at me when you spoke. Like you do with those on the pier. It is only polite, after all."

Shaking, Cedo quickly nodded, brushing handfuls of hair out of his eyes. "Y-Yes S-Sir."

The man inclined his head.

"These creatures, they will come." He licked his lips, voice quivering a little, and he made sure to focus on the eyes that were as green as emeralds and just as hard. "They will come from the farthest stretches of the universe. They will not come from the Moon, or from Mars. They will come from worlds that we will neither see, nor ever dream of. These will be worlds where objects will be created using the power of minds far greater than ours.

Their modes of transport will be far superior to ours, able to jump entire stretches of space and time. And they will arrive in the darkest hours, their attack well plotted and prepa—"

A flick of the man's wrist silenced Cedo, his voice dying as he looked at the other's slightly lowered head.

"Enough," the man said and Cedo felt his heart fall at the minute gestures of dismissal.

It appeared, from the way the man was acting, that this had been a wasted journey. With his voice, so died the tale, fading to black in Cedo's mind. Perhaps it would be used again. Yet Cedo had a feeling that it would never see its climax.

A sound, as loud as a hammer against nails, filled the silence and Cedo lifted his head to see the man tapping neatly trimmed fingernails against the varnished desk. His lips were narrowed and eyes bored into Cedo. Finally, the flame-haired man let out a deep sigh, eyes falling shut. Cedo swallowed, throat quickly closing as the eyes opened a moment later to once more stare back at him. The fingernails carried on their rhythmic clattering, slow and never-ending, like a train over tracks.

After what seemed like a century, the smooth voice spoke, "Mr. Reilly, do you believe yourself to be good enough for the entertainment halls?"

A tiny tremble took over Cedo's body. Every night, when he dropped into his bed, he dreamed of walking the boards of the theaters. Flicking his tongue over his lips, he stalled for time.

"I—I believe that I am good enough, Sir," he answered.

The man nodded, yet something flashed through the emerald eyes as he pulled himself from the monstrous chair. As slow as the death of time, he began to circle Cedo. Cedo shook as he stared straight ahead, fingers idly picking at the frayed hem of his jacket.

"You are good, Mr. Reilly." Words flowed like the smoothest of liquors. "But that is it. There is better than just being good, which was why you were holding court at the end of the pier. I can make into you the best." The man stopped, eyes mere inches from Cedo's own and he felt himself shrink back. "But you need to put your trust in me."

They stood, each looking at the other. Cedo did not move, limbs heavy. His body flared hot with panic as the man closed the gap between them, eyes flicking over his face. Still looking over the man's shoulder, Cedo swallowed, feeling himself on the point of breaking, and gave a small nod.

"Good." The man looked down his nose at Cedo, a slow smile on his lips as he pulled away. Red hair flared out behind him as he turned for the door.

A hand was raised over a broad shoulder, gesturing to him. "Come. It is late. You can rest and we will begin tomorrow."

Cedo quietly followed.

"Sir," he said, flustered. His mind went to his comfortable room, where Misty would be patiently waiting for him to return. He could imagine her confusion at the disappearance of her master and the sound of her pitiful mewls pained him. "I have a home to return to."

With a hand wrapped around a carved banister topper, the man turned, eyes glowering from beneath a mane of hair. "No, Mr. Reilly. You have a room in a boarding house and a cat who is very capable of looking after herself."

Cedo felt his mouth open to protest but thought better of it as the green eyes narrowed. Silenced by a mere glance, Cedo stepped back, head lowered. Peering from beneath his ragged fringe, the man nodded, stepping onto the stairs. Cedo let his eyes follow the long fingers up the long banister. The ending of the banister, the carved topper, caused Cedo's eyes to widen.

It was a dragon, the symbol of power and in an outstretched claw, it held a tiny, crouching mouse. For a moment, Cedo studied it; he had seen it elsewhere but could not place it.

Heart pounding, he felt like a chastised child, his eyes on the scuffed leather of his aging boots. The house felt too empty and tidy for his liking.

Always in the pride of place at his mother's side, it was there, among the aristocracy, that he had honed a storyteller's skills. While other children had been beaten for daring to speak of an imaginary friend or spook beneath the bed, Cedo had had any army of invisible friends, all ready to charge at the strange sounds that haunted the hours of darkness.

And now, these same friends who had melted into muses in his mind were crying out, something paining them. Closing his eyes, Cedo let out a low groan, the fear growing as the atmosphere of the strangely clinical house bothered him.

Reality resettled around him as a door creaked open. The man gestured to the open door. Like the rest of the house, every other door in the corridor remained firmly closed.

"You may sleep here. Rest, and tomorrow we shall begin."

For a flicker of time, a terse smile appeared on the man's lips. Nodding, Cedo stepped into the room. Like the study below the stairs, it was beautifully decorated. Drapes the color of the setting sun hid the window. A vase of flowers sat upon a single dresser, their delicate scent hiding the acidic scent that permeated the rest of the house. Yet it was the bed that made him stop. It filled the heart of the room, four carved pillars heading to the ceiling. Once more, dragons sat atop the dark wood pillars, protectively watching over the room. Cedo's heart shuddered a little, the fear wavering at the thought of the still sentinel dragons. Snow white material fell from the top of the bed.

"Sleep well." His thoughts were interrupted and Cedo turned to watch the door click home.

Pausing, Cedo looked at the door, loneliness settling over him. The single room he shared with Misty seemed like a lifetime ago, a lifetime that belonged to a different person. Carefully, he pushed the drapes aside, sitting on the finely woven bed linen, eyes on the floor as he toyed with the cuffs of his jacket. Silence hung in the air, a bleak cloud of uneasiness.

Inching back the covers, Cedo slowly stripped the dusty clothes from his thin frame. Cooling air touched his bare skin as he carefully placed them on the floor beside the bed. There was no mirror in the room, not that he would have wanted to have seen himself anyway. The dirt of the city had settled itself beneath his fingernails. But there appeared to be nowhere to clean himself. Feet moving over the soft carpet, Cedo approached the far wall of the room. A door was set in the wall, blending so perfectly with the room that, for a while, he had not seen it. Quietly he pulled it open, the hinges giving a slight creak.

From somewhere, a light flickered on, the gentle hiss of gas filling the tiny room. A sigh of relief left Cedo's lips as he peered into the small water closest. There was a lavatory and a basin with golden taps. Filling the basin, Cedo began to wash, watching as the water turned murky, the tiredness of the city splashing against the ceramic. The gentle movements of the water soothed his mind, quieting the voices that lay beyond his eyes. Drying himself with a rich towel, he quietly made his way back to the bed, and laid back in the cool cotton.

Jumbled words rattled through his head; so many questions that remained unanswered. The stress of the unknown plagued him, sleep unwilling to take over his already tired body. Desperately he fought against his body, trying to will it to rest, even for a moment. But it did not, the questions screaming in his mind.

Finally Cedo found himself drifting into a fitful sleep plagued by strange noises and even stranger dreams. The clank and hiss of machines, giant pieces of metal architecture built for the kill, roamed through his dreamscape. Bipedal metal monsters that shuddered as they moved, razor-sharp claws and knives slashing through the air. Unseen beings screaming and crying while the faint metallic smell of blood hung in the air. A river twisted through the dream, a slick, blood-red river that never seemed to drain, forever filled from massive waste pipes that jutted out from high, curving bricked walls.

CHAPTER 3

The eternity of night eventually gave way to dawn. Sunlight seeped beneath the drapes and slipped across the floor, gentle tendrils crawling over the carpet and bed, waking the sleeping occupant. Eyes slowly opened, quiet murmurs leaving his lips as Cedo ran a hand over his face, happy to finally escape the confines of his mind. Sighing, he pushed himself upright, leaning into the full pillows to take in the room that was that was bathed in a warm light. Heart falling, he realized that he hadn't fully escaped; he was still trapped in the house that seemed a million miles away from the comfort of his boarding house room.

Sliding from the bed, he wearily moved to the water closest. He wanted to dress and make an escape, return to the city he loved so much. With eyes still heavy with sleep, he looked for the neat pile of clothes. Yet they were not there and fruitlessly he searched for them. After an age, he finally turned to the dresser, brow furrowing as he moved toward it. Tugging open the heavy top drawer, the frown deepened as he looked at his neatly folded clothes. They had obviously been laundered and pressed, the care of a housekeeper evident in the carefully pressed creases.

Suddenly, from outside the door, there was the sound of voices.

"You *stupid* girl," he heard the distinct sound of the

man's voice hiss. "What the devil do you think you are doing, bringing food, scalding hot food at that, up the main stairs?"

Another voice, feminine, mumbled, and Cedo assumed she was apologizing. So the house was not completely empty. There were other people, servants obviously, who were secreted away in another part of the house. His eyes widened, attention turned back to the door, to the scene he could not see but could easily visualize as he heard the sound of flesh slapping against supple flesh.

"You have worked here long enough, *girl*, to know your role. Now deliver that to Mr. Reilly's room."

Heart thudding, Cedo shrank away from the door, quickly collecting his clothes as he hurriedly began to dress. There was a click and his eyes widened, body stilling, as he watched a small hatch at the bottom of the door swing upward. A tray slid through and the hatch closed. The panic once more began to rise and Cedo ran to the door, unbuttoned trousers flapping as his fingers wrapped around the heavy doorknob. Twisting it, he pulled, but the door would not move. A quiet cry, that of the imprisoned, filled the air and he sank to the ground.

Clothing himself seemed to take an age, and Cedo found himself sitting back in the middle of the room, the tray of untouched food still beside the door. Like a moth attracted to a flame, he had been drawn in, his wings now scorched and singed. Self-loathing washed over him in giant crashing waves. The hunger that had clasped him awakening was gone, replaced with an emptiness that no amount of food could ever fill.

Cedo felt his throat contract, a tiny whimper escaping as the door clicked and opened. He tried to stand, but found that his legs would not cooperate as the man walked in. A snug-fitting suit, the same shade as his eyes, hugged a tall, lean body, well polished black boots stopping before his face.

"I see you did not eat." It was a firm statement.

Shame flushed him and Cedo felt himself nod, hiding behind a veil of thick hair. The fight, the will to speak out about his confinement, had died, vanishing as the green eyes bored into his head.

"You will soon find your appetite again."

A hand with perfectly manicured nails dangled before his eyes. Taking it, Cedo stood and looked into the man's face, a face that, in daylight, looked like it had it had barely been kissed by time. A smile touched the lips, a twinkle flashing through the deeply-colored eyes before fading away.

"Let us begin."

Cedo followed, trying to ease the sense of dread that followed him like a black cloud. Perhaps the locked door had been a mistake? Or perhaps it was some kind of precaution in case the house was raided? Yet the feeling stayed with him as he walked along the corridor, taking a sharp left turn down an identically decorated hallway and down a set of bare wooden stairs. Taking in the firmly closed doors, Cedo wondered if these were the servants' quarters. They were far from the richly painted ones above the stairs. The uncomfortable silence still hung over the house as if the people behind the doors were waiting for their master to pass before they resumed their work.

He watched the man pause before a closed door, fingers flicking a tiny brass cover open and pressing his eye to a tiny lens. Rapping the door with his knuckles, he moved on. Eyes searching the corridor, Cedo saw spy holes on every door, and above each door, a brass tube jutted out, an orb of glass trapped in it. His heart stiffened; the man could look in while the occupants could spy out. Very strange.

The long corridor ended in another door, sunlight streaming through the curved panes of stained glass above it. The door revealed a courtyard, closed in on three sides by the walls of the house, the fourth side open and leading out onto a wide garden. Cedo smiled as he glimpsed trees and well-tended flowerbeds, the warm sun dappling the neatly trimmed grass. Over the sound of birdsong, he could hear the babbling of a stream, hidden somewhere behind the gentle rise of the grass. It was a stark contrast to the winding, smog-filled streets of the city. Beautiful, peaceful, devoid of the noise that rattled the windows day and night. His heart soared at the sight and gentle smells, spirits lifting.

One final step to the right and Cedo found himself walking through the door of a large outbuilding. Although, from its light and airiness, he would not have realized he was inside except for the three walls of mirrors that reflected him into infinity. A chuckle filled the airy space and Cedo turned back. The other man stood against the unmirrored wall, face lit with a joy Cedo had yet to see the man express as he beckoned him closer.

"Come closer, Mr. Reilly, and let me talk to you."

The man carried on smiling as a curious Cedo stepped up to him.

"Mr. Reilly. Have you ever heard the names Betty Nickolai, Edward Morgan, and Donald Smith?"

With a furrowed brow, Cedo nodded; of course he had heard of them. He had seen all of them at various parties and entertainment halls around the city. Their names had been on the lips of every person on every street, stars that shone brighter than those in the heavens above. Betty had been a singer with a voice that could shatter glass.

Edward had done a turn as a comic with a puppet called Cecil, while Donald had been the city's most renowned pianist. All were now sadly gone, bright lights snuffed out in their prime. Some said that they had died in strange circumstances, but Cedo had shunned the idea, believing that they had just been cruelly taken by natural causes. Died in childbirth, heart attack, and opium overdose according to the newspapers. The penny dreadfuls, on the other hand, had woven other tales.

"I created them, Mr. Reilly." There was an unnatural, almost supernatural, gleam to the man's eyes. "All of them came to this house and were molded by my very hands."

With a jerk of his head, the man said, "Begin. Tell me something. Weave me a tale. Something from the depths of your mind, something your soul screams to speak about."

No longer could he take the intense emerald gaze, so he turned away. But through the mirrors the man's eyes were forever peering over his shoulder. An uncomfortable gaze, the way the eyes looked up from beneath strands of bastard red hair, and Cedo let his own eyes fall shut. Normally the stories came when they were ready, not when some demon eyed stranger demanded it of him.

Cedo began. "We are not alone in this city. For below our very feet, deep below the pavements and roadways is another world. A world locked away from prying eyes, from those of us who would disrupt its natural workings." Behind him, Cedo heard a sharp intake of breath but chose to ignore it. The words burned through his very being. "It comes to life at night, using our long-forgotten tunnels for their homes and bases for things that no mind could ever imag—"

"NO!"

Shocked at the outburst, Cedo swung around.

Anger lined the previously smooth face and Cedo felt himself take a step back, trying to keep himself away from the rage that burned within the other.

"That is not what I want to hear!" the man bellowed." The people, those who will pay to see you, do not want to hear of the dark side of life. They do not want to be reminded that they have to go back to such lives. They pay good money to be entertained!"

The man was before him, hot droplets of spittle landing on Cedo's face. He dared not flinch, the fear he had first felt now coming back in heavy, painful waves. He stood, hands clasped before him and head lowered, letting the man berate him for what had been a perfectly innocent tale.

Cedo did not know how long it went on for before a knock rattled the door of the mirrored room. There was no apology as the man turned and left, the door slamming behind him.

Heart thudding, Cedo stood in the middle of the room. He felt like a schoolboy who was being punished for something he believed was right. That was what he thought the man wanted! Fantastic tales of things that did not exist and would never exist. For a while, the painful anger kept him from hearing the voices that drifted from beyond the door. Yet slowly they began to worm their way into his mind.

On the balls of his feet, Cedo crept toward the door, flinching at the creaking floorboards. He paused, listening as the voices continued, becoming more tense with every word.

"Mr. Black," there was the distinct voice of the man, gruff yet well spoken, "that machine has to be ready. Has to! There are orders for it that we can ill afford to refuse."

A heavier, older voice sighed deeply. It was male and tinted with a distinctive, rough accent, one that Cedo had only heard used by the common folk of the city.

"Erus, Mr. Veetu, Sir."

Cedo's eyes went wide and he pressed himself to the wall as a cool feeling prickled his skin. Erus—Erus Veetu—that was the man's name. Rabid, he leaned closer to the door, desperately trying to catch the rest of the conversation.

"Silence, Mr. Black! I want that machine finished, tested, and ready to roll out within the next week. I do not care what it takes."

There was the crunching of gravel beneath heavy boots and Cedo moved from the door and back to his position just as the man—now named—swung back into the room.

For a heartbeat, they stood staring at one other. Knowledge was power, names were even more powerful, and the man seemed to know that Cedo knew something he should not. With a flick of his wrist, the man dismissed that, eyes still scowling as he barked, "Impress me, Mr. Reilly. Make me feel better. Make me forget about this world that wants to tear me apart."

Cedo wanted to stay silent, wanted to wear this man down until he confessed all. But the sudden world-weariness and downcast eyes, the fingers delicately pressed to the bridge of the nose, told Cedo that now was not the time for such games. With a thundering heart, Cedo found himself walking closer, wanting to heal whatever conflicted inside the man, just like his mother had taught him.

Some people need to be helped. Some people are broken, deep inside, and they do not realize it. You are here for them, Cedo. You are here to help people, to heal them, to lead them toward the light.

Once he could feel the man's tiny breaths upon his skin, he stopped.

"Do you ever take the opportunity to wander around your gardens, Sir?" The deep green eyes flicked to his and the man shook his head before dropping his eyes to the floor. "I implore you to go there, go in the evening, just as dusk is taking over. It is called the magic hour for a reason, for that is when the beings we cannot see by day come out to play." Flicking his tongue over his lips, Cedo watched the man breathe, a small tinge of pink touching his pale cheeks. The man's reaction made Cedo shudder, unsure of what to expect.

"Sit beneath a tree, just as the sun touches the horizon and the sky is a canvas of pink, red, orange and purple. Rest your eyes and watch, for these beings, small and with glittering wings, will dance from beneath the bushes and trees, reveling in the darkening night, welcoming it as they come to work their magic. They are fairy folk and only we, the ones who choose to believe, can see them. Rest, good Sir, and extend a welcoming hand to them. Let them, in their flowing clothes of petals and leaves, step into your hand. Let them sit with you and tell them of your dreams and fears. For they have the power to change your life."

Pausing, Cedo looked to the man he dared not call by his given name, trying to gauge his reaction. All he could see were waves of that demon-colored hair, the man looking at the polished floor. Cedo wanted to rest his hands at the man's slender hips. Odd desires he had never before felt pulsed through him, desires that had crept in over the past few moments. They gripped him, making him flush yet chilling him to the core. Why did he want to touch this man? Was it because Erus had turned other people into music hall stars? Or something far deeper?

"Continue."

Swallowing around his dry mouth, Cedo nodded, wetting his lips before continuing, "The fairy folk, they have a queen. She lives in the twisted roots of a great oak tree, sitting on a throne carved from the finest fallen woods. These are not malicious folk. They are folk of love and kindness, using only what they find on the floor of the forests. The queen is not a harsh ruler. She rules with her heart and sees the good in all. Once a year, on the longest night of the year, just before what we call Wintermass, she grants one wish to the mortal human she sees fit to receive it.

"On this night, as the moon rides through the velvet sky, she goes to them and grants them one wish. It can be anything but it must be a wish that is given in love— they can wish to have their broken life repaired or for a poor neighbor to be blessed with wealth. They can wish for happiness for themselves or for another. But if they ask for the wrong wish, if they are already rich and they ask for more wealth, then she shows them what their life would be like without wealth, shows them the poor and the needy. So, good Sir, should you come across the fairy folk, or indeed the queen, then wish carefully."

The heavy silence that hung between them as Cedo's voice died could have been used to cast bells. Slowly the man lifted his head and Cedo found himself close enough to see the minute flecks of gold in the other's eyes. For that moment, they stood and stared, neither moving as unseen electricity crackled through the air. Then, as if fingers were snapped, it was broken, dashed away, as the man turned for the door.

"Better." There was a note of praise to the man's voice and Cedo felt his heart momentarily soar. "There are blank books in your room. Go there and write your ideas. We will continue later."

The bedroom was as lifeless as Cedo felt. The bed, smartly made when he had walked in, was now a rumpled mess of linen, tightly screwed balls of paper peppering the folds. Cedo lay on the bed, head resting on his hands as he stared at the chest of drawers. He could smell the odor that began to rise from his body, the cloying smell of sweat, yet he made no move to go and bathe. This was like no situation that he had ever been in, trapped and uninspired. Never had he been forced to write the thoughts that crept into his head. It felt wrong, as if it were a crime against those voices that spoke to him. All he wanted was to walk the boards of the finest theaters, not kill the muses that would put him there.

Standing, he picked up a lamp and pressed the tiny, metal switch. A flame leaped up the tube and Cedo quietly walked toward the stairs, feeling as if he were disobeying some unwritten and long forgotten rule. Unlike the previous night, the door to his room had remained unlocked. Cedo had pondered it for a moment, a shard of guilt slicing his heart, before he had decided it must have been left that way for a reason. What the reason was, he did not know. The heavy door to the study was ajar, the light from a single gas lamp lighting a narrow path in. Again, he shivered, a sense of foreboding gripping him. But he could not let go of the sense of adventure that had forever lived deep within him, the light drawing him closer.

Peering through the door, Cedo saw that no shadow was cast over the desk; the room was as empty as when the house had first been constructed. Closer he inched, and lightly he nudged the door open. The fear of getting caught was greatly overwhelmed by his curiosity, his need to know the facts behind the turbulent, secretive man far outweighing all else.

The single gas lamp threw a flickering circle of light

41

over the now cluttered desk. It seemed that the man had also been at work: pages of drawings were scattered across the writing block, an ink well with a fine pen laid over it to one side.

Breath hanging on his lips, Cedo stepped into the hallowed space, feeling like he was violating a specially tuned place. Leaning over the desk, his eyes scanned the abandoned papers, taking in lines and numbers, all written in a flowing script. Carefully, he moved the sheets aside, pulse increasing with each diagram that his eyes took in.

Machines that could only have come from a mind as dark as their purpose were etched onto the heavy paper. Machines of war, machines of torture, machines that lived off the blood of others, huge shining hulks that would soon carry the blood-rust badges of war.

Suddenly weakened by the thoughts that overwhelmed him, the voices of pain that cried through his mind, Cedo leaned against the desk, perspiration forming on his brow as the realization set in.

Veetu.

He knew now where he had heard that name before. It had been scrolled on the headlines of newspapers, discreet advertisements that were placed in the back of specific broadsheets.

Veetu Industries—the city's largest employer, owned and run by the man whose roof he slept beneath. A man with a deadly intent and nothing to lose. Not a lord of war but *the* Lord of War. It was a name that was breathed in fear by enemies and praised by those who used what the green-eyed man created.

Warm wisps of air lifted the hair from the back of his neck, his hackles rising, and his head snapped up. His body became motionless, eyes watching the towering shadow that danced across the curtains.

CHAPTER 4

J ust what are you doing, Mr. Reilly?" The question made Cedo's stomach turn, bile burning his throat as looked into anger-darkened eyes, his breath finally coming out in a pained whine.

It appeared to be a constant battle of wills as Erus stared at him, silently pressing Cedo to crumple beneath his gaze. Finally Cedo found the strength to move and he stepped away from the liquor-heavy breath. Erus was quick to follow, body straight and firmly poised as he stood before Cedo, hands clasped behind him and his eyes locked onto the hazel ones that threatened to spill over with tears.

"Mr. Reilly." The man's voice was filled with menace. "Why have I found you in my study?"

Cedo managed to swallow. His body sagged beneath the hard gaze, hands balling against the hot material of his clothes.

"You..." he managed to reply, a red tinge of anger beginning to prick at his body. "You are Erus Veetu, the man who has killed thousands and injured thousands more. How *could* you?"

Cedo did not have time to move before a hand that was filled with the strength of the machines connected with his face. He let out a cry before he slowly lifted his head, peering through the heavy hair that now covered his eyes.

"Why?" he heard himself ask, knowing that he was risking more wrath.

Fingers balled into his shirt, lifting him and pulling him closer, the man's face twisted into a snarl. Teeth bared, Erus hissed, "Because I can. Because somebody has to build such machines, and it may as well be me.

"Is that not right, Mr. Reilly? Because without them, you would not be here, boy! You would never have been born! Your parents would have been killed long before they could even think of conceiving you. Without me, this nation would not be as great as it is."

The strong grip freed him and Cedo slumped, trembling and sobbing pathetically. He was weakening, he could feel it. But that was what strength did; it broke and ruined those who could ill afford to be strong. He felt the man step closer, a hand gripping the back of Cedo's neck. The fingers, what he could feel of them, were surprisingly soft, not giving away the power that lay within the rest of the body. They tightened, bruising his flesh as the man lifted Cedo's eyes to his own.

"This country needs me," Erus hissed. "It needs me to stay alive, to keep the wars going that keep our industries powered. Without it, there would be no work, no one would eat, and you, my little tale teller, would have nowhere to lay your pretty head at night."

The fear was still there, ebbing deep within Cedo, but it was being eclipsed by something else. Something far more powerful. The feelings, those which he had felt earlier, were beginning to return as they stood and stared at each other. The electricity also returned, crackling between them and stirring strange emotions in Cedo, emotions that constricted his chest before shooting like bolts straight to his groin.

Erus' hands moved, stroking possessively over the contours of Cedo's neck, before settling at his jaw, forcing his eyes to look upward, to the war god above him.

"You live because of me and you shall continue to live because of me."

Beyond the curtains that hung from the great bed, candlelight danced, casting mysterious, twisting shadows. Lying against a mound of pillows, Cedo gazed, breathless, at where the four bedposts met the ceiling and splayed out into hundreds of branches, twisting and coiling, turning the room into a magical forest. He barely had the chance to brace himself on his elbows before lips touched his throat, taking his breath away as bourbon-soaked gasps tickled his skin. Cedo did not know what had changed, what had snapped within him, for him to be spread out on such a luxurious bed with hands and lips gently caressing him.

The buttons of his shirt were pulled open before lips worked their magic against his skin. Tremors eclipsed him, quietly mewling as he reached out, hands finally tangling in the devilish red hair. Instead of ripping the demon's head from his shoulders, Cedo pressed it closer, wanting, needing even, for those lips to trail lower.

And lower they went, brushing against the concave dip of his stomach, tongue briefly dipping into his navel as if trying to draw his soul into the other's body. And that was where Erus stopped, just above the painfully tight bulge that threatened to burst from Cedo's trousers. Green eyes shimmered, filled with a lust that Cedo that knew was going to tear him apart. A lust that Cedo found himself not caring what it did to him as long as it left him alive.

Strange feelings swirled through him, odd emotions that he had craved for so long. Acceptance and, somewhere underlying it, the murmurings of something akin to friendship.

Fingers curled their way back over his body, finding hidden spots between his ribs that made Cedo jump from the bed with tiny cries of unexpected pleasure. Hair was brushed from his ear as whispers grazed over it.

"Erus..."

The smile fell and Erus' lips were pressed to his, teeth digging into his lower lip. Crying out, Cedo flailed, hands finally forcing Erus' mouth to his own and hungrily returning the kiss. Coppery blood touched his tongue, blood that he hungrily lapped down.

"You know my name," the lust-filled voice hissed, "and, to you, it is not the one that I am known by."

Hands crawled into his hair, tugging his head back until Cedo found his neck painfully arched, eyes wide and staring up at the still-clothed dervish that towered over him.

"Say it." Lips curled into an ugly sneer, a sneer that, by its very nature, said its owner could, and would, turn nasty at the mere flick of a wrist. "Say it, Cedo."

Cedo's breath hitched in his throat, the warm room seeming all the more close as his given name was spat in his face. This man, the beast that held him, had the power to kill and maim millions of innocent souls. Yet he seemed to want more, seemed to want to control all that fell into his path. Cedo had felt himself try to fight but he knew he could not, not against someone who surveyed the world as his own personal chess game.

Groaning, he closed his eyes, head still arched against the swell of the pillows, the pain of his tautly pulled hair making him bury his feet into the sheets, legs inching invitingly apart.

"Yes, Sir!" His voice was suddenly a confident bark.

The cruel hands slipped away, Cedo quietly begging

for them to return, before they found their way back to his hips, fingers, inching his trousers lower.

"You are such a tease, Cedo. A terrible tease. But you are a good boy nonetheless."

Eyes still heavy with sleep, Cedo pushed himself from the bed. In the center of the room stood Erus, the man Cedo now found himself humbly calling Sir. Cedo found himself ignored as Erus finished dressing, fingers deftly fastening silver cuff links. Erus snapped open a pocket watch, glancing at it before looking at himself in the mirror.

"It is time." He never looked to Cedo, the previous night forgotten. "Mrs. Sugden, if you please."

Quickly he snatched a sheet from the bed, managing to retain his modesty as a middle-aged woman walked in. She was dressed like a servant, in clothes that were dull and practical. She towed a small, upright contraption with four wheels and a pole that ended in a loop. From the loop dangled a finely-tailored, pea green suit.

The woman looked up, eyes that seemed as hard as diamonds sweeping over Cedo.

"Girls!" Her voice matched her eyes. Three girls walked in to stand patiently beside their mistress.

Once more the woman looked to him and nodded and Cedo felt a lump grow in his throat, face flushing with embarrassment as they all approached him. Gentle fingers tugged the sheet from his bare skin, none of them ever looking at him as they dressed him. His skin tingled beneath their fingers, allowing them to lift his arms, easing them into the silk cocoon of the shirt.

Eventually, Cedo studied himself in the large mirror on the opposite wall. The suit fitted him perfectly, the long coat cinched at his waist before flaring out and falling to the backs of his knees, its cuffs delicately stitched with lace. Beneath it was a waistcoat of a lighter green, the fabric stitched with dark green vines that coiled around his body.

Erus stood beside him, face gentle for once as his fingers touched Cedo's chin, forcing him to look into his eyes.

"You look wonderful."

He pressed himself closer, wanting to taste Erus, even if only for a second.

"Later." Erus turned away. "This evening. Once you have performed. Then you can have a treat."

"Performed?"

"Yes." Erus looked over his shoulder, face now painting a completely different picture. "Tonight you will have your first performance in an entertainment hall. Why?" A wicked grin graced the red-head's lips. "Do you not think you are up to it? Or was everything you proclaimed last night while you were between my sheets a bare-faced lie?"

Quickly Cedo shook his head, a grin tugging his lips. "Oh no, Sir. It was not lies. I would never lie to you. Lies get you nowhere Sir, except into the courtroom, the workhouse, and the punishment chamber. Lies are for those without an imagination, as I am sure you well know." He could feel Erus' breath against his face and he leaned in to close the last teasing inches, lips just grazing against his. "Lies lead a downward spiral to pain and poverty."

Silently they stood, nose to nose, lips tentatively touching for a brief moment before Erus snatched himself away. "Indeed they do, Cedo. And should you ever lie to me then I can assure you that you will be punished. Understood?"

Quickly Cedo nodded, the heavy lump returning to his throat, wondering what kind of punishment Erus would give. No doubt, from the lord of war himself, it would be slow and painful. Silent once more, he followed, hoping he would never get on the wrong side of Erus.

CHAPTER 5

The Rose Theater was down a cramped and decrepit side street, a ramshackle building that looked as if it were ready to be pulled down. Cedo took in the rundown building with a quiet disgust; it was not the type of place he was used to frequenting. Already there were people on the tiny balcony, cavorting and shouting, drunk on cheap ale.

A hand came to rest against the back of his neck. "Everyone must start somewhere. This is where you will start."

Sighing, Cedo looked over his shoulder, distaste obviously showing, for Erus brought up a hand, silently warning him. "Obey and you shall be rewarded with greatness. Disobey and..." The word lingered, a sharp-edged threat.

Cedo was led down a small alleyway, the soot-covered bricks nearly disappearing beneath a barrage of old and new bill posters, screaming their wares in bold print. A rickety door creaked open and a thin, reedy man with straggly, nicotine-stained hair filled the void that the door had created. He looked at Cedo in all his finery with a disgusted look. Then the dark, button-like eyes flicked away to Cedo's left and the man's face broke into something of a smile, black holes showing missing teeth.

"Mr. Veetu, nice to see you again." The tone of voice

was somewhat condescending. "See you're still dabblin' in the arts then."

One of Erus' eyebrows raised. The movement silenced the man in the doorway.

"Mr..." Erus closed his eyes and snapped his fingers. With a brash grin he pointed toward the man. "Mr. Wilks. I spoke to Mr. Farns and he is expecting us, so if you would be kind enough to let us in."

Glaring through the plume of smoke, Mr. Wilks melted away from the door. It seemed that everyone, not just warmongering nations, lived in fear of Erus Veetu. Yet why did Cedo find himself becoming so comfortable around him? Was it because he had seen the creator of death laid bare, his soul creeping through as he had taken Cedo to his bed? Or was it for a different reason, one that Cedo could feel tickling the back of his head but could not quite reach?

Outside there had been the usual chilled night air of a seaside town that was lulling itself to sleep, but within the cramped backstage the heat was stifling. Pushing his way through tiny corridors, Cedo watched as other performers eyed him with the suspicion of the unknown. The acrid odor of sweat and grease paint made him gag and he resisted the urge to bring a hand to his mouth.

They walked down one corridor after another, each looking much like the last and each alive with hustle and bustle. The only light in the cramped pathways came from behind the frosted windows of the few that were afforded dressing rooms. On each door was a small plate, a name carefully handwritten onto it in neat copperplate. Names that conjured up images of magic that only such a building could produce: *The Tumbling Timbalinas, Alfros Magnifico, Titty-Ho*. Silently, Cedo followed the gilt-edged coattails of his Master.

Master—it was an odd thought for Cedo. To be under

the command of another laid a certain heaviness on his shoulders. Yet, at the same time, Cedo found himself feeling a sense of unhinged freedom.

A door as flimsy as the others loomed before them, a small, neatly printed plate upon it.

Mr. Farns

Erus did not let it stop him. Behind a cheap-looking desk sat a rotund man. His bald head was reddened and damp either from the heat or the bottle that sat upon his desk. Or possibly both. He looked up from his frantic scribbling, the first genuine smile Cedo had seen all night breaking his face.

"Erus." The man stood, clasping one of Erus' hands in both of his own stubby ones. "So good to see you again, my boy. Please, take a seat, both of you."

Carefully placing a jeweled and winged costume hat upon a wooden head, Erus folded himself into what appeared to be the only seat. Mr. Farns looked apologetically to Cedo.

"I'm sorry, I'm not used to receiving company very often. So, Erus, Who do you have for me today?"

"Allow me to introduce Cedo Reilly, probably the best storyteller you will have ever heard."

Mr. Farns nodded and smiled, politely looking over the piles of paper that all but hid him from view.

"Well, as I told you, we can put Cedo on just before the interval, after Mr. Fawkes the fire magician." Noble eyes swept over Cedo, and he felt himself nervously return the man's smile. "It is always a pleasure to première your acts, Erus. After the help you have given me. It is just a small way to pay off the debt."

Cedo wondered what the debt was as he waited in the wings. The speculation did little to alleviate his nerves. This was not the polite company he was used to. They were bawdy and drunk, happy to boo those they disliked from the stage.

Peering through a gap in the heavy stage curtains, Cedo could see them sitting at long lines of wooden tables. Food and tankards were scattered over the tables, flaming lamps hanging above their heads. Just out of sight to his left sat the amicable Mr. Farns, acting as chairman, a lamp and a heavy hand bell by his side.

His heart quickened as he heard the crowd roar and Mr. Farns bellow, "Ladies and gentlemen, the great Mr. Fawkes!"

Silence fell over the room and Fawkes, who had just been on stage, hurried past, head down and sweating a little. Eyes still pressed to the tiny gap in the curtains, Cedo watched as Mr. Farns announced in a dramatic stage whisper,, "Now, a special treat for you. He comes to us fresh from the salt waters of the pier, a storyteller like no other. Please, ladies and gentlemen, give a warm welcome to Cedo Reilly!"

Cedo took a deep breath and stepped into the circle of light that spilled onto the stage. He couldn't see very far, only catching sight of the first few tables. The audience stared up at him, tankards and forks halfway to their mouths, eyes sparkling with tiny flames of drunken wonder as they waited for him to speak.

He'd had several hours of coaching in the mirrored room, Erus walking back and forth, a riding crop tapping against his thigh as Cedo had dug deep to find something especially fitting for the evening. Unfortunately, the tale he had planned seemed shockingly out of place now.

"Have you ever thought of other worlds?" he asked the assembled audience. Not one responded to the question and the nervousness grew. "There are worlds away from here, away from Svenfur. Some do not exist on the same isle as us. Some do not even exist on the same planet. Many are far away, up in the heavens, watching down upon us as we look up to them, wondering what they hold. Some are planets of war, their populations forever engaged in gruesome bloodshed." He knew, deep down that he was skating on thin ice mentioning war. *They are here to be entertained, not depressed.*

His voice softened. "But some. Some are peaceful planets. Their people live in harmony and love. They care for each other. No one is ever left out just because they are young or old or ill.

"On these planets people do not live in buildings like we do. They live among the trees and flowers, happily warmed by a sun. In the evening, they retire into the canopies of the trees and it is then that the clouds swoop in, refreshing and cleaning the land, ready for the next day. The sound of the rain against the leaves lulls these peaceful people into a deep sleep, a sleep where they dream of us and wonder what we do. They ask the same questions of themselves that we ask about ourselves. *Are they happy? Do they love? Do they fight?*

"Finally, day breaks, the sun welcoming them back to the world. Happily, they awake, perhaps having seen a little of our lives during their dream time. Maybe it confuses them, or angers them, or makes them happy. But they place it aside as they take care of their world. Every day they collect plants and flowers. These plants are not stifled by the smog of Svenfur, so they grow big and strong and colorful. So very bright are these plants and flowers, hues that we will never see here. Some tower high above the population of the forests, their scents heavenly. These plants are harvested and used for everything—eating, brewing into the sweetest wines, building the tree huts or turning into dye to color their bright clothes."

Pausing, he opened his eyes and looked to the audience. Some seemed captivated while others seemed bored. Forcing himself to smile, Cedo began to relax and he paced the stage, aware that his short allotment of time was racing away from him.

"These people, they may not even look like us. Oh, of course, they will walk upright on two legs like us, but their language will be different. We could not understand them as they could not understand us. Their skin may not be the same color as ours. It may be colored by the sun or by the brightly colored plants or perhaps by the people themselves.

"They are free from the burdens of life that we are. Free to live how they see fit, sharing and caring among themselves, sharing skills and caring for each other. There are no families but are one big family that knows no boundaries or divides."

Out of the corner of his eye, he could see Mr. Farns nodding, telling him that his time was nearing an end. Turning to the audience, he gave them a smile. "I believe that their greatest wish for us, should they ever meet us, would be that we were more like them, that we would learn from them in the same way that they would want to learn from us."

Thankfully, the crowd did not boo him but neither did they cheer for him. Silence, as still as a quiet sea, hung over them as it had done when he had stepped onto the stage. Cedo turned toward Mr. Farns, an empty feeling of disappointment taking over him at the realization of his failure. He had not entertained these people. Perhaps they were not used to people like himself? Everyone else listed on the bill did other things—they juggled or sang songs. None of them told tales.

Quickly, Mr. Farns stood, clapping heartily as he

addressed the audience, "Ladies and gentlemen, the great Cedo Reilly!"

With a small bow, Cedo exited the stage. He did not feel very great, no matter what the proprietor said. The wrenching in his gut told him that this was not going to be the end of his evening. Head hanging and humiliated, he walked back toward the office. He had wanted to stay and see the rest of the acts, to laugh and smile and applaud them. Not tonight. Cedo could only hope that Erus was not drunk. He could not cope with the overbearing and demanding Erus in a moment like this. To have to cope with a drunken one as well would be akin to a nightmare.

CHAPTER 6

Quietly, he pushed the door open. Erus was still sitting with his back to the door, his feet propped on the cluttered desk. A dark bottle dangled from the long fingers, its slow swinging circles the only indication that Erus was awake.

Cedo's heart dropped to the floor: his suspicions had been correct.

Giving a polite cough, he tried to rouse Erus' attention. But the bottle still moved back and forth. Cedo shivered. He had not expected to become a wonder in a single night, but he sensed that applause, no matter how sparse, was a sign of victory to Erus. No applause would be a failure.

After what seemed like an age, Erus stood. His breath quickened as Erus faced him, eyes reddened by booze, angered by the obvious silence that had followed Cedo's exit from the stage.

Erus did not look him in the eye as he swept past. No one there to watch over them as they walked, an ominous presence followed by a silent shadow.

On they went, winding through corridors, Cedo trembling as they approached the exit. He felt his jaw tighten, muscles aching as he tried to work up the courage to explain himself.

The coach ride was dreadful. Erus never looked at him,

instead staring straight ahead as he sipped from the silver flask. Cedo leaned his head back against the padded seat and watched the city slide by. Street hawkers stood beside the road, screaming their wares as people passed—*City's finest gin! Just one florin a glass! Evening 'paper, get your evening 'paper ladiesan'genllemen! Step this way for the greatest show on earth!* After a time, their voices became one, a single sound selling a multitude of things.

Their carriage juddered forward, men on ladders holding up colored lights at junctions to tell the traffic when to make its move—red for stop, green to move again. It was a city Cedo had seen many a time, mostly on foot. From the back of the fine carriage it took on a whole other life, that of a great living, breathing machine. The smells of the city were all around him, an invisible marker for each part they passed through; the poorer, Darker Quarter that they were leaving stank of rot and cheap food.

The Darker Quarter where the Rose Theater was located, was exactly as its name described. It was a collection of narrow cobbled streets and tightly packed buildings hidden just beyond the sea road and stretching up towards Parson's Way. The title was unofficial, known only to the locals. To the tourists it was known and marked on the maps as *Lasciate ogne speranza, voi ch'intrate*. An unsuspecting person would never know it was there unless they accidentally took a wrong turn, a wrong turn that happened all too often according to the newspapers.

Gazing out of the window, Cedo noticed that the moon had disappeared from his life, hidden behind clouds that appeared heavy with rain. A storm was coming to wash away the grime and dirt and, Cedo hoped, to hopefully wash away the memory of tonight. He so desperately wanted another chance to prove himself.

Obviously, once his mother had disappeared there had been no more dinner parties, and the other events he had spoken at had dried up, her friends speaking to him only when they needed to. They had not been there once she was gone, offering no knowledge of her whereabouts. Just their sympathies at him being left alone, but he was an adult and therefore could look after himself.

The brougham pulled up in front of the house and wearily Cedo looked out to the softly lit windows. He did not particularly want to go back inside the house. It was not a stable place to be, at least in his mind. But he was here now, trapped by a man that he deeply desired. Manners told him that he should wait until Erus had exited the coach and so he did, giving the other ample time to put some space between them.

A moment later, Cedo stepped out into the cool night air. Standing a few feet behind, Cedo listened as the door ticked before swinging in. Erus flowed inside, the silent anger still clinging to him.

"Follow me."

Cedo looked up at the command. Erus did not look over at him. They walked past the study and to another corridor that Cedo had never seen before. It ran behind the stairs, well hidden from prying eyes and wandering feet. He wondered where it led. To the kitchens? To more servants' quarters?

Erus pushed open a door, eyes briefly flicking over his shoulder to Cedo before he disappeared down a set of stairs. Fear again rose in, an almost blind panic that should have had him running for the door and away.

Instead, he followed, feet carefully finding each darkened step, the sound of his heart loud in his ears.

Before he could reach the bottom, gas lights flared to life, illuminating a large room. It was white and windowless and, like the rest of the house, impeccably tidy. A single desk, a drawing board mounted upon it, sat in a corner. it. In the corners of the room sat what looked like pieces of unfinished machinery. One looked like a clawed foot, beautifully turned and crafted from a dull metal. Pieces of woven cabling protruded from the top, neatly tied off as it stood, waiting, to be connected to whatever it had been created for. Quite frankly, Cedo did not want to know. He had seen etchings and drawings of some of the pieces that Veetu Industries created and he could feel the stinking fear that anyone facing such a machine in battle would feel.

"Turn around." The order echoed through the room.

Doing just that, he turned and looked at Erus. The riding crop from earlier had made a reappearance, placing cold dread deep within him. Green eyes, chilled with a still ebbing anger, stared straight at him.

"Remove your trousers." Erus' voice was still cool, still emotionless and Cedo stood still, hair drifting into his eyes as he gave a small shake of his head.

CHAPTER 7

N o," he replied, heart thundering like a machine within his chest. "I will not be bullied by you."
Something flashed through the emerald eyes, something hot and raw and as primal as the forges that Erus used.

"You will obey!" he barked. "You live beneath my roof and therefore will do as I command."

"Then release me," he said softly. "You do not need to hold me here. You can let me go. I proved to you tonight that I am obviously not worthy of whatever you have to offer." His eyes flicked to the riding crop, a lump creeping up his throat.

Quietly, Erus snickered and closed the space between them, a hand finding itself in Cedo's hair, forcing him to look into Erus' furious face.

"You have had plenty of chances to escape, Cedo. You could have left the theater tonight. Yet you have continued to follow me. And why do you think that is? Because you don't want to, that's why. Because you want to see what you can become. You know you have it in you, but you don't know how to channel it, don't know how to make yourself a success."

He made no more sounds as he was pulled across the room. He watched as, with a swift flick of the wrist, Erus made the drawing board fold in on itself, revealing shackles protruding from the wall.

Cedo felt his breath quicken into erratic pants. His body was pressed across the desk and the shackles were dragged from the hole, a low grinding filling his ears. The cold metal was snapped around his wrists, his arms and body pulled tight as somewhere the chain clicked to a stop. He hissed as the trousers were pulled from his body, skin dimpling with cold.

"Just this once," he hissed over his shoulder, "I shall let you do this."

Erus chuckled. "Every good turn deserves a reward. Just as failure will be punished. Failure is not an option within these walls."

His legs could barely hold him and he shivered, the waiting tearing him to pieces. He was kept upright by the strained position, arms already beginning to ache as the metal circles dug into his flesh.

There was the sound of air being broken and a breath later the leather stung against his bare skin. A howl ripped from lips and he tensed against the desk, fingers wrapping tightly around the chain. Stinging pain made him shudder, his knees buckling as again the whip cut into him. He could feel the shame begin to rise, his body shaking with each lash, the tears welling.

Eventually, it stopped and quietness hung over the room, broken only by his coughed sobs. He did not hear Erus move, assuming that the man was admiring his handiwork, work that only a merchant of death could effectively give out.

Another tiny cry, one of shocked pleasure mumbled from his lips as fingers coated in a cool, soothing paste began to gently work over his sore buttocks. They dipped, stroking the gentle swell where his thighs ended and his rear began before creeping between them. The tiny cries turned to moans of pleasure as the fingers carried on rubbing back and forth between his buttocks.

As quickly as they had appeared, the fingers disappeared. The shackles fell away, his wrists a mess of angry, red welts. Arms eased him upright, guiding him as he was carefully clothed. He felt himself grimace as the material was pulled over the cream coated skin, pain raw and hot. But he was safe, his bloodshot eyes turning to look up at the man who held him. All hint of violence and anger had melted from Erus' face, the hardness replaced with the tiniest of smiles.

Supporting him, Erus brushed hair away from the Cedo's eyes, laying the smallest of kisses to his forehead. Still Cedo could not draw his eyes away, watching, waiting, wondering what would happen next as he leaned limply against his master. There was something there, something in those eyes that Cedo had found himself searching for over the past days. It was only there for the briefest of moments, but it was still there, a hint of something that looked like concern fluttering through them before disappearing back into the depths of the glittering emeralds.

Cedo had not expected Erus to be so strong. Erus commanded attention from all and his physical strength was no different. Carefully he guided the now-tired Cedo toward the comfortable room that beckoned. Upon reaching it, Cedo found that the bed had been made, a fire had been laid and a lavish meal had been placed to one side. He stood, weakened, as hands carefully undressed him before he was delicately moved to the bed. A sudden hunger began to wrench at him and he moved onto his side, flinching a little as sore skin rubbed against the smooth bed linen.

The drapes parted and Erus, dressed in a long, silken gown, sat on the edge of the bed, face soft and positively relaxed.

"I trust you have regained your appetite." A plump peach was held before him.

Eyes as round as the fruit, Cedo snatched it from the outstretched hand, ignoring the pain as he hungrily devoured it. Teeth tore at the rich flesh, juice dripping from his lips and to his chin. Amid the divine pleasure, Cedo looked up, catching the amused look that danced across Erus' face.

"My, my." His voice had become low. "You are hungry. Must be all the energy you used to convince that audience to love you."

Cedo ate—cheeses, meats, fruit—anything that was held out to him until he finally fell back to the bed, panting heavily, his belly full, washing it down with a glass of offered wine. Droplets of the ruby liquid slid over his lips, dangling from his chin before falling to the crisp linen, staining it with blood-like splashes.

"It will be laundered," the other whispered, glass dangling precariously from his fingers

Belly full, Cedo watched as Erus slowly approached, that damned hair now free of its restraints and rippling like snakes. Fingers curled around his jaw, wine-tainted lips touching his own. His eyes fell shut as kisses whispered over his lips and to his throat. Teeth nipped at the throbbing vein in his neck, his throat exposed. He gasped, hands reaching out to cling to Erus, teeth threatening to open the vein and drain him dry.

Not that he would have cared. He never thought that he would ever give himself over to someone so easily, so willingly, never resisting or giving it a second thought. But it had happened, sending ripples of lust and passion through him. It had been as if the sun had dawned, awakening a new day within him, a new day that was filled with hope and a renewed lust for life. It was intoxicating and Cedo knew that he would have a difficult time ever pulling himself away from this new passion.

"Sleep," Erus hissed, teeth dangerously close to his ear. "Sleep and wake on the morrow."

Cedo was sure he could hear something in the voice that had not been there before. It sounded gentle, soft, perhaps as if he suddenly meant something to Erus, instead of just being a plaything of the rich and dangerous. It was something that warmed his heart and gave him a hope that his affections would be returned.

The kisses kept on coming, his throat warming and reddening where teeth dragged across his skin, and he found himself being laid within the ripples and mounds of the bed. He never moaned, nor did he complain as the pain of his earlier beating once more flared through him. Instead, he just clung to the man above him, willingly giving everything over to him as he was spirited away, ready to begin this strange and new life.

Sleep eluded him, mind racing as if loud cogs were turning over and over. In the darkness, he watched the silent figure sleep, body stretched the length of the bed. Hands were tucked neatly beneath the pillow, hair spread behind him, frozen in the hours of night. The shadows were harsh, darkening the pits and arches of the face but even with them, Cedo could see the innocence of sleep that lay over it, the rumbling monster quieted, if only for a few hours.

So he lay, his head buried against the pillow, watching, until the sun began to peek through the window. It danced over Erus' sleeping face, gently lighting it with a pure, warm light. Cedo could not help but smile; his Master was even more beautiful now than he had been in the coolness of night. Sunset-colored lashes dusted sunrise tinted cheeks, eyes beginning to flutter as the start of the day began to wash over him.

Breath touched Cedo's face and he looked to the wakening man. Eyes still held the gentleness of sleep and the daze of finding another in his bed. Erus stretched, hands uncurling from beneath their pillow hideaway, lips curling into a tiny smile, recognition of the other person beside him finally setting in.

Erus lifted his head and leaned closer to breathily whisper a greeting. Cedo smiled, reaching out to lift the hair that had fallen so innocently into the other's eyes. The smile on Erus' lips deepened, eyes closing at the brief touch. Cedo felt a paternal streak flare through him, as if this man, for whatever reason, needed someone to look after him. It was blatantly obvious to anyone that Erus needed no others in this world, yet Cedo still wondered. Surely this man could not look after himself all of the time. Surely there were times when he needed to break down, needed to let the barriers fall even for a second, needed to let the outside world into his innermost being.

Or perhaps he did not.

Erus strained forward, a childlike movement, his eyes focused on Cedo. Suddenly feeling like their roles had switched, Cedo leaned closer, lips brushing against those that were offered. Cradling Erus' head, he closed his eyes as he became the strong one. He sighed as arms looped around his neck, holding him close. He deepened the kiss, tip of his tongue touching against soft, parted lips. They clung to one other, lips pressed together, hungrily moving in rhythm, tongues sliding over plump, rapidly bruising lips.

Power, as Cedo knew well from his nights holding court

on the pier, was an addictive feeling and holding a quietly whimpering Erus in his arms was no different. For those few heartbeats, Erus had become almost like a lost child. It was as if he had never been treated in such a manner, something that Cedo found to be an impossibility. There had to have been lovers before. He could not be the only person in this man's life. Erus' experience and confidence told a different story, a story that he was probably, despite his occupation, a darling around the city. But the way he was holding onto Cedo seemed to cry an entirely different tale.

It did not take Erus long to catch himself and the power crackled and flickered, switching back to its original owner. The hands fell away from Cedo, moving to straighten thick curls of hair away from a face that was now falling back into its everyday, businesslike manner. Green eyes lightened, more becoming impartial, and Erus pushed himself from the bed, seeming to have forgotten the moment and the night before.

"Come." His shadow moved back and forth beyond the hangings as clothes were collected from a large wardrobe. "I must go to Svenfur. You may come, if you wish, and collect some of your belongings from your room." The drapes were roughly pulled back, a silent order for Cedo to rise.

"You may bring your cat, provided you keep her under control." Erus began to dress, completely void of any kind of embarrassment.

Biting his lip, Cedo let his eyes drift over the strong, toned body. Muscles rolled in well-built shoulders, working down to a perfectly curved back and over tight buttocks and strong legs. The blush he had tried so hard to prevent came flooding back.

"I do not mind animals, per se, but..." Sliding his arms into a stiff, white shirt Erus looked over his shoulder.

"But I do mind if they begin to take exception to my furniture." A smile played on lips. "But if she makes you happy, then I shall be happy."

"Thank you, Sir."

"You will find the few clothes you have here in the dresser beneath the window. As I have stated, I should like you to move in on a more permanent basis. You have great potential, Cedo, and it would be such a shame to waste it out in the provinces and on your pier."

Quietly, Cedo pulled out the suit he had arrived in a few days before. As before, it had been beautifully laundered and pressed before being neatly folded between sheets of scented paper.

"As you know, Cedo, I am not holding you against your will. You choose to stay here and, at any point, should you choose to leave, you may."

Standing, Cedo sighed and nodded, turning to face Erus as he began to dress.

Erus' voice became lower as he spoke again, "I quite think you like being under the control of another. Am I right?"

Cedo quickly nodded, not wanting to face Erus.

"You were tired of being a free radical, were you not?"

Again, he nodded, arms suddenly becoming heavy as he struggled to find the appropriate holes on his jacket.

There was no sound of malice, nor amusement in Erus' voice. "Then you shall fall under my control. And if this is your wish, then we shall make it official at a later date."

Cedo's eyes snapped up at the words, suddenly wide with a fear he thought had all but disappeared. He took in Erus' gentle, caring smile, wondering what was meant by the final statement. It sounded like a commitment akin to a marriage, and Cedo debated if he were prepared for such an event. A nervous excitement played through him.

But Erus gave no more away, though the smile remained on his lips. Turning, he snatched up his cane and offered Cedo his arm.

"Come then. 'Tis time to begin a new life, my boy."

CHAPTER 8

Despite running north to south, the main thoroughfare of Svenfur was called West Road. No one knew why, any such records having long since disappeared into the annals of time. This was the main artery of the city and all amenities were located here, from those who ran the water and gas companies to the Patron of the city's offices. It was an attractive road, each building more impressive than the last until you reached the corner of West Road and Sea Front Road.

There, a huge white and gilded monument to architecture stood, windows looking over the people that walked the two roads and out to the sea. There, the Patron of the city worked, somewhere high above the ocean, quite possibly now waiting to receive Erus and whatever plans the creator of war now held deep within the locked case that was at his feet.

Since it was daytime, the streets were empty of the fine walking contraptions and lavish carriages. The people who owned them were probably far off in their manor houses. The mere peasants were back at work, manning the water and gas mains and keeping the pneumatic postal system in working order. Cedo had only seen this new fangled way of sending letters once before, a few hours earlier in Erus' office.

Standing just behind Erus, he had watched as a note

had been scrawled before being rolled up and dropped into a little brass tube. At the press of a switch, a little door had opened in the desk, a little round door that Cedo had previously thought hid an ink well. But no, the little tube was dropped in, the door was closed and another little button was pressed. There had been a *whoosh* loud enough to make Cedo jump and the little tube had gone on its way, disappearing into a network of tunnels and tubes he had only heard stories about. He had no idea how it would find its destination and Erus had divulged no information other than that it would arrive safely. Now Cedo was fascinated; any post he had ever received had come via the normal service.

The carriage pulled up outside of the big, white building. Erus stepped from it before it had come to a complete stop. As patient as any servant, Cedo stood before him as he awaited any orders.

Peering over a pair of blue tinted spectacles, Erus addressed him, face already lined with the stresses that lay before him, "I do not know how long this is going to take, so go do what you need to and come back here. Tell them you are waiting for me."

Giving a small nod, he watched as Erus turned away, one hand clutching the briefcase, the other pulling handfuls of wind whipped hair from his face.

"Good luck, Sir," he said, an odd feeling of despair suddenly clutching his heart. "For whatever you have to go and do."

Erus stopped at the peak of the grand steps. "Thank you, Cedo."

Cedo could not help but break out into a small smile. It was the human reaction that had just been graced upon him that caused the smile, the fact that Erus seemed to be, in part, human and not just a soulless, senseless killing machine. There was something within that body other than a man who created the supreme tools of war. Cedo

71

had seen tiny flickers of that person over the past few days. Cedo wondered if that person could be capable of anything other than the extreme black and white of human emotion. Could that person, for instance, love? Or did he just mete out beatings when things did not go his way and pleasure when it did?

He waited until Erus had disappeared into the great building before heading for the sea. Dodging the few carriages and trams that were winding their way along the road, he leaned against the railings and looked out to sea. Wind whipped at his hair and Cedo closed his eyes, taking deep lungfuls of the fresh, salty air. Even from here, just standing on the brink of the beach, he could hear the water calling to him as it rolled against the sand. Sometimes he was sure he could hear the sirens' voices when he stood upon the pier. They were there, calling to him to join them.

West Road sliced the English seaside city neatly in two. From where he stood, gazing out to sea, Cedo could have turned either way. To his left was the Darker Quarter. Above Parson's Way was the slightly more upmarket area of Whitmoore. It was within these few square miles that Cedo had his lodgings. It had offered an easy, and often interesting, walk through the Quarter until he had reached the Sea Road.

To his right was the Hinckledon area of the city. Here there were the places that were frequented by those who had money—shops, bars, hotels and theaters. There were also row upon row of gabled houses, jostling for attention beside the tiny shops that sold everything from fine jewelry to unidentified items from foreign lands. It was the playground of the wealthy. The city, it seemed, had unconsciously divided itself into those who could afford it and those who could not.

Only a few days had passed, yet he felt as if it had been much longer. His soul ached to walk the boards of the pier and reconnect with the world that was quickly fading from his memory. Yet he knew that he had stepped away from it for a good reason. There was so much more to life than the biting taste of the salt and the calls of the strangers who found him. No longer could he deny the dreams that had lingered in the depths of his mind. The dreams that wished him well, that wanted a better, more prosperous life for him. A life filled with happiness and love.

For a moment, his eyes lingered on the pier, and on the area that lay beyond it, an area that he knew well yet spent so little time in. He may have been welcomed there but he felt uncomfortable in the presence of the people his mother had consorted with. They were so unlike her, so false and pretentious, believing themselves to be something that they were not. Their inability to even try to understand people from other classes had angered him often. They were now the people he no longer wanted to associate with, the false aristocracy who paid for their titles with the blood and sweat stained cash of the poor.

His body suddenly froze, stomach lurching. *...who paid for their titles with the blood and sweat stained cash of the poor...*

Much like Erus. His money came from the stinking rot of death, his machines quite possibly built by underpaid, undernourished and bullied workers. What made him different from those he now disliked so much? What had blinded him to Erus' arrogance?

The answer was simple, as blindingly obvious as the changing of the seasons.

Erus had taken him in when he had needed it. Had scooped him from the creaking end of the pier and whisked him off to another life. Cedo had gone as far as he could on his own, and this was the boost he needed to fulfill the promises he had made to his mother.

Cedo stared at the great building across the street. It was not just that, was not just the pride of finding his way that had blinkered him to Erus. It was the strange, shivering lust that overtook him every time he looked at the red-haired man. It was the odd realization that he had found the person his mother had spoken of time and again, the one person who would make such an impact on his life that he would never want to leave. He felt hypocritical that he would once more be mixing in those circles, but he was not doing this just for himself. He was doing it for his mother, for the one who believed, and now for the new person who believed.

Arms clasped around his knees, he sat for a while longer, just gazing at the building before him as his thoughts whirled around his head. To be with Erus, he would have to let go of at least a few of the opinions that were trying to pull him down. Erus was not like the people in his previous life. He did not pretend he was something he was not.

Cedo suspected this was the tip of the iceberg and that Erus had plenty to hide, but for the brief snatches of conversation Cedo received, the warlord did not mince his words and he did not make any preconceptions about why Cedo was there. For that, Cedo was grateful. It proved, for now, that Erus was not these other people. To his knowledge, the weapons designer was not malicious other than in his job, and those were qualities that Cedo admired.

The Quarter was heaving with activity. It was here that the tradesmen lived and plied their wares after struggling through the undulating streets of the other side of town. Horses and carts clattered over the tight, cobbled streets, drivers and pedestrians alike yelling and bawling at each other.

"Bloody 'ell, can ye not gerra move on? I got places to be, me."

"Ah, shurrup ya whinin', 'cos if ya dunt you'll be gerrin' a buncha fives."

"Will ye git that cart moved, son? You havin' a three day week 'ere or what?"

It was a quagmire of different voices, people, sights and smells. This was where Cedo liked to wander, taking it all in. It was said that some people, those from the bigger cities, and even from Svenfur, came to study such places, trying to find out what made the residents tick.

As he walked, Cedo studied everything around him, searching for the next tale to tell. And it was then that he spotted it, stenciled on the side of a building. At first, Cedo was sure it was a trick of the light, a hallucination or a figment of his imagination but, as he crossed the road, his eyes widened, realizing that what he had seen was, for once, completely real.

It was a fading outline hidden beneath the grime of the city and Cedo was surprised he had seen it at all. His breath hitched a little as he brushed his fingers over the rough bricks, wiping the dirt away. But it was there, a small image quickly painted onto the brickwork—a dragon with a mouse crouching in its outstretched claw.

His mouth dried, eyes wide as he backed away. Now he knew where he had seen the images. Tucked away down alleys, beneath the lips of fountains and at the entrances to tunnels, the images were painted in places where the average person would not see them. But Cedo was not the average person. He had seen them on his walks around the city, quietly tucked away in discreet corners.

He hurried along the streets, mind a blur with the strange image—what did it mean? Were they a code? Were they hiding something? He wanted to know, wanted to get to the bottom of the strange little image. Were they promoting something? Perhaps Erus used them as a small trigger image for people, to remind them of his products and for people to make inquiries. But if so, then why was it so small and in such obscure places?

The steps of his old home loomed before him, and Cedo suddenly felt grateful to be there. For a moment, at least, he could be among his old belongings, picking the ones he wanted to take and carefully collecting Misty.

Silence swelled through the big house as he climbed the stairs, the other residents being elsewhere in the city. It was with a heavy heart that he pushed open the door to his room for the final time. He had liked it here, had liked the company of the other residents. It had been interesting to sit with them at meal times, talking and debating deep into the night. It had been a friendly little community, one that Cedo found himself loathe to leave.

CHAPTER 9

With Misty in her basket and his suitcase of meager belongings at his feet, Cedo looked around the Patron's offices. White walls were lined with the portraits of past leaders while a staircase no doubt led to the offices. At a desk at the foot of the stairs sat an elderly man, spectacles balanced on his nose, disapprovingly watching Cedo.

"Young man." It was the gentleman at the desk.

Looking up, Cedo watched as the snowy haired man walked toward him, cool eyes twinkling with a hint of fear.

"Young man," he repeated, voice now as quiet as the waves beyond the window. "What do you know of Erus Veetu?"

"Not much, other than that he creates weapons of war and has created some of the finest entertainment stars this city has ever seen."

Peering over his glasses, the man nodded. "That is very true, but I advise you not to get too deeply involved with him."

The comment shot into Cedo's heart, flaming hot before chilling him to the bone. "Why not?"

The man looked over his shoulder before continuing.

"Walls have ears, young man, walls have ears. But you know this. Do not wrong that man. Do not wrong him, because he will tear you apart in a death so slow and so painful that whatever afterlife awaits will be a relief."

Cedo leaned closer, looking at the man with worried eyes.

"How do you mean?"

Once more, the man looked up, shaking a little as he did.

"Like I said, the walls have ears here, as does the pneumatic postal system. Terrible, unspeak-"

"Cedo!"

The man paused, face paling and writ with terror. Looking over the suited shoulder, Cedo smiled as Erus descended the staircase, briefcase and hat in hand, face a picture of joy. Beside him was another man, tall and extremely thin. A black suit hugged the man's figure, dark hair short and styled around an angular face. A tiny smile, one that was condescendingly directed at Cedo, was the only emotion being shown.

"Terrance, old boy," the Patron said. "I see you've been getting to know Erus' young gentleman friend. Nice of you to make him welcome. Shame you couldn't do that with more of our visitors."

Terrance glowered and got to his feet, silently stalked back to his desk. Erus, still smiling, stopped with his hand on the door. His attention, for the moment, was firmly on the Patron.

"I'll see you again soon, Jules," he said, firmly shaking the Patron's hand.

Then Erus' eyes were back on Cedo, the happiness that was on his face seemingly unshakable. "Come, let us leave. I see you have collected your belongings. Good, good."

Returning Erus' friendly smile, Cedo stooped and picked up his belongings. Despite having known him for only a brief period, he was not used to seeing or hearing this level of emotion from Erus. He had no idea what it was for, but was sure he would find out in due course.

They settled into the brougham, basket and suitcase at Cedo's feet. They pulled off into the intensifying traffic and Cedo turned to look at Erus. If he had been shocked by Erus when they were in the building, then the grabbing of his head and rough kiss to his lips eclipsed all of that. Eyes wide, Cedo pulled away, chuckling a little. "What was that in aid of?"

Erus leaned closer, one hand tenderly stroking the curves of Cedo's face.

"A business opportunity has been sealed, one that I have been chasing for the past several years." Lips touched his cheek, softer than they had ever been before, gentle breath shimmering over his skin. "Finally it has come to fruition. The papers have been signed and now I shall begin to supply the Navy with the most advanced weaponry known to man."

The fingers moved into his hair, cradling the back of his head and pulling his parted lips to the ones that had been pressed to his cheek. "You cannot begin to understand what this means. The advancements that have been made, which have been lying dormant for the past two years, waiting for just this day. Now they can finally be freed from the sheds that hold them and find their way out into the world, where they will continue to protect this great isle."

Trembling beneath the light touches, Cedo looked into Erus' face. Never, in the short time that he had known him, had this man been so gentle, so tender with him.

Feeling himself drawn ever deeper into the mystery of this man, he ignored what Terrance had said. Kneeling up onto the padded seating of the carriage, he swung a leg over Erus' knees, settling himself onto the man's lap. His hands crawled into the waves of thick hair, mouth hungrily seeking Erus', pressing himself closer as his heated kisses were feverishly returned. His body shuddered and bucked as the hands that had previously punished him rode over his body.

Tilting his head back, Cedo looked down into glazed green eyes, taking in bruised lips and tiny breaths.

"I have never known someone to hide such passion within them. Cedo, dear Cedo, I find you awakening things within me. Things that dare not speak their names. Even I cannot speak their names." Hair became a veil as Erus shook his head, hiding his eyes and whatever they revealed. "I may never speak their names but they are there, within me."

Cedo felt his heart skip a beat. Surely Erus could not be speaking about how Cedo himself felt? Surely he could not be speaking about the soaring feelings that flew him to clouds of pleasure whenever he found himself in the other's presence? Leaning forward, he brushed the hair away, looking into green eyes now tinged with pain.

"Tell me," he said softly, "Tell me what now lives within you."

Another shake of his head, but the gaze could not be hidden, not now that Cedo had hold of his head. Eyes were windows to the soul and, slowly but surely, he could see Erus' innermost feelings battling to come to the surface. They wanted to be known, yet Erus appeared to be fighting to keep them hidden.

"You are not a monster. You are allowed to feel."

"If I feel, then I shall grieve."

"Why? Why shall you grieve?"

Cedo was sure he could see tears glistening in Erus' eyes. "I shall grieve for those who have died at my hands. Sons, brothers, fathers—all of them children, all of them loved."

"Then grieve! They did not die at your hands. That is

a complete lie. As you said yourself, you create what is needed to protect this country and to keep it a free land. It is not as if you went out and killed them yourself. You have done nothing except keep this country safe."

Erus sighed, making no move to escape Cedo's desperate clutches, turning his eyes downward instead. "If I were to grieve, then I would spend my lifetime grieving. I would spend my lifetime shedding tears for those whose names I shall never know. If I were to feel, this is what would happen."

Grabbing Erus' head, Cedo forced him to look into his eyes, eyes that he hoped showed the deepest and most passionate of loves. His lips touched the cheek of his Master, gently kissing the tears away.

"Then let me help you. Let me hold you while you grieve. I shall not go. I shall not think any less of you, should you shed tears. And I shall not tell those who wish to destroy you."

Erus was shaking as he reached up and pulled Cedo closer to him, lips brushing over his jaw and to his forehead.

"You have a good spirit, Cedo." Erus' eyes flashed with happiness. "And soon, I shall do something I have never done before and officially invite you into my life. Is that what you truly want?"

Heart rattling against his chest and mind whirring, Cedo hung limply in Erus' grasp. "Yes. It is something I would greatly like."

Erus smiled once more, lips once more finding Cedo's and giving him the gentlest of kisses. "Then you shall have it. You shall have everything you desire."

CHAPTER 10

The days passed, stretching slowly into weeks, until the night of their union was upon them. An ocean of paperwork had been filled and filed before the Council of Companion Relationships approved their joining. It was, as Erus had explained, a necessary evil, affording them protection from the laws of the land. Without the approval and subsequent papers, they could be arrested and charged with deviant behavior. The Council, Cedo discovered, were a group of men charged with overseeing the relationships between Masters and Mistresses and their companions. When a relationship was forged, a Certificate of Union was applied for, contracts were drawn up, and a letter confirming Cedo's consent was filed. A medical was demanded, to prove that he was of sound mind and body. It was an intrusive examination, and Cedo had been glad when it was over. Finally, on a moonless night, Cedo changed into the specially-commissioned, collarless suit.

Standing before the mirror, Cedo admired himself one last time. Lavish embroidery danced over the corn-yellow jacket, the breeches disappearing into a pair of long, black boots. He looked almost virginal, and his heart skipped a beat. The last moments of freedom were upon him. Soon he would walk into a new life. It was not a life he had expected himself to have. He had assumed that he would find an elegant girl and get married. Never, in all of his dreaming, had he seen himself giving his life over to another man. But he was and it felt completely natural. No longer did any doubts eat way at his mind, having melted away. They would most likely return from time to time, but every relationship had its good times and its bad. He would just have to accept and ignore them as best he could. The only hope he had was that he would never act upon what they said.

Straightening the jacket, he took a deep breath and made for the door.

Feeling light-headed and oddly optimistic, he strode into the dining room, a smile sweeping up his lips as he saw an equally finely-dressed Erus before him.

Around the large dining table, their faces lit by the soft light, were a group of people Cedo could only assume were the staff of the house. Toward the head of the table, he spotted Mrs. Sugden. Beside her sat an older man, his face as impartial as the woman beside him. The rest of the table was occupied by men and women, young and old alike, all with the same, impartial and hardened expression, as if no matter what their age, they were all as old as the hills.

Feeling a cold sweat begin to break over his body, Cedo turned back to Erus, taking in the warmth that radiated from his face. Yet it did little to calm his racing nerves.

"Are you ready?"

Quieted by a lump in his throat, Cedo nodded.

"Good." Erus placed two sheaves of paper on the table. "These are contracts—one for you and one for me. They state what you can expect from me and what I expect from you."

Flicking his eyes between the papers and Erus, he shivered with the slight fear of the unknown.

The contracts were written on heavy, creamy paper,

each part numbered for ease of reading. He scanned over it, taking it in as he tried to hold the papers still between trembling fingers.

I, Cedo Reilly, (hereinafter "The companion") do willingly swear, by almighty God, on this fifteenth Day of the Month of April, in the Year of Our Lord Eighteen Hundred and Ninety Five, to abide by the following clauses and stipulations.

The companion does willingly and wholly cede their corporeal physicality to Erus Veetu (hereinafter known as "Master").

The companion does willingly, wholly, and of their own free will, herein swear to obey all orders, instructions, commands and requests with unwavering dedication.

Within the confines of the private household and its immediate environs, the companion shall refer to the aforementioned master as "Master". In public spaces, open society and polite company, the companion shall refer to him as "Sir."

The companion shall willingly undertake any education, scholastic travails or practice, so as to perform upon the stages of the theaters, Music Halls and entertainment halls, without geographical stricture.

The Companion shall execute tasks in a timely, competent and contrite manner to the limits of personal ability.

When in public spaces, open society or polite company, the companion shall not seek to disagree, make argumentative commentary, act in contrary to others or make complaints in contradiction of the aforementioned Master.

The Companion promises to forswear all others in perpetuity, or until such time as this contract is amicably dissolved.

The Companion, being of sound mind and body, and

free from any ulterior motives or extraneous obligations, fully understands the scope of the contract herein, and that failure to uphold the clauses, willful ignorance or disobedience of said clauses, will lead to punitive action or stricture.

Both parties do hereby, undersigned, freely enter into the contract elucidated herein.

Signed: _____ Date: _____
  Erus Veetu ("the Master")
Signed: _____ Date: _____
  Cedo Reilly ("the Companion")
Witness: _____ Date: _____
Witness: _____ Date: _____

Letting the papers fall back to the table, he took a deep breath. "I consent."

A relieved smile crossed Erus' face. "Thank you."

Next, Cedo read Erus' promises to him.

I, Erus Veetu (hereinafter "the Master), do willingly swear, by almighty God, on this fifteenth Day of the Month of April, in the Year of Our Lord Eighteen Hundred and Ninety Five, to abide by the following clauses and stipulations.

The Master is of the understanding that the companion is an individual upon whose life cannot be placed a price. The Master shall keep the companion safe from harm, including the provision of a house from which the companion shall never be cast.

The Master shall nurture and encourage the companion, so that the companion may grow and blossom to the full extent of their abilities in order to perform upon the stages of the theatres, Music Halls and entertainment halls, without geographical stricture.

In accordance with the decrees laid down by the

Council of Companion Relations, the Master gives assurance that he shall be firm, yet kind, understanding that the companion has needs. Any needs that the companion alludes to shall be met in a way thast the Master deems fit.

The Master promises to return the companion's affections and the great love that the companion has so willingly bestowed upon him.

Should a disagreement arise from any of the clauses within this contract, the Master agrees to listen to all that the companion has to say and to weigh it carefully before making a final decision.

The Master promises to forswear all others in perpetuity or until such time as this contract is amicably dissolved.

Both parties do hereby, undersigned, freely enter into the contract elucidated herein.

Signed: _____ Date: _____
  Erus Veetu ("the Master")
Signed: _____ Date: _____
  Cedo Reilly ("the Companion")
Witness: _____ Date: _____
Witness: _____ Date: _____

With another nod, he handed it back, swallowing against the heavy lump in his throat. The man before him emitted a powerful energy that Cedo could not help but find himself drawn to. It was a magnetic force that, no matter what the elderly gentleman in the city had said, Cedo could not break away from. It was all or nothing and he was ready to hand over everything, including his soul, to the arrogant man before him.

An opened box was held before him and Cedo looked down. Lying on a bed of claret red velvet was a silver, rope necklace. Lifting his head, Cedo nervously brushed the hair from his face. He gave a trembling nod, the room suddenly hot. Erus lifted a hand, gently brushing the hair over Cedo's shoulder, eyes cool with a fearful compassion.

"You can still leave, Cedo," he said softly, a hint of fear in his voice. "But both you and I know that, for the rest of our lives, we shall both regret the moment you leave. Do you consent to this?"

Taking a deep breath, Cedo finally found his voice, "I do."

The emerald eyes warmed a little as another question was placed to him, "Do you consent to the contract that has been put before you?"

His voice was beginning to find a new confidence, "I do."

A smile finally broke Erus' worried face. The necklace was lifted from the box, and Erus pressed some tiny, hidden switch to release the catch.

"Cedo, this is a symbolic token of ownership and I want you to realize that once it is placed around your neck, it can never be removed. Not just figuratively, but literally too. It has a permanent locking device which, once activated, will seal it forever. There is no way that it can be removed without destroying it. Do you consent to wearing it?"

Breathing heavily, Cedo eyed it warily. It was the final step toward this new life he had been promised, one that he had never thought he would embark upon but that he now realized he wanted to grasp with both hands. Standing firm, he looked Erus square in the eyes and brought his hands up behind his neck, lifting waves of honey blond hair clear of his neck. "I do."

CHAPTER 11

The heavy necklace was placed against Cedo's skin, cool and possessive as hands locked it firmly behind his head. There was a tiny jolt, the feeling of something being removed and, for one heart-stopping moment, he thought that Erus had changed his mind. But when the other pulled away, the necklace was still firmly in place, the metal loosely hugging his throat. Cedo brought a hand to his throat, fingers finding the metal that was rapidly warming to his body. It felt heavy, almost out of place, but still it felt right, as if he had been accepted into a world he had never known he wanted to be part of.

Discarding the pin, Erus clasped his face and pushing it back, lips pressing to the center of his forehead. "My precious, beautiful Cedo. You do not know how long I have waited for this moment. You may have only known me for a short while but I have known of you for so much longer. Ever since I heard your name whispered upon the lips of bar men and street urchins I have known that I wanted to be a part of your world. "

Cedo stilled for a moment. Erus had known of him for how long? He had thought it had only been a matter of weeks, but obviously the arms manufacturer had known about him for much, much longer.

"How long have you known of me, Master?"

Lips brushed against his ear. "Far longer than you can imagine."

Hands limp by his side, he trembled beneath Erus' touch, the weight of the moment still lying upon him. From the corner of his eye he watched as the people around the table began to file out, only Mrs. Sugden and her gentleman partner remained. Picking up the pen, Erus signed the papers with a flourish. Cedo took the pen and watched, almost as if he were detached from his body, as he scrawled his name onto his own contract. His stomach clenched in a mix of sickening fear and heady excitement. For now, in the truest sense of the word, he was owned. Mrs. Sugden and the gentleman signed the contracts, then silently left the room.

From the corner of his eye, he was aware of the table being laid with silver cutlery and splendid glasses. Seating himself, Cedo tried to ignore the almost choking weight of the necklace.

"How do you feel?" Erus' voice shocked him into looking up, realizing that Erus was now seated across from him, a polite, almost businesslike, smile on his lips.

"I am not sure, Master. I am not sure if I have done the right thing, but I know that it is too late now."

"It is natural. Completely natural." Eyes followed the smile, warming a little. "You shall become used to it. It may take a while, but soon you shall find yourself becoming more comfortable." Elbows came to rest on the table, Erus resting his chin in his hands.

Feeling himself flush, Cedo quickly looked away..

"That others will judge me. That I will judge myself. That I will hate myself for losing my freedom." It took considerable effort to force out the last word and with burning cheeks, he finally looked up.

"Perfectly normal things to be worried about in such a situation. There are many, many arrangements like this throughout the city. It is why we have the Council to oversee and regulate them. While you have made a promise never to leave, you have to view this as a marriage."

Erus gave a husky chuckle, one that made Cedo shudder and squirm. "You may not view it as such, at least not at the moment, but in time you will. There are others like you in this city, and many more across the nation. You will not know them because, like you, they wear a discreet symbol of ownership. It may be as simple as a ring. Others may have an initial or image carved into some unseen skin. You will not know them and they will not know you, but you are all out there, in the houses across this fair land."

An hour later, passion raged. Lips were sealed to his and hands groped at each other's bodies as Cedo found himself being pushed toward to the bedroom.

The bedroom door was heaved shut, Cedo's panting frame pushed up against it as heavy hands roamed over him, lips pressed to his jaw. He shuddered and moaned, body aching with the need that had gripped him ever since he had stepped into Erus' predatory glare. Dragging himself away from the wood, he grasped a handful of hair, pulling Erus' mouth to his own.

With a grunt, Erus pushed him away, Cedo looked up into a face now darkened with passions that could only have come from the fires below. Lips were chapped and raw, a drop of blood nestled beneath his lower lip, eyes glazed nearly black.

The jacket fell and crumpled in Cedo's wake, forgotten as he snatched at tight shirt buttons, growling with frustration before it rumpled to the floor behind him.

Twisting on the balls of his feet, he faced a now nude Erus, a being who seemed as comfortable naked as he did clothed. Falling beneath Erus' Cedo let himself be swept up into strong arms and carried to the bed.

Hands held him as hot skin pressed close. Lips found each other once again and Erus commanded his full attention. He craved his Master's attention, found himself now silently begging for it and for approval.

Cedo arched against the hands that clasped his back, wanting whatever was offered and giving into the animalistic desire that now clenched his body. A growl that could only have come from that animal within rushed against Erus' lips, Cedo bringing his hands to his lover's shoulders and pressing him to the bed. He had waited long enough for this moment, had battled with every imaginable feeling and now he was ready to give in to desires that, in other parts of the country, , would have seen him shunned. But here it was not. Here, in the house of Veetu, the few girls he had courted and loved, a number so small he could count them on one hand, could disappear, wisps of memories that would never return.

A halo of red hair caught his eye, sliding over the crisp white linen, a face as pale and as open as an angel's wing smiling up at him. In those eyes, Cedo was sure he saw a glimmer of something, another world that was hidden behind the glazed windows of the face. It was a world that seemed to not want to be known, that wanted to remain hidden. Stretching himself over the sprawled body, Cedo pressed his mouth to Erus', hair falling over their faces as they closed themselves off from the world. He quivered beneath Erus' roaming hands, heart fluttering as he was guided to the lap of his Master.

Pain, red hot and jarring, jolted through him, a scream tearing from him as Erus entered him. Sweat beaded his forehead and he leaned forward, hands against his lover's chest. Fingers stroked his hips, lips brushing against his arms, gentle and soothing.

With time, he began to move, swaying on his knees. The pain came and went, the savage waves of Inferno becoming gentle swells of Heaven. His cries of pain became groans of ecstasy, a great pleasure like he had never felt before growing within him. Finally able to open his eyes, he looked down and found his own feelings mirrored in the face beneath him. Together they moved, now a single being, Erus crying his name as Cedo whispered his Master's. Hands slid over sweat-smoothed bodies, gripping and stroking, teasing and tormenting, the pleasure tightening deep in his belly.

Faster he rose and fell, impaling himself with such vigor he wondered if he would break the man. But as he slowed, those cruel and tantalizing hands pushed him onward. Fingers gripped his aching cock, sending lightning bolts of ecstasy straight through him. Head thrown back, Cedo cried out, body on the brink of release and collapse.

"Come," Erus whispered. "Finish what you have started."

And he did, every muscle snapping to attention as he spilled himself against his Master, cock throbbing against the man who could show him the extremes of pleasure and pain.

Opening his eyes, he looked at Erus, studying him for a moment. Hair streaked a damp face, green eyes wide with a sudden child-like naivety. With a vicious quickness, it became a look of terror, of suddenly being caught with no guard before him. There was something in that soul wanting to get out and unable to because of the fortress that had been built around it.

Slowly Cedo slid to the bed, lying beside Erus and draping an arm over him. His fingers tickled beneath the damp hair, cautiously encouraging his bed-bound Master to look at him. As slow as time, Erus moved, the panic in his face beginning to subside.

"What worries you?"

Erus closed his eyes and the final drawbridge crashed down. "It is nothing. Leave it be."

Cedo did not want to leave it be and he would come back to it, time and again. Almost as if he could read Cedo's thoughts, Erus pulled away, giving Cedo his back. Cedo wanted to know what went on within that head, what made the other tick. It would be a struggle to find, if he ever could.

CHAPTER 12

In the depths of his dream world, the sounds rose and fell, haunting cries and screams coupled with the sounds of machinery. In the waking moments, they stayed with him, refusing to die with the night, as cold and clear as the night-time air.

Snatching the covers away, Cedo all but fell from the bed, catching himself against one of the sturdy pillars as he turned a light on. The flame burst upward, showing him that the room was entirely empty. Empty of everyone but himself. Yet the voices kept on coming, pounding into his skull.

He pulled back the drapes of the bed, his worst fear rising. The bed was empty and all that remained of Erus was a slight indent against the pillows and a few loose hairs. Panting, Cedo felt the world swim before his eyes, coming in and out of focus as he battled to keep the sickness from rising further. Those sounds, those specter voices, the ones that he had heard every night since he had arrived, they were real. Real and somewhere within the four walls of the massive house.

Tearing open doors, he found his Master's immaculate clothes. Grabbing one of the seemingly limitless cloaks, Cedo wrapped it around himself and made for the door.

The noises were louder and he wondered why the house was not in turmoil. Surely others could hear them?

It took him a moment to find the clarity to think and to remember. They were probably locked away as he had once been, shaking in their beds as they listened to the horrendous sounds that came from somewhere below him.

He followed what he could hear, heart wrenching with each sound. They came and went, carried on the wind from somewhere in the bowels of the house. Cedo stopped at the bottom of the stairs and tilted his head, a blissful pause rippling through the air. Then it came again, the indisputable scream of a woman in pain, the high-pitched shriek of terror and agony making him curse and jump.

Cedo followed the narrowing corridor that went beyond the study. The corridor was darker than he remembered, the gas jets dimmer than before. Cedo shuddered as he pressed himself to the shadows. From where he stood, he could make out the door to the lower part of the house, the door which was once more firmly shut. Another cry, this one broken by tiny whimpers and the sound of begging, caused the spiteful taste of acid to rise within him. Inside his head, in the dark recesses of his mind, the images of a now-forgotten dream flashed forward, as fresh and as cruel as when it had first come forth in the depths of the night.

A river of blood running beneath buildings in a tunnel unseen by any man except its creator. Huge pipes jutting from stained brick walls, joints and bolts rusted and stained with years, perhaps decades, worth of this thick, red fluid. Perhaps it wasn't rust at all. Perhaps it was just stains, stains in memory of the hundreds, perhaps thousands of lives the river had carried away.

The sound of the scream was still ringing in his ears when Cedo realized that a blessed silence had fallen. Whoever it was, whoever had been going through such unbelievable pain, had become quiet. Too quiet, in Cedo's opinion. It was with a heavy heart and tears hanging from his lashes that he realized the silence was a lasting one.

Below him, Cedo could hear muffled and indecipherable voices. Pressing himself to the wall, he desperately tried to understand them. After a moment, they fell silent and Cedo groaned, the weight of the tragic night pressed closely to him. Close by, something creaked and his eyes snapped open as the cellar door swung open.

Cedo watched as a stout man clothed entirely in black left the inferno below. He walked with a purpose, thankfully away from where Cedo was hiding. Cedo wanted to escape, but something was holding him there, an unknown force that wanted him to watch and learn, to see the grave danger in which he found himself.

A child, no older than four and dressed in the clothes of a street urchin, gamboled beside the stout man. The child's tiny hand was held by a much larger one, a matchstick against a shovel. Round eyes in a face as innocent as a newly bloomed flower looked up hopefully.

"Will I see my mummy?" the child asked in the gentle voice that only children possessed.

The man smiled and Cedo's gut rolled as he spoke, recognizing the voice.

"Yeah. She's just down 'ere, sweet'art." Mr. Black. There seemed to be more to Erus' right-hand man than he had first thought. Something darker and far more sinister.

The child smiled, filled with the hope and joy that only a mother's love could bring. Tears began to fall as he watched them arrive at the door.

"No... No, please, no," Cedo whispered.

Mr. Black looked up and Cedo felt his voice catch in his throat. Eyes that were filled with an oily evil stared at him for the briefest of seconds before he disappeared into the darkness.

His feet nearly gave way as he made his way back toward the stairs. Strange, deathly affairs were happening beneath the roof of the house, away from prying eyes. Away from the supposed transparency of the outside world. Erus had to know what was happening beneath his own roof. Surely the child and its mother could not be kept a secret?

Leaning against the banister, he took a deep, labored breath. Mr. Black was embedded in his mind, the child's tiny hand clasped in his own. What would become of the child now that its mother was dead? What would become of him? Had his pursuit of a better life become his downfall, one that would spiral to a fiery death? He did not want to think about it, wanted to shove it all to the back of his mind. But the tiny child refused to allow the thoughts to die.

Erus never returned that night, leaving Cedo to only speculate on what his mood would be come sunrise.

Spread beneath the covers, Cedo stared at the intricate ceiling above him, taking in the irregular, winding patterns of branches. It was only now, in the early morning light, that he could really appreciate the beauty of it. It was as if Erus desperately wanted to be a part of the natural world, but had found himself trapped in a maze of metal and cogs, unable to reconnect to the world from which they had come.

It sickened him to think he may well be under threat within the walls of the Veetu house. He refused to let it happen. Erus could have everything else; his body, his soul, and every emotion known to man, but he would never take his mind, would never take what lived within it. If that day came, Cedo concluded, then it would be the day that he took his own life.

I shall escape, and I shall throw myself into the sea, because if he should destroy me then that is where I belong.

Despite the riot of the previous night, Cedo found himself looking forward to the coming day. The constant changes within the house and Erus' moods interested him. Who or what had created such a beastly monster, not the monster that created giant killing machines, but the one who could change as quickly as the weather? What fed that insanity, and what kept it burning just below the surface?

CHAPTER 13

With the day dragging into afternoon, Cedo wandered the narrow hallways that lay beyond the study. Past the deathly door that led below he went and to the end, the hallway coming to a junction. Before him was a door, the arched glass above it telling him that it led to the outside. To his left and right were identical corridors, both narrower than those of the main house, and as unfinished as other such quarters he had seen.

An odd smell of burning engine oil and cooking food mixed in the air around him, giving him the impression that some great, metal beast was behind the doors he passed, moving with slow, clunking movements as it passed food from one of its many hands. Leaning against one door, Cedo was slightly surprised to find that no such machine existed, that the loud metallic noises were made by a disgruntled young man bending over a deep sink.

The kitchen, a large, white tiled room with high set windows, was a bustle of activity and noise. A fire roared in a large, open pit, the heat escaping up an open chimney. Over it, a piece of meat slowly rotated via a chain crank. Pots, from which the smells of cooking vegetables escaped, were slung alongside the meat, a rotund cook periodically checking on them in between shouts to younger members of staff. Beside the fire was a long work surface, covered with well-used chopping boards and a variety of dirty knives and utensils, any of which Cedo felt would be thrown in the direction of anyone who dared step out of line. And he had a feeling that the cook probably had the best aim in the house.

Letting the door shut behind him, he walked a little farther into the kitchen. Everyone who moved around him had the perpetually red face of someone who had either been in the sun too long or who worked in the hot confines of a workhouse that never slept. A man, white clothes splattered with blood, raced past to dump a piece of unidentified meat onto a chopping block. It was only once the cook swept her eyes up to look at the new arrival that Cedo's nervous figure was discovered. He felt sweat begin to drop down his neck as dark, beady eyes focused on him, the cook's lips pursuing as she studied him. Swimming against the tide of activity, she stopped before Cedo, hands clenched at her sides.

"What do you think you're doing?" she demanded.

"N-Nothing."

Her eyes swept over him once more, taking in his clothing.

"And who the blazes do you think you are?"

Cedo's voice caught in his throat as he felt himself wither beneath her dark eyes. "I-I belong to Erus."

She held him still with her cold, narrowed eyes. "Oh, do you now? Another one of his flunkies. Well I hope you last a bit longer than the last one did. Poor bugger."

He was about to turn away when her voice called out to him, "What's your name?"

"Cedo Reilly."

The cook was leaning against the work surface.

"Well, Cedo Reilly, if you last longer than the cold winter that's coming then I'll say you're a keeper." He felt her eyes settle at his throat, taking in the heavy necklace.

"You just be careful, Cedo. He's got a temper on him, which I'm sure you've seen. Do your best to stay on the right side of him, all right?"

With a nod and a smile, she turned back to her work.

Compared to the heat of the kitchen, the garden was a welcome relief. Collecting Misty and her basket, Cedo had sought out a spot to hide from the world. He did not want to know what went on behind the closed doors of the house, be it murder or beatings. Nothing was out in the open. Erus, it seemed, saved face by keeping it all locked away. And so he should, because Cedo doubted that the outside world would want to know what the country's greatest weapons designer did in the silence of the night. Or perhaps they already knew and just turned a blind eye.

Taking his leather-bound book from the bottom of the basket, Cedo drew his knees up and propped the book against them. He wrote, the blank pages quickly becoming covered in his slanted handwriting. It was a way to relieve the pain and turmoil that was bubbling within him, the thoughts and fears of living under the watchful gaze of such a man.

Page after page was filled, Cedo never pausing to correct anything. To erase or correct would take away from its power.

A soft *chirrup* interrupted him and he let the book slide from his knees. Paws delicately came to rest in his lap, the rest of Misty's white body following. She looked at him with understanding cat eyes before curling into a ball, engine-like rumbles shaking her. She had always been a great healer in times of trauma, and now was no different. Stretching out a hand, he ran it along her back, eyes falling shut and letting out a sigh as he stretched out beneath the tree, the sounds of the garden lulling him into a light sleep.

Behind his closed eyes came images that filled him with warmth. They were not the harsh and bloody pictures of previous nights. Instead, they were filled with wonder, laughter, and cries of appreciation. They were there, it seemed, to encourage him to carry on, to not give up the fight. This man so obviously needed someone in his life who would listen rather than take. He created great machines and others took them, putting them in far flung places to injure and kill. The others he had kept in the house and turned into darlings of the entertainment halls had obviously done the same. They had taken all they could from Erus, leaving him a bitter and cold gentleman.

Cedo was not another plaything to this man; at least he hoped he was not. He wanted to be the one who could warm the chilled heart and find out what lay beneath the hard exterior. Cedo knew it was there; he had seen glimpses, if only for a moment.

Yes, he seemed to have more wealth than anyone could ever desire but Cedo's soul sang a new song as he realized what Erus could do with his talents if only he looked beyond the darkness. He could create great machines that would *help* people. They would make the lives of normal, everyday folk so much simpler. Machines that could create clothes or cook meals or even ones that could transport them at high speeds through the air.

"Ah, there you are!"

With the sigh of someone who had been on the verge of a deep and peaceful sleep, Cedo opened an eye. Erus stood over him, his fingers tucked into his waistcoat and a gentle smile on his lips. Almost instinctively, Cedo pushed himself upright, leaning heavily against the tree.

"Sorry."

Erus crouched beside him, the smile staying as one hand reached out to push hair from Cedo's eyes. "No need to apologize. You have the freedom to roam wherever you may wish in this house. All I require is that you do as I command of you, and that you do not leave the boundaries of this property.'"

Carefully, he placed Misty back in her basket, thoughts of Mr. Black roaming through his mind. He wanted to know what was happening, wanted to know if Erus was behind the noises that haunted the night. Instead, he asked, "What do you require?"

"To prepare yourself. We are going to the city, to another theater. This one has... a better clientele. We shall leave within the hour."

"As you wish, Master."

Svenfur had already become a hive of nocturnal activity as they drew up before the theater. People dressed in their colorful finery were jostling and shouting, ducking and diving as they avoided carriages and clanking machines. Touts called out their wares—gut-rotting booze, tickets to sold out showgirl performances.

Cedo felt almost at peace with himself as he stepped from the warmth of the carriage and into the bitter night air. The jovial night time hustle of Svenfur and the prospect of an evening entertaining strangers excited him.

"War in East rages on!" cried a street vendor. "Military says they have too few weapons! Veetu Industries unable to keep up with demand!"

Beside him, Cedo heard Erus sigh and he turned just in time to see him slump against his cane.

"Excuse me." Erus strode off, producing a single florin from a pocket and returning with a folded broadsheet.

"Look at this!" he exclaimed, turning the paper for Cedo to see the headline. "They expect bloody miracles yet only pay for the impossible! What am I supposed to do? *Give* them the weaponry?" He snorted and shook out the paper. "My factories are already working around the clock. Everything is assembled and ready to be shipped but they refuse to release the funds to do it. They seem to believe that these things materialize out of thin air. These parasites seem to think that raw materials, labor, and research cost nothing. They think we can all live on fresh air!"

Angered eyes appeared over the top of the newspaper, and Cedo instinctively took a step backwards. The paper was snapped in half and tucked beneath an arm. "The government are florin-pinching bastards who care only for what they can drain from others. I know this, Jules knows this, *everyone* knows this, yet nothing is ever done. They sit on their thrones behind their high walls, and bleed the men, *our* men, in the East for everything they are worth." Erus sighed, fingers pinching the bridge of his nose as he shook his head slowly. "Tomorrow. Tomorrow I will sort this out."

Gently Cedo wrapped a hand around the back of Erus' neck and pressed his lips to his temple. "You have survived before and you shall again. Now you have me beside you and, just like contract said, I am here to support you."

Eyes that showed the slow progression of time turned to look at him, a smile that had no doubt seen the creation of the planet etched beneath them. Heavy fingers stroked through his hair, cradling the back of his head to close the tiny gap between them.

"You are too good to me," Erus whispered, "and I thank you for it."

Something tugged at the hem of his jacket. Freeing himself from his Master's grasp, Cedo looked over his shoulder and into the bright eyes of a young child. Torn, ill-fitting clothes hung from the tiny form and dirty fingers stretched up to him. Memories of the night with Mr. Black stung his mind. Wiping a hand across his eyes he tried to bury them back into the darkness.

"Master..."

A coin was pressed into his hand. Kneeling, Cedo stared into the child's dark, button eyes, hopelessness making him feel suddenly alone. There were thousands of children like the one before him. Thousands who had no home, no parents, and no hope. Smiling, he dropped the coin into the small, outstretched hand.

The boy mirrored his smile and touched the peak of an imaginary cap. "Thank you, mister."

"You are welcome." His voice was tinged with sadness. "Take care of yourself."

The boy gave him another sparkling smile before disappearing into the crowd. Getting to his feet, Cedo faced Erus. But, before he had the chance to ask about the child he had seen in Erus' house, a hand came to rest in his back, guiding him towards the theater. People surrounded them, staring at them, hands cupped around mouths and eyes watching them. It was not a good time to start questioning his Master, especially if he had no idea what was occurring beneath his roof.

Holding his head high, Cedo looked straight ahead, the attention making him more than a little uncomfortable. It was not like these people did not know who Erus was; all the papers were emblazoned with huge headlines about the apparent failure of Erus' business.

But he knew he should not be worried; these were free times, people could be seen with whomever they wanted. He had seen more than his fair share of oddities on these streets—a mermaid cavorting with a sailor, men dressed as beautiful women, naked girls pressed against the walls of the beach. This was not a city of temperance but one of gaiety and glamour, of songs and high spirits.

The front of the theater was painted in red and gold, the pillars decorated with the figureheads from ships, a commemoration to its place on the seafront. Standing before the steps, Cedo smiled as he watched jets of flame dance before the fine woodwork, illuminating the strange ship-like building. A hand pressed into the small of his back and he glanced over his shoulder, Erus returning his smile.

Beyond them it looked as if the city had already come inside. People darted around, adding the final touches for the evening's performance. A wide set of stairs arched with fine gold banisters disappeared off to the stalls, while a row of doors beneath them led to the pit and cheaper, but far more entertaining, seats.

As if by magic, a smiling man stepped before them, a hand outstretched beyond Cedo and toward Erus. The tall, gaunt figure of his Master stepped forward, taking the rather large hand in both of his own and giving it a hearty shake.

"Mr. Smithson, so good to see you again!"

"And you as well, Mr. Veetu. Always a pleasure to have you with us. Please, follow me."

Like all theater owners, or at least the ones that Cedo had met in his short twenty-three years, Mr. Smithson was rather rotund. His cheeks were red from the heat and he swayed a little as he walked, leading them down winding corridors. Unlike the Rose Theater, the atmosphere backstage at the Ship Theater was rather jovial.

Here, the smell of the greasepaint made Cedo tremble with excitement. There was a good feeling in the pit of his stomach, as if tonight would be his night. Tonight, he would take the stage and he would mesmerize everyone before him. They would clap and cheer and demand more.

A door painted the brightest green and red was pushed open and the forever smiling Mr. Smithson ushered them in.

"Come on, lads. Make yourselves comfortable. Do you want a drink?"

Cedo seated himself in a well used chair. "Water, ple—"

Erus twitched a finger in a movement that Mr. Smithson did not see. Tilting his head, Erus gave him a warning glance, one that told Cedo that anything he required would be ordered by one person only. There was a flurry of hair and Erus resumed his conversation with the theater owner, who was none the wiser to what was happening.

"Whatever you feel obliged to serve us with, good sir."

Erus, now transformed from the haggard man of outside, now sat beside him, laughing and with eyes filled with a childlike wonder. As Mr. Smithson served them steaming hot mugs of sickly sweet tea, Erus fired questions at him, leaning forward in amazement as his questions were answered. Did they have anything special planned for the evening? Would there be music and dancing?

Finally, the conversation began to lull and Mr. Smithson turned his attention to Cedo. "Erus tells me you're a teller of tales. What have you brought for us tonight?"

He gave Erus a quick glance and, once the other had given him a barely visible nod, he returned his attention to the smiling man before him.

"I do not know yet. Something will arise when the moment is upon me."

"How very unusual. A storyteller who makes it up as he goes along. But, whatever works for you, m'lad, whatever works for you." The smile returned and Mr. Smithson rose, a pudgy hand clasping around Cedo's shoulder.

The theater owner stepped up to the door, calling along the corridor, "Miss Wells! Miss Wells, can you please come and accompany the lovely Mr. Reilly to the wings, please?"

A young woman stepped into the small office. She wore a fetching red dress and her blond hair was braided and wound around her head. Nervously, Cedo got to his feet, finding himself stumbling a little as he walked toward her. She said nothing as they left, waiting until the door was closed before speaking.

"I've heard your stories," she said in a gentle tone. "I saw you once or twice. At the end of the pier, right?"

With a blush staining his cheeks, Cedo nodded. "Yes, that would have been me."

Her eyes, as blue and as crisp as the early morning sky, sparkled up at him, one of her hands giving his own a reassuring squeeze. "You will be fine, Cedo Reilly. You just have to pretend that you're back at the end of the pier and that you can hear the fishes singing to you. The audience, they will be your fishes. They will clap and jump for you."

Heat rose to his face and he retreated behind his hair, the hand that was pressed to hers suddenly warm and clammy. "Thank you, ma'am."

She stopped in the strange half-light of the wings. Just looking down at the soft, delicate face made his heart race a little faster, his own skin tingling as she reached up and pressed a kiss to his cheek. "You will be fine, trust me."

She looked out through the curtains as she came to rest back on the tiny heeled shoes. "You're on after me. Just watch and then follow."

And with that, she was gone, skipping out onto the stage to a volley of applause, shouts and whistles.

CHAPTER 14

From the stage, the auditorium looked small, cramped with upturned faces, all eager for the next show. The heat from bodies and the many gas lights was overwhelming, and Cedo lightly fan himself as he stepped into the lights.

A million pairs of eyes stared up at him, all of them leaning forward to get a closer look at the boy in his finery. Miss Wells and her angelic voice and bawdy songs had left quite an impression, one which he would have to live up to.

For an eternal moment, he stood before them, savoring the crisp silence of an expectant audience. Then, in a break from every protocol of every theater in the land, Cedo stepped forward and nestled himself between the conch shell lamps at the foot of the stage. Swinging his legs back and forth, he took in the bemused looks of the orchestra.

Finally, he broke the silence. "Don't you think the sun is a strange thing, ladies and gents? It climbs into the sky, stays for a while and then disappears again!" He threw his hands up in mock aghast. "You would have thought that such a creature would have wanted to hang over our beautiful land forever. For we have so many fine things to see, especially here in gay Svenfur." A mild cheer rippled the crowd and Cedo beamed.

Leaning against his thighs, he surveyed the front few rows as he spoke in a hushed whisper that would carry to the furthest stalls, "Let me tell you that it would stay, if it were allowed to, but many years ago, long before you and I walked this fine city, there was an argument between the fire dragons and the lamplighters. The lamplighters had decided that it could not be light all the time. They saw the people of the land having too much fun beneath the fire dragon's warm breath. They believed that darkness was better. Of course, the fire dragon disagreed; he enjoyed sitting high up in the sky, looking down onto the land and sea beneath him.

"It infuriated the lamplighters; they could not stand to see such happiness below them. So, one glorious midday they took their lamps, they jumped onto the backs of their white steeds and went after the fire dragon. Across the sky they went, a million or more of them, chasing this fiery beast. Faster and faster they went, the flames in their lamps rocking and bobbing. But the fire dragon saw them coming and reared his noble head, breathing wide flames toward them. This stunned the lamplighters and some of them fell back to the ground, their lamps whistling behind them.

"For days the battle raged, the lamplighters coming and going as they battled with the great creature. For days, the fire dragon stood guard over the land, his warming flames lovingly keeping watch over us. But alas, it could not last and, after many months of battling, after many weeks of dark tendrils creeping across the sky before being bravely batted away, the fire dragon was forced to give up. He did not want to, for he loved what he saw below him, so he decided to play a prank on the lamplighters.

"It is the same prank he plays to this day. Whenever he sees them coming, their lamps swinging back and forth, he dives for the sea. Sometimes it takes him a long time before he disappears beneath the waves, other times it only takes a few moments. But it always catches the lamplighters off guard. They do not expect anything to happen so quickly and so it takes time for them to light the lamps you see in the sky at night."

He paused for a moment, taking in the upturned faces, each one filled with wonder. Not one person below him took a breath. They just waited, frozen, it seemed, by the sound of his voice.

"But the fire dragon is not stupid. Every now and again, he reaches out a talon and takes aim at the lamplighters, just to remind them that he is still around. It is said that if you catch a tumbling lamplighter, then all your dreams will come true. If you see one streaking across the sky, be sure to make a wish.

Lamplighter, lamplighter,
See me tonight.
I ask you to bring me
My heart's greatest delight.

It may be my sweetheart,
It may be my wealth.
But lamplighter, lamplighter,
See me tonight."

Cedo felt himself tremble as he carefully got to his feet. The theater was still silent as he inched back from the footlights. He could feel his heart beginning to tumble, the cold chill of fear once more taking over: again he had failed. It would no doubt be far worse than the punishment that followed his first performance.

Backing away from the foot of the stage, he took a timid bow and, as he did, the crowd erupted, cheering and clapping and stamping their feet. Stunned, Cedo stood, taking it in, basking in the riotous noise. Looking to his left and he flushed with pride as he saw Erus clapping. He had been a success! Turning back to the audience, he gave them one last, flourishing bow.

Backstage, Mr. Smithson clapped him heartily on the back, while stage-hands and linesmen alike clapped and whistled. Through the thick curtain, Cedo could still hear them clapping and cheering, demanding an encore. But what would he say if he went back out there? He looked to Erus. Slowly, his Master shook his head, smile lingering on his lips.

"Not tonight." He stepped closer so that only they could hear the words. "Another night, once you have perfected it a little more."

Lowering his head, Cedo felt the seemingly ever-present redness touch his cheeks. There was still more work to do; tonight obviously not being grand enough. Obviously, Erus had higher expectations of him. He wondered where this success would take him. Perhaps to the grander halls opposite the pier? Perhaps out of the city? Perhaps, even, overseas?

An arm draped around his neck and, still engulfed in the heady haze that surrounded him, Cedo let himself be led away from the wings.

"Mr. Smithson would like you to return," Erus whispered. "He would like to offer you a contract, to stay over the winter months."

Could he do that? Could he find a different tale to tell every night for so many months? Surely he could, having done it night after night at the end of the pier. But before an audience that was paying to see him, people who had *willingly* parted with their money.

Licking his lips, he nodded. "I shall do my best."

Once more, Erus' face lit up, hand tightening possessively around his neck. "And that was what I wanted to hear. Now, let us go and celebrate!"

It was not a gin house that they visited. No, it was one of the finest restaurants in Svenfur. Everything was made of gold, or plated with it, or reflecting it. Everyone who walked through the door was dressed in their most expensive clothes, all of them cloaked against the salty chill air, some with their eyes covered in brightly colored and beautifully decorated masks.

Men dressed as satyrs and women dressed as fairies drifted from table to table, memorizing orders before disappearing into the hidden confines of the eatery. From beneath the tables, on a gentle slope, tiny tracks appeared, wrapping themselves around the tables. Little trains, each pulling small, flat carriages rode along them, dispensing drinks and aperitifs to the diners before their main courses were served, elegantly dispatched to the tables on gold platters that flew overhead on wires. Still drunk on his happiness at the evening, Cedo watched, fascinated, listening to the chatter of those around him.

"Drink! Be merry!" Erus exclaimed as the train pulled up before him, an empty glass and another bottle of exceptional red wine delicately balanced on the truck.

Removing them, Cedo poured himself a glass. For a moment, Erus' eyes flashed with something dangerous and Cedo tilted his head to hear him whisper, "Manners."

With the sudden chill replacing the happiness, he picked up the filled glass and placed it before the theater owner. Looking to Erus, he leaned across the table, somehow managing to work his way around the grand candle sticks that separated them. He poured another glass of the dark, red liquid.

Gripping his glass, Erus raised it, his cheeks already tinted pink from the warmth and the alcohol. "To success and to happiness."

Smiling, Cedo returned the gesture, gaze firmly planted on Erus. "To success and happiness."

From above, platters of bloody venison gently glided to land on the table. Once more, Cedo found himself on his feet and he politely served the two gentlemen. It was certainly not a role that he had ever dreamed he would see himself in, but it was one that he found himself relishing.

Over dinner, the conversation spiraled from one subject to the next. Cedo listened, smiling and replying when questioned. The evening rolled on, every course better than the next and wine flowing like water. Heady heat and drunkenness began to take over and Cedo found himself laughing and joking, feeling at ease. Odd tales fell from his lips, the Master and the theater owner laughing and clapping him. He could not have been happier.

As they left the restaurant and walked into crisp and clear air, bells chimed in the distance. *One. Two. Three.* Tilting his heads heavenwards, Cedo smiled to the stars, the ones that now seemed to be writing his name. Leaning heavily against Erus, he laughed as, high above him, a speck of light flared before dying just as quickly.

Raising his arms above him, Cedo cried to the stars above,

"Lamplighter, lamplighter,
See me tonight.
I ask you to bring me
My heart's greatest delight.

It may be my sweetheart,
It may be my wealth.
But lamplighter, lamplighter,
See me tonight."

Above him, Erus laughed heartily and tightened an arm around the swaying and singing Cedo.

"It seems that it is not only a long time past your

bedtime, but also that you have drunk too much of that fine wine. Mr. Smithson, we bid you good night and thank you. Young man, it is home time for both you and me."

Still laughing and singing, Cedo allowed himself to be pushed up into the carriage.

Lying on the wide seats of the carriage, he laid his head in Erus' lap, an inane grin stretching his mouth. Strong fingers brushed the hair from his face and the normally stern face of his Master showed a different light, at least for tonight.

"Well done, Cedo. Well done indeed."

CHAPTER 15

With the depths of night cloaking him and just a candle for company, Cedo leaned against the headboard of the bed, the large journal resting against his knees as he lovingly filled pages with his writing. The warmth of success still rode within him, making him more than a little dizzy.

Beside him, the bed depressed and Erus lay beside him, chin firmly planted against Cedo's breastbone. Green eyes twinkled and fingers curled tenderly around his breast before coming to rest at the base of his throat, lovingly caressing the necklace.

"And what story do you tell your book tonight?"

Returning the smile, Cedo stroked through the hair that fell over his body. "I am telling it of a handsome prince. A prince who everyone seemed to despise but who had all the love in the world to give."

"Carry on." Erus' voice seemed distant, as if trailing away on the winds of the story to come.

"He lived in a castle in a far off land, a castle in which he surrounded himself with magnificent creations and beings. He felt that, if no one would love him, then he would build a home that, one day, someone might fall in love with."

He watched as Erus' eyes lazily opened and closed, Cedo's hands clasping the suddenly fragile-looking Erus to him. It was only in these moments, he was discovering, when they were locked away from the world, that a different Erus made an appearance.

"This prince, with hair as red as the setting sun and eyes to match the forests around the castle, tried to put his loneliness out of his mind." He was surprised when Erus did not move at the description, instead lying as still as a sleeping cat. "He tried to carry on, to make his life as beautiful as possible, but all the while there was that missing link, that ache in his heart that would not go away. One day, it became too much for him, and he went to the quietest part of the castle, the part where he built and created and sculpted and crafted.

"He let his hands begin to talk, fashioning pieces of metal and cogs, building them upward until, before him, stood the creature he wanted. It made the prince happy and, as he wound the key in the creature's back, his heart sang, for the creature moved, walking and smiling with him. He took the creature's bony, crafted hand and walked with it, showing it the castle. He gave this little biped machine a room, the most glorious room in the whole castle. It overlooked the forests and the rivers, the blue mountains in the distance, snow clinging to their peaks. The creature, with a click and a tick, looked at the prince and smiled, its arm wrapped around its creator's waist.

"With a lighter heart and step, the prince left the creature and retired to bed. As the sun rose, so did the prince, and he went to the room of the metal creature. It sat before the window, unmoving, unblinking, and the prince's heart grew cold. For a while, just a few moments, it had been the company he craved. As he touched the key it returned to life, his love for it returning as its glass eyes turned to look at him. The prince gave it a name. He had wanted to give a simple name, something simple yet beautiful, so he called it what his heart desired the most. He named it 'Love'.

"Every day, Love would wander the castle, patiently clattering along beside the Prince. Yet, as the clockwork ran down, so Love would die, leaving the prince feeling as dull and as sad as before. "Zealously, he worked on Love, making it better and stronger, perfecting the clockwork so that Love only needed to be wound once every few weeks and, eventually, adding a simple voice box. Day after day, he taught Love to speak, smiling and laughing as it learned new words, new ways to express itself. The prince was happy, his frosty heart warming to the creature he had made.

"One day, they sat side by side in the garden. Turning to Love, the Prince asked, 'What would you like to do?'

"Turning and looking at him with clear, glassy blue eyes, Love replied, 'I want to be free. You made me, and every day you come to see me. You made me tick every day, but then you changed me. Now you only see me when you need to. You only see me when you want to talk. Before that, we spoke with gestures. Life was simpler then, before the words and the big key.'

"Crushed, the Prince nodded. It was true, he had taken something simple and beautiful and turned it into something more complicated than it needed to be. And so he freed Love, setting it off into the world for someone else to discover. He had learned from Love, learned that things did not need to be difficult or elaborate, that the simplest, easiest gesture could bring the most joy."

Slowly Cedo found the trance that had surrounded him fading, leaving him in the bed, Erus in his arms. Erus was shaking softly, damp spots beginning to cool against Cedo's naked skin. Concerned, he carefully touched Erus' head, tilting tear-reddened eyes to him.

"Whatever is the matter?"

"It is true," was the barely audible reply.

"What is true?"

Erus clung closer, face becoming pained. "I do not know how to love."

Cedo felt his heart drop and he tugged his now fragile Master into his arms." You do know how to love, Master. Why do you think that I have stayed? Because you have shown me what it is like to be wanted and cherished by another. I would not have stayed if all you had shown me was pain."

Shimmering emerald eyes turned to him. Reaching out, Cedo clasped Erus' face and let his lips brush against the rumpled forehead. He shook beneath Cedo's touch, a strained sob echoing from his chest. Why was he crying?

The skin beneath his fingers was cool and clammy and the words that Erus uttered chilled him to the bone. "I never knew my family."

Carefully, he cupped the delicate face, thumb sweeping away tears.

Erus continued, "I was abandoned, so the story goes, on the steps of an orphanage. It was a cruel place.

But they all were. You were not dumped there if your family had money. It was where you went if you were unwanted and unloved." There was disgust and disdain in his voice. "I was always the smallest child, the weakest boy. Nobody wanted me. I was beaten, not just by staff but also by the other children. They were merciless, always screaming and baying for blood."

Erus trailed off, his voice becoming dark and haunted. "They would whip me, and laugh as my blood spilled against flagstones. It was there that I started the work that I still do today." He chuckled, the sound seeming to come from a different place, a different age. "It is amazing, the damage a small, simple stone can do when it is launched correctly." His eyes snapped open, once more filled with the glint of a cold-hearted killer. "Needless to say, that boy never hurt anyone ever again."

A shiver broke along Cedo's body as the green eyes bore into him, trying to silently pass on what lay beyond them, trapped deep within their owner. Emotions crashed over him and he pressed a fierce kiss to Erus' lips. Erus had confessed some of what lay in his soul, and it was a moment that Cedo would treasure.

"Mr. Reilly, sir." It was Mrs. Sugden who wakened him the following morning.

As before, he was alone in the large bed. He did not know how much sleep Erus took, or even if he slept at all.

He opened his eyes to see the housekeeper standing over him.

"Mr. Veetu would like you to go down to the mirrored room."

Once she left, Cedo quickly bathed, washing the sadness and pain of the night before. More fine suits had arrived. Some were gilded with embroidery while others were merely trimmed with lace and tucked at the waist. All gave him a slightly more feminine air than that of his Master.

With tiredness still clinging to his body, Cedo wound his way along the corridors until he reached the mirrored room. Politely he knocked, waiting until a voice called for him to enter.

The room beyond the door was not the same one in which he had learned Erus' name. Where once there had been a plain wooden floor, there were now huge trees and bushes, all giving off the mossy scent of a forest. Riotous colors burst from branches as heavy blooms let go of their scents. Somewhere, within the room-bound forest, he could hear the sound of birdsong.

Cedo gasped quietly. His Master stood, one hand firmly planted on a hip as he grinned. "Your fairy forest."

Tiny lights, powered by goodness knows what, flickered in the trees and something ticked by his head. Swinging around, he was quick enough to catch sight of a tiny creature flying by. It skittered around his head before flying toward Erus and landing neatly in the palm of his hand. He smiled down at the creature before flicking his wrist and tossing it back into the air.

"All clockwork, Cedo, I'm afraid to say."

The clicking creature flew back and hung before Cedo. Slowly it dawned on him as the tiny fairy-like creature came to rest on his outstretched fingers.

"Did you...?" His voice trailed off as Erus gave the smallest of nods.

The Lilliputian creature, on closer inspection, was beautifully made. Little eyes blinked at him, a head inlaid with finely spun hair cocked, as it looked at him. Gossamer-thin wings slowly flapped back and forth, light fragmenting through them.

"But why...?"

Erus slumped against the trunk of a tree.

"I was asked to create a new kind of execution device, something humane and relatively painless. There was no money in making things for the theatricals but there was money in death. The government drew on the pain I went through in the orphanage, told me to channel it. I was young and naive."

"How many did you make?"

"Execution devices? Too many to count." Erus smiled a melancholy smile of remembrance. "War is money and I have come to enjoy what I do."

"But it is blood money! Why do it if this—" He gestured to the enchanted indoor forest. "Is what makes you happy?"

"Because," Erus' voice became as dull and as hard as iron. "We cannot live without money. I am one of the fortunate ones. Without this money you would not have this fine home and new clothes. You would still be daydreaming at the end of the pier."

"But you could give it up now!" His voice raised against the deathly coolness of Erus. "Build these for theaters or the piers of the country. They would pay good money for this kind of enchantment."

"It is too late to go back and what you say is untrue. Do you not think that I tried to sell these ideas to others? Of course I did. I am not stupid. Every tiny idea that I have ever had has been up for sale, yet it is only the ones that cause mass destruction that sell. And it is damn expensive."

Redness fell before his eyes and Cedo snatched himself away from beneath the trees.

"Then change the people's views! You are obviously a strong and well enough known figure. Just think of what you could do. Just think of what you could change in this world. You could take this war that has been raging for so long and you could crush it! You could turn the world into the peaceful place that you have built here."

The rage that had been boiling within him was replaced by stinging pain, his head snapping to his shoulder. Stunned, Cedo stared at the floor.

"You know nothing, Mr. Reilly," Erus hissed, dangerously close behind him. "And you obviously did not hear me the first time around. Peace only sells if it comes with bloodshed, death and destruction."

"Then tell me," he quietly pleaded, never lifting his head as fingers slid over his shoulder. "Tell me why you do not want to change."

Erus did not reply, his fingers lying on Cedo's shoulder before he silently slid away. A moment later, the door clicked shut.

The floor was hard beneath him, the forest now dark and foreboding instead of the pleasant hideaway it had been just moments previously. The heavy scents seemed to rot around him, becoming musty and sickening. He had no idea where to turn or how to communicate with such a man when every comment, every suggestion was thrown firmly back into his face. It appeared that nothing he could say would have an impact on how this man ran his life.

And why should it? Erus had been at the forefront of his industry for years; there could be no turning back. Even if the money and the war dried up, he would no doubt go back to creating devices of execution. It was just a dark spiral of blood and pain, a spiral on which Erus stood at the brink, safely held back by his reputation and a barrier of wealth. Wealth which, until that moment, Cedo had felt no guilt using.

Picking himself up from the floor, Cedo wound his way among the trees and bushes, listening to the near-silent clicking of the flying creatures that zoomed above his head. Guilt swept through him. The guilt of turning against, albeit in good faith, the man who had obviously spent many long and labored hours creating a beautiful place for him to come and hide. In a moment of impassioned rage he had taken that beauty and thrown it straight back at the one who had created it especially for him.

The pain and sorrow of the moment gripped Cedo. Erus had actually lain there and listened before deciding to show Cedo a side to him that no one else knew existed. And he, the passionate young man with the quick mouth, had erased everything with a few short words. He felt terrible. He wondered how far Erus had gone. Perhaps too deep into the house to be found now, but he still had to try.

With his heart still heavy, Cedo walked past the row of doors, their glassy eyes watching him. He wondered what went on beyond them. Is this where the servants cavorted after hours? Or did they live in constant terror of being caught?

Each door was firmly closed and Cedo assumed that the occupants were elsewhere in the house, going about their daily lives. However, as he approached the end of the corridor, he became aware of a dull thudding.

It sounded like the heavy fall of a steam press, thudding against sheets of metal. Halting before a door, he carefully pushed the tiny brass door out of the way, eyes widening as he looked into the room beyond.

A woman sat bound and gagged in a heavy chair, her face twisted in pain. Beside the chair sat a small, metal box, wires protruding from it and wrapped around one of her bare ankles. Whenever the hulking figure of Mr. Black pressed his foot against a pedal, the woman convulsed, her back slamming against the chair creating the heavy thud as she desperately tried to cry out around a sodden gag.

Shock rolled over Cedo, bile rising and burning his throat. Finally a hush fell over the corridor and Cedo sighed, hanging limply against the door. It appeared that the torture beyond the door, torture that seemed to have no reason behind it, was over.

CHAPTER 16

His relief did not last for long. His gaze came to rest on the dazzling eye that glared at him from the tiny spy hole. Terror quickly grasped him and he desperately tried to escape. But the door still opened, the scorned jinn released from its bottle as it flung itself at Cedo.

"Spying on me now, boy?"

Hands wrapped around his throat and he flailed, trying to pull them away. Anger rose, questions whirling through his mind. The image of the child flickered behind his eyes, the darkness engulfing it.

"Why?" he snarled. "Why do you do this?"

Mr. Black snorted and swung a fist at him, Cedo plunging out of the way.

"'Cause I have to, that's why. 'Cause someone has to. Just you wait 'til I tell your Master."

The fire refused to die, burning in his stomach. "Does Erus know you do this? Or do you just think you can do such things without his knowledge?"

Something akin to hatred crossed Mr. Black's face, twisting it and darkening his eyes.

"You know nothin', boy. Nothin' at all. It doesn't concern you so keep your nose out of it."

Cedo laughed, a rough, grating sound. "But it does concern me. I live beneath this roof and whatever happens in the dead of night is of concern to me."

A thick hand snatched at his hair, Cedo hissing and cursing as Mr. Black pressed his face close. Rotten breath washed over his face and he hissed, lips curling back.

"You keep quiet." Stinking spittle landed on his face. "What you've seen is nothin' an' it's going to stay that way."

Again, Cedo laughed, the insanity boiling through him. Did Erus even know what was going on beneath his roof? His laughter obviously angered Mr. Black further and he grunted, hauling Cedo along the corridor. Hissing and spitting, he clawed at the burly man. He would stop it, would stop the pain of the house, even if it killed him.

They travelled to the Ship Theater with the same agonizing hush hanging over them. Mr. Black had hauled him before Erus, demanding to know why Cedo was spying on him. Yet his Master's right-hand man had said nothing about the act on which Cedo had been caught spying. Erus had dismissed it with a sigh and shrug, citing something about boys being boys. Now Cedo felt forgotten, as if he were being silently punished for what he had seen. The silence, however, told him everything: remain quiet.

Standing beside the stage, he watched as the curtain went up and the chairman announced the first act. To the riotous applause of the crowd, a group of tumbling acrobats in sparkling costumes fell about the stage. Even Cedo could not help but smile. As the applause died and the group brushed past him, Cedo heard a gentle cough. Turning, he saw a grinning Miss Wells standing beside him, a rose clasped close to her breast. Curious, Cedo tilted his head as he shyly returned her smile. Once his smile had fully opened, she offered the flower to him.

"For me?" Carefully he took it from her. "From you?"

Laughing, she shook her head. "Alas, someone else has beaten me to it, I'm afraid."

"Who?"

The singer gave him a cheeky grin, her eyes sparkling with a cheery mischief. "Oh, I am sure you will find out soon enough."

Cedo felt a little crushed that the beautiful rose was not from Miss Wells. He had remembered her friendliness fondly, warmed that someone would take the time to make him feel at ease in his new home.

Slowly he turned it in his hands. It was as fresh as the morning, its petals only just beginning to part. Hearing his name called, he deftly slid the rose into his buttonhole before stepping out into the bright lights of the stage, his body feeling a little lighter than before.

Enchanted, he stood upon the stage, feeling at home with the hundreds of eyes all watching him, all glistening in the dainty flames of the gas jets. Their awe was evident in their faces as he told the tale he had told Erus of the prince, his castle, and his robot called 'Love'.

From time to time, Cedo lifted his eyes, looking toward the wings in the hope that perhaps Erus might be there listening to him. But there was no sign of his flame-haired Master; the liquor probably warming his belly more than one of Cedo's tales could. But still, the audience's cheers and applause went straight through him, making him smile as he left the stage.

Beside the stage, a ventriloquist and his dummy waited to follow him, a tall man beside them. The young man smiled and nodded, eyes hidden by shadows and the mop of long, unruly blond hair. Returning his smile, Cedo disappeared into the maze of the theater, flushed with success.

He walked the corridors, finally finding the door that concealed the small office. Raising a hand, Cedo moved to knock but paused upon hearing the obviously drunken laughter of his Master. For the moment, at least, he was alone. Retracing his steps, he found himself out in the cool night air, the sounds of the city swallowing him up as he began to walk.

Moving away from the theater, Cedo found himself heading through the center of the city and toward the Terminus.

The Terminus was a swelling mass of glass and brick, eating its way through the heart of the city. Beneath its roof, engines as large as buildings would glide in on rails of polished metal, groaning and spilling jets of flame and smoke. Behind them would follow miles of carriages, all of them creaking in protest. From these would flood crowds of passengers, some of whom had come to join the fun, some of whom had come to find their fortune.

Sitting on a cold, wooden bench, Cedo watched as one such train slowly pulled in. Twin smoke stacks pumped flame and grime high into the air as she snarled to a halt, her sharp and angled nose gliding down to the rails. To say she was beautiful was an understatement and Cedo found himself staring at this marvel of metal. The men who began to race around her were tiny in comparison as they scrambled up lengths of ladder to cool her boiler and firebox. People spilled from the carriages, some hauling trunks while others arrived with nothing more than the clothes on their backs. All jostled to remove themselves from the Terminus, never taking a moment to admire it.

Quietly Cedo sat, watching as they raced around him. Among them ran the porters, all plying their trade to the weary travelers, voices joining in the great din of the cooling train. Many went unnoticed, while a few lucky ones were able to pick up loose change as they guided unknowing travelers on their way.

As quickly as it had begun, it ended, leaving Cedo, a few engine-men, and the stench of a hot train behind. They were busy cleaning and preparing the great beast for her next journey, their eyes flicking to giant clocks that hung from the girders, knowing that another such beast would be arriving shortly.

Getting to his feet, Cedo wandered the Terminus unheeded, passing over swooping bridges and beneath sweeping archways. Along the platforms there were various traders, some selling food, others selling newspapers and cheap books. A few more were selling themselves. But even they melted away the further he went.

Soon he found himself in what appeared to be a service yard. A few sets of rails sat side by side, small shrugs growing between them, while the platform was cracked and stained with oil. Only a few, spluttering lamps were lit, casting jittering, uneven light across the ground. There was a general air of disarray, as if this were the area that engine-men came to rest. It was, in the terms of the Terminus, the end of the world.

He was about to sit on the edge of the platform when something caught his eye. Walking slowly toward the platform buildings, Cedo studied the markings. Stretching out a hand, he dusted the wall and his heart skipped as he revealed the crudely etched dragon and mouse. The machines were already here and Cedo was sure that Erus had no hand in them. Perhaps this was the yard from which the weapons left in the depths of night?

Feeling a chill stroke his skin, Cedo straightened up and listened, waiting for the familiar clanking and hissing of a train to pull in. Yet none came, and he went back to studying the small picture. The claw of the dragon was extended along the wall, the mouse clasped precariously in the center. Eyes narrowed, Cedo leaned closer, trying to catch what he believed he had seen in the low lamplight. The mouse had the tiniest of paws lifted as if pointing to something. Cedo brought his head in line with the wall, eyes following the small paw. Where perhaps there should have been some kind of adornment, maybe a display of flowers, there was nothing, just darkness as the platform drifted off into the distance.

Cedo traced his way along the platform, studying the walls. There were boarded up doors and windows and, at the pinnacle of the platform, there were rails that carried on into nothingness. There was nothing for the mouse to gesture to. They were just odd adverts for a population of people who already knew what was happening.

Standing back beside the mouse, he impatiently looked at it, frustrated by not knowing what it meant or where it had come from. With a groan of frustration, he kicked at the wall, something crumbling beneath his toes. Crouching down, Cedo inspected a dislodged brick. Pressing two fingers into the opening, he slid them across something slightly sloped and as cool as ice. Beneath his fingers, the curved surface slid away with a click and he sat back, confused. His eyes widened, heart leaping as the uncared-for door clicked and swung open.

CHAPTER 17

The room beyond the door lay in semi-darkness, the odd ray of light straggling through the high windows. There was nothing there, but still the room gave off a sense of foreboding. With his breath tight in his throat, Cedo started in fright as something scuttled across the floor.

Slowly his eyes began to adjust to the murky light and he brushed away the cool spot of water that landed in his hair. The room was as empty as any abandoned house and all that lived there were mice and rats scuttling. Again something fell into his hair and, again Cedo brushed it away, looking up in frustration to see where it had come from.

Hanging above him, hidden high in the rafters above the windows were what appeared to be some kind of carcasses, legs splayed and stretching downward. It was only then that the smell of raw meat touched his nose, turning his stomach. But what made him retch was the iron wheel that reached out into the room. It could just be seen in the shadows, the large, pivoted arm holding it as the light clung to raw, jagged spikes. Whatever was up there had met a gruesome and painful of death.

Cedo weakly moved toward the door, the stink of vomit and stomach acid suddenly far more pleasant than whatever was above him. Again something scurried in front of him and wearily he aimed a foot at it, ignoring the metallic clang it made as it bounced away. He had to escape before the chamber of death began its work once more.

It was a struggle to leave the Terminus. From every side, people jostled and yelled, ignoring the fleeing man.

He felt the night could not get any worse, but as he rounded the corner to the theater he felt faint as he looked up at the now darkened building.

Clutching the thin jacket close, Cedo looked around for someone to help. But there none; he had been shut out. Not even Erus had waited for him, something that confused him and scared him.

"Lookin' for someone?" Cedo jumped at the voice.

A figure stepped from the shadows and into the light of a street lamp. Cedo could have collapsed from happiness as he looked at the blond stagehand. The tall, gangly man was clad in thick woolen trousers and a jumper that was several sizes too big for his frame.

"Erus," Cedo leaned heavily against the front of the theater. "Erus Veetu."

The boyish-looking man rolled his eyes and angled his body against the lamp-post. "Now why would a smart lad such as yourself get messed up with that?"

"What makes you say that?" he retorted, arms folding over his chest.

He snorted, hunching himself over a little as he moved to study Cedo. "Because I know what that man's like. 'E's a bastard to everyone who steps into 'is path. If you ain't got somethin' 'e wants then you're scum. But 'e's the scum."

Narrowing his eyes, Cedo leaned back into the

shadows. What the man was saying was true; Erus was a bastard, but it did not stop Cedo from loving him and trying, as desperate as he might, to understand him.

"You have no right to comment on my life!" he retaliated.

The man chuckled and stepped beneath the theater's canopy as the first drops of rain began to fall.

"I've got every right to comment on your life." The man's face was mere inches from Cedo's. "I used to work for 'im."

Cedo felt his jaw slacken and the man broke into a wide smile, thrusting a hand toward Cedo.

"William Burton." The man pumped Cedo's hand. "Survivor of Veetu Industries."

"What did you do for him?" Cedo softly asked.

William shrugged, his wide grin still in place. "Worked in 'is factory. Buildin' 'is weapons. Floor boy—I fetched an' carried." He waved a hand of long, bony fingers. "Those could get into most parts of 'is machines. Nearly lost a couple o' fingers along the way."

Cedo frowned, looking up into the face of the man who towered over him, impossibly long legs disappearing into the jumper. "That does not explain how you came to the conclusion that he is a bastard, though."

William's face darkened, eyes becoming hooded as his lips pulled back into a snarl. "'E's power crazy." He pressed a finger to his forehead. "Gone in the 'ead, that one. Likes to think 'e rules it all. It's the government that's done it. Thrown too much money at 'im an' 'is crazy ideas. 'E don't want to win the war. 'E just wants a world that's empty of everyone but 'im."

Cedo stepped up, neck arched back as he looked up. His heart was chilled to hear such words about his Master. The cook, the gentleman in the Patron's office—both had told him to beware of the man he lived with. Yet none had spat the venom that William did.

"I advise," Cedo began, "that you stop reading what the tabloids have to say and get to know a person before you pass judgment on them."

Tossing a handful of hair over his shoulder, William snorted. "Oh, I know 'im all right. You know 'e tests 'is so-called weapons, torture instruments, an' execution devices on people 'ere in Svenfur?" Cedo nodded, the memories of the woman flooding painfully back. "Well, 'e nearly 'ad me."

"Y-You?"

William looked almost mournful as he nodded. "Promised me an 'onest wage if I just 'elped 'im one day. I don't care, I'll 'elp anyone, me. Took me to some place under the city. There were others there, just like me an' you. He lined us up, or rather some lackey of 'is did. 'E's never there when it 'appens, at least not in the same room anyway." William sighed and Cedo stepped toward the suddenly frightened young man.

"We were lined up against this wall. I remember, there was me an' another bloke standin' shoulder to shoulder. We didn't know what was comin'. None of us did. There was this rumblin' sound, shook the whole floor it did, an' that was some mean feat seein' this place probably used to be a sewer. They built 'em well, the sewers an' tunnels. Anyway, this machine suddenly burrowed up through the floor. Sprayed brick an' mortar everywhere. Damn near killed a few of 'em. It was a great hulkin' thing, looked like a big metal cigar only it 'ad some great drill at the front an' these movin' tracks where there should 'ave been wheels."

William slumped against the wall, appearing smaller, quieter. Cedo reached out and draped an arm around his shoulders.

"This thing, I think 'e calls it *The Mole*, the drill bit,

it suddenly changed, opened up. Next thing I know, two lasses just down from me were splattered on the wall. Nothing left of 'em! Well, of course, we all ran after that, but it kept firin', kept turnin' them into this crazy red mist. I managed to escape, an' so did the bloke next to me. Got out through a sewer pipe. We tried to make our way along this tunnel, find our way to the outside, but you'll never guess who was waitin' for us?"

Cedo already knew the answer. "Erus."

The man looked up, his head coming to rest on Cedo's shoulder as he gave a small and knowing smile.

"Got it in one. Mr. Erus fuckin' Veetu. 'Ad some kind of fancy gun with 'im. Didn't even blink as 'e blew the other bloke away. Then 'e turned to me, an' I'll be damned if 'e didn't 'ave a grin on 'is face that wouldn't 'ave looked out of place on some blood-sucking monster. Told me 'e'd let me live if 'e could 'ave me. Just one night an' then I could go back to the factory floor. 'E's not my type but it was worth it to see another day. I left that fancy 'ouse of 'is the next day an' never looked back. Came to work 'ere. They needed someone good with their 'ands. So I'd watch your back, Cedo Reilly, really I would. 'E may like you now, but you get on the wrong side of 'im an' 'e'll put you before one of 'is fancy guns."

Cedo forced a smile. "Thank you, Willi—"

"Please." The dazzling smile returned. "Call me Billy."

His own smile softened into one that reflected how he really felt—thankful. "Thank you, Billy."

Fingers ruffled his hair." Now, Mr. Reilly, we should be seein' about gettin' you 'ome. Don't want to keep 'is royal 'ighness waitin' longer than we 'ave to."

Billy split the air with a whistle and a moment later a small cab rounded the corner.

"Dougie'll see you 'ome." William smiled as he opened the door, keeping it ajar as Cedo climbed in. "I'll see you tomorrow, Cedo. You take care."

The door slammed shut and a hand thudded on the roof. A moment later, they swayed off into the night, Cedo daring to lean against the window and catch a small peek at the blond. But he was already gone, melting into the darkness as quickly and as easily as he had melted out of it. And Cedo did not blame him; he had already had one nearly fatal run-in with Erus, so why risk there being another?

CHAPTER 18

The ride home was filled with the kind of dread that one met while facing their last moments. The "what ifs" and "whys", the memories and the horrors were riding high through Cedo's mind like warriors in battle. He knew that he would be punished for his disappearance.

His heart sank as they rocked up the gently sloping hill toward the house. Every house they passed lay in darkness, the occupants having long retired on such a foul night. The rain had long since stopped and in its wake it had left the bitter coldness of the cleaned world. Cedo wondered if Erus used nights like this to appease his soul for the blood that ran through it.

As desperately as he tried to accept his Master's choice of occupation, it was a struggle. It tore at Cedo's soul, pulling him apart as he found himself loving a creature who lived off death. But, as his mother had once told him, *"You cannot help who you fall in love with."* A statement he was finding to be painfully true.

The terror began to claw at him again as they idled past the water pump and drew up beside the house. Lights blazed in every window and, even though Erus kept less than normal hours, it was still odd to see the house lit up. Cedo slowly alighted the carriage, nodding to the shadowed driver as he made his way past the towering trees and to the front door.

He reached out to lift the brass knocker but as he did, the door swung effortlessly inwards, as if it had been primed for his return. Cedo went to quietly close it, flinching and grinding his teeth as the bolts that lay deep within it thudded home. He looked around, waiting for the fury that no doubt lay in wait. Yet it never came and he took one nervous step after another, leading himself toward the stairs. He would hide in his room. There was no need or use in disturbing Erus, for he would only get a tongue lashing, if not more, for his unscheduled disappearance.

The lights in the hallway, unlike the rest of the house, were out, giving his surroundings a deathly feel as if somewhere, the pipes had been cut, killing the lifeline of the house. With his breath still heavy, Cedo walked to the stairs, aghast at what he saw. The foot of the stairs was blocked by a tall, twisting candelabra, the candles throwing off a soft, flickering light and guiding him towards the study. The floor beneath his feet was as soft as silk and, upon looking down, Cedo was shocked to find himself walking upon a carpet of petals.

Cedo followed the trail of dancing flames, trying to keep his composure as he entered the study. Erus was seated behind the desk, hunched over another of the magnificent drawing boards. He appeared not to notice Cedo's arrival, instead focusing with immense concentration on whatever lay before him. A brass-tipped pen swept over the paper in flowing lines, briefly disappearing into a hidden inkwell before resuming its journey.

Feeling weak, Cedo stood before the desk, hands clasped behind him, wondering if this elaborate setup was just the calm before the storm. He stiffened as Erus lifted his eyes, peering over the board. A smile began to find its way across his Master's face and, for once, it showed no signs of being malicious. He pushed himself up, the pen still trapped in his ink stained fingers, the smile warm and welcoming.

"So, you return." The pen dropped into the ink well.

Cedo fought to find his voice. "Yes, Master. I-I apologize, Master, for disappearing. I did not mean to leave the theater an-" Erus lifted a finger, silencing him mid-sentence.

"Call it a test, if you will. A test of faith. You left, but you came back, just like I hoped you would. The prodigal son. You've proved your loyalty to me by returning, a gesture for which I am greatly humbled."

The room was uncomfortably warm, the heat beginning to claw at Cedo's skin. Erus moved closer to him. The weakness returned as the finger inched along his cheek, curling beneath his chin to lift his eyes. A hand came to rest in the small of his back, guiding him as his knees buckled.

The world around them could collapse around them and he would still be unable to resist the gentle touches of the man who had taken him from the streets. It was what bound him here through the pain and the blood and the horrors. It was these moments, the tender touches and caresses, which stopped the guilt from tearing him apart.

Lips kissed him, warm and hungry, and he collapsed onto the loveseat. Erus knelt over him, hands fervently tugging at their clothing. One foot dangled to the floor as Erus pressed himself close, kneeling over him as his hands roamed.. Feeling his cock begin to swell, Cedo reared up from the upholstery, sighing as he gripped the back of Erus' head, pulling him closer, needing to feel those hands and lips claim him.

Clothes fell away, piling on the floor around the carved legs of the cramped seat. Confidence brimmed as the warm air wrapped around his nude body, Cedo viciously attacked his lover with lips and fingers, his teeth nipping at supple, welcoming lips. He twitched as his Master fought back, trying to regain control of the passion-stricken man. But all too soon, Cedo triumphantly straddled Erus' lap.

"My, my. It seems as if there is more fire in you than I first thought." Fingers slid over his ribs, making him shiver. He arched upward, moaning as Erus continued, "I never would have expected it from such a prim and proper boy. But it is always the quiet ones who harbor the darkest desires."

Teeth dug into the soft flesh above his collarbone. "We shall have to take advantage of this, dear one. I quite believe that you enjoy having the rod taken to you, and I am sure that there are delicious pleasures that we can amuse ourselves with over these long, dark nights."

Cedo whined and pressed himself closer, rubbing himself against Erus' still clothed lap. The rough material felt delicious, sensual, almost begging him to spill himself over it. There was another of those damned chuckles as searching fingers slid away from him. Clothes rustled and Erus released himself from the confines of his garments.

Cedo laid his hands against his Master's shoulders, guiding himself to Erus' cock. Again, he howled as he was entered, knowing that beyond the initial pain lay the blissful fervor of release.

It was the pleasure that drove him on, through the pain and to that blinding moment. Laying his forehead against Erus', he watched as the man beneath him bloomed, opening up like a flower. Rich eyes became unshielded, his strong body relaxing beneath silken touches. He gave himself over to Erus, an understanding building that, beyond the walls that Erus built, he needed these moments as much as Cedo did, needed some chambered knowledge that all was not lost in the world.

Cedo delicately peeled linen from his lover's body,

leaving him exposed in a way he suspected Erus feared. For he appeared to hide behind clothes and machines and high built walls, both physical and metaphorical, scared that a scathing world may discover some trivial truth about him. Cedo did not care for such matters, instead wanting everything from the handsome man.

Erus groaned, guttural and shaking. Brushing his hands over the expanse of naked skin, Cedo let his thumbs play over nipples that had become hard, watching as Erus trembled beneath him. Feathering kisses on Erus' throat, he cried out as the liquid feeling rushed through him, his own cock now demanding the same attention.

Cedo leaned back onto his heels, Erus' softening cock still buried within him. He moved upon it as he stroked himself, twitching as it brushed against something inside of him. He could hear Erus, composure obviously restored, calling to him, pushing him onward like a flagging horse. Hands gripped his naked thighs, groping at the join of leg and groin, curling around his tight balls. Finally, Cedo came, lifted by angels as sticky fluid splattered his naked skin. He hung there for a moment, panting heavily, before beginning to relax, trailing fingers through the mess he had left behind.

Erus grinned at him, nodding toward where his fingers lay, idly tracing circles in the rapidly cooling liquid.

"Taste yourself."

Newfound confidence flooded Cedo's body and he did just that, tongue lapping gently at his fingers as he tasted the heavy salt flavor. Erus hissed and pressed Cedo's tainted lips to his own.

"You do not taste bad. Better than the last one at least."

"Who was the last one?" he forced himself to ask.

Hands idly drifted back to his flanks. "I do not remember. It was so long ago now. There was somebody, but he did not stay. He chose to leave, just as the others have done. I have not seen him since."

"Was it a blond-haired boy?"

A wistful looked glanced over Erus' face, the sharp tongue remaining dormant. "Perhaps. As I said, I do not remember."

CHAPTER 19

*T*he further you go down that rabbit 'ole with 'im, the 'arder you're going to 'ave to dig to get yourself out," Billy's voice disturbed his dreams, and Cedo finally lifted himself out of the bed as the first, gray claws of dawn began to disturb the night.

As had become the norm, the bed was empty. Cedo wondered if the man ever slept a full night or if he had become so used to this lifestyle that, even if he had nothing to do, he would rise and find himself a quiet place to be alone. It was certainly an odd lifestyle, yet Erus showed no signs of being affected by the sleeplessness.. His face was strangely unlined and free from dark shadows. It was as if he were untouchable by even the hands of time herself.

Cedo looked out over the garden. He rarely had time to ponder the beauty of the village from such a vantage point. Beneath him, the garden rolled away, down to the stream, before undulating up into another low hill. Houses were dotted along the hill, and beyond them, trees formed the beginning of a wood. Through the trees, he knew, was the road to Svenfur, twisting down the hill before flattening itself to the winding coastline.

Cedo drew himself into the window, knees pulled up as he balanced his journal on them. Thoughts mingled in his mind, thoughts that wanted to be free and written down, and so he placed pen to paper and began to free them.

For a while he sat and looked over the words, feeling oddly guilty that they had now come out. Why should he want to write such things about the man who had taken him from that grotty boarding house? It seemed terrible to even think them, let alone write them, but Cedo knew what would happen if he didn't. The anger and resentment would build, a black tar that would seep from his soul and through his pores before he finally boiled over and let the wrath and anger spill free in spoken words rather than written ones.

There seemed to be no point in dressing and so he slipped a nightgown over his head, the thin material flapping around his ankles as he walked barefoot from the room. He could not believe that a few hours earlier, they had romped upon the loveseat before lying upon the floor, wrapped in heavy blankets as they had talked and gossiped deep into the night, drinking wine and lolling against each other like two tired dogs. It had only been when the clock had begun to call the early hours of dawn that Cedo had crept upward, leaving Erus with a small kiss and a heavy heart to do whatever he needed. Just one night, that was all he wanted, one night where he could wake up and Erus would be beside him.

It made him feel like a plaything, as if he were the living version of the fairy that Erus had created, born to be happy before being put back onto the shelf as his own mechanism wound down.

Trying to distract himself, Cedo wandered the shelves, taking in the volumes that stood upon them. There were such great titles as *The Sciences of Great Engineering,*

Mathematics and Calculations for the Building of Moving Structures and *Mathematical Methods for Physics and Engineering.* Shelf upon shelf was dedicated Erus' job and not one seemed to be a book that could be read for pleasure. Working his way into the corner of the room, Cedo moved the loveseat and knelt down, curling himself into the corner as he studied the books. Some were great tomes, all with equally unpromising titles. Others were unmarked, slender black books. Curious, he pulled a blank covered book into his lap.

The cover was slightly worn, the corners battered and peeling as if the book had been placed upon the shelf and pulled off a number of times. Opening it to the first page, he began to read the spiraling handwriting.

Day 1. Time—1400 z.hrs.
Subject—D.S. Age—33 yrs.
Location—Test ward 009
Appears well, if a little agitated.
Day 2. 12.01 z.hrs
Subject—D.S. Age—33 yrs.
Location—Test ward 009
Subject is beginning to question his surroundings. Is constantly agitated. Staff informed to sedate if necessary.

Quickly, Cedo flicked through the pages, the world around him becoming focused on the distinctive black handwriting. Cedo wondered who the poor soul was whose life was being detailed in quick sentences, and what became of them.

Day 13. Time—03.15 z.hrs.
Subject—D.S. Age—33 yrs.
Location—Test ward 009
Subject has entered the realms of complete insanity. No longer knows who or where he is. Talks incoherently to himself non-stop. Self inflicted wounds are being treated.

Breathlessly, he skipped over dates and pages, taking

in the downward spiral of an unknown life.

Day 16. Time—19.09 z.hrs.

Subject—D.S. Age—33 yrs.

Location—Test ward 009

We have discovered that new device works exactly as planned. The subtle changes to the body's chemical make-up allows the user to extract information that is needed before either sacrificing the subject or re-aligning the make-up and releasing them.

Subject of experiment 98-23DM sacrificed at 19.00 z.hrs. Time of death—19.01 z.hrs.

The blood drained from him as he slammed the book shut. Fumbling, Cedo pulled the next unmarked ledger from the shelf. It detailed, in all too perfect handwriting, the life and death of someone known merely as B.N. Whoever they were, they had died at around the same time as D.S., the ledger pointing out that, while they had tried to make it as painless as possible, it had been difficult due to the nature of the device they were testing. Tears sprang to his eyes as he ran through pages of dates and times and nameless initials, all of them signed and counter-signed by Erus and a signature that he could just make out as the official mark of the Patron. Everything was authorized and aboveboard, and that made it all the more painful.

Slamming the book home, Cedo let out a pained sob, his fingers running into his hair. Tears already warmed his cheeks as he tried to hold back the cries. They were for those who had died, but also for himself, a new found dread beginning to swell inside of him. The initials, they seemed so familiar, a tiny flicker of a memory from somewhere in his mind. Once his usefulness was over, he feared that he would be next, that he would become C.R., sacrificed to provide some new weapon or execution device. He sobbed for the woman in the room, the woman who had been burned with electrical shocks. What would become of her? Would Erus begin to apply more power until the slight smell of singed flesh became stronger as she cried out to be allowed to cross to the afterlife? What would *his* fate be?

Cedo whined as he tried to back away from the shelves, stumbling and falling onto the seat where they had made love the previous evening. Now the blood red velvet screamed accusingly to him. *You live with a killer! You are at the mercy of one who does not care! You cannot leave!*

How many more had Erus fucked upon that seat before they had been so cruelly "sacrificed"? How many had known their last moments of pleasure riding upon the cock of the man who would later murder them?

Cedo screamed. It was a strangled scream, the cry of the condemned. It was the cry of the man who knew that there was no way out. Knees buckling, Cedo caught himself against a shelf as he fell, too filled with blinding fear to notice as a book swept down from the shelf, scattering pages across the floor.

As he slumped to the floor, he remembered the words of warning that Terrance had uttered to him:

"Do not wrong that man. Do not wrong him because he will tear you apart in a death so slow and painful that Inferno itself will be a relief."

Then it began to fall into place, subtle twitches in his brain forcing him to his knees and pushing him weakly across the floor. Crashing into the shelf, he tore at the books. Rifling through them, he did not rest until he had found the last set of initials.

E.M.

Edward Morgan, Donald Smith, and Betty Nickolai - the three people Erus had plucked from obscurity and turned into stars. Cedo felt himself retch, clutching his stomach as bile dripped from his teeth. They had not died the deaths others believed. They had died at the hands of Erus. Still coughing pathetically, Cedo slid to the floor, the world around him becoming dark.

CHAPTER 20

A low clicking brought him to, the world slowly swimming back into focus as he painfully eased himself from the floor. Swaying slightly, Cedo crept in the direction of the sound. For a while, it eluded him until, through pain-weary eyes, he noticed a small, flashing light on the desk. It blinked beside the portal for the pneumatic tubes and he flicked it open. Inside sat one of the message tubes, the light obviously indicating its presence.

Taking it out, he could see his name written on the paper inside.

Cedo removed the paper and unfurled it.

Cedo,

I am with Jules and request your presence in Svenfur. The carriage is on its way to collect you. I shall see you shortly.

Erus

Peering through the window, he let out a groan. Through the shrubbery he could see the carriage. His head pounded and joints ached from the fall. Muttering darkly to himself, he quickly shelved the books before gathering the sheaf of papers. He stopped to study them.

They were schematics, but they were like no other creation of Erus' that he had seen. Instead, they were breathtaking, soft lines creating animals and birds like the ones within the indoor forest. Others were fairies, one was even a dragon. All of them were amazing and it pained him to see them hidden.

A heavy knock rattled the door and Cedo quietly cursed as he hurriedly returned the designs to their hiding place.

The driver did not spare the horse as they raced toward the city, the carriage leaping and crashing as much as the poor beast between the shafts. Cedo could feel the color draining from his face as they closed in on the smog-choked sprawl.

As the brougham skidded to a halt, he dashed from the cab, taking the steps two at a time. Perspiration dotted his face as he pushed open the door and Cedo knew that he did not look at all presentable, not that he cared now that he had arrived intact.

Terrance was seated behind his desk, face darkened with annoyance. An eyebrow arched as steely eyes lay upon the thick necklace. Suddenly self-conscious, Cedo placed a hand to the rope-like jewelry and followed the man's gaze over his shoulder.

Behind him, sprawled in a chair, was Erus. Fingers were pressed to his temple as he eyed Cedo with the same irritated disdain as Terrance had.

"Nice of you to finally join us." He rose, taking his time.

Instinct told Cedo to take a step back, the stinking aura of power beginning to clasp him. Eyes swept over him, taking in his disheveled appearance.

"You certainly took your time getting here, even if you did not take your time dressing."

"Do not keep me waiting. Ever," Erus snarled quietly in his ear.

Head lowered, Cedo nodded. "Yes, Sir."

"Good." Erus straightened up, collecting his cane as he headed for the door.

Outside, the sun had finally made an appearance from behind the dark clouds but it did little to warm Cedo's chilled flesh. He could feel the anger radiating from his Master, the way his shoulders were pulled back telling him more than the few words had. Silently he walked behind Erus' rapidly disappearing back, not daring to taste his wrath.

They had, according to Erus, an appointment to keep at a gentleman's outfitter to collect a number of new outfits for Cedo. It was a suit of green and gold that he wore as they left the tailors, Erus beside him. As they approached the seafront, Erus finally broke his silence.

"You look wonderful," he murmured, a hand resting in the small of Cedo's back.

Pressing himself to the warm touch, Cedo smiled, looking to his lover as he noted the pride in his voice and the gleam of happiness in his eyes.

The air was brisk and laced with salt as it lifted the hair from his shoulders. Tiny chills flickered along his bare neck, cooling the necklace on his skin. Cedo suddenly realized how exposed he felt with no collar to protect him, but he no longer cared. The curious, accusing glances no longer bothered him. He felt proud of his status at being Erus' hand-chosen prince.

Grief still ripped through him, the pain of what Erus did still haunted him, but he could not live with that shadow creeping behind him. His heart lay with Erus the man, not Erus the arms dealer. The darkness needed to be cast off so he could explore this man further, delving into his very soul and discovering what made him like he was.

It was a fascinating and quite delicious prospect. Cedo knew that he would care what happened, but it would need to be placed to one side to further expose the inner workings of the very man he had fallen in love with. A man who had showed him that relationships did not have to be between just men and women, indeed, they did not need to be between of people of the same social status. He was realizing what an honor it was, despite the misgivings of the people he spoke to. He, Cedo Reilly, was going to be the one who was not cast aside by Erus. He would not be murdered or made to disappear. With his head held high, he would be the one to walk with the necklace proudly on show until the end of time.

"Would you care for a coffee?" Erus' voice snapped him from his thoughts and he gave a smile and a nod.

The beach was dotted with small vendors, all nestled in the arches beneath the road. Here they sold a variety of different items—from grease-laden foods to tourist trinkets. He was led into a small and steamy coffee house, a place that was a riot of noise and activity. Voices called out orders while an overworked youth made cups of rich-smelling coffee. Crockery clattered in a sink while cakes and pastries jostled on a brass topped counter. A great coffee making machine took pride of place behind it, its pipes and outlets creamy with an ever-present mist.

Guiding them through the cramped space, Erus took a seat in a tiny corner booth, placing his hat on the table as he did. Feeling a little nervous, Cedo sat opposite him, quietly studying his surroundings before returning his attention to Erus. There was a strangeness to the situation, to seeing Erus out of his normal environment. It was a welcome change and Cedo's heart warmed as he watched Erus look around.

A waiter, a floor length apron wrapped around his

waist, came to take their order. Once he had walked back to the counter, Erus turned to Cedo, relaxing as he leaned on his elbows.

"I used to come here all the time when I was a child." Green eyes twinkled playfully. "I would take money from the matron's office and come here to have hot chocolate."

Erus sighed happily before returning to his story." It did not take the owner long to work out where I was from and he made a deal with me. If I washed his dishes for him I could have hot chocolate. Ten mugs equaled one hot chocolate. Twenty mugs and I could have hot chocolate and a slice of whatever cake took my fancy. It was hard work, but it became my home. That coffee machine..." His voice trailed away and Cedo suspected he knew what was coming next. "I built it for the owner in my spare time, once I had managed to leave the orphanage and was working on government contracts. It was installed just two days before the owner died."

Erus paused, breathing heavily. "The one man who was like a father to me was murdered in the most brutal fashion. Body parts were left all over Svenfur for us to find."

Stretching across the table, Cedo gently took Erus' hand. Eyes glazed with tears looked into his own and Cedo brushed the diamond droplets from his lashes.

"Did they ever find the culprit?"

"Indeed they did. It was a group of men, not from around here. There did not seem to be a clear motive for why they killed him. In court they all gave a variety of different reasons—he owed them money, he had raped one of their daughters—all the usual horse shit you hear. Yet, each of us took to the stand and testified in favor of his character." Erus once more looked up, eyes a little harder. "The men were each put to death in a machine that I had designed. And you know what, Cedo? That was the only time I was happy that someone would die because of me."

His fingers tightened around Erus' hand. Finally, he managed to speak, "Erus..."

The man swallowed, his Adam's apple bobbing as he fought back tears. "I am cursed by whatever loveless gods watch over us. Everyone I love is taken from me. My parents, whom I never knew. The single person who became like a father to me. Gone."

Cedo listened carefully, unsure of what to say. Had Erus loved the others who had lived beneath his roof? Or had they just outlived their purpose? Finally he dared ask, "What about the others?"

Erus' eyes flickered with confusion. "Whom do you speak of?"

"The ones before me, who you made into stars? What became of them?" He could hear his heart, thudding with the same deep sounds as the machine on the counter.

"They became ill. All of them. It is common, you know that. I-" He became flustered and pulled his hand from Cedo's. "I had scientists create medicines to try to cure them but they failed. They all died. Again, it was because of me."

Erus shook his head, hiding behind waves of hair as he stared at the wall, as if trying to etch his memories into the dark wood. Cedo could feel his skin tingling at each tiny secret, the painting beginning to complete itself. The logs with the horribly cold terms were the details of medicines that might have changed the world. Or that might have let Erus hold onto someone for just a little longer. The penny dreadfuls that had detailed the deaths in all their gory glory had, to some extent, told the truth.

"What would have happened if they had lived?"

"They were all in their prime." Erus did not look at him. "They were ready to go out without me, to spread their wings and fly."

The answer appeased him but still there was one other thing Cedo needed to know. "Did you love them?" His voice became quiet. "Did you love them like you love me?"

Erus' eyes had a distant look to them, forgotten conquests and hidden thoughts coming out. "I did. I loved each in their own way. But if you mean did I take any of them like I have you, then the answer is no. You are the only one who has been joined to me in such a way."

Relief spread through him as the darkness he had dreaded evaporated to nothing. Not caring where they were, Cedo leaned across the small table and gave Erus the barest of kisses.

CHAPTER 21

Sliding across the seat of the carriage, he laid his chin on Erus' shoulder.

"Tell me," Cedo purred into his ear. "Tell me you love me. Tell me you cherish me. Tell me you want me to be here forever and a day."

Erus' stern expression was reflected in the carriage window, eyes momentarily lifting.

"I gave you my token of affection. What more proof do you need?"

Those few words stung more than any punishment Erus could have meted out, burying deep into his heart. Wrapping his arms around his Master's slender waist, he melded himself against the warm, stiff body.

"Tell me what you feel for me."

Beneath his touch Erus barely seemed to breathe, instead staying in his fixed position, staring at the reflections in the window.

"What do you want me to say, Cedo?"

Sighing heavily, Cedo buried his face in the warm hair. "I want you to tell me what you feel for me. I want to know that you love me and that I'm not just another pawn."

"How do you mean, 'pawn'?"

He was so close, yet still so far. Erus was close to giving in, yet every time they even came close the walls would thicken, the defenses becoming prickly and cold. His hands travelled over Erus' broad chest.

"Everyone in your life, Master, seems to have their place and their position. I just need to know that you are not using me as another stepping stone to wherever you want to be."

Beneath his strong grip, the body weakened, slumping against his hands. "You were never a pawn. I never intended to ever use you for anything, and I apologize if that is how you feel. Yes, there is money to be made from your talents, but I keep none of it." For a brief moment, Cedo's blood ran cold. "The money is in trust for such a time as—" The strong voice cracked. "For such a time as I am no longer here. Then it will become yours. Anything you need between then and now, you can have."

Cedo froze. He knew, from adding his signature to a contract, that it would be hard to break what they had. But he had never thought of what could happen in the meanwhile, had never thought that death would, at some point, come for them all. Easing his grip on Erus, he gently stroked him, head lolling against his Master's.

"Let us not think of that," he said softly. "Let us never think of that. We are both young; there is still so much time ahead of us."

In the glass of the window, he held the cool gaze of the unmoving man he held.

The theater was in full swing when they arrived, the audience already streaming into the auditorium.

Backstage it was the same pandemonium, with artists running back and forth and, somewhere, someone calling that it was five minutes until curtain up. As with the previous nights at the Ship, Erus bid him farewell before disappearing into the murk of the theater. Making his way through the melee, Cedo fought his way to the side of the stage.

Up swept the curtain to the cry of the crowd, the band crashing into their opening number. The first act of the evening, two male dancers in spangled costumes, raced by. One of them handed a rose to Cedo, giving him a knowing smile before leaping out onto the stage. Crouched in the wings, Cedo quietly watched them twist and twirl to the band's thumping music and he found himself wondering if they, those two men on the stage, were like him and Erus. There had to be others in the city, those who chose to live with someone of the same sex. It could not be that hidden, could it?

Leaning forward, he studied them intently, looking for any clues that might answer his questions. Both, he noticed, wore earrings, but that was it. There were no fancy necklaces and nothing that might tell him otherwise.

"Oi!" Twitching with fright, Cedo looked behind him, crawling out of the way as a dark figure loomed over him, hidden by the shadows of the wings.

The figure knelt down, revealing himself in the flickering light. Gasping for breath, Cedo buried his hands into his sides lest he should thump the blond man.

"You gave me a right fright."

If he had sounded menacing, it did not show on Billy's face, the wide smile in place and eyes dancing with the lights of the stage.

"Was wondering where you were." Billy shuffled a little closer, pressing himself into Cedo's hiding place. The other was warm, no doubt from the exertion of running around backstage. "Can you escape tonight?"

"What do you mean, 'escape'?" he coolly asked.

"I mean—" Billy's smile widened. "—that me an' some of the other lads are 'eading out tonight an' I was wonderin' if your royal 'ighness would like to join us."

His throat dried at the suggestion. "Me?"

"Yes. You. Now, you comin' or not?"

Cedo stared at the stage, mind a-whirl. Stay and go home to another evening confined to the room of the man who appeared to have no feelings for him? Or go out and discover what really happened when the sun dipped beneath the sea? There had been no problem when Billy had sent him on his way the night before. In fact, Erus did not even seem to have particularly missed him, despite signing a contract that said otherwise.

Looking back to Billy, he gave a nod. "I will come, but only for a while, you understand."

Billy ruffled Cedo's hair. "You're a good'un. I'll see you after the show, take you to this place. Trust me, you'll love it."

The chairman's deep voice called his name and, with a renewed lightness in his step, Cedo walked out onto the stage to an accompanying cry from the crowd. From the noise alone, he felt accepted, welcomed into the world of his dreams. He did not sing or dance, nor did he perform acrobatics, but the spoken word, his spoken word, had wormed its way into their hearts.

The roar was deafening, the crowd drinking in his tale, and he breathlessly ran from the stage. Exhilaration sang through him and it was Billy's hand on his arm that stopped him.

"Quick," Billy panted in his ear. "We 'ave to go now."

"Why do we have to go right this moment?"

"Because, 'is good lord Mr. fuckin' Veetu is lookin' for you."

Peering past Billy, Cedo tried to make out the shadows that moved in the darkness.

"Gotta get outta 'ere an' get gone. Cedo, you ain't backin' out on me now, are you? Not gonna go runnin' back to 'im?"

"I have to," he hissed. "Billy, I am sorry, but I did promise him that I would not go wandering."

Billy snorted, warm breath hitting Cedo's face. "Get ya to put it in writin', did 'e?"

"Actually." His voice became cool. "he did."

Billy's hand relaxed against him, the tall figure slumping a little. "You stupid fucker, Cedo. Stupid, silly fucker." Fingers stroked though his hair, making him glance up at the lanky figure hovering over him. "Never put your name to anythin' that man 'ands you. Not unless you 'as got the money to buy yourself out. An', from lookin' at you, even in all your fancy clothes an' all, you ain't got nothin'."

An arm was loosely draped around his shoulders and they made their way toward the back entrance.

Another pair of boys joined them as they wound through the narrow corridors, Billy briefly greeting them before they were joined by three girls, all of them dressed with the finery of dancers. Feeling a little uncomfortable at the fine clothes he wore, Cedo moved away from Billy's protective grasp and stepped behind them, listening to them chatter about the evening that lay ahead. This was their one night of freedom this season, for soon holidays filled with decorations and colorful gifts would be upon them and no one would see the outside world until the frosts lifted.

As Cedo left with them, he heard an echoing voice call his name, a voice laden with the dark promise of what was to come.

CHAPTER 22

They raced through dark, narrow alleyways, feet scuffing and clicking against the cracked cobbles, the girls laughing and grabbing his arms.

Cedo laughed with them, the lightness of it lifting his soul as he escaped. There would be horrors untold after tonight but, as they sped along, oblivious to anyone or anything following them, he knew he needed this. The defiance played a sweet song to his soul, carrying him through the criss-crossing streets of the city, further from the one who professed love but preferred pain.

It was another narrow back street, shielded from the prying eyes of the world by high walls, that led them to the back door of a windowless building. It was like some strange tale come true; a single door in a faceless wall, a solitary gas lamp creaking in the light breeze. All that changed when the door was thrown open, light and music flooding the street.

As the others melted off into the crowd, Cedo took it all in. The room was bare except for a bar stocked with colorful bottles. Set to one side was a band comprising of a piano and several men with hand-held drums. No one sang, and no one seemed to care, as this was not a place for drinking to forget. It was a place where memories were created.

Groups of people leaned against the bar and the

paneled walls while others danced, linking hands and arms as they galloped and twirled over the floor. Their bodies glistened with sweat but they did not appear to mind, caught up in the joy of the moment.

From nowhere, a jug of foaming beer was thrust into his face. Taking it, Cedo looked up into Billy's grinning face. Already Billy's eyes were alive with the atmosphere that clawed them.

"Drink!" Billy cried, voice almost lost in the music.

Eyeing the glass with suspicion, Cedo finally took it, sipping at the heavy liquid. Drinking, he watched, the itch in his body urging him to join the dancers. But the old reserve reared its ugly head and he remained a passive watcher. He watched until the nearly empty glass was snatched from his fingers and thrust toward a nearby stranger. In the blink of an eye, Cedo was whisked from the corner and into the rabble of dancers, struggling in Billy's strong arms before giving in.

For a moment, he panicked, wondering what others would think of two men thundering through the dancers. Yet, as he whirled and stamped and clapped with the rest of them, Cedo began to notice those who were not part of the troupe on the floor. Some stood, secluded to one side, arms around each other. Others were part of the melee of music, partnered up with their sweethearts. Each one flickered into view before melting away just as quickly; not one of them was with someone of the opposite sex.

Desperately Cedo took a deep breath to quiet his racing heart, his body nearly falling limp in the strong arms that held his hands. Gripping Billy's hands tightly, he looked up into the blue eyes that swam like fish in the sea, emotions racing through them.

"Billy!" he cried. "Billy!"

Blond hair tickled his nose as the taller man leaned closer. Blowing it away, Cedo huffed and he gripped the back of Billy's head, trying to force them to at least slow down.

"What is this place?!"

Billy chuckled, chin resting on Cedo's shoulder as he pulled them back toward the epicenter of the dancers. "This is where your real fairies live, Cedo!" The bemusement must have shown on his face for Billy laughed heartily, gesturing to the room with a grand sweep of his arm. "This is your real 'ome, Cedo! They're all kamps, Cedo. Every last one of 'em."

The world could have chosen that moment to stop and he would not have noticed, for everything faded into an abyss that held just himself and Billy. He hung in the strong arms, breath coming in labored gasps.

"Kamps?"

"Those 'oo like their own kind." Fingers stroked the nap of his neck, cradling him close, Billy's face a mess of soft shadows and swimming eyes.

"But." Carefully Cedo guided them away from the dance floor, trying to seek out a quiet corner. "I thought you liked girls?"

His face was clasped and turned upward, Billy's hot, cloying smell raking up his nostrils as warm, beer soaked breath whispered against his lips.

"I do." The barest hint of a beaming smile pricked Billy's. "But I like boys as well. I'm what they call bibi."

Every fiber of his being was crying for him to clutch Billy close and press their lips together, but beneath the passion was a smaller, darker voice, one that whispered his fate to him. With his heart turning to stone, he reluctantly let go, sliding from beneath the gentle fingers. Desperately he tried to ignore the agony of rejection that hung in Billy's eyes. Tried to ignore the pain that inched through his belly on sharpened tracks, so many unspoken words hanging by invisible threads.

Muttering an apology, Cedo slipped away, out of the door of what could have been his new home and into a bitter and misty night. It was fitting that the night was as bleak as it was, mirroring what ate away at him. Just one kiss, one innocent little kiss, and it would have led to other things. It would have led to dark corners and warm beds and finally to the confrontation that he did not want.

Crossing from alleyway to street, Cedo heard raised voices, their displeasure only just muffled by the smoky fog. Walking through the murk, Cedo watched from the safety of the shadows as two men, lit by a lamp high above them, took pipes and mallets to a downed walking machine. The shiny contraption lay twisted on the ground, its entire being groaning as it tried to right itself before being brutally smashed back down. The air held the sharp feeling of hatred, an anger that was directed at the battered metal frame.

Inching forward, Cedo felt himself begin to say something before clutching himself, his stomach turning violently over. Amid the wreckage of the machine lay what must have been its rider, its skull splattered against the cobbles, red blood mixing with the machine's dark, sticky hydra-fluids.

Before he could vomit and before the men could turn their pipes on him, Cedo stumbled out of view, leaning helplessly against walls and railings, fighting to keep himself upright.

Home. Cedo did not know the way there, to the building somewhere on the edge of Svenfur that contained his belongings and his lover. It was not really home, more of a dump for the things he needed and the person who kept him.

He could feel the mist of blind panic beginning to rise, blurring his vision as he hunted for the means to return to the imposing house. The brightly-colored trams that coasted tourists along the seafront most certainly did not run that far out of the city, where the drops and inclines of hills posed problems. He had no idea if the great machines of the Terminus went there; he had certainly never heard them. An omnibus would go that far from the city but that in itself caused yet more problems to arise: he did not know where they departed from, and he did not have the fare.

Leaning against a soot-stained wall, Cedo stared into the distance, watching lights sparkle and dance upon water-soaked cobbles. The walk would take him well into the next day and he did not want to do that, images of what no doubt waited for him imprinted in his mind. Tears filmed over his eyes, the colored lights blurring until they merged into nothing more than a smear.

Arms around himself, Cedo pushed himself onward, walking in the direction he hoped would lead back to his abode. Untangling one arm, he curled his fingers toward the few people he passed, his meek voice asking for change. How quickly the great fell, his face not yet recognizable enough for them to spare him a few coins. Each person looked at him as if he were the dirt on their shoes, unworthy of any kind of comment, eyes accusingly looking at his beautiful clothes.

Disheartened, he stopped, wiping his hand across his eyes. No one was willing to help, not one person wanted to give a little kindness.

"Excuse me, Sir," his voice was pitiful. "Would you be so kind as to spare some change in exchange for a tale."

A man, face as gnarly as an old tree, glared at him from behind an armful of parcels before guffawing.

"I won't pay you for no tale, lad, but I'll pay you for a suck."

Cedo felt his already shivering body cool still further

at the frank request. Eyes that sparkled with a devilish lust stroked over his body and he recoiled still further.

"Pretty lad like you, out all alone. Surprised someone hasn't already made you their wife. But, for a moment, you can be mine."

It was a vile experience, kneeling in the filth of the city while making faux appreciative sounds around the stranger's stinking cock, but it had to be done. The few coins that were tossed into his outstretched hand did little to quash the feeling of disgust that ate away at him.

CHAPTER 23

Stumbling onward, he was able ask, just barely where he could catch the Witheybrooke omnibus.

"The front," the woman has said, eyes saddening a little as she took in the dirt that cloyed his clothes. "Opposite The Grand."

Cold gripped him but Cedo willingly pressed on, pushing the shock of the previous hour's events somewhere they could be forgotten.

The stop was one of many that littered the busy seafront road, each marked by a small tin sign proclaiming the bus number and destination. Leaning against the railings, Cedo walked along them, the disgraced whore looking for his next fix.

23... 32... 37... 45... 58.

That would be the one to carry him home, the paupers' carriage. Buses came and went, moving between the trams and their iron tracks. Drivers called out the destinations, hustling people onto their advertisement-clad coaches before pushing the horses onward. Through the traffic, he could see the splendor of the Grand Hotel, swirling iron railings decorating the precarious balconies, an ode to modern technological advancements. Once upon a time, he would have dined there with his mother and her friends late into the night before one of them dropped him into a bed.

"All stops to Dalry! Callin' at Baddeley Green, Oatnell, Thunderbarrow Hill, Witheybrooke, and Dalry! All aboard!" A creaking bus pulled up before them, passengers spilling out onto the windy pavement, a set of four horses chomping at their bits.

Shuffling along the queue, Cedo wearily pulled himself into the two-tiered omnibus, eyes on the scuffed and dirty floor. A large lady, swathed in a heavy animal skin cloak, sat next to him, a cage of clucking birds balanced precariously on her lap.

Absolute silence gripped the hallway as Cedo stepped through the unlocked door of Erus' house. Darkness accompanied it, every lamp left unlit. It was as if someone was telling him something, telling him that now was the time to turn and never come back.

As when he was a child, Cedo pressed his hand to the wall, guiding himself. Along the wall, over the door to the dining hall and across the open mouth of the corridor that led away from the stairs. Safety was just a step away. His fingers brushed against the smooth, varnished wood of the dragon's head and Cedo let the air back into his lungs as he pulled himself upward.

"This disappearing lark of yours seems to have become an awfully bad habit, Cedo."

Terror clutched him. He stopped, hands gripping the banister tightly. Bile rose in his stomach when Erus' breath touched his cheek, silken hairs brushing against his skin. Fingers locked over his mouth and the panic broke its stranglehold, a cry, muffled by the tight fingers, tearing from him as he was jerked back from the stairs.

Through the darkness he was hauled, cries unheeded , the fingers nicking his skin as they closed tighter around his lips. A swift kick and the kitchen door thundered open, Cedo released only to go sprawling across the hard flagstone floor. His knees throbbed from the heavy fall, his face was taut with the terror that held him, trying to escape the snarling demon above him. Around him, accusing eyes stared, yet there was not a murmur from any of the members of the house. Despite the heat from the roaring fire, the kitchen felt frightfully cold.

"Mr. Morris, if you please."

Cedo found himself being roughly hauled to his feet, the strong arms of the elderly groundsman holding him firm. Terrified, he looked straight into Erus' blank face, hard eyes staring straight back at him.

"I bring you into my home," snarled the arms dealer. "I give you everything you could ever dream of, and all I ask in return is that you stay beside me, an effortless task, one would think. Yet you cannot even do that. Instead you go gallivanting off into the night without so much as the good grace to say where you are going. To say that you have had me worried is an understatement. Mr. Reilly, you knew your place the moment *this* was placed around your neck." Fingers jerked the heavy necklace. "Your place is beside me, not running around the city like some overpriced harlot. I gave you one chance and you returned, yet I have not the slightest idea where you went. Second chances do not come so cheaply."

Cedo watched, shaking in the iron-like grip, as Erus wrapped his hand in a thick glove and delicately lifted a shaped iron from the fire. The heady terror returned in abundance, Cedo pressing himself closer to the groundsman as the back of his hand was offered.

The tears came before the white hot metal touched his skin, his scream a dull sound compared to the pain that ripped through him. Cedo found himself crashing back to the floor as the iron was pulled away, taking not just his skin with it, but another layer of himself. Deeper and deeper he was falling down the rabbit hole, unable to scramble back out and now, with this, the final act of ownership, he was at the bottom, sitting in the darkness.

Crumpled on the floor, his hand outstretched across the cool stones, Cedo screamed again, one long sound of pain and terror, a cry for those who fell through the cracks. wailing for the gift of hindsight. Not for the first time, he wanted to die. Erus would not let him die, no matter how hard Cedo tried to make him. He would just be patched up and once more put out for target practice.

As the searing pain began to subside so did his voice, falling to a sob before dying completely. The kitchen was empty, the spectators having left, no doubt having received their lesson in what would happen should they cross Erus' path. Even Mr. Morris had melted away, leaving them alone.

"Why do you defy me?"

With difficulty, Cedo lifted his head, looking over his crumpled shoulder at the figure hiding in the shadows. Erus stepped forward, the heartbreak on his face causing a fresh wave of guilt and sorrow to flood Cedo. Every morbid thought that he had ever had, every inkling that he was just a mere toy began to ebb away.

"Because..." he finally whispered.

Erus made no move toward him, instead standing in the dying light of the fire, face cast in shadows that only highlighted his own pain. "Because why?" The iron hung at Erus' side and, for the first time, Cedo noticed the shape it had been cast in: a claw with a mouse sitting at its center.

Quickly he looked to his still smarting hand. Flowing red welts showed the image, burned for all eternity into him. Putrid bile began to rise, threatening to choke him. Marked. Scarred. Forever. Nothing would wash away that stain. Everybody would know where he had come from. A sign to the people of the city that Cedo was not to be approached, that he was an untouchable of the highest kind. An unsellable slave, shackled to just one person.

Cedo heard something he never thought he would hear, as Erus pleaded with him, "Why, when I give you everything, do you defy me? Why are you like the others?"

Drawing in deep breaths, Cedo sat up, cradling his injured hand. There was a haunting sadness in Erus' face but it did nothing to quash the rigid anger that was beginning to rise within him.

"Master," his voice quivered, but only a fraction as the pain of the burn began to disappear. "You can give me baubles and beautiful clothes but you cannot give me the one thing I truly want. You can shower me with all the gifts you want, but they are not love." And so the tears fell. "I love you, Master and that is all I want in return. Trinkets mean nothing if they are not given in love."

"Balderdash!" cried Erus, the iron clattering to the floor. "I brought you here to make you a better person. I took you from the draughty room in a desolate boarding house and gave you a home where you would not have to worry where your next meal came from. I took you away from the cold clutches of the pier and placed you upon the stages of the city. What more could you want from me?"

Clutching his hand to his chest, Cedo struggled to his feet. "Then why did you bind me to you? Why did you place me upon your bed? Why do you smile when I lie next to you?"

Erus' expression changed, eyes widening as he began to back away, a haunted look crossing his face as Cedo slowly closed on him.

"You do not know how, do you Master?" Cedo continued, body aching from the effort of moving. "You do not know how to love. You are as cold as the machines as you build."

Instinctively, Erus brought up a hand, hiding his face.

"No."

"No?" Cedo repeated. "No, you do not want to hear what I am saying? Is that not always the case? You want the trappings of someone permanently by your side, but none of the strings that come with it? Are you as soulless and heartless as the people on the streets make you out to be? How many lies have you told me, Erus? How many times have you fabricated the truth in order to make yourself appear the victim?"

Erus did not look up as he leaned heavily against the wall, one hand wrapped around the doorknob.

"Never," was the hushed reply. "I have never lied to you. Yes, you have heard the warnings from those outside of these walls and it is good that you have done so, for you now know the monster you reside with. But I have never lied to you and I never plan to lie to you. I cannot feel for those who have inadvertently died at my hands for if I do I shall weep until death takes me. Yes, I am a cruel and heartless person but I have been pushed here by those before me. Yes, you are correct in saying that my heart is as cold and as senseless as the metal I build with."

Before him, Erus slid to the floor, becoming a shadow of himself. Knees drew up and arms wrapped around them, all of it vanishing behind a shroud of hair as he laid his head against his legs. Red and black were stark against one another as the proud man became a whimpering child, shaking as sobs echoed from the tiled walls. Unsure of what to do or say, Cedo watched in shocked amazement, the change filling him with a dull sadness. The man who had been shaped into a leader had lost his dignity.

Kneeling before him, Cedo let his hand fall upon the bowed head, fingers slowly working through his Master's hair as he listened to garbled words. Words that were lost in the torrent of pain and sorrow that spilled from the aching body.

"Once—once I was like you.... I. I was lost. Once Papa Brokoveich had died, I was lost." Another sob followed by a coughing fit. "I had everything at my feet. The world. My designs. My first factory. But I was lost. I. I needed direction. Needed a firm hand. Needed guidance. That."

A sigh and a shudder, Erus obviously too ashamed to look up. "That was when he arrived. From another land. James." There was a small laugh, hoarse and dull. "Such a common name for such a powerful man. He was a businessman, looking to invest. He wanted something new. Mainly he dealt in precious metals, jewels and the like. But, after a while, he chose to deal in me."

Quietness fell over them. Eventually, Erus picked up the tale. "As with you and I, he placed a sentiment around my neck. Made me his. I did not need his money. But, for that time, I needed someone to guide me. For several long years he kept me locked in the cellar of a hotel. From there, he came and went, going back to his homeland. Returning only when he needed what I had been working on.

"I admired him. I believe I even felt affection for him. But never once did he return my affections. Instead, once he had what he needed, he set me adrift. By then I understood better what I had to do. I took in people like you, not just because I enjoyed your talents. Not just because I wanted to make you better performers. I took you in because—" Again he stalled, shuddering fitfully beneath Cedo's touch as if it were too much to bear. "I took you in because I craved the company. I wanted people who were not fearful of me. I wanted what I had given him. And, in you, I got it."

His hand slowed against the mane of hair. Instead, Erus took his uninjured hand in his own, his touch light as he lifted his face to Cedo's. Despite the tears, despite the redness that marred his face, there was once again a proud look in those green eyes. They held his own gaze as his fingers grazed over Erus' collarbone, taking in the gentle sweep of it. Cedo felt his eyes widen as his fingers drifted over something other than skin and bone. Tiny lumps, unmoving and as hard as nails lay along the bones. Yet never, in all the times they had spent unclothed together, had he noticed them.

"This is how he marked me." He held Cedo's hand against his breast. "You may ask why I do not have them removed and I will reply that I would if I could. But they are fused to the bone and to remove them would leave far more damage than he inflicted upon me."

Peeling the shirt away, Cedo took a closer look, squinting in the dying light. There was not a mark where the lumps lay, no scarring and no indication of what lay beneath the skin. Perfect and untouched, as clear as day.

Knowing that his own eyes were filled with sadness, Cedo reached out, arms wrapping around his Master. The man fell against him, body limp as arms hung around Cedo's neck, Erus shaking in his grip. His own pain, the pain of a skin wound, was nothing compared to pain Erus sobbed out against him. Legs curled beneath him, he sat, a mother rocking her heartbroken child.

CHAPTER 24

Morning came as every morning did, heralding them to a new day of work as it distributed a gentle warmth to a world on the brink of the changing seasons. Summer was dying, leaving behind it crisp days and cool nights.

When Cedo finally awoke, it was with little surprise that he found himself in his own bed, Misty purring away by his head. Erus had locked himself away somewhere, mending his wounded pride. The man he called Master had taken a great fall.

Drifting into the strange, mechanical forest, he swept Misty up into his arms, placing her onto his shoulder. Taking in the elegance of the trees and their ability to live beneath a roof, he quietly began to sing to himself, the cat's soft, bushy tail swinging against his neck.

'O'er the mountains,
And o'er the sea,
On wings of
gently spun gold,
He came to me."

Winding among the trees and bushes, he sang, Misty muttering in his ear. It took very little for him to forget that the surreal forest was set beneath a roof. Something fluttered by his ear, the sound of gently clacking gears catching him off guard before he lost himself back into the world that lay beyond his eyes.

"O'er downs, ,
And o'er fells,
Caught on the
rays of the sun,
He came to me."

From among the arched, trailing roots a tinny sound made him pause and look up. It was gone in the flicker of an eye and Cedo moved on, the sound quickly becoming a distant memory.

"He landed a'fore me,
And gave me his hand,
His eyes a-glowing
as he carried me high."

Tilting his head, he listened as the sound returned, the quiet tapping of fingernails against stone. It came over a tree root, Cedo freezing when the thing came to rest at his feet. Because a *thing* was all it could be described as, two halves of a metal clamshell fixed atop eight bolted and jointed legs. The crab-like creature appeared to have no way of seeing and tiny but lethal looking tools extended from what should have been its mouth. Pincers, knives and a minuscule teethed wheel all chattered against each other as the creature surveyed them.

Claws dug into his shoulder and he yowled as Misty dived for the creature. Back arched and tail high, she hissed, trying to ward off the vicious looking being. Remarkably, rather than leave, the crab lowered itself until its back end was in the air, tool teeth chattering at the suddenly startled cat. As Misty looked up at him with big blue eyes, Cedo concluded that if the cat could have a shocked look then this would be it. Dipping his shoulder in a shrug, he gave her an apologetic look, one cautious eye still watching the crab.

The cat took a new tactic in an effort to scare off the monster. Sticking her nose forward, she gave it a cautious sniff, followed by a pushing paw. The thing did not move, once again returning Misty's gesture as a beveled leg ran along the cat's shoulder. Misty shivered from top to tail at the touch, inching a little closer to the brass and bolts machine. Gingerly placing one paw on its curved back, she began to wash it with long, slow licks before Cedo's surprised eyes. His curiosity grew as the creature gave a clanking shudder beneath the barrage of cleaning, a dull shaking of gears accompanying the movement.

His silent surprise stayed as he watched the once-shiny machine turn a dull yellow beneath the tongue of its new friend. The crab appeared to have lost its earlier fight, now lying down beneath the cat's paw. Deciding to leave them be, Cedo turned away with the plan to find somewhere to rest for a while and nurse his aching hand. The wound had not been dressed and the dead skin was peeling away to leave a red mark behind. He would need to find something, a dressing for it at the very least, before he dared to venture out in the evening.

He had not walked more than two steps before the ear splitting scream of a pained cat caused him to turn back. The metal monster had Misty by the tail, pincers digging in as it began to drag her away. White hair began to fill the air as Misty tried to dig her claws into the lightly grassed floor, screaming and howling in a desperate escape attempt. Bearing down on them, he caught hold of the cat, bundling her into his arms and kicking the creature away.

The brass crab ricocheted off the floor, the metallic clang of it stilling Cedo in his escape. Turning to look, he watched as it rocked on its upturned shell before righting itself. That *thing*, that beast, it must have been one of them that he had kicked as he had escaped from the slaughterhouse at the Terminus. Instantly he felt ill at the memory and, before it could come back for another go, Cedo raced with Misty to safety. As the door slammed behind them, another of the clangs filled the air, the sound violently turning his stomach.

With Misty's tail and his hand bandaged, Cedo sat in the window of his room. Upon his lap sat the leather-bound journal, a mystified Misty lying at his feet, bandaged tail sticking up as straight as a sail. He could not help but smile as she waved it to get his attention, obviously dissatisfied with the neat bow he had tied at the tip.

"It will come off when it is healed and not a moment before."

The cat turned her head, giving him the disdainful look that every cat had worked into perfection.

"You can be grumpy about it, but you should be grateful you still have your tail. In fact, you should be grateful that you are still alive, because I believe that machine was going to eat you for its supper."

Taking up his pen, he began to write. The words flowed, covering the pages. He did not know how long he sat, the passage of time creaking to a halt.

Billy, dear sweet Billy, if only you could see me now. I promised my mother that I would never turn into my father, that I would never leave the one I loved to go after another. But you, the angel of the night, are not the harlot he left my own kind mother for. You are of a different kind entirely.

Closing the book, he leaned his head against the cool glass. Beyond the house, the sun had begun its descent down toward the roll of the Downs, the sky ablaze with deep shades of red, orange and purple. The world was beginning to sleep while for Cedo it was time to wake.

"Mr. Reilly," a voice he did not know called through the door. "It's time to go."

The unknown voice belonged to Mr. Morris and those nine words were the only ones he had uttered as he whisked Cedo to the brougham. The driver's silence made him wonder if the servants were under some kind of command, one in which they were not to speak to him unless it was to tell him to dress or wash or come for dinner. Instead, he was kept for one person only. He thought of never having another friend.

The Cartier was one of the grandest buildings in the city. Situated in the heart of Hinckledon, it boasted visiting royals and ambassadors among its audience members. To Cedo, it was a dream to be standing on its pure white steps, staring up at the names that adorned the marquee, names he had seen featured in theatrical newspapers. Ones with which he had never thought to be sharing a stage.

No one was there to meet him, nor to guide him through the usual labyrinth of the backstage. Rather he found himself speaking to a young woman at the box office. Running a long fingernail down a list, she finally looked up and reached for a contraption on the wall. It looked like the horn of an instrument and was made from the same highly polished brass. A tube ran from the slender end of it and into a box. She pressed a button and waited, the horn held close to her ear before announcing his arrival to whomever answered.

After a while, a door beside the box office opened and a tall, thin man with a gaunt face walked out. Striding over to Cedo, he offered a hand and a smile.

"Mr. Reilly, ever so pleased to meet you. My name's John Cartier." As they descended into narrow passages, he carried on speaking. "I've heard plenty about you. Not just from Mr. Veetu, but from people who have seen you. I trust that you have something spectacular prepared for us tonight."

With a thin, tense smile, Cedo gave a small nod. "I always try to have something special for wherever I am."

It was not necessarily true, of course. Not having had Erus around all day meant that he had not known if he was to go out. Of course, it also meant that if tonight did not go as well as Erus liked then no one would be any the wiser. Although deep down, he knew that sooner rather than later, Erus would find out about any abysmal performance.

There were not many others before him, although the caliber of performers was far better than at The Ship and The Rose. Most were musical acts; women dressed as men, men dressed as women, couples and groups and a smattering of soloists. There were those employed to impress; fire-breathers and jugglers and stilt-walkers in vivacious costumes.

A gentle hush fell over the theater as he stood in a circle of pure white light. Expectation itched toward him from the waiting crowd and he began.

Caught in the darkness of the wings following his performance, he could have sworn he was back at the Ship. But when Billy's familiar voice did not ring out, his heart dropped. Billy was gone, another of the many people to pass through his life.

Outside, the carriage waited to whisk him away. With no one to issue orders to him and no one to take him to unusual dance halls, it seemed only right that he should go home. Am emptiness swam over him as he settled into the carriage.

CHAPTER 25

And so it carried on: spending days by the window, journal in lap, and evenings at the Cartier, slowly building a new group of listeners. But the house was empty, his meals left outside his door, clothes appearing, clean and laundered, as if by magic. From time to time, Cedo heard the quiet murmurings of the servants but other than that, nothing. Erus had gone, vanished as quickly as he had appeared.

The nights were drawing in, becoming darker and colder. Gradually, decorations began to appear, not just around the house, but in the windows of other homes and businesses. Wintermass, the annual celebration of the changing of the seasons, was quickly descending upon them, bringing with it an unspoken excitement. For on the longest night of the year, when the moon hid itself away, people across the land exchanged gifts and feasted upon rich foods. For weeks beforehand, shops hawked beautiful gifts, each trying to outdo the others with extravagant window dressings, while families and friends threw spectacular parties.

One such party was being planned for the house of Veetu and it had been hard for Cedo to ignore as the bustling of the servants grew with each passing day.

Most of the rooms he wanted to explore were locked, off limits, so Cedo had taken to lounging in his room as he awaited the break of evening. One night, it never came, the sharp rap at the door never echoing across the room. Instead, the stern voice of Mrs. Sugden called out, urging him to open the door.

Sliding from the window, he did as was asked, the tired looking housekeeper holding a laden hanger.

"Master asks that you shave all hair except for your head, dress in this and join him downstairs as quickly as possible."

His heart leapt as he took the hanger from her, but was soon replaced with dismay as he gazed at what he held. For once, it was not one of the many handsome suits that had been gifted to him. Rather it was a long, red silk dress, not unflattering but still something that a woman would wear. Looped around the wire hook were a pair of long, red evening gloves.

Dropping it to the bed, he hid himself in the water closet and lathered his face and arms and legs before taking his razor to them. With his heart still in his throat, Cedo returned to the mirror and let his clothes slip to the floor before sliding into the delicate dress.

Sad eyes stared back at him as he took in what he had become. The dress sat comfortably just below his shoulders, wrapping over his chest and accentuating hips he never knew he had. Like every other piece of clothing, it had been stitched especially for him. Before he left the room, he pulled a brush through his hair and stretched the gloves over his hands, watching the strange portrait move in the reflective glass. This had to be a test or a punishment or both. Catching one last glance at himself, Cedo forced himself to smile, for that would be what Erus would want. A smiling, beautiful wife.

Pausing once more before the mirror, Cedo let a wicked passion rage through him, the smile turning into sinful smirk. Whatever Erus wanted from him, whatever the reason behind the dress, Cedo would play along. He would give him the wife that he seemed to so want. Ruffling his hair into slapdash waves, he went for the stairs.

Candles and garlands of evergreen trees adorned the banisters, a pair of large, wrought iron candlesticks sitting at the foot of the stairs. There, at the bottom of them, arms folded behind his back and eyes watching the door, was Erus. Cold eyes turned to him as he ascended the stairs.

Unsure of how to stand or act in the unfamiliar garment, he chose instead to return the glance with the barest of smiles. "I have missed you, Master."

He received a small smile for his words. They stood beside one other, watching as the servants carried food and gifts, the smell of spices and fruits accompanying the preparations.

The sound of Erus' voice was enough to make him twitch a little and he turned to look. "This evening, you shall stay beside me. You will speak when spoken to. You are to be seen and not heard."

He gave a curt nod, feeling cold. Here he stood, waiting for the world, dressed in women's clothing and being told how to act. Never had he thought his life would slump to such a place.

Beside him, there was a flare of red and Cedo turned to look at Erus, cold eyes mirroring how he felt. "You may wonder why you are dressed as you are. You have had too many liberties and you have pushed against boundaries that are not meant to be broken. You are a simple slave, here to do my bidding, and tonight you shall finally act like it. Understood?"

The chill crept over his exposed skin and Cedo managed to suppress a shudder. How could he reply to that, reply to the question that had haunted him since the damned dress had been laid out before him? In short, he had been put firmly in place, not through anger and pain but through silent humiliation. It was a punishment he would not forget.

Before long the house became the hub of Svenfur's social life. Everyone who was anyone appeared to be there, all of them dressed in their finery as they passed the time drinking and eating. Small, box-like creatures picked their way through the throngs, trays of drinks balanced on their backs. They moved with an ease that Cedo had never seen in such things, never spilling a drop as, with some unknown intelligence, they wandered from room to room. Everything about Erus' life was set out to impress, and no doubt people were on some level, but they knew what his business was and such things at a mere party were nothing.

Demented pleasure tore through Cedo as the thought crossed his mind. Standing beside Erus, listening as his Master and an older, portly gent, spoke of the complexities of harnessing energy into small power sources. Just the topic of conversation was enough for Cedo to want to turn any kind of weapon on himself, although he knew that if he dared so much as yawn that Erus do the damage himself.

"You must introduce me to your young lady!" the man exclaimed. "She's been standing here looking fit to drop from boredom."

Color rose to his cheeks and he could feel the smirk on Erus' lips.

"This is Claudia." Cedo looked to Erus, the smug look on his Master's face making him fit to burst with anger. "She has not been with me long, but she is settling in well. Is that not correct, Miss Reilly?"

Pursing his lips, Cedo scowled darkly at Erus before putting on his sweetest smile and turning to the man.

Obviously the man needed one of the many doctors in the room to check his eyes if he could not tell that Cedo was a man.

Forcing his voice into a falsetto, he gave the man a curtsey. "It is a great honor to be living here. Much more pleasant than the smoky streets of the city."

If he had not already been so red from the drink and the warmth, Cedo would have been convinced that the gentleman was blushing. "Indeed it is, Miss. We have many great industries in Svenfur, but they do clog up the streets and the skies with their by-products. Still, I suppose it is the price one must pay for progress."

"Indeed it is, sir." Cedo's mind wandered, thinking over the things he had seen and heard, of the machines that could tear a man to shreds in mere seconds. So that's what progress was known as these days?

The evening dragged on and Cedo found it more and more difficult to stop himself from yawning. Every person they spoke to was exactly the same, obsessed with politics and money. Even the partners of these people looked as bored as he felt, glassy eyes looking at him. Sometimes they smiled; mostly they just ignored him, no doubt wishing they were elsewhere.

Eventually a face he recognized walked up and greeted Erus.

"Erus, how are you?" Mr. Farns said as he stretched out a hand in greeting.

"Very well, Mr. Farns, thank you. And yourself?"

"I'm well. I have news for you."

Erus' face lit up. "And pray, what is that?"

Mr. Farns appeared to relax as he took his hand back. "I have the rest of the debt. While I appreciate your help in rebuilding the theater, the debt has been a great weight around my neck. I hope that my final offering will be enough to finally clear it."

Cedo's blood ran cold, his hackles rising as Mr. Farns continued: "I have my meager offering with me, but such a gathering is not the place for it. Shall I leave it in the cellar for you to look over when you have a moment?

Straightening up, Erus let out a contented sigh. "That would be very good of you, Mr. Farns. I appreciate your forward thinking."

"Then I shall do that. And now that we have resolved that, I shall leave you to enjoy the rest of your gathering. Thank you for extending your invitation to me."

Erus gave a small nod, Cedo shivering as a hand was placed in the small of his own back. "You are more than welcome, Mr. Farns. I shall speak to you later."

Cedo gave Mr. Farns a small smile as he was guided away and toward the stairs. "The evening is ending," Erus whispered. "Go and rest; I shall join you later."

He knew better than to react to Mr. Farns' words, especially with so many people still in the house. The warning of the dress was enough to keep him silent. Perhaps later he would approach Erus over what had been used to pay off the debt because he was sure that it was not money.

Mouth filled with the bitter taste of rejection and the cold chill of loneliness, he lay within the folds of Erus' bed. Tonight he had been shown exactly what he was, and that was the mere trophy he had suspected himself to be.

The familiar creak of the door never came and, irritated with waiting, Cedo slid from the bed. Wrapping himself in a heavy robe, he walked out into the dark hallway. The house now lay in darkness, the last embers of the fire burning in the grate. Other than that, dark and silence prevailed. Following the lead of the house, Cedo made his way toward the cellar.

Beneath the stairs, the cellar was as silent and as deserted as the rest of the house, the thick darkness enveloping the capacious space. No one other than himself was there and Cedo felt the coolness gripping him. Something else, other than the ghosts of weapons past, lived here. He could not see it but he could feel it, mingling with the smell of long dried oil and once molten metal.

Sliding carefully across the uneven floor, he noticed the tiniest glow of light coming from one corner. Reaching out, Cedo grasped only at air as he closed in on the faint, yellow light. Drawing closer, he could hear several voices along with other noises, all of them too faint to make out.

Cedo allowed his fingers to dance across what he believed to be rough hewn wall. Instead his fingertips found something that was smooth and strangely warm.

A low grinding sound filled the air and Cedo stepped back, shocked, as whatever had been guarding the entrance slid back. Light filled a small entranceway and steep, narrow, stone stairs, carved from the very being of the building, disappeared down and around a corner. The noise intensified as Cedo stepped out and slowly descended, unsure of what he would find.

As he reached the final step, Cedo froze and he surveyed the scene. It was dominated by a giant, bipedal machine, its entire body built from metal and tubes. Long legs swung back and forth, its towering body swaying easily as it moved, joints hissing and creaking as it walked around the cavernous room. Like its legs, it had powerful-looking arms which, instead of hands, ended in a pair of deadly cannons. A pair of glowing lamps sat on its shoulders, swiveling back and forth. It was not built to look human; it was built to instill fear in whomever saw it.

But he could not run, not even when he managed to tear his eyes away from the beast. Like the stairs, the huge room was chiseled from the foundations of the house. It stretched away into the darkness, a monolith that had been there long before the building of the house.

Unguarded gas jets billowed from the walls, lighting the room with long shadows and making it warmer than the rest of the house. In the center sat a rough circle of chairs, each of them occupied. At the head sat a large, throne-like seat, much like the one that occupied Erus' office. No surprise to Cedo, the man himself was seated in it, a bulbous glass in one hand and a large cigar in the other. Roars of laughter and jovial conversation could be heard above the creaking of the giant machine.

Still shivering on the steps, Cedo forced himself to step into the room. No one saw him sheltering in the shadows, watching the soiree that unfolded before him. Glasses were refilled from bottles that sat on the floor, and varnished boxes of cigarettes and cigars passed from around, the air filling with sickly smelling blue smoke. He could not make out the conversation. It would no doubt be filled with violence; toasts being made to the upcoming success of the gruesome metallic machine. Cedo closed his eyes, trying to ward off the thoughts that were already beginning to fill his head, thoughts of bloodshed and of the rivers of blood that flowed beneath the city. These were the men who brought about such things. They were the ones who tortured and tested and injected until they had what they wanted to keep the war efforts going.

The noise around him died away and Cedo opened his eyes. Panting, he slammed against the wall as he looked up into the glowing lamps of the machine. One of the great arms lifted, the cannon clicking. His heart thudded in his chest, breath taken away as he stared into the dark abyss of the muzzle.

CHAPTER 26

Suddenly, a voice cried, "At ease!"

Slumping against the cold wall, Cedo sighed with relief as the machine stepped away. What had gone came flooding back as he saw Erus look up, eyes searching the darkness.

"Who goes there?" his Master called.

Hands gripped in fists, Cedo stepped forward, shaking. "Please, Sir. I'm sorry. I did not mean to interrupt."

Instead of the tongue lashing he was expecting, Cedo was rewarded with a smile. Erus motioned him closer.

"Cedo! Come a little closer. I have something for you, a little surprise."

Hugging the robe closer, Cedo walked to the sweeping, carved seat that his Master so obviously loved. Erus pointed to the bare floor before him. Until now, the hunched figure at his Master's feet had been hidden by the circle of men, only coming into view as Cedo stepped closer. Long, ruffled blond hair hid its face, bare arms hugged around a naked body.

"A gift. For my beautiful Cedo, courtesy of Mr. Farns."

Cedo gave Erus a curt smile and then followed his Master's line of sight to the kneeling figure.

"He's going to be your assistant." A foot stretched out and hooked beneath the figure's chin, lifting a fear-filled and dirt streaked face to look at them. "Aren't you, Billy?"

Instinctively Cedo brought his hand to his mouth, stomach turning as he looked down into Billy's shimmering blue eyes. Billy was as scared as he was disgusted. How could they trade humans to pay off a debt?

Cedo managed a smile, trying not to let on that he knew Billy. "Thank you, Sir, for your kindness."

He offered a hand to the filthy man but was quickly knocked back by Erus. Tearing his gaze away from Billy's tear streaked face, Cedo only just managed to remain quiet as he looked into hard green eyes.

"No." The firmness had returned to Erus' voice. "He lives down here. Filthy street scum does not live above stairs. Do not worry, Cedo, he will be well looked after and will accompany you when you go to work." Erus smiled. "It will allow me to catch up on some work. It is not that I do not enjoy your stories, far from it, but there is so much that I need to do. Now, return to bed. I shall be along later."

Gritting his teeth, Cedo silently left, fuming as he returned to bed. He felt awful, leaving the blond man at the mercy of Erus once more. His helplessness angered him as he fell into bed, body heavy and leaden with the knowledge of what lay beneath him.

"I am going out."

Groaning, Cedo lazily brushed hair from his face and opened one eye. Above him was the sharp, straight back of his Master, hair lifted from his shoulders as he eased himself into a tailored jacket. The scent of soap and cologne lingered over them, sweet and sharp.

"I will be back later. Under no circumstances do you leave the house unless it is to go to the theater."

Balancing a hat on his head, Erus turned, eyes dark.

Cedo did not shrink back, holding the gaze. Always Erus left him, always to some unknown destination. It chilled him to think that the man he loved with a burning passion should go out and orchestrate the deaths of people.

Face still cold, Erus held out a hand to him. Strong fingers stretched toward him, one of them adorned with a heavy, jeweled ring. Coolness etched his own face as he looked between the outstretched hand and the face of his Master above him.

"Kiss it."

Stomach churning with Erus' attitude, Cedo pursed his lips and bent his head, briefly pressing his mouth to the slightly cool metal. Redness flushed his face and he fell back to the bed, staring at the man above him. Erus said no more, a small smile flickering over his face before he turned for the door.

"You are becoming a well-trained little courtesan," he said with an animal-like smirk. "Silence, from you, is golden. Save your pretty little voice for those who pay to hear it and for beneath the bed sheets."

Bile rose at the words, poisoning his throat with its acidic heat.. That was all the sadistic man was about: power and money. There was nothing else to him, and nothing Cedo could do would thaw that frozen interior.

Behind him, the door clicked softly shut. For a while, he lay still and stared at the wall, mind turning over. It was with a start that he stood, suddenly remembering Billy.

A few moments later, dressed in clothes that would suit a work house, Cedo quickly made his way to the cellar. Now that the house was clear of its Master, he could find out what was happening.

The gas jets flared, flooding the cellar with light. The large desk that he had had the misfortune to meet still sat against the wall. Everything else seemed in order and the only thing that was missing was the large leg that had sat in one corner. Cedo could only imagine that it had become part of the monster he had met the night before.

He had not expected the door to the hidden room to be open, but he also had not expected it to be locked either. Frustration burned his skin as Cedo let his hands wander over the dark wood, desperately trying to find the invisible spot that would open it. But it was to no avail and he let a fist thud into the door.

Feeling his options melt away, he sank to the floor, brushing sweat-drenched hair over his shoulder. Leaning against the door, he let his fingers wander over the tiny opening between the floor and the door. Cool air gasped over his fingers and, with his heart twitching, he stretched himself, mouth pressed to the gap.

"Billy!" he hissed. "Billy, can you hear me?"

Nothing. Cedo cringed, panic beginning to ride through him. Digging his fingernails into the wood, he let out a soft cry as splinters flaked off, trapping themselves deep into his skin. The pain was momentary and seemed fitting, yet his only concern was the man beneath the stairs.

"Billy?" he called a little louder. "Billy! Are you down there?"

Again there was nothing. Rich blood, as red and as fierce as the dying sun, dripped from the splinters beneath his fingers and to the cobbled floor. Hopeless tears prickled his eyes. Now they came for someone he barely knew, someone who should not be mixed up in something so sinister.

"Billy?!" His voice was becoming more frantic, filled with the notion that time was rapidly running out.

"Cedo Reilly? That you, mate?"

Cedo could have sung for joy. Stretching his fingers as far as he could, he looked past them, catching a glimpse of clothing beyond the door.

"Are you hurt?" he asked, breath labored.

There was a soft chuckle and an azure eye peered from beneath the door. "Only as much as can be imagined from 'im. 'E wants me alive, not dead."

Cedo's face ached as he smiled. But he was not going to go anywhere, not yet. Wriggling his fingers, he forced one beneath the door. A second later, Billy wrapped a finger around his, holding him tight.

"You okay, Cedo?" There was concern in Billy's voice.

"I am fine," he softly replied. "Better for knowing that you are alive and well." He sighed and leaned his forehead against the door. "I cannot get you out. The door is locked."

The long finger tightened around his own. "It's okay, mate. I'm alive. That's all that matters right now. Well, that an' that ruddy great walkin' cannon 'e's got down 'ere."

Happiness drained from him.

"What has he done with it?" he whispered, fearing the worst.

"Oh, just left it guardin' me, that's all. Nothin' to worry about, Cedo, lad. It's not goin' to do anythin' to me while I'm locked up. Only if I get out without 'is permission."

Cedo relaxed, finger rubbing soothingly back and forth against his imprisoned friend.

"You will be getting out later though, won't you? To come to the theater with me?"

"Oh aye, lad. 'E's left orders with that thing an' with the staff to let me out well in advance. I'll be waitin' for you, all scrubbed up as if nothin's 'appened, don't you worry."

Lying in silence, he held onto Billy, not wanting to let go in case it was all a mirage. Someone obviously knew the combination to the door, knew how to convince it to open.

"Billy?"

"What's up, mate?"

Weakly he smiled. "I am going to see if I can find someone to open this door. Try to get them to let you out."

From beyond the door there was a sharp intake of breath. "You sure you want to be doin' that, lad? You know what 'e's like if you upset 'im too much."

Gently he squeezed the hand that he still had a hold of. "For you, anything."

Billy chuckled huskily. "Cedo Reilly, I 'ope you're not fallin' for a wretch like me."

Laughing softly, Cedo felt himself tingle, a lost happiness coming back. "Now, that would be telling. I will try not to be too long."

"You take your time, an' take bloody care!"

CHAPTER 27

His first stop was the wretched heat of the kitchen. From his experience, cooks knew everything, even if they never left the kitchen. Grapevines spiraled everywhere and always seemed to end in the kitchen.

The kitchen was its usual controlled melee. Roasting meat, bubbling sauces, and simmering vegetables filled the kitchen with their delectable scents. Cedo stood and watched, listening as the rotund cook shouted orders back and forth, never moving from her spot at the chopping block. Working up the courage he needed, Cedo approached her, hands meekly folded before him.

"Excuse me?"

Her reddened face looked up at him and she let out a sigh, placing a large knife to one side. "Yes, Mr. Reilly. What can I do for you?"

Beneath her heavy gaze, Cedo withered, mouth drying as he tried to word what he wanted to say. I'm l-looking for someone to u-unlock the cellar. To let out the new boy down there."

An elbow propped the cook against the well worn chopping block. "So I've got another bloody mouth to feed then?" she demanded." Nice of him to bloody well tell me!"

Cedo gave her a pained smile. "Yes. His name is Billy.

He arrived last night. Only I feel he is in need of some food and some clean clothes. And I think he may need medical attention as well."

Cook sighed and went back to working on the pile of colorful fruits. "Well, that don't surprise me. No one's safe around here. You'll need to talk to Morris. He's the one who can get in there."

"Do you know where Mr. Morris is?"

The knife paused in midair and Cedo became light-headed. A second later it fell back to the board, neatly slicing some exotic pink fruit in two. "He'll be out in the garden."

The garden stretched away before him, devoid and dead of life. Skeletal trees extended their branches over frostbitten grass. Flowerbeds, bare of anything other than a light dusting of frost, slumbered, waiting for the coming sun. Hugging the thin shirt closer to him, Cedo walked over the brittle grass, looking for the elderly gardener. What kept such a man working in the twilight of his age? The house had an odd assortment of staff; they were either strangely young or strangely old. No one who lived there seemed to be in their middle years.

At the bottom of the gentle slope stood the gardener, a shovel in his hand as he worked at the bank of the stream. Beside him sat a soggy pile of steaming mulch. Taking a deep breath, he made his way toward Mr. Morris. He did not expect any sympathy from him; Cedo was the kept house husband, never having to lift a finger other than to look after himself.

"Mr. Morris?"

The man did not look up. "Yes?"

"Mr. Morris, I believe you know how to get into the lower part of the cellar?"

Another shovel of mulch was flicked onto the pile.

"Aye, I do, lad. Why d'you ask?"

Swallowing his nervousness, Cedo stepped around the man and looked up into his weather beaten face. "There is a new boy down there. I believe he needs medical attention. Could you possibly unlock the door and disable the machine down there?"

The shovel crunched into the unforgiving ground, Mr. Morris leaning on the curved handle. His fingers reached into a pocket and he pulled out a small watch, flicking open the dull, worn lid. "Not for another couple'a hours. Master's orders. The boy's been looked at, so don't worry yourself. He'll be fine. Now get yourself back inside before the Master returns and finds you catching your death out here."

Stretching himself back across the floor, he relayed the bad news to Billy, news that was shrugged off.

He spent the day there, whispering back and forth beneath the door to Billy. The young man, he discovered, was much like him, alone in the world. He had left home young due to arguments with his mother, a father who had disappeared into a haze of alcohol and cheap, imported opiates, and sisters who had been sold into goodness knew what to pay a growing mountain of debt. His heart wrenched as Billy twisted his dark tale. Yet he had conquered the darkness that had threatened to swallow him. A weaker man would have wound up in the asylum long before the first act had finished.

It was at Billy's insistence that he left, the stagehand assuring him that, sooner or later, someone would be coming. He wondered if Billy would spend every day locked behind the door, watched over by a machine that had just one initiative. It still sent shock waves through him that Erus would accept a living, breathing person as payment for a debt..

Outside, the sky had turned to inky black. For a while, Cedo sat on the edge of his bed, head cradled in his hands and muscles aching from having lain in the cold, questions rolling over in his mind. Was there a way to free Billy? It all seemed impossible, a mountain that could never be conquered. Erus would not let another pair of hands and eyes slip through his fingers so quickly. Billy would be forever trapped with him, but at least they had each other.

A knock at the door brought him back to reality and he stepped from the bed to open it. A smile crossed his face as he looked up into the Billy's welcoming face.

"Told you I'd get out, didn't I?" Billy gently teased before giving a low whistle. "Smart digs you got 'ere."

Shaking his head, Cedo began to search through the drawers, knowing that their departure was imminent. "Not every night. I mostly sleep—" He paused as he turned to look at the other man.

Billy nodded knowingly, assuring Cedo that he did not have to say another word. Silently, he studied Billy, looking at injuries that had been expertly tended to and the nondescript clothing that he wore. He looked like every male member of staff he had seen, dressed in suit trousers and a stiffly starched shirt. Cedo felt for him, the free spirit who had now been captured and detained, a song bird who no longer had a reason to sing.

Stepping behind the decorated vanity screen, he began to shed his clothes, his groin already embarrassingly beginning to tighten with a red heat. Sliding the silken material of his suit over it did little to help and he let out a tired groan. This could not happen, not now. Pulling the dazzling blue jacket over his shoulders, he stepped from behind the screen. Billy was seated on the floor, Misty curled in his lap.

"You like cats?" he asked softly.

"Oh, aye." Billy looked up, a relaxed look on his face as he kneaded the cat's upturned belly. "'Ad 'em all my life. I used to look after the theater cat. Me an' 'im were the best of friends. I'd feed 'im an' 'e'd keep me warm at night, make me think there was someone sleepin' next to me, like." He nodded to the puddle of fur in his lap. "She's friendly enough, ain't she?"

Cedo shrugged and walked closer, Misty giving him a curious glance as he scratched her ear. "I would not know. I am the only person she's ever known. She likes you."

Billy tilted his head and returned the smile, blue eyes never having lost their boyish glitter. "Course she does. Natural with animals, me."

Crouching beside them, he watched for a little longer, a sense of guilt making him uncomfortable. What was the point of having Billy with him? What sick game had Erus decided to play now? Running his fingers over Misty's head, he stood, backing off as the guilt and knot of need and lust crashed together.

Raindrops dappled the windows of the gently swaying carriage but they did nothing to lull or comfort Cedo. Beside him sat Billy, quiet as he stared out at the heavy clouds. Neither seemed to know what to say in such close quarters, not after their previous meeting, one that tormented Cedo with the reality of who he was.

Queer. Strange. An unspoken oddity, one that was far more widespread than he had first thought.

Trying to escape his thoughts, Cedo let his fingers run over the steamed glass of the carriage, watching strange shapes and swirls appear, unconsciously mapping his mind.

He was quick to exit the carriage as it slowed before The Cartier, almost as if he wanted to lose Billy in the throngs that lined the streets. But the tall stagehand had no problems in keeping in step with him.

"Whatever is the 'urry?"

Cedo barely registered the question, looking over his shoulder with a silent shrug. Reaching the smartly painted green door, he pulled a folded note from a nail, flipping it open as he stepped into the small room. Sitting on the low stool before the mirror, he read it. It was nothing important, a mere gesture telling him that he was now the first act of the second bill. He smiled and placed it to one side: Popularity finally seemed to be catching up with him.

"So what do you want me to do, then?" Cedo jumped a little and glanced in the mirror, the realization that Billy was still close behind him.

He gave a small smile as he took in the gentle giant, hunched over slightly and hands clasped before him, awkward at the strange situation he found himself in.

"I've never been into all this 'elping the performers lark," he said softly. "I just do everythin' else, you know."

"Why don't you go and fetch us a drink? Something warm for me, please."

Blue eyes lit up, sparkling now that their owner had a task. Once Billy had left, Cedo let his head drop to the dressing table and sighed, tugging on his hair. He could see where this game was going, the thickness of dread snaking through him.

Master.

He was sure that was what Erus wanted him to play at. The sick bastard wanted to watch as someone else was corrupted at a hand other than his own.

When the door clicked open, Cedo snapped upright, eyes terrified as Billy returned, two elegant china cups dwarfed in his large hands. He stopped when he saw Cedo.

"You all right?"

Quickly Cedo nodded and looked away, studying himself in the mirror. "Fine. Just fine," he rushed.

The mug was placed before him, the smell of rich coffee curling to his nose. He stared into the dark depths of it, studying it rather than the man who stood beside him.

"You sure?"

He gave another nod and sipped at the drink, cringing at the heat. "Perfectly."

For Cedo, it was an easy evening. Being mid-week, the theater was not as full as it would normally be.

Those who were watching and patiently listening were those who had been born into money, those who would never lift one of their delicately powdered hands to work. They were professional socialites, interviewed and sketched for various publications, their sordid lives laid bare for anyone who had a florin to spare. Everything about these people was for sale, including the tales of whoever their current bed partner happened to be.

That evening, he wove a charming tale of a star-bound princess who, after travelling across the icy, glittering galaxy, found herself stranded among the citizens of Svenfur.

With his legs dangling over the edge of the stage, the darkness of the orchestra pit threatening to swallow him, he watched as the audience warmed to him, all of them leaning forward to catch his every word.

"It took many years before a craft arrived to ferry her home, a craft of glistening metal of a type that had never been seen before.

"The princess looked at it, diamond tears clasping the corners of her eyes. Her home, the one she had spent so long crying to return to, seemed dull compared the vibrant city she had slowly come to love. Trying to hide the tears, she looked at those gathered on the coastal road and painfully raised a hand to bid them farewell. The crowd returned the gesture and, as she placed one dainty, glass-clad foot on the craft's steps, she heard a low gasp go up.

"She was going! Leaving! Abandoning the people who had accepted her, who had taken her in and taught her the ways of their land. No judgment had been laid on her when she had arrived; her strange, scaled features and narrow yellow eyes had not frightened them. Here, she was one of them.

"Tilting her head, she looked toward the sky, toward the star that was her home. Her heart ached at the thought of going back, of having to sit upon on throne in a soulless room, where none but her courtiers would visit.

"Staring at the craft's captain, she shook her head and took a deep breath. 'No,' she whispered hoarsely. 'I do not want to go back.'

"With that, she stumbled back along the beach, heart soaring as she climbed the beach steps and ran back into the welcoming arms of the city.

"There were no tears, no painful feelings of guilt when the craft took off, plumes of flame lighting the night sky as it surged through the sky, the deafening noise rumbling the earth beneath them."

Pulling himself back onto the stage, Cedo took a proud bow as the audience politely applauded him. Pride swelled him, the feeling a far cry from his first evening in a theater all those dark nights ago. Taking one last bow, he exited the stage, the inky dark engulfing him.

"For you." He jumped at Billy's disembodied voice.

Eyes adjusting to the darkness, he saw Billy's murky shadow, something clutched in one hand. Stepping into a small square of light, he waited until Billy appeared beside him.

He plucked the rose from Billy's fingers, but not quickly enough as the man caught hold of his hand. Fiercely, Cedo tried to pull it back, but Billy's grip only tightened more, puzzlement and finally anger settling over his face.

"That bastard!" Billy quietly exclaimed as he studied the claw-and-mouse brand. "That low-lying, controllin' snake."

Cedo pulled his hand away and tucked it beneath his clothes. Carefully Billy stroked his face, lifting his eyes to the blue orbs above him. "You deserve so much better an' you know it. Why'd you go get yourself tied to *that*?"

Cedo could not reply, instead trying to hide the tears as he grasped the flower close. Unmoving, he studied it for a moment, stroking its silky petals. "Did you—?".

Billy meekly nodded, shifting from one foot to the other, the fury draining away.

"You sent me the other flowers?"

Again Billy nodded. Grinning, Cedo twisted his hair into a knot and pushed the stem of the rose through it. Manners told him that he should thank Billy for the gesture; he wanted to stand on tiptoes and peck the blond man's cheek. But he knew that would lead to other things, to acts that would never remain secret.

Instead, he peered up from beneath his thick lashes, trying to hide his embarrassment. "Thank you."

Stealthily, he raced through the theater and to their carriage. There was nothing to collect from the dressing room and he threw himself into the cushioned seats, fighting the emotions that coursed through him as the black horse threw itself against its bonds, the leather and metal creaking around it. He had betrothed himself to

Erus, and now there was someone else, someone who had made no move to hide how he felt about Cedo.

"You all right?"

Tears stung Cedo's eyes as Billy clambered up beside him and he shrank back, pressing himself against the door.

"Billy, please..." he softly begged.

Settling himself into the opposite seat, Billy stared at him, tall frame hunched over.

"Cedo, mate, what's up?"

Fingers swept over his knee and he jumped, stung.

"Just, please... Please do not."

Billy never moved his hand, even as Cedo squirmed, pressing himself further back into the seat.

"You've gotta talk to me, Cedo. I don't know what you want unless you tell me."

He wanted to scream, wanted to tell Billy to leave him alone but the words would not come. Instead, a single tear made its way down his cheek, the man's tenderness equally pulling at and breaking his heart.

"Billy, I am with Erus. You know this. I," he sighed. "I cannot do anything with you." *No matter how much I would like to.*

CHAPTER 28

Quietly he cried out as an arm draped around him, pulling him against a broad shoulder. Softly Billy stroked him, fingers ghosting over his head and whispering soothing words. The act reminded him of his mother, the final person to have shown him such kindness.

He begged the tears to stop, hating himself for showing such weakness to another. Rough fingers delicately touched him, hushed whimpers leaving Cedo's lips. Tentatively he returned the gentle touches, fingers sliding over skin and hair.

And oh, how soft Billy was, his skin just beginning to pucker as the stubble pressed its way to the surface. Lips, plump and delicate like the petals of a flower, parted when his thumb pressed to them. An excited thrill touched him, his skin beginning to rise in tiny goose bumps. Here he was, with someone who finally treated him as an equal, who did not push him away or scold him.

Panting softly, he pressed himself closer to the wandering hands, melting when one slid to the small of his back. Cedo did not move when the petal lips pressed against his own. Cupping Billy's face, he hungrily returned the soft kisses, parting his lips to allow him entry. The cloying heat of desire clung to him, making him moan, suddenly wanting what he had previously denied himself.

As it reached its peak, Billy pulled away, the flush of

passion just visible in the passing light of the city. Giving a whine, Cedo stretched himself closer, wanting another taste of the delicious forbidden fruit. Instead, he frowned when Billy pressed a finger to his nose, chuckling but never saying a word as he slid to the floor of the carriage. Cedo could only watch as hands gently pushed his legs apart.

Cedo's heart thundered in his chest and he sat back, legs coyly spread.

"We don't 'ave to do this..." Billy whispered.

His voice hitched in his throat and he gave a small, desperate shake of his head. "Please."

Fingers that had been roughened by work carefully pulled his breeches down, revealing, much to his embarrassment, his already-hard cock. His ears burned and Cedo turned his head away. Billy chuckled as he gently guided his head back around.

"Don't 'ide. There ain't no need to." Fingers crept along his naked thigh, causing him to twitch and whine. "Besides, if you've been with Erus then you got no need to be embarrassed." Cedo all but flinched at the final remark, but the husky voice was filled with the warmth of jest.

The man's hands kept up their gentle motion, stroking along the insides of his thighs, thumbs hooking against the taunt base of his cock before moving away. Slowly Cedo found himself relaxing into the touches, head lolling back against the window of the carriage, lips parted and gently panting.

And then his world exploded into a million bright colors as soft, welcoming lips gently wrapped themselves around the head of his cock. Resting on his elbows, Cedo managed to look down, just making out the sea of blond hair that fell over his thighs.

Tightening his fingers against the seat, Cedo could not

help but let out a deep, guttural groan, a noise he had only ever heard Erus make. Now it came from him as a velvety tongue worked its way around him, one moment tracing throbbing veins before working into the slit at the head. It tasted him and made him rock his hips, begging for more. And how he wanted more. How he wanted to fall into those pools of eyes and never surface, drowning in them and making his new home in Billy's heart.

Billy seemed only happy to oblige, feeding off the tiny, almost pitiful noises that Cedo made, humming around him, fingers sliding over his tight balls and his tiny, flower-like entrance. Closer it pressed, just breeching and causing his body to quiver. A heartbeat later and Cedo gave a tiny cry, a tear sliding down his cheek as he spent himself into the welcoming mouth.

Hooves and wheels clattered over the cobbles, the only noise that echoed eerily around the gently sloping street. Cedo fixed his disheveled appearance and then alighted, shivering at the brisk air wrapped around him. Before him, the house lay in darkness, the only light coming from the softly hissing street lamp. *Home.* Not the place he particularly wanted to be at that moment, but it was a place to lay his head and think. Think about what had happened and where that left him.

Dead, most likely. It had long been the feeling that Erus would not let him go without a fight. A fight that would probably end in his death because, if Erus could not have him, then no one could.

And it was with that leaden thought he slowly walked to the door, Billy quietly walking in his wake.

Beyond the door, and giving Cedo a frightful turn, was Mr. Morris. A lantern was held aloft, throwing deep shadows across his face.

"'s back to the cellar for you, Burton. Master's orders." It was an order that was spat with every ounce of hatred for those he had been forced to awaken for.

"Master wants you upstairs, Reilly." Cedo flinched as the stony attention was turned to him. "Wants you to get to your room. Says he'll come for you."

When he did not move, Mr. Morris leaned closer, whisky soaked breath stroking Cedo's nose. "Now!"

The sound reverberated from the wood paneled walls and, giving Billy an apologetic shrug, he made for the stairs. Halfway up, and shrouded in darkness, he glanced over his shoulder, sadness setting in as he watched Billy become a quivering child at the hands of the groundsman.

A single, spiraled candelabra sat atop his dresser, tiny flames doing little to appease the dark. What chilled him was what lay before the candles: a cane, its handle wrapped around the vines of candles.

It was with a pounding head and an aching body that Cedo awoke the next morning. He dared himself to peel away the blood-red sheets and peer beneath them. Red. Everything was that damned color.

Beneath the sheets, his eyes rode over what he already suspected. Bruises and welts decorated his skin, speckles of crisp, dried blood staining him. With an agonizing slowness, Cedo eased himself from the bed. His body howled in pain, his lower back a knot of agony while his marked hand echoed them. He slid to the floor. Deep within him, his stomach rolled and Cedo let out a tiny cry. Never had he felt so alone, so abandoned.

Above him, the door opened but he refused to lift his head.

"Cedo." Knees appeared before him and a hand touched his chin. Gritting his teeth, he stubbornly refused to look. But the fingers stroked at his cheek, gently tilting his reddened eyes to Erus'. They were devoid of their normal harshness, instead filled with a soft sadness.

"Darling Cedo." Erus' voice matched his eyes, yet Cedo felt nothing toward him. Whatever he had felt for the man he called Master had died the night before, escaping with the blood he had shed. "I wish that I could turn back time. I should not have punished you, for you had done nothing wrong."

A lump turned over in his throat as he battled with what lay inside of him. He did not want to give in again. There was a way out from this; he just had to find it. For now, the tunnel may be dark but, sooner or later, that lamp that would guide him to safety would be lit.

Erus tightened the hand to his cheek, voice peaking with desperation, "Cedo, I rarely, if ever, tell you what you mean to me. You are my light in a horrific darkness. You stepped in when no other would and took my hand. You loved me unconditionally, gave me your all and, despite that, I was still not happy. I wanted to tear you apart until you were empty and I could make you whatever I wanted. You let me, you never gave up and last night I went a step too far. You had done nothing wrong and I saw fit to punish you. I wanted to see you bleed for me. Such a selfish and childish act. There are no excuses for what I did."

His throat tightened. However, the small voice in his mind would not be quiet, bawling at him not to listen to another lie. This had been spelled out to him time and again and, every time he had gone along with it, believing that Erus would lift him to a status that many only dreamed of. Instead, he was being used as a ladder, a stepping stone to elevate the Erus' meager ego.

Pulling the hand from his cheek, Cedo held it, caressing the strong fingers. "No," he quietly answered. "I will not believe another of these lies. You tell them time and again. I have loved you and have fallen into your arms. I have given you everything, as much as is possible of me, and it is never enough.

"I understood the contract I signed with you, yet no matter what I have done it has always fallen short of your mark. I have tried to improve, and damn if I haven't. I have gone above and beyond your expectations. You have taken me from the pier and now I am playing to some of the finest theaters in the city. But you expect a lover who is patiently and quietly waiting for you, come rain or shine."

Erus shuddered and Cedo watched a tear slide over scarce freckles.

"Erus, love is like anything. It dies if it is not nurtured. I understand that the blissful period of our relationship is gone now and we have settled into a routine. The initial love has died, to be replaced with pain and beatings. There is nothing for me to wait for now. All I know is that I will either be ignored, abandoned, or beaten. I want to be perfect, want to be yours, but unless there is something more than a courtesy kiss then I will wither and die before I have been given time to be crafted."

Patiently he waited for the unhinged anger and floggings that would come with his unsolicited words. It never came, Erus folding before him. Strong shoulders shuddered, hair muffling quiet cries, arms reaching for Cedo.

He tried to resist but it was futile and, after a moment, he gave in. Who was he trying to kid? There would be no break from this. No matter what he tried to shield it behind, he still loved the man who held him. Still loved the fiery and unpredictable temper. It was a kinship he would never fully understand nor appreciate. They would fight and bicker, yet they needed each other. He needed a protector while Erus needed someone to show him that life did not always have to be a bitter battle of wills.

Touching the hair that lay against his shoulder, he pressed a kiss to Erus' bowed head. "I love you. I will love you 'til the end of time." He dared himself to softly ask, "Do you even know how to love?"

Gently Erus shook head and Cedo felt the last of his own defenses crumble away.

"Is it because of your past?"

Erus nodded and Cedo slid closer. "If you let me, I shall teach you. I shall show you the wonders of what it is to love. It burns deep within me, a hot flame that eclipses my entire being. Such is the power of it that I feel as if I could create whole other worlds, whole other universes." Shivering with the excitement of the ideas that flitted through his mind, Cedo pressed his lips to Erus' temple. "Let me woo you. Let me show you what it is like to truly fall in love."

They stayed curled on the floor until Erus saw fit to take his leave. In the intervening hours, Cedo went to work with a vigor he had forgotten. Now he had the briefest of moments to break the monotony of his day, a chance to shine in the eyes of the one he wanted to impress.

Racing through the house, he collected what he needed: flowers, a blanket, and the most delicate of candles. He left a picnic basket with the cook, and changed into the finest clothes he had. By the time he had finished, he, and his chosen space, looked like they had been plucked from the most beautiful tale ever told.

Patiently he waited beside the front door, confidence brimming as it slowly opened. Erus, head slightly inclined and weariness lining his face, stepped in. Tucking his hat

beneath one arm, he gave Cedo a puzzled look.
"You should not be here."

CHAPTER 29

He stepped closer, linking his arm through Erus'. "Tonight I play for you. Those out there can wait. They will come back." Giving Erus a teasing wink, he led him into the house. "Absence makes the heart grow fonder."

Silently they walked past the study and out the back. Erus leaned against him, a warm whisper touching his ear, "You look divine."

Cedo stepped into the large forest room and gave him a gentle smile. The slender candles were woven into the trees and bushes. Scents of rich flowers filled the air, sweet and rich and exotic, telling unsung yarns of faraway lands. Beneath one tree lay the checked blanket, surrounded by candles. A crystal chandelier dangled mysteriously above it.

Taking the hand of the silenced engineer, Cedo sat them amid the candles. He watched as Erus' eyes wandered over the forest. For once, the silence that hung between them was one of quiet pleasure. Cedo savored it, the silence and the look of childish wonder upon Erus' face. A man who had never known a childhood, who had never known the wonders of make-believe, was getting his moment and it made Cedo happy. Very happy.

Reaching into the overflowing basket, he pulled out a pair of finely spun goblets. They looked as if they would break under the merest touch, light sparkling through them. He filled them with a thick red wine and handed one to Erus. Quietly his Master studied the glass, trying to work out what was real before he took a cautious sip.

"It will not kill you," Cedo whispered. "Nothing will kill you tonight. Well, perhaps it will kill you with pleasure but certainly not with pain."

Kneeling up, he pushed the jacket from Erus' shoulders and loosened his cravat. "Relax, if only for tonight."

Finally Erus smiled, body sagging slightly as he exhaled. "It is beautiful," he said softly. "I did not know that such beauty could be created."

"You created it." Cedo took another sip of wine before lying down, one hand behind his head. "I just took the liberty of making it that little more beautiful. You have a wonderful talent, Master, one that you do not realize you have. I know that I have told you before, but you must choose your own path and if that is in making weaponry then I cannot change that. But tonight is not about that. Tonight is about romance and the blossoming of love."

With a small nod, Erus raised his glass. "To love."

Around them the creatures quietly sang as they dined on delicious and divine foods. Cakes that were decorated with glitter and icing. Fruits that ran with fresh and sticky juices, tantalizing the taste buds, and wine that had come from the very spring of life itself.

They smiled and laughed, exchanging more than mere pleasantries or cruel words. Erus told stories that no other soul would ever know, ones that made Cedo cry with laughter. In return, he spun tales that had lived long inside of him, waiting to come out. Tales of magical places filled with adventures, of sorcery and bravery and people who lived in the craters of the moon.

As the basket emptied so the heavens above them opened, a gentle rain beginning to fall. Cedo could not help but give a gentle laugh as Erus looked around himself, the wonder of a youngster playing on his face.

Passing his hand before Erus' face, he grasped at thin air and chuckled. "Magic."

Green eyes never turned to him, captivated by the world surrounding him. "Indeed."

The rain fell above them, captured by the leaves of the tall, sprawling tree. Pushing the basket to one side, Cedo leaned back against the thickset trunk. Spreading his legs a little, he patted the ground between them. "Come."

Stunned, Erus turned to look, hesitating. Cedo could see the fight that was going on behind his eyes. Could he surrender? Eventually, the fight drained away he sank back between Cedo's legs. Wrapping the blanket around them, Cedo laid Erus' head against his chest, the strength of the protector taking over him. Shivering at the pattering of rain, he caressed the thick, red hair. Like spun silk, it fell through his fingers and beneath his touches he felt Erus begin to relax. Beneath the sound of the raindrops came purrs, low rumbles of noise. The smile refused to leave Cedo's face and he showered the head beneath him with kisses. Everything in him tingled, feelings reborn, the excitement of love brimming over.

Fingers wound into the nape of his neck, pulling his face down to Erus'. He did not need to hear the words he longed to hear, for they swirled in depths of his Master's eyes. Parting his lips and closing his eyes, he pressed a heartfelt kiss to the welcoming mouth.

Morning dawned with the aches and pains that came from sleeping on the forest floor.

A weight lay against his chest, pinning him to the tree behind him. Cedo could not help but smile. Between his legs, curled beneath the blanket, was Erus. Hair that shone gold beneath the sun, curved over his chest and shoulder, mingling with his own, lighter, hair.

Tingling with an innocent excitement, he ran his hand across the sleeping head, lifting a weight of hair away from Erus' peacefully resting face. It was a beautiful pause in the fabric of time, a time when the hands of the clock stopped, letting everything rest just as it was. Cedo cradled Erus to him, every fiber of his body relighting with the love he had originally felt for this man. The fiery man may take him to pieces. But he always seemed to put him back together, allowing his love to reignite more passionate and powerful than before.

Green eyes, serene and clear, looked up at him, a lucid smile gracing still resting lips. Cedo returned the smile and gave him the briefest of kisses.

"Good morning, Master."

"Good morning, Cedo."

Warm and happy, Cedo carried on letting his hands roam across the relaxed body. "I trust you slept well?"

"Wonderfully. It was such a comfortable night, by far the most restful I have ever had." He tilted his head to look up and Cedo felt his beat quicker. "We must do this more often. Must escape more."

Rubbing his thumb across Erus' forehead, Cedo listened as the other man purred.

"We must rise soon," Erus whispered. "There is something I want to show you today."

Despite the chill that hung in the air, Cedo found himself to be unimaginably happy. He had every reason to be and he was not going to let it pass him by. Stepping from the carriage, he walked to the railings and looked out to sea, watching the glistening waves crash against the shingle. Beside him stood Erus, eyes hidden from the sun by tinted glasses, brim of his hat casting fleeting shadows across his face. Slyly looking toward him, Cedo noted the new posture, the absence of stress giving the strong shoulders a relaxed slump. There was no hurry, no need to rush.

"I often wonder what other lands are like," Erus commented over the sound of the breeze.

Lifting his head, Cedo leaned languidly against the railings. "You mean you have never been? Never followed your weapons into war?"

Erus laughed warmly, looking to Cedo from behind wind swept hair. "Why would I want to go into the theater of war? Once they leave my hands I do not know what they are used for. And in answer to your other question, I have never travelled from this fair land."

"But why?"

The wind caught Erus' hair, whipping it into an arc as he looked back out to sea. "Because I have never felt the urge. The desire to travel the globe has never crossed me. Yet now, as your tales of the sky and the planets and of the lives that lie beyond this place take hold, I feel that I should."

Stepping closer, Cedo defied his instincts and draped an arm around Erus' waist. Leaning up on his tip toes, he whispered, "Then come. Travel with me. We will find a ship and we will go. We will find lands where the spices are as bright as the sun and where the jewels are as big as your fist. We will find cities that are draped among the trees. We will walk and dance and study. We will drink wines that are as sweet as honey; we will kiss and make love in the streets because no one shall care. It will be a liberated society where we can be ourselves."

A look of romance crossed Erus' face and he sighed,

head resting against his Cedo's. "I should like to do that. Perhaps one day I shall. Before I grow too old, mind. I would like to enjoy it on my own two feet and not from some powered bath chair. Those chairs are all well and good but they are hopeless when it comes to climbing mountains or travelling up hills. Besides." Once again his attention turned to Cedo, the wistfulness changing to brashness. "I would rather grow old disgracefully than gracefully."

Rolling on the balls of his feet, Cedo placed the quickest of kisses to his Master's cheek.

Fingers ruffled his hair. "We will talk about this more later on. Onwards! I want to show you my latest creation."

Excitement and joy bubbled through him as they walked along the sea front, giving an elated spring to his step. Seeing the wide sea front as his own personal stage, Cedo pulled away, spinning on his toes and laughter spilling from his lips.

Presently Erus raised an arm, his free hand catching at Cedo and pulling him close. There was no chastisement for his behavior, just a small, warm smile. Face ruddy with excitement, Cedo let himself fall into the embrace and pressed kisses to his jaw. The skin beneath his lips turned a soft pink, Erus bundling him into the hansom cab that drew up beside them.

"You bring me such great joy, Cedo," Erus mused.

The hired cab only took them so far before depositing them at the side of a stone-littered dirt track. Confused, Cedo looked to Erus. The engineer gave him nothing but a smile before setting off along the rough path, his trusty cane picking the way. Beneath the warming sun, Cedo followed, feet crunching against the sandy stones. On either side of him, the ground rolled away, brown and yellow scrub just waiting for spring to arrive.

Up and over the undulating Downs they went, Erus striding away and Cedo following in his footsteps. Dust flicked up before him as he kicked at stones, sending them scuttling away. When Erus had told him he wanted to show him something Cedo had not expected to be taken to the middle of nowhere.

Cedo slowed as the thought hit him. Perhaps Erus had brought him here to finish what he had started. To kill and dissect him and throw his remains to the wind. It would not be beneath Erus to do such a thing, especially now that he had laid himself bare.

Up and over the brow of the hill and Cedo stopped, staring at what lay beneath him in the dip of the Downs. Long, domed white buildings stretched the entire length of the valley, the sun turning the roofs a blinding, desert white.

"My research facility," Erus stated proudly.

His mouth dried, leaving Cedo to nod bluntly as he followed Erus down the winding track. Now there was a subtle bounce to his Master's step, an innocent movement as he gallivanted toward the buildings.

The once toy-like buildings grew until they filled his entire line of sight, roofs studded with arched windows. Erus slowed until he fell into step beside Cedo.

At first glance, there was no obvious way into the unmarked buildings, the massive facility looking as if it were built from one continuous stretch of tile. But as Erus reached out a hand, the outline of a perfectly normal door appeared, swinging out toward them.

Eyes twinkling, Erus calmly exclaimed, "This is the boring way in."

His excitement was infectious, a child at Wintermass who could not wait for the rising of the sun. His own body tingled with the familiar sensation, stomach turning at the excitable unknown.

Warm air, laced with the smells of grease and hard work, enveloped them as they stepped into the building. From above, the mounds had looked like separate buildings. But, once inside, they revealed themselves to be one, continuous space. High above them, gantries ran back and forth, people moving over them with rattling footsteps. To look up gave a sense of inverted vertigo, eyes instead forced to settle on the windows.

When his head had stopped swimming, Cedo gasped. There, nestled among the gantries was a huge airship, bolts and ropes shot into the floor to hold it still. Beneath the inflated envelope dangled a gondola like none he had ever seen. It ran the length of the massive ship, arching delicately upward like the bow of a ship. At the stern, two propellers dropped down beneath it and, to the fore, the gondola was decorated with guns.

Moving to the bow, Cedo found himself staring down the darkened barrel of a cannon. The entire craft, right down to the tiniest of rivets, was as black as a storm-laden night.

"Stealth warfare." Cedo could not tear his eyes from it, turning circles beneath it. "It becomes completely silent once you've factored in the ground noise of a battlefield."

An arm draped around his shoulder, guiding him toward a metal staircase. Quietly he climbed the slightly shaking stairs and stepped through the open door.

On the inside it looked like any other ship; smaller, almost claustrophobic. Along the ceiling, arching from a spine-like structure, hung fragile light bulbs, their waspish filaments buzzing to life.

The gondola was empty except for seven skeletal chairs. Three on either side of the ship were set before tiny portals of tinted glass, the butts of the guns nestled beneath them. And there, in the nose, was the final chair, its rib-like back silhouetted against the soft light of the controls. Dials and levers, buttons and switches reached out beneath the darkened front window. .

"What do you think?" Erus' voice was touched with a higher pitch.

Walking across the wooden floor, Cedo let his fingers roam over the cool metal of the captain's seat. They drifted to the brass and wood of the levers and the smooth glass of the dials. Leaning closer, he let Erus' question hang in the air as he read the intricate numbers and letters of the control panel. He caressed the dark, warm wood, almost fearful that it might jump to life beneath his fingers. His fingers lingered over the tiniest of brass inlays: A claw and a mouse. Behind him, Cedo knew that Erus was waiting for his approval. For a while, he basked in the power before leaning against the captain's seat.

"It is beautiful," he said, eyes settling on the suddenly nervous Erus. "A work of art like none I have seen before." His hand swept over the chair, taking in the starkness of the rigid design. A design that seemed to exemplify the deathly purpose of the ship.

Those few words seemed to appease Erus and he relaxed, leaning against one of the gunners chairs. "Of course, it has not been fully tested yet. We need to make sure that the guns will not rattle the frame apart. That is why we work out here, in the wilderness. Lots of space for us to run tests." The joyous smile returned to his lips and he moved toward the door. "Now, if you don't mind, dear Cedo, I have more that I would like to show you."

They exited through a door on the opposite side of the craft, one that led them onto one of the high gantries. Looking down, Cedo's stomach turned and his vision begin to sway. Ahead of him, Erus laughed and looked over his shoulder eyes sparkling.

"You will soon learn not to do that! I do not want to be sending someone up here to fetch you down."

Nodding weakly, Cedo kept his eyes on Erus' back as he inched along the walkway.

Finally they ascended a stairway. Smiling broadly, Erus placed a hand on his shoulder. "It is just along here. Something a little more special than everything else."

They walked through the open expanse and he desperately tried to take in all that was housed within the facility. In one space there appeared to be a large telescope, folded barrels pointed toward the heavens. It sat on a base of circular tracks, winches and round handles attached to one side of the dull object. As they passed it, Cedo discovered it was for shooting slugs of metal at the stars rather than staring at them.

Along from that was an odd, wooden structure. It took on the same appearance as the gondola of the airship except that beams stretched out at right angles from the top and bottom. On the front was a carefully crafted propeller. Cedo wondered if it would follow its light as air cousin upward to space.

On one sturdy table lay an upturned creature, spindly legs bend at odd angles as a workman hovered over it. Peering a little closer, he soon pulled back in disgust. The thing on the table was the same kind of creature that had nearly dragged Misty to her death.

"Master?" he weakly asked.

"Yes?" Erus turned and looked at him, eyes clouded with the dreamy look of someone who had been deep in thought.

"What is that creature?" He nodded toward the work bench.

"It is a head crab. A wonderful little creation if I say so myself. It's an assassin machine, able to creep into places where snipers cannot get. Once in there it stuns its target with a poisoned dart before drilling into the brain."

A shiver of disgust rattled his body before he tugged

Erus away. "Please. Let us carry on before I find myself succumbing to sickness."

Erus gave him a smile, tipping his hat to him as he linked his arm through Cedo's. "As you wish. I have something that has been built especially for you. I hope that you like it."

Turning his gaze from Erus, Cedo looked to what stood before him, his breath taken away.

CHAPTER 30

Before him stood a graceful, skeletal horse built from warm-colored brass. Cedo looked through the whisper-thin gaps, taking in its inner working. Its mane and tail were fashioned from fine filaments of wire. A bridle of supple leather encased its head, the reins hanging on its neck. Standing before it, Cedo looked into the strong eyes, watching the tiny lamps that burned behind them.

Walking beside it, he ran a hand along its metal flank. "Beautiful," he managed to softly utter.

"It is like any horse." There was a tone of nervousness in Erus' voice. "It can be ridden. All you have to do is mount it."

Bunching the reins into his hand, Cedo sprang onto the horse's back. For a moment it was uncomfortable, the hard metal odd beneath his buttocks. Staring straight ahead, he touched his heels against the unforgiving sides, gasping as the horse eased itself into a walk.

With shocked amazement, he turned the horse in circles around his Master. Heavy metal hooves rang out against the floor, the movement feeling just like every living horse he had ever ridden. Another touch of his heels and the horse picked up the pace to a jerking trot. He swayed with the movement, legs dangling almost uselessly at its sides before he pulled up beside Erus.

"But how?!"

Erus did chuckled and touched the side of his nose. "Magic, my dear boy, magic."

Sliding down from the magnificent creature, Cedo held onto the reins, joy rushing through him.

"But why?" Beside him, the horse had fallen completely still.

Erus stepped closer, one arm going around his waist and tugging him close. Warm breath touched his forehead and he tilted his head to look into eyes that sparkled with joy.

"Can you imagine the reaction of the crowds when you ride out onto the stage on something so splendid? They will think they are dreaming! It will seal you in their memories forever." Lips tenderly kissed his forehead. "Also, you deserve it."

Clasping his free hand into the small of Erus' back, Cedo stayed pressed against him, feeling his heartbeat. Eventually Erus pulled away, looking at him with almost tired eyes.

"Come, let us take the exciting route home."

The exciting route home was certainly different. A hand-cranked lift had taken them to the bowls of the earth where waited an uncomfortable bench in a tiny train carriage. It was one in a number of carriages, the others, according to Erus, carrying a myriad of things to be delivered to the factories in the center of Svenfur.

The carriage was oddly silent as it glided through the dark tunnels, powered by some unseen engine. A sweet, musty smell filled the air, making the odd world even stranger. How such a place had come to be so deep below the earth, Cedo had no idea. It was yet another of Erus' strange projects, most likely created to impress those he wined and dined into buying his machines.

"*The Mole.*" It was as if Erus was reading his thoughts and Cedo turned to look at him in the dim, electric light of the carriage.

Slowly the realization dawned on him. *The Mole*; he remembered Billy speaking of it, the shocking digging machine that had opened fire on his blond friend. Erus' face looked deathly eerie in the dull light, an almost cruel smile written on his lips.

"It burrows down," Erus called over the clattering of the train. "We tell the driver where we want him to go and he comes down here. *The Mole* has a cannon within the drill bit that allows it to fire into the tougher rock. Behind it we have a team of men, 'tunnelers' we call them, who secure the tunnels with bricks and tiles. You can't see it in this light, but it is a work of art. Withstands pretty much anything."

Erus seemed proud of it, as if by showing off his wares he was somehow redeeming himself in the eyes of his bonded. As much as Cedo appreciated the gesture he could not help but wonder exactly what Erus thought he would get from their little trip. Seeing a childishly happy Erus had made him happy and the metal horse was a gift beyond all imagination. But it was the dark knowledge of knowing just how everything came about that prevented him giving Erus the praise he suspected his Master so desperately craved. He wanted gestures of true love, not some shiny trinkets of war. He could only suspect what would become of the designs for the horse.

Resting his head on the window, Cedo stared out into the darkness ahead of him. It was strange to be whisked around in such a way, the only sense of motion being the swaying and noise. For all he knew, they could be at a standstill with a horde of people beyond the train creating the entire spectacle. It was only when the train pulled up to a brightly lit platform that he let himself believe.

He looked through the grubby window and out onto what looked like a normal railway platform. The only difference were the gently curving walls, covered with intricately locking ivory tiles, the light of the gas lamps turning them a blinding white. Archways that led, he assumed, to other tunnels, branched off from the platform. There was a whole other world down here, one that his Master was building. It impressed him, but he dared say nothing, at least not yet. For now, Cedo knew that the power lay in his hands.

From the archways spilled a small group of men, their faces dirtied with the efforts of a day's work, their arms bulging as they pushed large, flat trolleys to the train. Cedo listened to them yelling to one another, loading the trolleys with cargo from the train. There were boxes and trunks and what appeared to be partially completed machines, all of them being whisked away by the burly men.

It was all over in moments, the platform emptying just as quickly. Silence reigned for a time before somewhere in the recesses of the subterranean world, the motors picked up and the train began to move. Cedo settled himself beside Erus, head resting against his Master's cheek. He was preparing himself to get comfortable, to enjoy the moments of the ride, before something filled him with dread.

It was as they exited the little station that he saw it, curved above the platform: a large pipe that seemed rusted red. Cedo would have believed that it was nothing more than mere rust if he had not seen a single drop, suspended in the air as they moved past—a single drop that was as red as the blood that now chilled his very veins.

The train drew to a stop and he tried to put the sickness from his mind. Hustled from the carriage, Cedo made his way up a badly lit spiral staircase that groaned beneath his footsteps. For something to be so badly built, or at least left to rot, seemed out of place with the rest of the Veetu lifestyle.

Once he had finished his ascent, hand tightly gripping the rail, Cedo found himself faced with a door. He pressed his fingers to it, expecting it to react like every other door. Instead, the dark air around him filled with a husky chuckle and he was gently pushed to one side. From deep within his jacket, Erus produced a bunch of keys and, upon finding the one he wanted, inserted it into the door..

"Now you may enter."

They stepped into the gloom of the lower part of the house and he could hear the distinct sound of the large, mechanical gunman moving. It took all of his power to step into the cold area. Walking toward the stairs, he watched it move back and forth, trapping a hunched figure in a shadowy corner. Slowly he stepped closer, looking at the hunks of half eaten food that littered the area, the stench of urine and fear almost too much to bear. He wanted to cry, wanted to order the walking machine to open fire on its creator.

Instead, he crouched beside the figure, pushing wisps of matted hair from their face. Cold, haunted eyes looked up and a sob caught in Cedo's throat, a sob he dared not let out.

"Oh." Somewhere through the gloom Erus sounded exasperated. "If you must bring your toy with you then make it quick. At ease!"

With the walking cannon stilled, Cedo looped his arms beneath Billy's, carefully pulling him to his feet. Billy groaned and leaned against him, one arm draping around his waist.

"Honestly," Erus grumbled as they walked toward their chambers. "I do not know what you see in that boy."

Cedo forced a weak smile to his lips, softly squeezing Billy's waist as he helped him along the corridor.

"If you're going to clean it up then you will do it in your own room. I do not want it anywhere near me in that state."

Just a little, the weak smile widened. "As you wish, Master," he purred delicately.

Upon entering his own, sparse room, Cedo sat the weary Billy on the edge of his bed, listening to his pitiful groans. It was as if everything that had been good about Billy had been sucked from him, siphoned off for some dastardly use.

Trying to remain upbeat, he dragged the tin bath from the small wash closet and placed it before the fire. Drawing hot water into the jug, he began to fill the bath, finding towels and a cake of sweet smelling soap. Once all was ready, he knelt before Billy's hunched form and gazed up into eyes blackened by lack of sleep. The focus of the blue eyes came and went, eventually settling on him as Billy managed a tiny smile.

"'ello, Cedo."

His heart leapt with joy at the tiny spark of life within the other man. "Hello, Billy."

Up close, he could see the dirt caked into the other's skin, the cut that rode on the cheekbone. He suspected there would be worse beneath the layers of uncomfortable sack clothing. Gesturing to the filled bath, he climbed onto the bed and averted his eyes. Once Billy had lowered himself into the water with a gentle sigh of pleasure, Cedo looked up, taking in the tall body now folded almost uncomfortably into the bath. He smiled as Billy rolled his head back, hair brushing the floor behind him. It had turned from its normally radiant blond to something dirty and dull.

"What happens to you?" he softly pushed. "Down there?"

Billy took a deep breath, eyes focused on the ceiling above him. "I'm earnin' my keep. Put on that train an' sent off to that place of 'is in the country."

Cedo's eyes widened a little and Billy shifted a little, eyes dropping shut.

"No worries, Cedo. I just fetch an' carry. Fix things that them damn scientists of 'is 'ave no idea about." He snorted with disdain. "You know, they go off to some fancy school for years an' years, yet they know sod all about what they're workin' with. It goes wrong an' they look at you as if they've just dirtied their breeches."

Warmth touched Cedo's cheeks, the glorious feeling of happiness once more filling him. "I am glad you are safe and alive." He sighed. "I wish that you were not here, but there are some things that cannot be changed."

"Oh, they can be changed, Cedo, lad, but it'll take time. Like everythin'. I won't be 'ere forever an' neither will you. Mark my words."

The words filled him with a liquid mix of emotions; sorrow, happiness, panic, and hope. He adored living in the house and, for the majority of the time, he adored Erus. But there were things about the warlord that disgusted him, mainly the job he had given himself. All felt like it was changing with the gift of the horse but Cedo knew he was a long way from ever having Erus as he wanted him. He was a mere slave, a piece of flesh to be enjoyed.

Shifting to the floor, Cedo sat beside the bath, silently

taking in the body that was enveloped in water. Long, strong arms draped over the edge, and a chest rippled with muscles. He gazed at Billy's strained neck, the fearful excitement of being caught by Erus turning his breaths into quick, tiny pants. Picking up the soap, he dipped it beneath the water, nervously bringing it to Billy's exposed skin.

Billy chuckled, lifting his head just enough to look at Cedo, eyes returned to their mischievous state. "So, you wanna play, do ya? You can't resist my wily charms, can ya?"

The soap was snatched from his fingers and dropped into the water. Kneeling up, his heart hammered as he placed his hands on either side of Billy's head. Gripping the curved metal of the bath, he briefly laid his lips against the blond's. They stayed pressed together, lips sealed together until footsteps thumped along the hallway. Cedo scrambled to his feet and sat back on the bed, cheeks stained red as the door burst open.

"I am *not* your servant, Reilly! Do not send me running after you," Erus fumed, one balled fist planted against his hip. "Hurry yourselves up and get downstairs."

With that, the door crashed shut, the fear of reprisal churning Cedo's stomach. From the bath came a hearty laugh and Cedo turned to look. Billy laughed, the water rippling around his chuckling body.

"No people skills, that man. No people skills whatsoever."

CHAPTER 31

Cedo Dressed Billy in a long, silk dressing gown and led him down to the dining room, listening as the stagehand whistled at the richly decorated house. Dinner was a quiet affair, the atmosphere thick with Erus' disapproval. Thankfully, he kept his opinions to himself, for which Cedo was grateful. Either he was too tired to voice them or was just allowing Cedo to play his own little game of being Master. Whichever it was, Cedo preferred his own Master to keep his biting words to himself, at least for the evening. He wanted to tend to the tall blond for a while and make sure his friend was well before being forced to return him below stairs.

Following the hearty meal, they retired to the study. Cedo sat on the loveseat, and nudged his legs apart to allow Billy room on the floor. Nursing a glass of brandy and pursuing the newspaper, Erus sat across from them, one leg placed across the other. Cedo cleaned a fine hairbrush of tangled red hair and tossed it into the fire. The hairs popped and sizzled, curling to nothing and leaving a singed smell in the air. He had just seated himself, hand positioned above Billy's head when Erus looked up. Cocking an eyebrow, Erus looked at them for a moment, the quietness between them crackling like the fire.

"Touch *it* with that brush and you know what I'll do

with it." His lips twisted into a sneer before he turned his attention back to the broadsheet paper. "And I am certain, Cedo, that you would not want me to embarrass you before your little toy."

Rolling his eyes, Cedo got to his feet. He placed the brush back on the desk and his hand was just pulling the door open when Erus spoke again. "And do not roll your eyes at me, otherwise I will make it last all night long."

Skin tingling with excitement and fear, Cedo took the stairs two at a time. He did not want to be beaten, not in front of Billy. One did not admit to enjoying such things. Although he was sure that, in his exploration of the sexual underworld of Svenfur, Billy had seen far worse.

Collecting his own brush from before the mirror, he hurried back to the study, face reddening when Billy gave him the smallest of waves. Making himself comfortable, Cedo took the weight of the sun- and meat-fed hair in his hands and began to gently run the brush through it.

Before him, Billy began to relax, shoulders slumping and his head lolling forward. Cedo found himself following suit, eyes becoming unfocused, his hand rhythmically moving.

There came a rustle as Erus folded the newspaper and placed it on the small table beside him. Lifting his cane from beside his leg, he traced the tip of it along Billy's jaw, turning the man's head.

Beneath his fingers, Cedo felt Billy react, his body tightening. Hair fell away from his throat and Cedo watched his Adam's apple bob, veins throbbing beneath his tightened skin, trying not to react to the man who had tormented him. Cedo felt his own body stiffening as he watched the two men. The smell of fear began to impregnate the air, the acridness heightening when Erus ordered Billy to stand.

Obediently, Billy did, shoulders back and eyes on the

shelves, doing his best not to look at Erus. Hunching forward, Cedo watched, his entire body tightened like a spring, ready to fight or run.

As before, Erus' eyes ran over Billy's tall, lean body.

"Take off the gown," Erus commanded.

Cedo's knee began to twitch, his fingernails digging harshly into the palm of his hand. He did not want to watch, did not want to be in the room while his friend was humiliated. But still he needed to be there, because fleeing would break every rule of friendship.

Slowly, the gown slid from Billy's shoulders, crumpling behind him. Unabashed by his nudity, he stood before Erus, allowing himself to be admired. From his vantage point, Cedo could not see the look on Billy's face. But he could see his Master, green eyes darkening and glazing. It was a look that Cedo had seen a hundred times before, the look that announced Erus' innermost lust.

"Now I know why I did not kill you," Erus' voice was low, dripping with the very deepest shards of his soul.

In desperate attempt to stop his leg from shaking, Cedo curled onto the low seat, legs trapped beneath him. However, it did nothing to quash the terror that gripped him, the cold, hard fear turning his skin into a canvas of tiny lumps. It only grew as Erus unsheathed something from within the depths of his cane. Hammered and polished to a devilish gleam, a slender sword was held before his face, lips twisted into a hate-filled snarl.

The sword dropped, Billy flinching as it touched him. Cedo wanted to move, wanted to grab the weapon. But he dared not, for it would only be turned upon him. He needed to remain calm, no matter how much it hurt. If he remained calm, then they would all get out of this alive.

"Now, tell me why I should not cut you up." Erus had pressed himself closer, his face crushed against Billy's.

If Billy was scared, he did not show it, his body standing

tall and proud. Cedo suspected that such a gesture was causing the anger that seethed from Erus. He did not like people to defy him, and Billy knew exactly how to play the game.

"Tell me why, William Burton? Tell me why I should not hack you up and feed you to the hounds that live on the Downs? I see how you look at Cedo. I see the desire in your eyes. I know that you want him. Am I right?"

Cedo was sure he was going to be sick, his stomach turning over while cool sweat ran along his neck. Yet Billy never answered, remaining silent, the anger turning Erus' face into a map of reddened lines. "Answer me!"

Cedo didn't follow what happened next, such was the speed of movement. Billy brought up an arm. A heartbeat later, Erus stumbled back, eyes wide with shock and a hand clamped to his neck. From Billy's hand hung the sword, the tip glistening a silky red. Stunned into silence, the flame-haired man staggered across the room, hand firmly against the wound. He struggled with the desk, pulling open a cover and yanking out a speaking tube.

Eyes that flickered with anger and pain stared at them, forcing Cedo to shrink back. "Doctor Barnes, could you come to the house, please? Yes, it is rather urgent. Thank you."

Then he was gone, lurching from the room like a drunkard, the door slamming in his wake. A thick silence hung over the room. Cedo felt his vision come and go. He did not know what to feel, such was the wave of emotions that pounded through him. Eventually he found his voice, a harsh cry leaving his lungs.

He heard a clatter and was able to focus just enough to see Billy toss the sword carelessly onto a shelf. His voice sobbed, shaking his entire body.

"How could you?"

The broad back was turned to him, shoulders rising

and falling as Billy caught his breath.

"Billy!" Tears bled onto his cheeks and he shakily pushed himself toward Billy, laying a hand on his shoulder.

He wanted to maim him, injure him for hurting his Master. He wanted to watch Billy bleed and cry; wanted to watch the life blood flow from him.

Yet... Billy had done something no other dared to do. He had stood up to the power of Erus Veetu. Had defied the man who all but ran the city. He had shown him that not everyone was willing to take whatever was thrown at them.

Billy looked at him, face strangely unlined and empty. There was a faraway look in his eyes, as if they were following some spot on the shelves. Carefully they moved, in time finding Cedo's own horrified, face. Rough hands cupped his jaw and tilted it, a fresh set of feelings swimming through Cedo. The man who tended to him now had stepped straight from one of his own tales; strong yet caring, silently looking after the one he wished to protect. Billy's hands dropped to his shoulders, pressing him close to his naked body. Cedo could do little other than drape his arms around Billy's waist, holding himself up as if letting go would mean he melted straight through the floor.

Once Billy had wrapped himself beneath the gown, they walked to Cedo's room. The house was thick with a threatening silence, one that penetrated right to the core and caused fear to rise and fall in waves.

Behind the closed door of his room, Cedo stood and stared off into the distance. The shock of what had happened still hung over him. For the first time, the walls of the house felt like a prison, like the death house he would surely wind up in if they killed Erus. There were times he wanted the bitter warlord dead, yet Cedo loved him with a passion that many would never care to understand. He enjoyed the moments when Erus gave in and played along with him. Yet he also lived for one other thing.

"'Ey!" He looked up to see Billy sprawled naked on the bed. "This is one nice bed. I ain't been in somethin' like this since..." Billy's voice trailed off and he gave Cedo a small shrug before folding his arms behind his head.

Billy writhed over the crisp sheets for a while before finally settling down in the little crevice of linen and blankets he had created for himself. As hard as he tried, Cedo could not bring himself look away. Instead his eyes roamed over the white skin, taking in the skinny yet muscled legs, rippling stomach, and tight chest. Billy may have looked thin, underfed even, but beneath it all he was built like a champion race horse.

Eventually, the embarrassment of watching the naked body got to him and he moved to the door. He would leave Billy here for the night, allow him some luxury before whatever punishment Erus saw fit for them.

"Now, where you goin'?"

Cedo froze by the door and looked over his shoulder.

"To sleep next door," he replied with an apologetic smile.

Billy pouted and propped himself on one elbow. "An' leave me all alone in this 'uge bed all night?"

Temptation at its finest was there before him, sprawled on his bed. He knew he had to resist because Erus was expecting him to fall for Billy's charms. It would give Erus the excuse he needed to unleash all Inferno upon them. He gave a curt nod.

"Yes, and for that I apologize. But I know that you will understand."

Billy sagged back to the bed with a shrug, giving Cedo his back. Feeling utterly rotten at the abandonment, Cedo quietly crept next door to the empty bed there. Whether Erus would return in the night, he did not know. He only hoped that his loyalty would be rewarded.

The darkness of sleep brought with it the usual torment of dreams. However, this time the blood and the screaming was replaced with something far more agreeable. Dreams of lust, of naked skin; dreams of pleasurable moans and cries. Cedo woke with a start, his skin speckled with a sticky sweat. Sitting upright, he looked around himself, his eyes slowly adjusting to the inky darkness.

Beside him, the bed was empty, the crumples in the sheets being the only evidence that Erus had even been there. In the depths of his mind, he heard the cries once more, heard a voice that sounded very like his own.

Slipping from the sweat-sodden nightgown, he wrapped a sheet around himself and left the room. The sweet taste of anticipation clung to the tip of his tongue as he let himself into the adjoining room. There, in his bed, lay the creature from his dreams.

The gas jets whispered to life, a soft light filling the room. Billy did not stir, tucked deep beneath the blankets. Dropping the sheet to the floor, Cedo crawled across the bed, his lips wandering to the shell of Billy's ear.

"Wake up," he sighed. "Please, wake up."

Billy stirred, moving onto his back. He mumbled something incoherent, his eyes still closed. Fighting with himself, Cedo resisted just straddling the taller man's hips and having his way with him. The taste between his lips was exquisite, the sweet taste of forbidden fruit. Temptation had finally won. Letting his tongue touch the tender skin behind Billy's ear, he whispered again, trembling at the prospect of lying with Billy. His groin was beginning to tighten, blood rushing through him in a volcanic heat.

Lazily Billy opened his eyes, a slow smile lighting his face. "'Ello, Cedo."

"Billy..."

The blankets were lifted away and Billy wrapped him in strong arms, holding him tight. Beneath the broad chest, Cedo could hear the other man's heartbeat, could feel it pattering against his own. Tilting his head back, Cedo looked up into Billy's face. For so long he had tried to convince himself that Billy was nothing more than a good friend.

But that was dashed away as he tangled his hands in blond hair and pulled welcoming lips to his own. Never had he dreamed that another's skin could feel so delicious next to his own. His hands ghosted over the body that held him, taking in each curve and welted scar, dipping between bony hips and over the swell of powerful thighs.

Eventually his hands found their way between their panting, warm bodies, fingers flinching away as they brushed against Billy's hardening cock. Billy gasped into his mouth, hips swaying a little. With growing sureness, Cedo let himself touch the hard, silken skin.

They lay for a while, tangled together, lips and fingers exploring. His legs went around Billy's waist and he clung to him, never wanting to break away or come up for air. A warm haze wrapped around him, fogging his brain and making it difficult to breathe. Yet he would not have cared if he had died there and then, held in the arms of the angel who had stepped from the wings of a theater.

Pushing Billy to the bed, Cedo climbed on top of him, knees nestled against hard hips. Golden hair, capturing flashes of light, spilled over plump pillows, Billy's chest rising and falling as he tried to catch his breath. Locked together they sat, panting, their hips rocking.

Curling his fingers around Billy's neck, he pressed just hard enough to leave a subtle red mark. Blue eyes sprang wide and Billy gasped, his windpipe momentarily crushed. Sitting up, Cedo admired his handiwork, gloating a little at how fine Billy looked with the marks upon his pale throat. He pondered whether Erus would allow him to follow suit, to have Billy wear something upon his neck just for Cedo.

As quickly as they had risen, the marks faded, leaving Cedo to press a kiss to his dying fingerprints.

"Would you allow me to make you mine?" he brashly whispered, his tongue tasting the velvety softness of Billy's lobe.

There came a hiss and Billy writhed beneath him, his erection teasingly pressing against Cedo's thigh. "If it meant bein' able to watch over you for all the 'ours of the day then, yes, I would. Be proud to, Cedo Reilly."

The words excited him and he rocked his hips, pressing his hard member against Billy's stomach. "Then your first duty," he softly proclaimed, "is to make me happy. Very, very happy."

Billy growled deeply and roughly grabbed him by the waist, dragging him to the bed. Strong fingers wound around Erus' necklace, tugging his mouth back to Billy's, azure eyes sparkling with mischief. "I never thought I'd 'ear you say those words, Cedo. Never."

CHAPTER 32

The door rattling frantically in its frame caused Cedo to wake with a start. Sitting upright, he watched as it shook against its hinges, the noise overbearing.

"Reilly!" His heart stalled as Erus barked at him. "Reilly, you had best be awake!"

Struggling from the bed he hurriedly dressed and looked to Billy's still sleeping form. Deep in sleep, the noise had done nothing to awaken the man he had shared a bed with. Frantically he shook the sleeping figure, his own heart pounding like an engine against his chest. Dazed eyes looked at him and Cedo felt himself begin to panic as the sound of keys jangling dashed through the door. Painfully slowly, Billy roused himself, stumbling from the bed and into Cedo's outstretched arms. Between them, they struggled to the small water closet, Cedo shutting the door on the still dozy Billy just as Erus burst in.

If the planet of war could have a face then it would have been Erus Veetu. Nostrils flared and eyes that burned with the fires of wrath glared at him. Where there had been blood there was now a neat bandage hiding the wound below.

"Where is he?" Erus thundered.

"Who?" He could barely speak as nausea closed his throat.

Lightening fast, Erus was before him, a hand clamping

to his throat, fingers tightening into a painful stranglehold.

"You know who."

His oxygen was being cut off, flashes of light dancing before his eyes. Desperately he clawed at the fingers. But like some vicious puzzle the more he fought the more they tightened.

"Where is he?!"

Shaking and trying to fight back both tears and Erus, Cedo shook his head. He owed a great debt to Billy and he was not about to repay it by giving up his friend to the claws of the monster. His sight began to leave him, wavering into blackness. Precious air was becoming scarcer by the second as his knees began to sink beneath him. Erus never let him go, the demon above him screaming obscenities, belittling him with words of anger.

Then, like a butterfly against his lips, the sweet taste of air returned. Hungrily Cedo filled his lungs, savoring every ragged breath as he forced his sand-dry eyes open. Billy, freed from the confines of the small room, had Erus by the hair, holding the screaming banshee at arm's length.

"You might terrify 'im, Veetu, but there ain't an iceberg's chance in Inferno that you scare me," he snarled.

That only fed the fire. Erus reared against the strong arms as he attempted to grapple with the man that held him. Nothing seemed to surprise Billy and he landed a punch, quickly and squarely, to Erus' face, letting him hang by a handful of hair before tossing him to the bed.

Bruised and battered, Cedo nursed his aching throat. Grateful he might have felt, but it did not stop the deadness that engulfed him as he watched the two men fight. He dared not think what would become of Billy once Erus had recovered himself.

Splayed on the bed, Erus glared at them, nostrils flaring. Already a bruise was beginning to shadow his cheekbone, a painful reminder of the man who stood between him and his slave.

"So." He slowly rose to his elbows and Cedo slunk back. "It seems that your toy has more the mind of a dog than a human."

The air around him tightened. Disheveled and seething, Erus stood, one heavy foot after another approaching him. Cedo dared not look up when the booted feet stopped before him.

Humiliated, he stared at the floor, shaking slightly before his Master. Before Billy, even before Erus, his heart had been a blank slate, waiting for someone to etch their name upon it and claim it as their own. One would have been enough; never did he suspect there would be two.

"You'll swing one day, Veetu, for what you've done," Billy snarled.

There was an indignant snort. "For what, dare I ask?"

"For them. For us. For Cedo."

"May I remind you, *toy*, that Cedo entered freely into this contract, as did many others. Their families were richly rewarded for their lives. *Your* family was richly rewarded."

Billy sighed. "My family needed the mon—"

Erus abruptly cut him off: "They all *needed* the money, toy. The difference between them and you, is that you escaped. I let you escape, and now I wonder if that was the wisest move. Luckily, you have kept your opinions to yourself, not that anyone would believe them of course. No one, not even the lowest tabloid hack, would believe some odd-jobbing whore. But I do wonder, now that you are beneath my roof, how long you will be able to keep your mouth shut." Erus snickered, the sound rough, rasping, wind through autumnal leaves.

Out of the corner of his eye, there was a flurry of movement. Cedo watched in shocked silence as the two men once more struggled. Never had he seen Erus act like this, and never had he expected him to. There was too much about the man's demeanor that said he would never lower himself to such trivial things as rough bar room brawling.

It was a blur of movement and it quickly ended with Erus standing victorious, a handful of Billy's hair clasped in his hand, the man dangling from it. With a grunt, Erus landed one final blow to Billy's stomach, winding him before he made for the door.

"Follow me, Reilly," he barked. "I really don't want you to miss this."

Filled with terror, he chased after Erus as he hauled Billy through the house, bawling the name of a man that chilled Cedo to the bone. "Mr. Black! Mr. Black!"

Servants scattered before them, pressing themselves against walls, waves that did not want to stand in the way of progress or punishment. From one such doorway stepped Mr. Black, falling into step behind Erus.

The door to the cellar was heaved open, feet thudding against the steps, the gloom coming to meet them. The macabre procession whirled past the desk and the neat shelves of tools and to the far reaches of the extensive room. Cedo hurried behind them, palms cool with perspiration as they went to the farthest depths of the building: The War Room.

It was coming; Cedo could feel it, a liquid hot rage that bubbled deep within him, threatening to burn him alive. He could stand up to Erus. He could stand up and make his voice count. He had done it in the early days but something, the silent threats that hung over him, had silenced it. But if Billy could take on the great warlord, so could he.

Letting the scalding feeling grip him, he snatched at Erus' elbow, swinging him around. A brief flicker of emotion flashed across Erus' face before it settled into indignation.

"What?" he demanded, eyebrow arching.

"Why are you doing this?" he hissed. "Why are you punishing him?"

Erus' face became blank, eyes widening before it fell apart and he bellowed in Cedo's face, "Why? Why am I doing this?" Erus grabbed a handful of his own hair and exposed the bandaged wound. "Do you expect this to go unnoticed? If I were to drag your toy before a court of law, they would do exactly as I am about to do. He is nothing but a reprobate, common street scum who will never learn how to behave. I highly doubt this is the first time he has received such punishment for his wandering hands and vicious tongue."

Snarling, Cedo snatched Billy from his Master's grasp, the rage raw in his veins as he faced Erus. Standing between his friend and his Master, he faced Erus.

"I shall not let you do this! Everyone is allowed an opinion, and just because it does not please you does not mean you can punish them."

For the time he regarded Erus with defiance, no emotion filling him as he took in the face that had caused him so many feelings in the past.

"How would you feel if that were your mother or father kneeling on the floor before some cold-blooded killer?" he demanded.

His Master's lip curled back, teeth bared in a vicious snarl. The fury rolled from him, gripping Cedo. But he refused to back down, refused to give in. Billy was relying on him to be a voice, just as he had been for Cedo. It was time to forget about the consequences and stand up.

"They are dead to me!" Erus roared. "As is every other person in this stinking city. Each and every one of you expects your life to be handed to you, to be freely given and nothing expected in return. You expect to become wealthy from meager jobs. Yet you know nothing about the fruits of hard labor. As I have said before, behavior is rewarded or punished."

"Perhaps so, but that does not mean by you. You are not a court of law, Erus."

Erus' eyes narrowed, nostrils flaring. Never moving, Cedo remained in front of Billy, protecting him. Tension stung the air, its sharp tendrils threatening to force him down. Finally Erus sighed and shook his head. "I have said in the past that I shall take all you say into consideration and I shall."

The shock hit him in the stomach, a hot, leaden thump. Staring up at his Master, Cedo shook his head.

"Excuse me?"

Pinching his nose, Erus refused to look at him. Instead he gazed at the wall before lifting a hand. "You're excused, Mr. Black."

His Master's aide grunted and shook his head. "You're makin' the wrong choice, Mr. Veetu."

Erus never reacted, never lifted his head. He gave another sigh and flicked his fingers towards Mr. Black. "We shall speak of it later."

Holding his tongue, Cedo watched as the bloodthirsty man finally turned and left. The dark threats he uttered towards Cedo and Billy could be clearly heard. Threats of violence, of pain, and of death. It left Cedo wondering exactly how much Erus actually orchestrated. Despite his temper, his Master had shown little violence, even toward those beneath his roof. And in this moment, in his haste to injure Billy, his anger had vanished to nothing in mere moments. Perhaps all he spoke of was a display to keep his competitors at bay and to keep his work shrouded in mystery? Or perhaps he was just giving up on all he had worked up?

Erus' eyes remained on the wall. "Billy, I wish for you to remain here in the cellar. I shall speak to you later."

Cedo reached behind himself to wrap his fingers around his friend's wrist. "Master, please."

"Please, Cedo, just let it be for the moment." Shaking his head, his Master refused to look at them.

"Let it go, Cedo. I'll be all right."

Gazing over his shoulder, Cedo caught Billy's forlorn smile as he drifted away, the shadows eventually carrying him away. Taking one of Erus' hands, he gently stroked his Master's fingers. Something was wrong. It felt as if the universe were shifting, as if everything were about to be shaken like dice in a cup.

"Master?"

Stroking Erus' cheek, he lifted saddened green eyes to meet his own.

"Master, whatever is wrong?"

"You were right," Erus said in a hushed whisper. "I should not be allowed to play judge, jury, and executioner. Billy is yours to do with as you wish, and I should not have taken a hand in that."

A shiver snapped along his spine and his hand tightened around his Master's. "Thank you, Master."

Erus gave him a weak smile and led him from the cellar, the anger having melted to nothing. Excitement and trepidation rolled through Cedo. There might be punishment for what he had done. Yet he had protected another from being hurt and that was all that mattered.

CHAPTER 33

It was not until evening, when Erus lay beside him and the gas jets were turned low, that all was laid to rest.

"What will become of Billy?" Cedo softly asked, dread filling his heart.

For a moment, Erus was silent, eyes searching the ceiling.

"He will remain here. There are things I need him to do. An extra pair of hands is very welcome at this time."

Brushing his Master's cheek, Cedo turned his face to him. Erus' eyes were sad as if the weight of the world were upon him. He wondered what was going on behind them, what he was thinking and feeling.

"Master, I wanted to thank you."

"Pray, for what?"

Smiling, he cupped Erus' face, fingers tracing over his cheek. Love swelled through him and he wanted to sweep the man beside him into his arms.

"For allowing me to have a friend. It means a great deal to me."

"You are very welcome. But remember that he was given in good faith."

Pressing a kiss to Erus' jaw, he asked, "Will you accept our friendship?"

Pulling away, Erus sighed and gazed at the ceiling, telling Cedo all he needed to know.

"I ask you for so little." His Master's voice was pained. "I will be yours if you only you will respect, love, and fear me. Yet time and again you tear at my defenses and bring them down. While I should have expected such a thing to happen, I never believed it would."

Cedo placed a hand on his Master's chest, feeling the beat of his heart beneath his palm.

"But I do not want to fear you. I have never wanted to fear you. All I have ever wanted is to know that you feel the same as me. I understand that there is great pressure on you at the moment. All I want you to know is that I am doing the right thing by you. Sometimes a person needs to step in and show another their reflection. I do hope you realize that I was not doing wrong by you."

Silence, broken only by the sound of breathing, filled the room. In his heart, Cedo knew he was right. Whether Erus would accept that would be another matter. Finally Erus turned to him with a sad smile. Gently his fingers stroked over Cedo's cheek.

"I know, and I should thank you for it. Now sleep, for tomorrow is another day."

It did not feel like a second had passed before he was being shaken awake. Coming to, Cedo looked around himself, finding the figure of his Master kneeling beside him.

Beside the bed stood the clothes stand, a suit of deep midnight blue hanging from it. Lace decorated the cuffs, and silver thread danced over the breast, picking out graceful, whirling patterns.

On a table beside him lay a light meal of fruit, eggs, and bread, a meal that he began to ravenously devour.

Erus leaned into a corner, legs artfully crossed at the

ankles. "We must get you back to the Cartier. It has been too many nights and I do not want you going stale."

Stuffing his cheeks with food, Cedo nodded, watching as Erus pushed himself upright and walked to the clothes hanger.

"Soon we will have you away from the Cartier. There is another place, a theater that takes away the breath of even the rich visitors. They have heard of you and want to offer you a trial."

"Which one?"

"Now, that would be telling. But please do not tell Mr. Cartier of our plans. He does not know and I would rather he didn't for the moment. Come, we really must go."

Cedo climbed from the bed, the ache of excitement knotting his stomach. A new place, at last! He wondered which boards he would tread next. Dressing in the fine clothes, he felt a tingle of anticipation make its way along his spine. Already he could smell the smoggy air of the city. It had been too long and now he longed to go out, to stretch out tired muscles and fill his lungs with fresh air.

The lights seemed brighter than in previous evenings, or perhaps it was the hope that burned in his soul. Letting them engulf him, Cedo stopped at the edge of the stage and peered through the glare. He could pick out the first few rows before everyone else disappeared into murky shadows. Turning his head, he looked to the gilded boxes that overlooked the stage. Looking down at him was Erus, John seated beside him. Giving Erus a small smile, Cedo turned his attention toward the hushed audience.

"Once upon a time, this city, this country even, did not exist. They lay beneath a shell of ice and snow. Cold winds blew over the hills and valleys, chilling everything in its path and causing the people who populated the area to hide within the shanty houses they had carved from the very wastelands around us.

"They lived in fear, for in one of the valleys was the magnificent castle of the ice king. He had come from nowhere and had claimed the land for his own, enslaving the people into building the mansion he resided in. He was a cruel master, his demeanor as cold and as hard as the land around him. Rarely was he seen, choosing to live behind the façade he had created. The people of the wastelands did his every bidding in the vain hope that if they could crack the icy exterior, then perhaps the bitter lands around them would thaw with him."

He paused, heart hammering. Cedo knew he was taking a risk and he held a hand above his eyes, peering through the light. Erus was listening, leaning closer over the edge of the box.

"Of course, it never happened and the ice king continued to rule with a heavy hand, emerging from his castle only when the people enraged him.

"On one such occasion, he arrived in the small town wrapped in the furs and skins of animals and driving a sleigh of glassy ice. Four white horses pulled it, moving silently through the downy-white snow. No one was expecting him and no one knew of his arrival until he stood in the town square, bellowing for attention.

"'Why does nobody come when I call?' he bawled. 'Why do you choose to ignore me?'

"Cautiously, the people backed away, fearful of what would happen if they spoke. The ice king swung around, watching each them with a crystal blue gaze. The silence that hung over the town was as stony as the ground beneath their feet.

"Finally, one brave soul stepped forward, a young

man with sun-touched skin, a young man with hair as yellow as the watery sun above them.

"'I will help,' he said. 'But only if you help us.'

"The ice king snorted and glared down his nose at the man before him. 'And what do you wish me to help you with, peasant?' he demanded.

"'If I help you,' the young man continued, 'you must bring the spring back to us.'

"Again the ice king snorted, stepping back onto his sleigh as he gestured the man closer to him.

"'The winter was here before I arrived, and it shall carry on regardless of whether I am here. I can do nothing. Now come.'

"The young man stepped aboard the sleigh and allowed himself to be taken from the town and to a fate unknown.

"For a while he was useful to the ice king, his hands nimble and skilled. He rebuilt crumbling parts of the castle, building the defenses against townspeople who would never attack. From the wastelands around the castle he foraged for food and encouraged to it bloom. He was everything that the ice king needed. Yet, at the same time he was not.

"The ice king watched him with interest, standing in the topmost windows of the castle as the young man tended to the small gardens he had created. The boy was magical, his fingers turning anything he touched to life. One day, as the boy carried in a basket of brightly colored berries, the king approached him.

"'Boy, tell me how you do it.'

"Stunned, the boy looked at him, the basket clasped tightly beneath one arm. 'Do what, your highness?'

"'Create life from nothing.'

"The boy just looked at him and shrugged. 'I do not know and perhaps I never will.'

"Something stirred within the king, something primal and warm and, for a moment, his lily cheeks were touched with the color of the berries. With the strange feeling twisting his stomach, the king left him, more confused than before.

"The days turned into weeks and the weeks into months. The cruel winds and harsh ice never left, never melted, leaving the land locked in an icy waste. But in a corner of the garden, a small tree began to flourish beneath the boy's tender hands, its leaves tentatively testing the cold air. In time, fruit began to form on its branches, expertly caught by the boy's hands.

"Watching this magical transformation, the king once more approached the boy. 'Boy, tell me how you do it.'

"Again, the boy just looked at him, giving him a small shrug and a smile. 'I do not know, your highness.'

"Taking the boy's hands, the king looked at them. He turned them, taking in the rugged perfection of them. Once again, the strange warmth twisted inside of him.

"Stepping closer, the boy took the king's hands in his own and looked into the cruel eyes before him. 'But if you let me try, I can show you.'

"Words abandoned the king as the gentle creature closed in on him. A hand brushed over his cheek and the strange feeling threatened to choke him. He let out a small cry and stepped away from the boy. His eyes glazed with something that hurt far more than the cold air. Again, the boy reached out and touched him, and the king trembled, his cries fading to nothing as the boy took him into his arms and held him close.

"The boy held the sobbing king as he sank to the floor, uttering five small words as he did:

"'It is love, your highness.'"

Pausing, Cedo once more glanced around himself. Although he could not see his audience he could feel them. Could feel them leaning closer, clutching his every word close to their hearts. He heard a few quiet gasps and what sounded like sobbing. Perhaps he had touched a few people. He glanced to the box just in time to see Erus' fleeing back. Smiling to himself, he turned back to the audience.

"No one knows what happened that day. What they do know is that, slowly but surely, the land around them began to thaw. Where once it was barren, there was now greenery. Grass and flowers bloomed. The sun beat down, warming chilled bones. Animals returned. And the people were happy.

"With the cold went the huge ice castle, the king also disappearing. With him went the boy. Why, nobody knows. Perhaps the king needed to be reminded of the magic that brought him to his knees. Perhaps he realized that there was more to his life than cruelty and ice. Wherever they are, I wish them the best and hope beyond hope that they are happy."

Retreating from the light, Cedo paused as quiet fell over the theater. It took a moment but suddenly the room was filled with applause, with whistles and shouts of "*Bravo!* " Smiling, he waved and stooped to collect a few of the flowers that fell at his feet. Allowing himself to wallow in the adoration of his crowd, he dared not to think what he would face once he stepped away from the stage.

Euphoria crashed over him, filling him with a sweet and heady sense of adoration. Barely able to bring himself down, Cedo all but danced into the wings. What he found in the darkness shocked him.

Erus stepped from the darkness and, laughing, Cedo linked his arms around Erus' neck, his lips seeking out the ones that spoke so harshly to him. For a brief second, Erus stiffened beneath his touch before his body sagged.

Arms wrapped around his waist and Cedo felt his own adoration, the fiery worship for the man he kissed, flowering in his belly. It swirled around him, making him groan. Beneath his fingers he felt his Master's body make the same tiny movements, his chest rising and falling against Cedo's as his tongue touched to his slave's lips.

"You know it is not easy to win my forgiveness," Erus softly panted into his mouth, "but do not think I do not appreciate you trying."

The words made Cedo writhe between Erus' arms, pressing himself closer to his Master's chest.

Finally Erus pulled away, one hand coming to clasp Cedo's face. "Let us go," he said, voice heavy and laced with passion. "I believe we need to take in some air."

Stepping back, Cedo followed the other man's heavy footsteps until they emerged into the light of the corridors. Silently they walked, one behind the other, as they made for the exit. People looked at them, some leaning in close to one another, peering and whispering from behind hands. It took a while to wind in and out of the crowds of performers and admirers before they stepped from the building and into a darkened loading yard.

A single, rusting gas lamp hung above the door, moths flittering around the glass, wings occasionally tapping against it. Mist had already begun to drift in from the sea and wind through the narrow streets.

Erus tugged at his wrist. "Come. It is a nice evening and I do not want to stay here any longer than I must."

Stepping between the crowds of people, they made their way along the street. As when Cedo had first met him, Erus showed no regard for anyone or anything as he stepped from the pavement and into the road. Nothing touched him and there were no cries or horns as he strode across the dirt covered street. Fearing for the other man's safety, as well as his sanity, Cedo hastily followed, dodging thundering wheels and hooves.

"You are a madman," he cried above the din of the city.

Erus just grinned, teeth glinting in the yellow light. "I know."

He did not have a chance to say another word as Erus hurried onwards, leading them close to the seafront. Already the smell of the sea pricked at Cedo's nose. He drew in deep breaths of it, filling his lungs.

Once more, his hand was grabbed and he found himself being dragged across the lanes of traffic and into the melee of the pier. Startled, it took Cedo a moment to take it all in. It was something he had never expected; Erus did not seem to be the kind of person who would frequent such an area. But he allowed himself to be pulled into the carnival atmosphere, slowly relaxing as he found himself walking across the familiar boards.

Walking beside a line of small booths, Cedo stopped, tapping at Erus' elbow. When his Master paused, Cedo beckoned him closer.

"Why have you brought me here?" he tentatively asked.

Eyes staring out to sea, Erus appeared to ponder the question before taking in a deep breath and turning back to the man beside him.

"Because we all need time to ourselves, time to escape and to talk. And, most importantly, to enjoy ourselves" Erus gestured around himself, face lightening with a smile. "And what better place to do it?"

Taken aback, Cedo could not quite believe what he was hearing. Had Erus just suggested that perhaps they needed to have *fun*? He was sure that such a word did not exist within Erus' vocabulary. He was not even sure if Erus knew the meaning of the word.

"Your little game with the forest had me thinking,"

Erus continued. "It made me realize a few things."

Cedo moved to ask what things he meant but he was not fast enough. Erus stepped away from him and back into the throng.

Leaving behind the gentle breeze and the slight spray of the sea, he chased Erus into the heart of the fairground. Around them carousels twirled and sealess boats swung, laughter and music filling the air.

"What did it make you realize?"

Beside the large swing boats, Erus stopped." It opened my eyes to a life I did not know."

Cedo's throat felt tight.
"What do you want?" he finally asked.

Erus grinned and stretched out a hand to clasp his face, thumb sweeping over his cheek. Whining softly, Cedo leaned into the touch.

"I want you," Erus whispered, voice soft yet domineering over the noise around them." Everything about you. And perhaps I have to change my thinking a little to get what I want."

Standing beside the carousel, Cedo watched as the horses danced on their gilded poles, pondering what Erus had said.

It opened my eyes.

How? Erus was still the controlling monster he had been from the start. Yet this tiny gesture, this time away from the routine of home and theater, pain and anxiety, made Cedo feel suddenly as if he were wanted, as if he were treasured.

Before him, the carousel began to slow, the horses finishing their race, the gaudy music cheering them on. Erus took his hand and pressed coins into his palm.

"Awaken what is within," he said, "and you shall see what I want."

Cedo's brow furrowed as he stared at the coins before

looking to Erus. His Master stood on the edge of the shadows, face already hidden from view. He gave a curt nod toward the painted, prancing horses. Feeling the nervousness of being forced, Cedo stepped up to the golden fence of the merry-go-round and held out the coins to a weathered carnie.

Walking over the creaking boards of the fairground ride, he weaved in and out of the poles, looking for a place to sit and hide. It felt odd to be there, a grown man enjoying a child's ride. Others were boarding around him, ignoring him as if he were just another of them; mothers and fathers with excited children at their hips; lovers canoodling in the high-sided carriages.

Of course, the usual oddities from Svenfur were there, people like himself, those who lived one life in the light and another in the shadows, majestic human-like peacocks enjoying the fruits of their evening's work before going back to find more. And that was just what he was; another of them, with nothing to fear except the moment that the ride stopped and life began again.

Cedo rejected the pig and the cockerel, instead pulling himself up onto a white stallion, its golden bristle hair braided down its neck. Swirling down its neck was its name: *Knight*. Sliding his feet into the stirrups, Cedo prepared himself for the sudden movement.

Slowly the carousel began to pick up the pace, his horse clumsily jerking upward before floating back down. Still Cedo could not shift the feeling that he was being watched and ridiculed, that this moment would be used against him. But as the ride picked up speed, its steam engine laboring, he could not help but let a childish rush of glee take over him. Laughter spilled from his lips and he tilted his head back, watching the colored lights above him. And deep within him, a tiny flame whooshed into life, the flame of curiosity and unhinged delight, of not knowing what lay over every hill.

People flickered by, strangely lit and moving awkwardly, looking like the brief snatches of the new-fangled photography. Faces distorted, all of them lit with the passion of the fresh evening.

All but one.

The face, nothing more than a snippet of an image, was there, trapped in the same place beside the carousel. Never did it move, instead intently watching the riders. Cedo's stomach began to churn as the ride began to slow, each revolution revealing a little more of the shadowed face.

Another sweep by, another snippet. One half dark, the other starkest white.

Slower and slower it went, his horse laboring upward before falling back down. A hollow where there should be an eye. The other side blank and featureless.

Stepping from the horse, Cedo stumbled dizzily toward the exit, the odd face somewhere behind him. It was etched into his mind, a beacon of horror. He wanted away from it, to hide in the mass of people and try and purge his mind. He swayed as he pushed against the crowds.

In the light of a fortune teller's stall the back of a hand, mangled white and red, was shoved into his face. As he careened sideways a voice that sounded like a whistle hissed a singular word.

Beware.

Then the man with the mangled oddity was gone, whipped away and swallowed up by the crowd, leaving nothing but the faint, sweet scent of charred flesh behind.

Gripped with terror, Cedo pushed through the hordes of people. Suddenly he felt claustrophobic, penned in. Faces flashed by, all of them suddenly twisted and battered. Panic churned through him and he felt bile, acidic and stinging, threatening to choke him.

Abruptly something clamped around his arms and terror screamed from him, tearing himself from the tight grip. Swinging around, Cedo looked into Erus' shocked face. The ruined face he had seen from the carousel flashed before his Master's and then disappeared. Erus clasped his face, forcing him to look into eyes that were filled with concern. Cedo could see his lips moving but no sound came out. All that filled his head was the engine hiss of that voice.

He rocked back and forth as Erus shook him, eyelids feeling heavy before snapping open.

"Whatever is the matter?" he heard Erus cry above the joyful sound of the funfair.

Feeling himself begin to sag, Cedo grabbed at Erus, catching the lapels of his coat as he pulled himself upward.

"Evil!" he replied, voice high pitched and screaming. "Out there. One of *yours*."

Erus staggered a little but Cedo refused to let him go, moving with him as he panted, body heavy.

"There was nothing left of his face! It was gone. Hidden by a mask. His hand was marked." Pulling the glove from his own ruined hand, he thrust it into the face of his Master. "With this!"

Giving Erus one final shake, Cedo stepped back. "I am not alone! "There are others. How many? How many more are there?"

Erus weakly leaned against the cold metal, body limp as he looked at Cedo.

"You are the only one. Others were marked for other reasons, many of which are unspeakable."

"What reasons?"

It took Erus a while to speak, as if he did not want to divulge the secrets that haunted his soul. "Some stole ideas, intent on selling them to other companies. Some were marked merely as workers in the factories.

"Some were marked as experiments. They were supposed to be exterminated at the end, but the carriage that was carrying came under attack. Only a few escaped before the carriage was resealed, but it was enough. I have never seen any of the marked people again, but I know that they are out there and I doubt that any of them have a good word to say about me."

Aghast, Cedo stared at Erus, stared at his lithe, silhouetted form gulping down the air as if it might be the last he was to ever breathe. He wondered how hard he would have to push to send the menace of Svenfur to his watery death? Instead, he gripped the railings, knuckles glowing white beneath the lights of the fair.

"I am not bloody surprised," he retaliated. "You branded them and sent them to their deaths! I cannot imagine one person liking you after that. You are a monster, Erus, a damned monster."

Erus' shadowy face turned to look at him. Even beneath the brim of the hat, Cedo could see the lines of sadness set into the face. "I know," Erus softly replied. "I know."

With that, Erus climbed down and began a slow, languid walk toward the end of the pier. Heart filled with stone, Cedo followed, watching the proud body slump, shoulders rolling forward, as he began to lose himself in the shadows behind the stalls.

Stopping beside Erus, Cedo looked along the final step of the pier. This had been his ground in a lifetime that now felt a million years before. His corner, the one where he would straddle the joining points of the railings, was empty. No crowd, no cat calls, no long tales. Instead, a couple stood there, staring out into the same expanse as they.

The wind picked up again and Cedo turned his face

into it, gasping as his breath was whipped away. Tilting his head back, he caught the breeze, and let it lift the hem of his jacket and pull at his hair. He felt the exhilaration of standing there, of feeling like the last person on the planet. Climbing onto the railings, he looked over the edge, daring himself to stretch that little bit further. His body reacted, filled itself with the brisk chill of deathly adrenaline.

"Do you miss it?" He cast a gaze over his shoulder to see Erus. A shudder of recognition danced down his spine. It had been like this in the beginning, the dark figure standing on the pier and watching. Now that figure had brought him back.

"I do."

Erus sighed. "I will give you a choice. You can stay with me."

Cedo felt his heart race. "Or you can come back to your life here. Time and again you have shown me up for what I am, and even though you have changed, I will never change. So, should you choose, you can have your freedom once again. You will never see me again, and I shall never see you again. It will be over."

Feet thudding against the boards, he looked at Erus. The man seemed... broken, defeated, as if his life were coming to an end. Stay with Erus... Or have his freedom?

Cedo could feel his lips chapping as he softly asked, "Shall I choose now?"

The shadow that was Erus gave a nod. "All I ask is that you weigh everything before you make a decision."

Lowering his head, Cedo brushed a handful of hair from his eyes. As he did, his fingers grazed the weighty necklace he had all but forgotten about. He knew that others had glimpsed it and judged him for wearing such a piece, but he had not cared. With it came so much responsibility. Responsibility, yet also affection and someone who showed him how much he cared in equally extravagant measures of pleasure and pain. Going back to his old life would mean the freedom to roam and to go as he pleased, to consort with whomever he wanted. It meant a life of being liberated, of being the roaming artisan he had always wanted to be.

He may have roamed but it was with sadness that he realized he had never left the city, forever hunting for his mother.

Biting his lip, he looked up. Before him, the shadow remained except that now something glinted from its hand. Long and silver, it appeared to be a cutting tool. Slowly he inched closer, letting his hand touch Erus' face. His Master flinched beneath his touch. Parting his lips, he cupped the back of Erus' head and pressed his mouth against the trembling man.

"I choose..." he whispered. Erus whined softly and Cedo pressed his mouth closer.

CHAPTER 34

Blindly he reached out and gently took the heavy tool from Erus' hand. Giving Erus another hungry kiss, he quietly finished what he had begun, "I choose you."

He was sure that Erus sobbed beneath his lips. Arms tightened around him, cinching his waist, the tool clattering to the floor between them.

Erus said nothing as he pulled away but he did not need to. As resolute as Erus was in not declaring his affection, Cedo could feel it in the other man's tiny movements. Erus took his hand as they began to walk back along the pier. Cedo was sure he could see the glisten of something upon Erus' cheek.

Leaning into Erus, Cedo allowed himself to be lulled by the rocking of the brougham. Achingly slow, it headed up the bustling West Road, making little time and allowing him to take in the brief snippets of a life he rarely saw any more. The road was jammed with every kind of vehicle imaginable, all heading for the Terminus and the roads beyond it. People jostled up and down the footpaths, ladies picking up the hems of their dresses as they wove around each other.

Erus turned to him, body tight with tension.

"This is horrendous."

Closing his fingers around Erus' hand, Cedo leaned closer, burying his nose in softly scented hair.

"Changes are afoot." Erus did not move when Cedo kissed his neck.

"What kind of changes, Master?"

A hand clasped the back of his head and pressed him closer.

"You shall see, precious one."

Resting his head against Erus', Cedo peered through the tiny window. Outside was the Terminus, its great glass and steel structure a glittering beacon in the dark night.

But it was not the building that caught his interest. It was the machines and engines that were parked outside that caused him to lean a little closer.

Climbing across Erus, Cedo pressed himself closer to the window. The machines stood, silent and unmoving, scoop-laden arms and wheels hanging still in the bustling air. Stout funnels, black with soot, protruded from the sides. Several of them were lined up along the road, standing several meters above all of those who paused to ponder what they were.

"Changes," Erus breathed in his ear.

Cedo looked over his shoulder to Erus. "Changes?" he asked.

In the orange glow of the street lamps, Erus grinned. "Tunnels. Beneath the city."

"For what?" Cedo could barely hold himself as gloved fingers found his bare skin.

"Trains. Similar to the one you rode on."

Sliding away from Erus' fingers, he moved back to his seat and stared at his Master.

"I did not know that you were planning on selling the

idea of the subterranean railways."

He could see Erus grin, face all peaks and troughs of light and shadow. "Oh, of course I have sold them, dear Cedo. Every great idea is up for sale. In fact, there has been a bidding war between several companies and I am thankful to say that I have come out the victor. The advancement of this city is very dear to my heart. It is a city that has served me well and it needs to be dragged out of the era of the horse and cart."

Erus moved closer and placed his hand once more at the base of Cedo's neck. "Would you not like to travel in comfort, Cedo, away from the peasants of the city? Would you not like this road to be clear, for us to make a hasty exit and return to a roaring fire on a cold, winter evening?"

Shivering beneath his Master's touch, Cedo nodded, eyes fixed on the shadowy face.

"Yes, Master, I would," he sighed.

Murmuring, Cedo's eyes closed as Erus stroked his face There were things he wanted to say, accusations he wanted to throw, and questions he wanted to ask. But his vision swam and his skin tingled when fingers crawled over his face and into his hair, pulling his lips to his Master's. Kneeling upon the seat, he linked his arms around Erus' neck and willingly gave himself over.

They swept along the footpath and into the house. As the door creaked shut behind them, Erus faced him, proudly smiling. At the foot of the stairs stood Billy. He grinned as they walked in.

"Go," Erus said. "Spend some time together. It is the least I can do."

A smile spread over his lips and Billy joined him, falling into step as they disappeared into the house.

In the cellar, the air was cool, the gas jets doing little to warm it. A pile of blankets were neatly folded in one corner, a pillow resting on top of them. They searched for a place they could call their own, a secluded spot to sit and talk.

"Billy, I apologize for you being down here."

Fingers touched his elbow and he looked up into dazzling blue eyes.

"It's all right, mate. Don't you worry. I've slept in worse places. Besides, I've got a roof over my 'ead, food in my belly an' somethin' to do with my hands."

The few words warmed him, making him feel better. Billy really was a good soul who saw the good in all that happened.

Cedo walked through the expanse of the cellar looking for somewhere to rest. Other than the desk and a few odds and ends of machinery, there was nothing. In one wall was the door that led to the subterranean railway and, mirrored beside it on the opposite wall, one that Cedo had not noticed before. Murmuring to Billy, he approached it.

Cautiously he pushed it open, reaching into the darkness for a switch. Instead his fingers brushed against a smooth metal plate and, a breath later, electric lights jumped to life, the darkness melting away. With it went Cedo's breath as he stepped into the room beyond.

In the heart of the oppressive room stood a polished table, chairs surrounding it. At the head was another towering, throne-like chair. Running his hand over the silken wood of the table, Cedo studied the inlaid map of the globe. Crisp white paper, an inkwell and pen, and a speaking tube marked each place at the table. The walls were dark with wood paneling, red and black striped wallpaper hanging above them. A door, made from the same dark wood as the paneling, was set in one of the walls.

Overwhelmed, Cedo stood and looked around himself. Beside him, Billy softly whistled in admiration. Neither said anything as they looked around the room, almost as if it were forcing them into silence.

Desks lined the next room in neat rows, each one set with a typing machine. Stunned, Cedo studied it, panting quietly as he looked at the large map on one wall. Before the map stood a large desk on a plinth. More paper sat upon it, set before an array of speaking tubes. An idea slowly formed of what the place was, coming through the mists in his mind. Such places had been whispered about since the outbreak of the war, stories and legends that had been passed through the shadows and along the streets.

Beyond the desks was another room containing a semi-circle of tables, each containing a speaking tube and, on closer inspection, a street map. Eyes wide and mind alive, Cedo read each one carefully. Each map coincided with a major city somewhere in the world.

Quietly they walked, finding dormitories, store rooms and a spacious kitchen. As well as the blazing electric lights, each room also held redundant gas lamps on the walls.

The underground rooms seemed to go on forever. Bathrooms, studies, drawing rooms, and even a bar. Each was carefully named with a brass plate upon the door. When they stepped into a closed corridor, it seemed as if they had finally reached the end of the world. All that was contained in the corridor were two doors, one labeled *Observation Room*, the other *Erus Veetu*. Cedo's stomach turned as he reached for the door knobs, first for what must have been Erus' quarters, and then for the *Observation Room*. Both, unsurprisingly, were locked.

They trekked back through the rooms, the quietness abruptly hitting Cedo. Nothing. There was not a sound. No footsteps creeping past doors. No strange noises coming from the cellar. No pots and pans crashing in the kitchen. No Erus shouting. An absolute and deafening silence.

Slowly they melted away from each other, not wanting to leave the hidden rooms. Billy remained in the cellar while Cedo returned above stairs. They did not speak, the shock and awe of their find leaving them speechless.

Behind the door of his quarters, he found Erus lounging on the bed, a book before his face. Other than the crackle of the fire and the rustle of pages, silence enveloped the room. As the door clicked shut, Erus looked up and slid from the bed, the book thudding to the bed.

"Hello my darling." Cedo stood still and allowed himself to be approached, smiling when Erus placed a hand on his shoulder. "Come and join me. I'm craving your company."

The pleasantness threw him a little and he moved closer to the bed, stilled when Erus lifted a finger.

"Stop there and undress." His Master dropped back to the bed, leaning into the mounds of pillows.

Feeling the weight of Erus' gaze upon him, Cedo picked at his clothes, letting them fall around his ankles. The warmth of the fire brushed against his nude back and buttocks. Rolling his head, he caught the predatory look on Erus' face, and felt himself begin to glow with confidence.

"Come closer."

Obeying the order, Cedo walked toward the bed, Erus shifting onto his hands and knees. Standing at the foot of the giant bed, Cedo shivered as fingers ghosted over his hip, tempting him closer.

"It has been too long since I last looked at you. Too

long since I last held you in my arms."

Proudly, Cedo pulled his shoulders back as he allowed hands and eyes to ride over the lines of his body. It took all of his strength not to fall into the arms that wanted him; for now, he held the power, the tables turned for a brief glimmer of time.

He remained like that, silent and strong, when Erus gripped his slender hips and pulled him to the bed. Falling into Erus' lap, he wrapped himself around his Master's strong body.

Erus' lips parted, breath coming in short bursts and Cedo took it all in. And what a sight that was before him! Flushed skin and lidded, heavy eyes, crisp night shirt slipping from one pale, lightly freckled shoulder. Bending closer, Cedo attached his mouth to the hollow of Erus' shoulder, teeth tearing at his Master's tough muscles. A howl of what could have been either pleasure or pain, tore through the air. A circle of teeth and a dark red welt were left behind, leaving his own mark on his Master.

With the barest of touches, Cedo allowed himself the pleasure of feeling the lines of his Master's body. Every inch was taut and muscular. Breathless, he inched his way lower, admiring the rise and fall of his chest. Heat began to rise in his own body as he curled himself into the foot of the bed. Above him lay Erus, body limp and arms outstretched.

Slinking back toward his Master, Cedo gasped as he eased the night shirt over spread legs and muscular thighs to reveal Erus' beautifully strained erection. It excited Cedo, for it was he that did this, he who caused the excitement, the sighs, and the flushed skin. He and no other.

Curling between Erus' legs, Cedo paused for a moment, taking in the heady, musky smell of arousal that rose from his Master's body. His own excitement grew as he touched his lips to the stretched skin. Beneath him, Erus moaned as Cedo let his tongue trace along veins and around glans, gently sucking on the head. For a moment, they lay there, the soft sounds of Cedo's lips filling the heavy air. Erus gave a strangled cry, pulling himself away.

"I must have you now!"

Grabbed from the end of the bed, Cedo was tossed to his back, limbs and hair draping over the rumpled sheets. Erus towered over him and gripped his hips, lifting them as he pushed himself in.

Hips arching from the bed, Cedo cried out, tears pooling in the corners of his eyes as he clawed at Erus. His heels came to rest in the small of his Master's back, and he felt filled, satisfied. Sliding against the bed, they moved as one, intertwined in the quieting light of the fire. Shadows slid over them, cloaking them as they touched and kissed.

Head falling back against the voluptuous pillows, Cedo sighed, tears trickling from the corners of his eyes, the yearning ecstasy wrapping his body in a tingling vigor. Another cry left his lips as temporary blindness fell over him, stars bursting through the darkness.

The fluid warmth broke through him and the blindness lifted just in time to see Erus open up, face flushing as he groaned, eyes flickering and laying bare the haunted soul. Suspended in between pleasure and release, Cedo stared into the wide green eyes. Through them flowed the horrors of the past, a loveless and painful childhood, a boy forced to grow all too quickly into a man. Cedo felt his heart ache at the lost innocence.

A strong hand wrapped around his aching member. Desperate, Cedo rocked against the welcome hand, shuddering and flinching before finally spilling himself against his Master.

Sighing, Erus sank to the bed beside him. Dirtied

fingers were offered to him and Cedo gratefully licked them clean, Erus watching him with a smirk. Once the fingers were clean, they crept over his face, drawing his lips to Erus'.

"My beautiful, precious, Cedo. I do adore these moments. It is just such a tragedy that they are far and few between. There are times when I wish that this life were not so busy. It frustrates me because I do believe that there is so much more to know, so much more to learn about you, yet the very moment I get that time something seems to arise."

Moving closer, Cedo let his hand stroke through Erus' damp hair, pushing it away from his face and eyes. There—it was what he had been looking for—the relaxed man, suspended from life for a while as exhaustion began to cloak them.

"Ask me, then," he softly pressed.

Erus was quiet, eyes flicking back and forth as if he were trying to peel away the layers that made up his slave. "Tell me about your childhood."

And so he did. Taking Erus in his arms, he recounted tales of his childhood: of walking the beach with his mother, of telling stories for high society, of lying in the garden and learning the constellations.

"Your mother," Erus whispered, head against his shoulder, "what is her name?"

His heart stilled with sadness. "Her name was Isobel."

Erus' face creased, pondering the name that had been given to him. Eventually, he shook his head.

"Such a familiar name." Cedo's heart momentarily stopped, eyes widening as he crept. "But I do not believe I know her."

The rush of euphoria was dashed away, hope fading with it. For a second, he had thought that perhaps Erus had known her, or even knew her whereabouts.

Fingers brushed through his hair, bringing his attention back to Erus. There was a peaceful smile upon his lips.

"Tomorrow we shall go out. Just you and I, away from all of this. You need a chance to forget, if only for a while."

Cedo gave a little sigh and relinquished his momentary role of protector, allowing himself to be pulled into strong arms as sleep began to fall over him.

CHAPTER 35

Once they had woken and dined on the simple breakfast that Cedo had come to expect, he found himself being led toward the forest room.

They passed beside the forest room and on through the small yard. There was a chill in the air and a light frost touched the grass, crunching underfoot as they walked to a part of the house that Cedo had yet to see.

He found himself in a stable yard. Never had it crossed his mind to wonder where the horses that drew the carriage were housed. Yet it was here, right beneath his nose.

In the center of the cobbled yard stood his iron horse, mysteriously transported from the heart of the countryside, tacked and silently waiting. Beside it stood a wild-eyed dapple-gray stallion, a wiry, yet strong, stable master gripping the reins.

"Thank the gods you've finally arrived," the stable master's voice was gruff.

"You should be thankful you do not have to drive this one, Mr. Turnbull." Erus grinned before he grabbed the reins and effortlessly pulled himself into the saddle.

The horse threw its head up and plunged back when the stable master's grip was lost. Erus gave a growl, tightening his hands against the leather as he looked to Cedo.

Taking the reins of his metal steed, Cedo pulled himself into the saddle. As his weight settled on the great back, the horse came to life, giving its head an experimental shake. Before he could take a breath, Erus had taken off. Touching his heels against his own horse's flanks, Cedo gripped the reins as it began to rock forward on strange legs.

Erus was gone by the time he reached the brow of the garden, fire-colored hair streaming behind him as his horse easily cleared the stream. Still gaining a feel for the strange horse, Cedo let it idle through the stream. It was a strange beast, and Cedo was curious as to how it functioned. He doubted he would ever find out, the secrets no doubt locked deep within Erus' brain.

Beneath the heavy hooves the earth rumbled, easily lifting them up and over the next rise. Ahead, Erus had come to rest beneath a tree. As they rocked up toward him, Cedo could see that neither horse nor rider looked exhausted. Erus looked positively alive, color touching his cheeks and hair disheveled.

"You took your time, lad." Erus laughed, the sound carrying notes of happiness instead of malice. "Shall we see what it can do?"

Gripping the reins, Cedo nodded. "It has been a while."

"Been a while since?"

Looking down, he took in the neat mane and strong neck. Unlike Erus' dainty-looking horse, the creation he sat astride had been modeled on the stronger cart horses of the city.

"It has been a while since I last rode." Cedo flushed as roguishness danced over Erus' face.

"You ride extremely well between the sheets, so I do not know what you are complaining about."

Grinning, Cedo could not help himself. "I am glad you

think that my bedroom prowess is a worthy substitute for horsemanship, but I have to disagree with you."

Erus guffawed, reaching out to slap a hand against Cedo's thigh. "I do enjoy your humor. It makes a great change from the gloominess we seem to live in every day. We need more of it, dear boy, so do not be afraid to let it fly. Now, let me see what you can do."

They moved out from beneath the tree, the rolling expanse of the Downs before them. Hills came and went, beginning to bloom into life as the winter melted away. Somewhere over the rolling mounds was the sea, and Cedo wondered how long it would take them to reach it. An hour? Several hours? All day? Beside him, Erus began to rise and fall with the movement of his horse and Cedo followed suit, pushing the great beast into its own rickety trot.

"Are you ready?" Erus looked to him, the playful glint still in his eyes.

A burst of muscle and the gray horse took off. Suddenly, his own horse may have been made of air as it leapt into life, chasing the apparition before them. The ground disappeared beneath them, the metal horse stretching its man-made body. It took them just moments to catch Erus, the warlord turning to grin at them as they sped onward. A fence came and went, the second of suspension causing Cedo to lose his breath. The competition was fierce, Cedo laughing with glee as the wind swept the hair from his back. Onward they went, crashing along the ground until they came to a halt atop a hill.

Beneath them stretched Svenfur. The near-permanent fog was settled over the rooftops, held there by the slopes around it. Stretching away along the coast was the city, disappearing into the distance as it tried to make headway over the hills. At the edge of the city stood great smoke stacks, pumping out the smog that sat over the city.

Soon, those factories would be left in the wake of newer developments, no longer the unofficial boundaries as the city. Already the tendrils of new buildings were beginning to grow, jagged wands of partly built houses stretching upward. Along the stretch of the hill were the shadows of quiet villages, which would perhaps one day be gobbled up by the advancement of the city.

"It is not much," Erus said, "but it is our kingdom and therefore must be defended. If we do not defend it, who shall? For once one defense falls, then they shall all fall, and we shall be slaves to whomever chooses us."

"Is that your excuse for the deaths of others?"

Erus did not look at him, instead staring out to sea.

"It is not an excuse, Cedo, it is a matter of pride. I may have come from the scum that coats the sewers, but I am proud of those who have kept and raised me. I am proud of my city and my country. No one else may share that pride, but it is there, a burning flame that never leaves once it has been ignited. I may be the angel of death, but I am proud of my realm, proud of the people who live in it and who go to the theater of war. They too have pride and it is the reason that they go."

"But just what are we fighting for?"

Erus' answer was as light on words as it was quick: "That, my dear boy, is a good question."

Staring out over the city and the sea, they remained quiet, taking in the view as the horses sighed beneath them. From their vantage point, the city looked quiet, as peaceful as Cedo felt. Relaxing as the salty breeze tickled over his skin and whispered through his hair, Cedo closed his eyes and filled his lungs with the sharp air.

At peace. It was a strange sensation in a world of such turmoil, a welcome quietness in his mind. His breathing became steady, matching the rhythm of his heart, the rise and fall of the water way down before him bringing the calm that it had always brought.

Eventually, and without a word, Erus turned his horse and made for home. Following, Cedo rode beside him in silence, watching the fells come and go, coppices of trees passing and falling behind them, their shadows as haunting as the house they were now heading toward.

The service corridors were a bustle of hidden noise and voices, something Cedo had never noticed. Whenever he was in the building it appeared to be quiet, as if the staff were waiting for the next outburst from their master. Servants politely bowed their heads as they passed, Erus pausing to peer into the looking tubes outside several of the rooms. Entering the dining room, Cedo found it set for lunch. Noiselessly Erus seated himself, plucking the newspaper from a tray beside him.

Finally, he could hold his tongue no longer. "What news?"

Erus sighed and shook the newspaper. "The usual; murderers and thieves. Some days I wonder what we fight for, as the place appears to be going to the dogs. The Patron would do well to speak to the city Guards. Although I highly suspect nothing would get done unless he bribed them." There was a long pause before Erus muttered, "Or threatened them."

Resting his chin in his hand, Cedo smiled at the burst of dark humor.

"Why do you not speak to him, Master?"

The paper moved and Erus arched an eyebrow. "And pray, say what to him?"

"You could tell him that you could do a better job with the law enforcement within the city."

A page was turned, Erus dropping his eyes back to the

tiny print. "Anyone could do a job better than those over paid, pie eating mongrels. Goodness, your cat could do a better job and it spends most of the day asleep. At least it is just most of the day instead of all of it."

Cedo chuckled softly. "She could have her own little badge and office."

"I would fix a bloody cannon to her back. That should sort the problem. Mouse *and* criminal catcher. We could have an entire force of cats and they would do a damn sight better than the shirkers we have now."

Once again, Cedo chuckled and he felt himself relax before Erus, a dreamy and light-headed feeling drifting over him. He had been searching for this, for the man who seemed to be buried beneath the prickly exterior.

"Dear gods," Erus groaned. "Willy Wingo is back in town. How people can abide to watch him I do not know. At least he is at the pier, so thankfully we are unlikely to meet him." Erus huffed from behind the newsprint, the paper moving with him. "I suppose that some people are attracted to such crude acts though. Such a shame, such a sign of lack of intellect. I pity such people."

"Why do you pity them?"

Another page turned. "Why should I not pity them? They spend their lives going between the factories and the public houses. There is nothing else, just an endless journey from one drink to another."

"That is an awful generalization, Master."

"It is true," replied Erus. "I came from nothing. Why should they not better themselves?"

Cedo could feel the first twinges of anger rising. "Perhaps they enjoy that life?"

There was a harsh laugh from across the table. "What is there to enjoy, staring at the bottom of a tankard night after night?"

"As I said, Master, perhaps they enjoy that life?"

The newspaper was folded and placed back onto the tray. Erus leaned forward, elbows resting on the table as he looked to Cedo. Staring into the stone cold eyes before him, Cedo shivered.

"I understand what you are saying, Cedo, but I still do not see an excuse for such a lackluster life. I do not see why some can climb and become the stars and why others spend their lives entirely in the gutter. I have seen it many a time in my own factories; workers who are not inspired. They mope around, creating pieces that mirror their humdrum lives. Of course, such people go on to other things in my factories."

The tone with which the last sentence was spoken, a tone as icy as the eyes that looked at him, sent another shiver through Cedo and he straightened up, pressing his back against the seat.

Erus shrugged and stretched a hand across the table. "It is in their upbringing, no doubt. Parents who never had anything to live for breed children who have nothing to live for. The schools are as uninspired as the parents, turning out little worker bees. I suppose I should not complain; they keep me furnished with a constant supply of workers. And a constant supply of cheap beer. It is what keeps the economy turning over, I suppose."

The door to the dining room opened and a small, wooden trolley was pushed in. It looked completely out of place in the house but was stacked with lunch. The smell of freshly baked bread tickled his nose and all but chased the thoughts of Erus' class generalizations from his mind. The usual small army of unspeaking maids emptied the trays onto the table, decanting wine and lavishing their spotless plates with delicious foods.

Lunch was eaten in silence, Erus looking through the small pile of letters that had been left beside the newspaper. Each one was read before being discarded back to the tray. Cedo felt the need to ask what they were addressing but thought better. Instead he picked over his own meal, still amazed at how quickly Erus could change between his moods.

Clearing his plate to one side, Erus pushed himself away from the table and motioned Cedo to him. Doing as he was bid, Cedo stood and stonily walked to his Master's side. Face relaxing, Erus patted his thighs. "Take a seat."

Carefully lowering himself to the proffered lap, he laid his hands on Erus' shoulders to steady himself. Hands wrapped over his hips, guiding him downward until they sat, awkwardly, nose to nose.

"Our outlooks on this world are very different," Erus began, fingers sweeping temptingly beneath the waist of Cedo's trousers, "and it is something I appreciate in you. Our life together would be extremely boring if it were not for our differences. It is why I do not punish you for these discussions. I want you to keep your personality. Besides, if you did not have one, if you were lifeless, I would not have permitted you into my home. As I have said, I watched you for many days before making that initial invitation."

Erus' hands crept up to Cedo's face and cupped it, gently stroking as he spoke, "I demand perfection when it comes to your performances and your behavior. But I do not demand it when it comes to anything that will promote discussion between us. I want somebody interesting in my life. I do not want some silent and performing animal. Now." Erus leaned in, brushing his lips against Cedo's. "I want you to spend the afternoon resting. I want you to be at your very best for this evening."

Lying upon the covers of his bed, Cedo stared at the ceiling. Misty lay on his chest, her purrs rumbling through him and the tip of her tail sweeping against his cheek. Moving his hand over Misty's back, Cedo allowed himself to relax. Things were beginning to change for the better. The barriers were falling, tiny shards of a hidden soul finally making their way to the fire. Erus had obviously, whether consciously or not, found it was the time trust him, attitudes changing with the coming spring.

His thoughts turned to Billy, pondering where he was. There had been no sign of him all day. Lifting Misty from his chest, he placed her on the bed and left.

CHAPTER 36

Easing open the door to the cellar, he stood at the brow of the steps and listened. Sounds of groaning metal and muted curses reached his ears, and he smiled.

Creeping down the steps, he hid in the shadows that lapped along the walls. In the heart of the carved, stone room, stood Billy. His sun-blond hair was braided down his back and his work clothes were stained with grime, once-white sleeves rolled to his elbows. A machine of monstrous proportions towered over him, four legs splayed outward so he could reach the parts he needed. Strong fingers moved back and forth, lacing wires before fitting them back into the great fighting machine. The guns attached to its sides lay silent, hanging towards the floor, and the head of the beast was strained upwards, showing off an array of wires and pistons. Soon, armor plating would be added and the great, clomping machine would be sent to the front line.

"Where in Inferno did this come from?!"

Billy cursed and swung around. "Where in Inferno did you come from?!"

Chuckling, Cedo stepped from the shadows. "I wanted to see you before I left for the evening."

Smiling softly, Billy approached him and slung an arm around his shoulders. "That's real nice of you,

Cedo. I appreciate it, 'specially after all you've done for me." He nodded to the huge machine. "Turned up on the underground railway a couple of days ago. I've been puttin' it together, makin' sure it all works. At least I'm not goin' back an' forth to that place of 'is in the country. Looks like I'm workin' for Veetu Industries again. Didn't think that would ever 'appen."

The irony was not lost and Cedo and he chuckled softly. "It is good to know that you are well. I have been worried."

Billy's arm tightened around him and lips touched the top of his head. "You 'ave no reason to worry. I'm fine."

They fell silent and looked at the machine before them. It was a marvel and no doubt able to carry several soldiers to places no conventional weaponry would. Cedo wondered where the inspiration for such creations came from. Wherever it came from, the great steel beast before them would put fear into the hearts of whoever saw it. Its great, clawed feet would be enough to crush a man to death.

The thought sent a shiver down Cedo's spine and he gently lifted Billy's arm from his shoulders. "I must leave. I just wanted to see you."

"Aye, you 'ave a good evening an' look after yourself. I'll see you later."

Standing at the base of the steps, he turned and smiled. Billy watched him, eyes sparkling, and Cedo felt an admiration for him. Billy had stepped into his life when he had needed someone and, despite all that was thrown at him, refused to leave Cedo's side.

"You look after yourself as well. I shall return as soon as humanly possible."

Upon arriving at the theater, his excitement grew as Mr. Cartier came to find him, personally escorting him to a dressing room. Cedo allowed himself a moment to let his fingers brush against the tiny, metal plate on the door, his name stamped in bold, black letters. Beyond the red door was a dressing table, its mirror surrounded by branch-like stems, each ending in a small oil lamp. There was a simple chair before the mirror and, placed just behind it, a chaise lounge. As the door closed, Cedo saw a table laid out with foods and drinks.

"Thank you."

Mr. Cartier inclined his head, returning Cedo's smile. "You're very welcome, Cedo. It is time that you're fully appreciated and I'm glad that we can accommodate you."

With that, Mr. Cartier swept out, the door swinging shut behind him. Standing in the middle of the room, Cedo looked at it, taking it all in with a sense of wondrous disbelief. He could not believe that his time was coming, that his love of telling tales was finally paying off.

Reach for the stars, my darling, but remember that such achievements can come with the most heinous of prices. He swung around as the words lilted through his brain, only for his heart to fall when he realized that she was not with him. Another apparition, a ghost in his brain, just like the stories.

Walking to the table, Cedo snatched up one of the bottles and poured a thick, purple liquor into a glass. It smelled delicious and he sipped from the glass, letting the smooth liquor slide down his throat. Savoring the sweet taste and the warm rush, he attempted to dash away the sound of her voice. She was not here. He wondered if she would ever see his success. Saddened, he poured himself another glass and fell to the chaise lounge.

"Drinking yourself into a stupor will do little to chase away those memories."

Startled, he turned to see Erus standing behind him; his Master creeping up on him was something he had yet to become accustomed to.

He offered Cedo a hand. "Come. Discard that bottle."

Looking between the deep purple liquid and his Master, Cedo regretfully lowered the bottle to the floor and took the proffered hand. Letting out a groan, he leaned limply against the poised redhead.

"Drinking will get you nowhere, Mr. Reilly." Erus clasped his right hand in his own, his free hand falling to rest at Cedo's hip. Swaying a little, Cedo looked into green eyes that swam with a rarely seen happiness. "It may make you feel better, but that feeling soon passes. To see you suffer any more than you are already suffering would make me sad."

Slowly they began to sway, Erus clasping him close as they danced a music-less dance. Gingerly, he slid his own arm around Erus' waist.

"I do not want to be here."

Their gentle movement never halted. "Whyever not?"

Cedo felt the pain begin to rise, the dark days haunting him, waiting for just a moment to spark him into such a state.

"Do not be so silly," the voice seemed to come from the distance, part of a different reality. "Dear Cedo, I know that it is your desire to find your mother, but if you leave you may never find her. There are ways and means of tracing her and I can help you. If you leave, I shall be unable to get the necessary details with which to track her down."

"I would greatly appreciate that." A tiny smile began to write itself onto his face.

Lovingly, he tightened his hands around Erus and slowly moved to the music only his Master could hear. Freeing his hand from the one that grasped his, he draped his arms around Erus' neck, pressing himself close.

The movements took over, hips rolling. His lips found the curve of Erus' jaw, his sureness of the man he held growing. It struck him that Erus did have his best interests at heart, something that had blossomed while he had tried to wage war with a man who seemingly just wanted him as some toy. Linking his fingers in Erus' thick hair, he moved his lips, gently pressing them to his Master's.

The moment ended all too soon, a firm knock at the door pulling them apart.

A voice called, "Mr. Reilly."

Giving Erus one last kiss, he stepped away, straightening himself. There was a feeling of hope as he walked toward the stage, a sense that the situation was not completely one-sided. It lifted his spirits, the happiness soaring toward the stars as he stepped out onto the stage to rapturous applause.

Arms filled with flowers and dazed from a successful performance, Cedo let himself be guided into the waiting carriage. It was only when he was settled that he realized that their ride looked different. A gas jet quivered in each corner, casting a warmth over the normally cool carriage.

"It is sad that I have had to leave the Cartier, especially in light of them giving me my own dressing room." It had pained him to collect his belongings from his room after only a single evening.

"Sad it may be, but you are going onwards and upwards. Mr. Cartier could see that is why he lavished you with the gift of your own room. Let me take those." Gently Erus relieved him of the heady flowers.

"Here." The posies his Master had been carrying replaced the audience's gifts. "These are far better."

Lifting the brightly colored blooms to his nose, Cedo inhaled deeply, allowing the soft scent to wash over him. Memories of the first time he had received such flowers danced through his mind.

"Take a closer look."

Reaching into them, he felt among the thorns until his fingers closed around a bundle. Pulling it out, Cedo's eyes widened as he gazed at a thick wrap of bank notes. Breath held, he looked to Erus. His Master's face was twinkling with happiness and a childish mischief.

"That is for you. Spend it as you will and enjoy it."

Kneeling over his Master, he cupped the finely boned face and pressed his lips to the quivering ones below his own.

"Thank you, Master."

They rolled on through the night, Cedo seated comfortably in his Master's lap as he lovingly kissed him. As they passed the Terminus, Cedo peered through the steamed-up window and looked to where the boring machines had stood a few days earlier. Now they were gone. All that remained were hoardings and piles of rubble, steam panting from the holes that had been left behind.

The brougham clattered away behind them as they entered the house. Leaning against the stair rail, Erus looked at him, face empty of any kind of emotion.

"I shall be in the study. The rest of the evening is yours. Do with it as you see fit."

Cedo sighed, feeling the coolness that radiated from his Master. Barriers fell and they rose again, floodgates that held back a sea of emotions, all begging to come out.

When it seemed that he had made progress, it was all washed away as the ice king once again returned.

The cellar was ablaze with light, the mechanical creature standing proud and apparently finished. Between its legs sat Billy, a pencil in one hand and a tankard in the other, a drawing board on his knees. Placing the flowers to one side, Cedo sat beside him, frowning as he watched lines appear on blank paper.

"What is it?"

A mapp, Billy scribbled in the spare space.

Frowning, Cedo hurriedly translated Billy's misspelled words.

"A map of what?" he asked.

Billy looked up, face filled with terror, and he shook his head, lifting a finger to his mouth. Swallowing, Cedo nodded, understanding. Silence was essential but, the secrecy chilled him and he leaned closer, watching. The pages filled with dark twisting lines until eventually Billy sighed and put the pencil to one side.

Still confused, Cedo asked, "Where will it take me?"

Billy shrugged and Cedo stared at him, confused.

"What is with the silence and why can't you tell me?"

Billy collected the pencil and scribbled in the margin. *Need to be quiet.*

They both stared at the page, at the streets and the strange symbols. Seeing his normally happy friend so solemn sent chills through Cedo. Something odd was happening and, whatever it was, it had scared Billy into silence.

"Will the map answer my questions?"

Billy shrugged again, the silence between them overwhelming, a hundred questions hanging in it.

Wrapping his arm around Billy, Cedo shivered, fear beginning to rise.

CHAPTER 37

Daylight came all too quickly. Cedo did not remember falling into slumber. Hands shook him awake and drew him from the bed. Lazily he stood as the hands washed and dressed him, eyes sleepily staring at himself in the mirror. In the heart of one of the whirlwinds he glimpsed Erus, tall and proud as hands pulled and prodded, clothed and brushed.

When the hands had excused themselves, Cedo cautiously admired himself in the mirror. Where there had once been a sleepy blond haired man, there now stood an angel. He was dressed in the whitest of suits, the scarcest of silver threads dancing over it. Lace decorated the hems and the wrists, while his nails had been filed and painted with a hint of silver lacquer, a white jewel sitting at the tip of each finger. His hair had been curled, the natural waves accentuated until it hovered around his face.

"There is to be a masquerade ball at The Noir Jewel. Your mask is in there." Erus nodded toward a box on the bed.

Lifting the lid, Cedo grasped the long, golden carved handle that slid up toward a molded mask. The mask was as white as his clothes, with a gentle sheen of sparkling paint. Feathers bloomed from the brow, while silver paint inched its way around the edge and the eye holes. The nose was prominent, perfectly hiding his own.

"And yours?" Cedo asked.

"Look and you shall see."

Dropping the mask to his side, he looked. Erus was dressed in the deepest of blacks, his hair electrifying against his suit. Before his eyes, he held a jet black mask identical to Cedo's.

"Black and white," came the deep voice from behind the mask. "Good and evil." Erus stepped closer, the mask falling to his and revealing a smirk on his face. "You and I."

Cedo breathed in sharply as lips hovered over his own. Sharply Erus turned, a darkness flickering across his face. "Billy will be joining us, so I advise you go and find him. I believe he may still be in the cellar." Erus' voice dropped. In my humble opinion the cellar is where he belongs, but who I am to complain?"

Cedo could feel the jealousy emanating from his Master. It came and went in waves, the obvious explanation to why he lashed out at Cedo's assistant. Pausing at the door, he painfully whispered, "I love you."

The back shuddered, head bowed. "I know, Cedo. I know."

Darkness came quickly and the carriage rolled away into the inkwell night. With his mask resting in his lap, Cedo studied Billy. His friend sat with his head bowed and dressed in the stiff black and white suit of their male servants. It was a treat to have him with them, yet he could still feel Erus' resentfulness. Erus no doubt wanted to keep him locked beneath the stairs, working on the great metal beasts he brought from the factories. A night together was an appeasement, no doubt, to keep Cedo happy.

The carriage rolled around a corner, its four wheels briefly mounting the grass, causing Erus to scowl and bang his cane against the roof. Across the fields, Cedo could see a building blazing with light. From a distance it appeared to be a stately home but as they closed in on it, Cedo could see that it was far bigger and far grander. Pillars of white marble held an ironwork balcony, which in turn held an array of colored flags. Large picture windows covered the walls, giving tiny clues of what waited inside for the eager crowds.

As the carriage slowed to a halt, Erus leaned close. "This is just a party. You will not be expected to perform, so you may relax."

Erus alighted, his suit briefly hiding him in the darkness. Collecting his mask, Cedo followed, Billy beside him. Grand ice sculptures of fantastical creatures stood upon ice white steps, sparkling beneath flaming torches. People, dressed in jewels, feathers, ornaments, and lace, milled around the entrance sipping from glasses, masks hiding their faces. Lifting his own mask, Cedo followed in Erus footsteps, his Master's boots and cane grinding over stones. Climbing the steps, Erus was greeted by a man in a red mask held by a stout hand, a baritone voice calling his Master's name.

"Erus, so good to see you, old boy! How are you?"

Erus dipped his head, humor in his voice, "Mr. Bailey, I assume. I am afraid your voice gives away."

Guffawing, the red mask tossed its head back, gut rolling. "Your hair gives you away. You may as well walk around in your birthday suit."

Erus chuckled. "I am afraid that should I do that, then I would most likely not escape alive. To answer your question, I am doing well. Could not be better, in fact. And yourself?"

"Same as, old boy." The stout man clasped a hand

over Erus' shoulder, guiding him toward the door. "This ball is just starting, so we should get ourselves inside. Do not want to miss all that good wine, do we?"

The two men walked into the tremendous building. Closing in on Billy, Cedo leaned closer, lips brushing against his friend's shoulder. "Are you okay?"

Billy peeked from beneath his hair with the barest of smiles. "With you by my side, Cedo, I'm always okay."

Touching the tips of his fingers to Billy's, he gently squeezed the strong hand.

Walking into the theater, he looked around. Plants and trees weaved their way over the walls and across the ceiling. Where the architect had been forced to use pillars, they were decorated with winged beasts. Tiny lights hung from the pillars, winding through boughs and leaves. The theater had been plunged into a murky blackness, and where once were seats there was now a yawning cavity. Lights twinkled from hidden coves and the only place that remained fully lit was the gallery's wondrous sky, showing clouds and stars dancing over the wild blue sky.

Standing in the midst of it all, Cedo gazed at the fantastic ceiling, ignoring those who jostled him. Lost in the strange tranquility of the theater, he listened to the tumbling music, groups partnering off and falling into dances. A devilish angel, dressed in scarlet and with black and white wings sprouting from its shoulders, slid past him, a platter of drinks held before the oddly feminine demon mask. Snatching a glass of sparkling wine, Cedo sashayed his way among the dancers, time lost on him as he drank, the liquor skipping through his brain. Deep within him, the thrill of finally being in the place so many had told him about made him shiver and smile.

The empty glass was plucked from his fingers and a disguised woman, dressed in a flowing, floating gown, stood before him. She grasped his hands and whirled him into the heart of the dancers. Feathers erupted from her shoulders in a collar of shivering colors. Beaming, Cedo moved with her, dazzled by his partner's mask. All he could see were her heavily made up eyes and the way they sparkled, curling at the corners. They danced, Cedo laughing as every color of the rainbow swirled past him. Finally, the woman released him, sending him spinning and roaring with laughter.

Cedo leaned against a pillar, vision rolling before him. He picked another glass of wine from another passing tray and took a welcome drink before looking to the spectacularly decorated stage.

The heavy curtain had been dropped and before it stood displays of flowers, candles and fantastically dressed acrobats. Colored lights moved across the stage, tracking flying acrobats. Cedo watched them, fascinated. Yet, as they whirled across the stage, his eyes were drawn to something partially hidden in the shadows of the wings. Glimpses of color beneath the light, bold flaxen and deep red, first in the light before hiding once more. Hints of limbs came and went in what could have been a dream, not quite of this world and not quite of another.

Closer he moved to the stage, the shadows moving into the full light of the stage. There they stood, kissing and clawing like starved animals. Neither appeared to protest at wandering hands and passionate lips. Neither saw him, nor did they hear his howl of heartbreak, his cry drowned by the music and cheers of those around him.

Erus was in Billy's arms.

CHAPTER 38

Unable to watch Billy and his Master, Cedo fled the theater, discarding the feathered mask as he flagged down one of the waiting carriages. Betrayed, he ordered the driver to take him into the city, aching with the anguish of what had transpired before his very eyes. He could not face going to the Witheybrooke house, could not bear to stare into the faces of those who had torn out his heart. They were burned into his mind, standing on the stage before everyone, his Master bending and submitting to the one person he loathed.

As they raced toward the city, the anger boiled over into bitter howls and cries, his fists raining into the upholstery and walls of the carriage. It may have hurt, it may have broken bones, but Cedo did not care. It was only when his hand shattered one of the windows that the driver howled at him to stop, threatening to abandon him on the darkened Downs .

The driver discarded his bitter passenger at the Terminus, and Cedo thrust a fistful of florins at him. There was no time for words, no time to contemplate the whys and wherefores of his dire situation. All that bred in his brain and his heart was the need for revenge and the desire for pain.

Bandaging his hand in his handkerchief, Cedo made his way along West Road, eyes roaming as he looked for a place to plot and plan. People bowled out of his way until the sounds of a public house drew him into the welcoming embrace of liquor.

The bar room was filled with scruffily dressed men and a few whorish women, yet none of them looked at him as he approached the bar. A barman put down the glass he was polishing. "What can I get ya?"

"Whisky. A bottle thereof."

The barman raised a dark eyebrow but silently did as he was bid. Cedo followed suit, eyes locked with the barman as he handed over banknotes. Their eyes narrowed until Cedo finally snatched up the bottle and glass, storming off into a corner of the bar.

Snarling at his throbbing hand, he poured the dark liquor into the glass. As quickly as it was poured, he threw it down his throat, wincing as it burned. But he did not care; he had never been a lover of liquor, but the pain that churned through him was enough to drive any man to drink.

He started to fill the glass, thought better of it, and lifted the bottle to his lips, the drink filling the cold void that had opened up within him.

All too soon the bottle was empty, Cedo's dreams mingling with the tiny drops that were caught in the crevices. Struggling to his feet, he stumbled to the bar and purchased more of his new love. His relationship with Erus had been far from perfect, but that had never stopped him from loving the bloodthirsty warlord.

It had been the same with Billy, a blossoming friendship that had been killed the moment he had seen their lips sealed together. How many others had seen them kiss? Erus had said nothing about taking others and had assumed that Cedo was the only one for him.

Besides, Billy had been given to him as a gift, a gift that had sickened and lifted his spirits in equal measures.

Cedo spent the night on the streets, sleeping uncomfortably in the doorway of a backstreet merchant. Sleep came and went, staying away far more than it came and, as the sun rose above the skyline of the city, so did Cedo. With a blind ache behind his eyes, he walked, staying within the confines of the back alleys. He walked until the sun began to set and, with his stomach aching, he fell once more into a public house.

Soon the money that warmed his belly with whisky and cheap soup dried up, taking with it the blissful moments of forgetfulness. Sitting with his feet in the gutter of the West Road and head in his hands, Cedo watched the feet of people walking around him. Uselessly, he fumbled in the pockets of the blackened and torn jacket, hoping that there was something other than filthy air within them. Pressing his fingers into the seam of the pocket, he groaned, chipped fingernails snagging at the stitching. With a tear it gave way, his fingers brushing against something papery.

Cedo tore at the pocket and pulled the paper out. Clambering upward, he stood beneath a gas light and unfolded the paper, praying that it was money. He nearly cast it away when he laid his eyes on Billy's meticulously drawn map, heartbreak opening once more.

But something stopped him and he lifted it to the light. In the center of the map was the clock tower that stood at the top of West Road, the words *Begine hear.*

Followe mouses. written beside it. From above him came the sound of grating masonry, grains of dislodged stone falling into his hair. Glancing upward, Cedo saw nothing except an overhanging ledge, a gargoyle perched on the corner.

Cedo approached the clock tower, looking up at one of its eight faces as it began to chime the midnight hour. Searching the base, Cedo noticed a small painting, the white paint nearly weathered to nothing; a claw with a pointing mouse sat in its palm. He found another painted on the adjacent door. It also pointed clockwise. Cedo ran around it, the last two doors also bearing the same image.

"They lead nowhere, Billy! Nowhere!"

Shuffling through the papers, he examined them in the low light, desperately trying to decipher Billy's badly spelled words.

Derains. Seweres. Cript.

Cedo caught himself as realization began to set in; everything was underground! Turning to the door before him, he leaned against it. Beneath his weight the door began to give, wood splintering, Cedo falling through and into pitch darkness.

CHAPTER 39

Sitting on the damp floor, Cedo looked around, the shadowy room touched by the scarcest of light from the faces of the clock high above him. Standing, he fumbled, tools falling around him. Strangely, he felt no fear as he blundered. There was nothing within him, as if he were the blank slate he had once been.

Grasping at whatever lay before him, Cedo picked up a cylindrical tube. Holding it to the meager light, he grinned as he recognized the lines of a workman's safety lamp. Groping around the base, he pressed the ignition. A flame sprang to life and threw a welcome light around him. Scrambling to his feet, Cedo turned, casting the light around himself.

"Okay, Billy. What did you want me to find?"

The lamp caught the curves of a handrail. Inching closer, he knelt and brushed dust and dirt away, smiling as the mouse pointed toward the steps. Holding the lamp above him, he cautiously climbed down the curving staircase. Leaving the scent of dust behind, the growing stench of the sewers caught his nose. Lifting his arm to his mouth and nose, Cedo found himself in an annex, tunnels branching off all around him. In the distance he could hear the sound of water and, beneath it, the sound of something that chilled him.

Grime all but covered what he was looking for, and

Cedo scratched it away to reveal a mouse. It pointed down a tunnel, toward the sound of the water. Taking a deep breath, Cedo coughed and stepped into the trail of water.

The flame of the lamp flickered, flaring a little as it picked up the presence of gas. His feet sloshed in the stinking water, moving until he reached another junction. Yet more tunnels stretched away, pipes spearing down into them from the ground above.

Finding the next mouse, he wondered how Billy knew about the tunnels and whatever lay within them. Pausing, he noticed that something other than muddy water splashed around his ankles and he leaned closer, trying not to vomit at the stench. Sitting on top of the water was something with color, tendrils moving toward his feet. Something red. Something that looked like blood.

Crossing one tunnel and exiting through another, his eyes were becoming accustomed to finding the barely visible paintings. As he walked through one, a sound from above ground caught his ears, the sound of grinding stone. Glancing up to an inlet, he caught sight of specks of falling masonry and something making a rapid escape. Cedo shivered with a sudden, unknown terror. Cedo had never thought that metaphors could be true but there was, quite literally, light at the end of the tunnel. Sliding along the wall, he splashed toward it, scum-laden clothes sticking to him.

Turning the final corner, he stood, stiffened, the ghouls of his nightmares coming to life.

A tunnel like every other, crept past him, its basin filled not with water but with blood. Narrow pipes arched from the walls, spilling their liquid death. A cloying metallic scent hung in the air, causing Cedo to gasp before he finally collapsed to his knees, vomiting phlegm and bile. Echoes haunted their way to his ears, the sounds of voices struggling to cope with what had befallen them.

Scrambling to his feet, Cedo edged along the tunnel, precariously balanced on a tiny ledge. What had once been hidden was alive, a sadistic dream come to life. His nose and throat burned and he inched slowly onward, eventually making it to a simple wooden door. There was no handle, just an image, one he had seen a hundred times before. Leaning his shoulder against the door, Cedo let out a horrified cry. How could all of this exist, mere meters from the surface of the street? He did not need to ask what it was; the answer already haunted his soul.

Over and over, he pushed against the door, feeling it bow against the frame. Finally, with a splintering of wood, the door gave way, sending him sprawling onto an immaculate, white tiled floor. A corridor stretched away, others branching off from it. Cedo made his way along it, heart pounding against his ribs. Doors glided past him, all of them bare except for brass numbers. Trying several, he found that they were all locked, keeping their secrets to themselves.

He turned left, shuddering with fright as the haunting cries grew to a crescendo. He found himself in another corridor where, unlike the others, the doors were made of glass. Slowly, as if marching to his own death, Cedo approached the first door.

The room beyond the door was tiled white, the floor sloping away to hole in the center. In the center of the room stood a suit of armor, arms suspended above it in chains and legs shackled to the floor. It was only when it lifted its head that Cedo realized a living, breathing human was inside, eyes already dead as they stared out at him. From somewhere above the door, a metallic, pointed tentacle darted out and tore into the man. Easily it ripped through the armor, the man arching and screaming before the appendage pulled back, leaving him to hang limply from the chains. It returned, wrapping around the man and yanking him from the chains. Muscle and bone ripped apart, splattering the room with blood, limbs remaining in their shackles as the unseen monster dropped the torso to the floor.

Cedo screamed, voice reverberating along the corridor, begging whoever controlled the facility to stop. Tears stung his face, as violent as the deaths around him. Beyond the glass, he saw all means of weaponry being tested, from the giant man that had had lived in the cellar of Erus' home to articulated suits of armor for the soldiers on the battlefield. Nearly every test, whether it was meant to kill or protect, ended in bloodshed.

Blinded by the pain of what he saw and his body aching with fear, Cedo stood before the last door, staring at a woman. She was seated on a metal chair, arms and legs restrained by leather cuffs, eyes pleading with him to free her. His very being ached and he slumped to the floor, head and hands against the door as he sobbed, mouthing apologies to her.

The room began to fill with a white smoke, the woman's eyes widening as she began to gasp. It was not long before her skin began to turn blue, hands clenching at the arms of the arms of the chair. Shaking his head, Cedo heaved with sadness, body rising and falling as the woman's life ebbed away.

"Ah, Mr. Reilly, we've been expecting you."

Stunned by the voice, Cedo looked over his shoulder. Above him stood a man dressed in a white coat, holding a syringe filled with blue liquid.

He may have screamed, or he may have begged. He may have fought against those in white, the killers of below. None of that mattered when they held him to the floor, mucus and tears gathering around his head as the ice-cold needle slid into the skin of his throat, casting the warmth of sleep over his weary body.

"So." There was the sound of a chair scraping over a bare floor.

Wherever he was, it was so cold that he shivered. Cedo opened his eyes before quickly closing them again, head aching. It felt as if something were burrowing into his skull, and slowly he looked up, trying to lift his arm. But something was restraining him and he groaned again.

Rocking his head back, he tried to focus, vision swimming. He was in a room of bare floorboards and open windows. He sat in a stiff wooden chair, arms and legs shackled with leather cuffs. There was not a thread of clothing anywhere on his body. Gasping and licking his lips, he was finally able to look in the direction of the voice.

Before him sat Erus, arms draped over the back of the chair, studying Cedo as if he were one of his experiments.

"You followed the trail. I must say that I am extremely impressed that you took it upon yourself. You have shown a spirit that I never thought existed in you. For a long time I thought that you were just here to appease me, to answer yes to whatever question I asked you. But you showed that you are far more than that. Far, far more."

"You are a beast," Cedo spat back. "A cruel and emotionless monster."

Erus laughed, picking up a glass that sat beside his booted feet. Drinking from it, he held it by his fingertips, swirling the scarlet liquid. "You know what I am, Cedo. You have known from the very start of our relationship and yes, you may have protested, but you have never left despite being given the chance to do so. This—"

He gestured to the bare room. "—has been the only occasion that I have fetched you back, and even then it was only to congratulate you on the person you have become. I know what happened down there. I know that you screamed and begged for the lives of those poor souls. I know that, given the correct apparatus, you would have fought to the death for those people.

"And that is what I have been waiting to see. You have fought for your toy time and again, and now you have shown that you will fight for all that is right in this world, even when faced with the darkest of evil. But the people that you encountered, they are the dregs of society, the ones with nothing. As with everybody who passes through my company, their families, if they have them, are richly rewarded."

"BALDERDASH!" Cedo cried, straining against his bonds. "No living being would would sell their families to a certain death."

"Ah, but they do, Cedo." His voice was softer, calmer as he stared into the depths of the glass. "They soon realize that there is nothing to live for except to help their country. It is their final act of patriotism."

Angered by the Inferno-spawn creature seated before him, Cedo snarled, lips peeling back to bare his teeth.

"And still you fight. I knew the fire was in you. You are what I want and you always have been. A fighter, a warrior. I never wanted some simpering, pathetic creature that would bend to my every whim. Besides," Erus toyed with the drink in his hands, eyes looking everywhere but to Cedo as his voice softened, "I wanted to end the experiments. We know that the weapons work and we know that they do their job. Why must we kill people in our own land just to prove that? Why not send the machines straight to the battlefield? Of course, there are certain tests we need to do, but none of them should involve the deliberate slaying of another person."

Leaning against the bonds, Cedo felt his jaw slacken in shock. Never had he heard Erus speak in such a way when it came to his work.

"How do you mean?" he asked.

Erus looked up. "I have listened to you, Cedo. I have always listened to you. It is one of the reasons I created the horse for you and left the forest in the mirrored room. You have always been right; there is far more to life and my intelligence is far greater than mere war. There are so many other avenues that I could take my work. But..."

Cedo could feel the anger melting away, his face settling back and his heart warming. "But?" he gently pressed.

"But there are others who deem such tests necessary, who believe we need them. I have pleaded my case but they will not listen."

"Who wants the tests?"

Erus' shoulders rose and fell. "The scientists. The defense ministry. The Patron. I feel as if they are press-ganging me into doing them. It feels..."

"What does it feel like?" he pushed softly.

"It feels as if they are trying to unseat me, like they are trying to find something wrong with what I do." Green eyes peered up at him, Erus' shoulders rising and falling. "It feels as if they are setting me up for a fall."

"What about the experiments that happened here? Why was Mr. Black torturing that poor woman? What happened to the child?"

Erus flinched and shook his head. "I did not want them to be performed. They were needless and painful. But Mr. Black insisted and I could not refuse."

"Why could you not refuse?"

His Master stared at the floor, his chin in his hand, body shuddering with deep breaths. "Mr. Black forged papers that said I had a hand in Papa Brokoveich's death. I would never have hurt him, not after all he had done for me."

Straining against his bonds, he tried to look into his Master's face, tried to read the emotions that haunted his features. "Why would Mr. Black do such a thing when you provide all he needs to live?"

"Because he is truly soulless and believes he deserves a bigger share of the business. I would never test the properties of an electrical current on any living thing. Not even animals. We have other ways of ensuring it works. And I would never take a child from its mother. Never."

"And where do I come into all of this?"

Erus did not move, still slumped against the chair. "You shall be the one who helps me to quash what is happening. I need you to remain with me. As I said, you have the fight to help me unravel all of this. It is your voice that will quiet the naysayers."

His blood boiled as he looked down at himself, naked and strapped to whatever contraption Erus had decided to drag in.

"If that is the case, then why am I tied up like some horse?" he snapped.

Erus' face rapidly changed, a darkening storm as he reached beneath his jacket and Cedo felt the atmosphere change as he held up Cedo's journal. "Because of this."

CHAPTER 40

What about it?" He already knew the answer. Erus kicked the chair away, sending it crashing across the room, holding the pages up for Cedo to see. "Notes! Letters! All of them to that toy of yours! Never once do you mention me unless it is in spite. The very person who you managed to change. The very person no one in this godforsaken city thought would ever change."

The book slammed into the floor at Cedo's feet, causing him to flinch. Hands, as strong as an ox, yanked at his hair, forcing him to stare in the heartbroken face above him.

"You have hurt me, Cedo. The majority of the time I have managed to restrain myself as I watch you lord it over all and sundry. Have done everything within my power to stop myself from snapping as I watched you cavort with your toy. I gave him to you as an assistant and a companion for you when I was not around. But that, that was the final insult. To see how you viewed each of us. I shall not harm your toy; he is yours to discipline. Point number eight of the contract I gave you, the contract that you *signed,* what does it say Cedo?"

Trying his best to not break down, Cedo closed his eyes. He had looked over that contract a thousand times, memorizing it. "Point number eight," he whispered, voice beginning to break, "reads as follows: *I promise to stand by my Master's side, forsaking all others for him.*"

"*Forsake*, Cedo. That is the operative word in that sentence. And what did you do? You disobeyed it. You stood there and you mocked me. I cannot speak like you, I cannot vocalize how I feel about you but, needless to say, there are deep feelings for you and you *mocked them.*"

Lowering his head, Cedo heard a strangled cry filled with the agony of a heart torn into a hundred pieces and dashed to the wind, a noise that he himself had made in the past. Shame flooded his cheeks, guilt an ugly weight around his neck, and he uttered not a single word as the blows began to rain down onto his fragile flesh.

Released from the chair, Cedo did his best to fight back but he was nothing compared to the wrath of a scorned man. Reduced to crawling across the floor, Cedo grunted as a leather clad foot landed in his ribs. Blood began to well in his mouth as the stout walking cane crashed into his head, feet stamped on his fingers as he reached to grasp Erus' ankles.

In time, the beating came to an end. Cedo lay prostrate on the floor, battered and broken, blood oozing from the wounds inflicted upon him. Unable to move, he lay with his eyes blooded shut, panting softly, ribs aching with every tiny breath. His mouth was dry, crusted with blood and saliva, fingers and joints bent at uncomfortable angles.

Erus said nothing, and the barely conscious Cedo was glad for the silence. A soft flurry fell around his head, partially burying him beneath the flakes before the door slammed shut.

Time drifted past, yet Cedo did not notice. He inched across the floor, collecting up the parts of his dreams that had been scattered around him. Aching with the agony, he held them close as if the shattered words would comfort his wounds. Bandages came and went, for what good they did. Food was placed before him and removed, uneaten.

They delicately cradled his head and whispered words of comfort. They offered his mouth food and water, yet he refused it all, desperate to escape, desperate to be away from his shattered world. Still his husk carried on breathing as if there were a slight possibility that it might recover. As if the pain of what he had truly done to Erus would heal and allow him to be returned to the arms that cared for him more than they had punished him.

Around his throat the necklace remained, a stark reminder of what had been. A reminder that only served to return him to the earthly body from which he was trying to escape.

"Cedo. Cedo, mate, you goin' to wake up for me?" A hand shook his shoulder.

Carefully he opened his eyes, flinching at the light that streamed from the bare windows. Quickly he closed them, groaning as the onset of a headache thundered through his skull. Trying to lift his head, Cedo coughed and spluttered, wheezing through mucus-filled nostrils and tinder-dry throat.

"Don't try an' move, ya daft bastard." A glass of water was placed against his parched lips.

The water tasted like the finest wine. Once he had drunk his fill, morsels of food were placed into his mouth and he wearily ate, tiny sparks of energy beginning to light his body.

"Coppers are 'ere." Billy painstakingly checked his wounds. "Takin' 'is 'ighness away."

Panic suddenly found its way through his tired body and he lifted his head. Billy was doubled over, one arm in a sling and a calm, yet tired look, on his face.

"War crimes 'pparently. There's talk that the Patron finally called the law on 'im. They're smackin' 'im with 'is rights right now."

Whining, Cedo forced himself from Billy's lap. The wail grew, hands clawing at the floor as he tried to pull his weakened and useless body along.

Splinters sliced beneath his fingernails, the emotions he thought had died the moment Erus had taken his hand to him rapidly reawakening. He needed to be there, needed to reassure Erus that he was not alone. Wanted to protect him.

And suddenly a blanket was draped over his nude body, an undamaged arm lifting him and cradling him close. Gratitude washed through him and he gave Billy a smile.

Heavy footsteps rattled throughout the house as they exited the soulless room, Billy carrying him toward the stairs. The room they left behind, Cedo realized, was the one given to him by Erus on the very first night he had stayed in the house.

He sobbed as they descended the stairs and were surrounded by the dark-uniformed and hatted men of the city Guard. They came and went, some carrying items from the house, others examining artifacts around them, bustling about as if Billy and he were not there.

Beside them, the door to the study opened and Erus, flanked by two officers, was escorted into the hallway. His hair was tied neatly into his neck, hands chained behind his back. Crestfallen, Cedo watched, the hatred he had borne toward his Master dying.

"No," he whispered. "No."

At the door, Erus lifted his head and looked over his shoulder. His face was blank and his eyes were dead.

One of the officers patted Erus' shoulder, prompting him toward the black, windowless carriage Cedo could see sitting before the house. Held tightly against Billy, he began to shake with fear of what was to come.

"Erus!" Heartache tore through his voice, Billy's unbroken hand reassuringly stroking him.

Erus paused on the step of the house and gave him one last look, a tiny smile finding its way onto his lips.

"I love you," Cedo said.

Erus' face creased as his smile deepened. Dropping his head, he allowed himself to be led from the house. Howling with despair, Cedo crumpled against Billy. It was over.

CHAPTER 41

I may not 'ave liked the bastard but whatever 'appens, I'll always be 'ere for you."

Limp with despair, Cedo sat hunched in the brougham as it made its way toward the city's court house. The weeks following Erus' arrest had passed achingly slowly, the house even colder without him as rooms and shelves were emptied by the city's Guards.

"You 'ave to remain strong, an' I'll be 'ere to help you."

Cedo offered a weak smile. His body was taking its time to recover from the beating. "I appreciate it. But, Billy. If you hate him that much, why did you kiss him?"

Billy's face screwed up in disgust. "I didn't just kiss 'im. I 'ad to go the full way with 'im. Not pleasant, my friend. I don't know 'ow you've managed to do it for so long."

"That does not answer my question."

"Well, I 'ad to keep the ruse goin', didn't I?" Billy continued, seeming not to have heard Cedo. "Was quite simple really. You 'ad to see us, 'cause I knew that when you did, you'd do a runner. You'd go to the city an' try and lose yourself. Which, if I might say so myself, you did a bloody good job of. An' what did you find while you was 'idin'?"

Slightly confused, Cedo shrugged. "I found his underworld domain."

"Bingo!" Billy beamed." An' what did you use to find that shit hole?"

Rolling his eyes, Cedo grinned. "You sly dog, William Burton. You knew what you were doing all along."

"I damn well did!" The grin never left the stagehand's face. "I knew what you'd do. Don't think I didn't 'ave a read through your journal while you were fetchin' water that time. I knew I 'ad to get you to see what 'e was doin', an' when I found the dreams you'd been 'avin' it all made sense. I wanted to send you there anyway, just so you could see what 'e was doin'. But then I got the chance to show you that you weren't losin' the plot as well. I'm just—" Billy sighed and shook his head. "I'm just a little frustrated that you've chosen to stay with 'im, 'specially after all you've seen."

Billy's words sent a chill through him and he reached for his friend's hand.

"We are all here for a reason, Billy. Perhaps, somehow, we are going to change the world for the better. That is why I have chosen to remain. That, and deep down, I believe that Erus can change too."

"What makes you say that?" Billy softly asked.

"Before he beat me, Erus confessed to why he was killing people in the experiments. He did not authorize them. The defense ministry, scientists, and even the Patron, demanded that they take place. There is so much that is hidden from view, so much that even he does not know. We must not be too quick to judge and hope that things can change for the better." Smiling, he linked his fingers through Billy's.

Cedo felt his heart leap as his smile was returned, Billy's eyes twinkling. "Okay, I can see where you're comin' from an' you know 'im better than any of us. Oh, an' the words you wrote about me were beautiful, by the way. I knew you always 'ad a soft spot for me."

A little shaft of happiness found its way into his dark world and he leaned closer, touching his mouth to Billy's. "Thank you."

He started to move away. Instead, Billy grabbed him and deepened the kiss. "Don't go yet. I've missed this."

Chuckling, he gave in, wrapping his arms around Billy.

The courtroom was a dismal mirror of a theater, staggered seats wrapping around the walls. In the center sat a pit for the judge and barristers.

And for Erus.

As they seated themselves, Cedo sadly took in the image of his Master seated in a hexagonal glass-walled chamber, looking disheveled and lost, staring at his chained hands. The chamber was a strange addition, its walls stretching several feet into the air before sloping into a copper pipe in the ceiling. Cedo drank it all in, a haunted feeling grasping his soul. Around them, the courtroom filled, ghouls coming to watch the spectacle of a trial.

A voice echoed around the grand room, "All rise!"

Cedo to clasped Billy's hand as they stood, the aching dread beginning to sicken him.

Cloaked in black, the judge swept in and seated himself, nodding for the spectators to follow suit.

"Erus Veetu," the judge began. "You have been accused of crimes against your own people and country. How do you plead?"

Tightening his hand around Billy's, Cedo held his breath and leaned forward to peer between the people before them. Finally, Erus lifted his head and looked to the judge.

"Not guilty."

Despite his appearance of unkempt hair and blue prison clothes, Erus' voice was strong and proud, giving Cedo a tiny glimmer of hope.

They sat in somber silence as the day dragged onward, a never-ending parade of witnesses being called to the stand. Cedo never let go of Billy's hand as the catalogue of crimes was laid bare, word after malicious word against Erus hurled at the judge. And never did Erus look up, never seeking out his supporters. They were in the minority, but they were there, hands linked in the shadows and voices silently whispering prayers.

The trial dragged on, unfolding over a number of ever-lengthening days, yet Cedo refused to give up. Diligently he rose every day and sat in the courtroom, Billy beside him, as they stared at the glass-encased Erus.

Every day, Erus seemed a little more pale and haggard, the fight seeming to drain from him as his life and work were picked apart. In the early days, he had snarled and fought back, rising from the chair he was chained to in a desperate bid to try and correct facts and figures. But the weariness appeared to have won and now he sat, head down lowered. Cedo wondered if he even knew that they were there.

One day, after lunch, the judge sat, shuffling through piles of paper before pushing them to one side. Cedo felt his heart begin to fall as the judge announced, "And now we reach the sentencing stage. Before that, I should like to read a letter that the Patron has kindly allowed me to look over. It reads as follows:

Your Honorable Patron,

I appreciate you taking time from your busy day to read through these few words. I hope that they will be accepted as a character witness for Erus Veetu. My name is Cedo Reilly.

As the judge announced the name of his lover, Erus' head snapped up, eyes wide and nostrils flaring, searching the crowd. Cedo raised a hand, desperate to catch the roaming eyes. Finally they settled on him and Erus forced a weak smile, Cedo's heart aching with the to be beside him in these final moments of his trial. He could feel his throat tightening, breath coming in short pants as agonized tears began to swell.

I have been acquainted with Mr. Veetu over the past several months and, despite his faults, he has shown that he has a heart and is able to care for others. He took me in when I was a part of the theatrics of the pier. I lost my father early in life, and my mother within the last few years. I know nothing of their whereabouts and would greatly like to find them. He allowed me the opportunity to search for my family, something I would not have been able to do while struggling at the end of the pier. I have lived, and continue to live, beneath his roof, rent-free. Everything is provided for me so that I am free from worry and debt. As a result of his generosity, I have gratefully given Mr. Veetu my complete devotion. A devotion to him is the only condition of living at the Witheybrooke house, devotion which I have gratefully given.

I implore that you investigate deeper before you pass judgment. I implore that you speak to those close to him to find out more of the truth. I implore that you do not rely on mere hearsay and rumor.

I may have yet to find my family but I hold out hope of finding them, in the same way that I hold hope of you looking more deeply into this case.

Yours in Truth,
Cedo Reilly.

Taking a deep breath, the judge surveyed the courtroom as he placed the letter to one side. "Mr. Reilly, I assume that you are somewhere in this room." The judge held up a hand. "I do not need you to show yourself, but I would like to thank you for your words. However, in light of the circumstances I do not think that anything will alter the decision I have come to."

CHAPTER 42

Cedo's heart was in his throat, terror gripping him as the judge swung his seat around to face the side of the glass chamber. Shaking, Cedo reached for Billy.

"Erus Veetu." His Master never moved as his name was spoken, instead keeping his eyes firmly on Cedo. "There may be some kindness in your soul, but I am afraid that it is too little, too late. You have caused great suffering among your own people, among the people that you were given the privilege of protecting. You took the weak and the hopeless, and snuffed out their lives in the name of progress. In light of this, I have chosen to sentence you to death."

Cedo felt the scream rise but it never left his lungs as Billy grabbed him, holding him close to muffle the sound of pained howls. From the corner of his eye, he watched Erus tighten, body becoming anxious as straps folded from nowhere to hold him to the seat. Tensely, Erus looked around, jaw clenched until he found Cedo.

"Do you have any final words?" asked the judge.

"Cedo." Despite being a condemned man, Erus' voice was unchanged. "Cedo, there is something I have wanted to tell you, but have never known how to say until now. I love you, Cedo Reilly. There was never a moment when I did not love you."

Jerking himself away from Billy, Cedo struggled to stand, legs watery beneath him.

"No!" he howled. "No! You cannot do this." The tears came freely, hot against his chilled skin. "I love you, Erus." From behind him, Billy supported him, hands guiding him to his chair as the glass-walled chamber began to fill with white gas.

Through his tears, through the crying of his dying soul, Cedo watched as Erus choked and wrenched against his bonds, eyes bulging and mouth gaping in a silent scream. As a black veil of darkness began to descend over his mourning mind, screams began to fill the air.

He never left the room, never moved from beneath the branches of the bed. It was here that he had spent so many hours with Erus. And it was where he chose to mourn as the hours after Erus' death turned into days and weeks. To Cedo, none of it mattered; his Master was dead, wiped from the earth by those who wanted him gone. What had he known for them to cause such a ruction? What had he designed that suddenly had them running scared, enough to send him to his death?

Outside, the sun was once again rising, feeding the fresh blooms that decorated the lawns and Downs. Beside him, Misty stretched her lithe limbs, purring and settling beside his head. Never had she left his side, not even when Billy slid into bed beside them.

The grief consumed him, at times a red hot fire that burned in his belly, at others a cold and icy aching chasm. It never seemed to lift, causing him to sob and scream and howl for the one he had lost. So many times, he wondered if he could have prevented it. Thoughts and ideas, all of them a moment too late.

The screams he had heard as Erus had choked to death had been due to a malfunction within the chamber. It was an untested design of Erus', one that they had decided to test out on its creator. It had been constructed without Erus' knowledge, the plans secreted away from somewhere and slipped into the hands of the Patron. The seals had been poorly constructed, causing noxious gas to fill the courtroom, sending people into a panic. Billy had carried Cedo to safety. Cedo had demanded to know why he had not been left behind. Each time he demanded an answer, Billy gave him a pitying look and walked away, muttering something about it not being Cedo's time.

Behind him, he heard the door open and, a second later, a silver tray of food was placed beside the bed before it was obscured by Billy's form.

"Did you make breakfast, or did cook make it?" he asked dryly.

A hand came to rest on his head. "As with every mornin', Cedo, I made it."

Sighing, he rolled away and wrapped himself in linen that smelled faintly of Erus.

"My cookin' ain't that bad, Cedo. You're goin' to get up an' you're goin' to eat somethin'." The bed depressed and arms pulled him close, Billy's heavy, musky scent wrapping around him. "I'm gettin' sick an' tired of lookin' at you in this state. Cedo, I know you're 'urtin' an' I know it's goin' to take a long time for that 'ole in your 'eart to 'eal but I'm not goin' to watch you waste away to nothin'." The hair was brushed from his shoulder and soft lips touched his jaw, pausing before moving to his neck. He made no move to shrug them away. "I love you, Cedo Reilly. You might not think it at times, but I do. An' I ain't goin' to let you rot in this 'ere bed. Erus wouldn't want it, an' neither do I."

Mustering a smile, Cedo reached out and placed his

hand over Billy's. The least he could do was make an effort for the man who, every morning, every day, made the effort for him.

"Any news on his body?" he cautiously asked.

"None whatsoever. Your guess is as good as mine as to where 'is body is."

Wearily he sat up and looked to Billy. Within Billy's eyes, he could see his reflection; skin gray and ashen, hair lank and unwashed. Despite the growing warmth of the changing season, he wrapped the blankets around himself. He did not feel hungry, but he heard his stomach growl at the smell of freshly cooked eggs and meat.

A crumpled and dirty envelope was thrust into his face. Pausing, he plucked it form Billy's fingers, studying the nearly unreadable handwriting and the scrawl of a hundred different postmarks.

> *Mr. C. Reilly,*
> *Verne Manor,*
> *Witheybrooke,*
> *The Great Kingdom of England*

Turning it over, he hurriedly opened it. From it he tugged a sliver of paper. Upon it were perfectly formed letters, a world away from those on the envelope, arranging themselves into a single sentence:

A man carries a torch to the stone-covered grave of the unsung hero.

He held it to the light of the window, turning it back and forth, looking for imperfections and watermarks in the paper. There were none and, frustrated, he dropped it to the tray.

"It makes no sense."

Billy's hands spirited the paper away and Cedo peered over his shoulder as it was turned back and forth.

"You're right. It don't make any sense. Who the 'ell sends somethin' like that, an' from so far?"

Scooping up the envelope, Cedo considered it. "I have no idea."

"What if..." Billy leaned against the doorway to the WC, a jug nestled in the crook of his arm, the tin bath at his feet. "What if it's a code?"

"How do you mean?"

"My pa used to send to them to ma all the time. A few sentences that looked like one thing an' meant another."

"Billy, I am not following you on this."

"It's simple. If 'e wanted to tell 'er 'e loved 'er an' wanted to meet 'er somewhere, 'e'd write somethin' like *And today, the apples are ripe, ready for the plucking.*" Billy shrugged. "Apples bein' a symbol of love an' all of that." His voice trailed off as he rose from the bed. "Oh, what do I know? Could've been a list of things to get from the shop."

"Billy, no! You might just be onto something."

Eyes sparkled before him as he was pulled from the bed. "Get into the tub an' get yourself clean first. I'm sick of lookin' at that filthy hair of yours."

Sinking into the warm, clear water, Cedo laid his head back, staring upward as he pondered the note. If it were a code, as Billy had said, it would take some working out. Breathing deeply, he slid down beneath the water.

"... could be a location!" Billy was chattering away excitedly, seemingly unaware that Cedo had disappeared.

Sliding from the water, Cedo looked to him. "Sorry, you were saying?"

Grinning widely, Billy held up the shard of paper. "The last portion of this 'ere note. I reckon it's a location. I can't be sure, but I've got a feelin', you know, in the pit of me stomach."

"What does the last piece say again?"

"*Stone-covered grave of the unsung hero.*"

Stone-covered grave. He willed his brain to think, to

search the darkest recesses and hidden corners. Finally he succumbed, the blackness falling and spiriting him away to a land of warmth and peace.

When the cup of steaming tea was placed before him, the clock was just beginning to chime the early hours of the morning. Books were piled on the desk, maps unfurled on the floor.

"Anythin'?" Seating himself across the desk, Billy sipped from his own cup.

There was something, an inkling of what the message might concern, but Cedo was growing weary.

"There is something. The final part, the part you believe to be a location. You might actually be correct."

"I am?" Billy sounded surprised and he leaned closer, examining Cedo's scrawled pages of notes.

Pulling the map closer, Cedo pointed to an area that, while only small on the paper, was a vast area of land, far greater than their own country. "Here, in the Kievan Dynasty of the Great Empire. There is a range of mountains called the Ural Mountains. Legend has it that Ural-Batyr was a great warrior and, when he died after drinking an entire lake, the local people buried him beneath a pile of stones. But what of the beginning of the passage?"

"It's simple," Billy butted in. "You've got to think outside the box. *A man carries a torch.* Who carries a torch?"

Cedo shook his head. "The lamplighters?"

Still grinning, Billy tapped his chest. "Who carried a torch in 'ere?"

"A lover?"

Instinctively he reached for the books, opening the

cover of one before Billy slammed it shut. "Not a fictional lover. Think about it. One that carried a torch on 'is 'ead an' in 'is 'eart. What color was Erus' 'air?"

Cedo felt his spine straighten, weary brain awakening and skin beginning to tingle with excitement and anticipation. "Red. Like the flame of a torch."

Billy's face lit up, eyes sparkling. "*A man carries a torch.*"

Cedo suddenly felt as light as air, his heart thudding. "He is alive."

His fingers traced over the map, following rivers and borders, imagining the route, and the time, that would take them to his Master. A strength he thought had died with Erus began to flood him. Breath shortening, he excitedly whispered,

"Do you fancy a trip, Billy?"

The blond man's face was a picture of exhilaration, hands stretching and clenching. "Cedo, I'm not goin' to turn down an adventure!"

CHAPTER 43

The house was in upheaval as they prepared for a trip across the Empire. Trunks and bags were packed, maps were gathered, and books consulted. The weather may have been changing around Svenfur but in parts of the Great Empire, it would still be the middle of winter. Routes were plotted in the great dining room, the large oval table hidden beneath papers, rulers, notebooks and pencils, every last detail debated at length.

"Cedo!" Billy stood at the foot of the stairs, bellowing in an effort to find his mate.

Opening a door, Cedo raced out, clothes and furs tucked beneath an arm. Standing at the tip of the stairs he looked down to the red faced stagehand, staring at the growing collection of belongings. "Yes?"

"Cedo." Billy gestured to the growing pile in the hallway behind him. "We can't take 'alf of this stuff. We might 'ave to walk or ride some of the way. We ain't goin' to get an airship or train all the way to Ural."

Pressing a hand to his perspiring forehead, Cedo nodded, flustered as he dropped the items that he held. "Okay. Right. What do we need?"

Another trunk appeared beside the door, the two male servants quickly disappearing. Billy gave it a wide eyed look of agitation before turning back to Cedo. "Clothes. Warm clothes. Cash. Food. Maps. Couple of guns. Ammunition. Nothin' more."

Picking up the furs, Cedo tossed them down to Billy before gathering the rest of the clothes and heading back toward the room. Behind him, Billy bawled, "Where does Erus keep 'is cash?"

Frustrated, more with the prospect of such a big journey than with Billy, he turned. "I do not know! Search the house! It will be in the last place we expect it to be!"

The door softly opened and Billy stepped in, concern written into his face. "Cedo, I got to ask this, before we step out that door an' into goodness only knows what. Are you sure you're strong enough to do this? I mean, 'e did give you one 'ell of a beatin'."

With a smile and a soft sigh, Cedo stood, his branded hand draping around Billy's waist. "With you by my side, I can achieve anything."

Laying his chin on Cedo's shoulder, Billy quietly replied, "An' that's what I wanted to 'ear. Now, 'ave you considered what weapons you're goin' to carry? I know you don't like all this fightin' an' bloodshed but we don't know what we're goin' to meet out there."

Stepping away from Billy, he swept up a sword that stood in a corner. Unsheathing it, he balanced it in the palm of his hand, gazing along the blade and into a mirror, studying his reflection. It was many years since he had last held such a weapon, and he had never used one in self defense.

"You ain't takin' that."

Turning on the balls of his feet, he grasped the hilt of the sword, the tip of it hovering before Billy's throat. That stagehand held up his hands, a look of shock on his face. "Any more of that an' you'll be gettin' me all 'ot an' bothered."

Chuckling, Cedo sheathed the sword and clipped it to his belt. It felt good, a satisfying weight. "What do you have?" he asked, turning back to Billy.

"Well." Billy stepped back out into the hallway, only to return with a trunk. A trunk that had once been fastened tightly shut, the hinges and lock now splintered and open.

Throwing open the lid, Billy tugged on a tray. Several trays, all of them loaded with an array of guns and ammunition concertinaed out, Cedo's eyes widening as he peered at them.

"An' that's not the only one," Billy said proudly, hands on his hips and chest puffed out. "There's 'undreds of 'em down there, in 'is bunker. An' I can bet you there's some other crazy weapons down there." He gestured toward the open case. "Take your pick."

Selecting a pair of pistols, Cedo picked up the leather harness. Draping it around his waist, he deftly hid them in the small of his back. As if they might bite, he picked up the cold, metal bullets, turning them over in his hands.

"You know, they ain't goin' to kill you unless they're in the gun. Now, take what you can carry. You don't know when we might need more an' if we're goin' to be able to get it."

Picking several small boxes from the trays, Cedo looked up to Billy. "Did you find any money?"

"I'm still lookin'." Billy sighed and leaned against a wall, face sprinkled with dust. "'Ave you called the bank? 'E 'as to 'ave some kind of account."

"I am sure he does." Cedo stacked the boxes to one side. "But I very much doubt that they will release the money to me."

Billy sagged against the wall. "Do you 'ave an account?"

"Billy." Cedo desperately bit his tongue against the insults that he wanted to toss toward his friend. "The last time I had a bank account was when I was a child. I withdrew all of the money when my mother disappeared. I am not the kind of person to whom the bank would give an account."

"We will find something. Go back to the bunker and see what you can find. I highly doubt that Erus kept all of his money in the banks. I get the feeling that he would not have trusted them."

"'Ave you found anythin'?" Their voices echoed through the corridors and doors of the underground rooms.

Peeling the carpet from beneath the table of the cabinet room, Cedo gave a frustrated groan as he came against nothing more than cold stone. Rapping his knuckles against it confirmed that it was as solid as it looked.

"No!" he called back, voice bouncing from one wall to the next until it found the ears of his friend. "Nothing in here!"

There was a brief pause before the reply came: "'ave you checked the walls?"

Cedo closed his eyes, exhausted. "Yes! I have tried the walls. And the ceiling. And anywhere else he might possibly have hidden it."

Chilled silence fell over him, the kind of silence that bore tales of horrors untold. Horrors that faded from his mind to be replaced by a chuckle when his reply arrived: "All right , all right . No need to be gettin' shirty with me."

Turning into the grand kitchen, he found Billy sitting amid an array of boxes and tins, eyes startled behind a layer of grime.

"Nothin' in 'ere. But we'll be dinin' like kings if we make it down 'ere." Getting to his feet Billy stood, hands resting at his hips. "There's one last place to check."

With his stomach churning, Cedo nodded, knowing where Billy meant. They had searched the strange rooms from top to bottom, unearthing a magnitude of different items, all of them either designed to sustain or destroy life.

Striding through the still rooms, they found themselves standing between the two locked doors. Cedo stood back and watched as Billy ran for the door on the left, crashing a sturdy shoulder into it. The door creaked and buckled before the lock splintered and gave way.

Stepping into the darkness, Cedo ran his fingers over the wall, eventually finding a flat panel of metal. As with the rest of the bunker, bright electric lights burst into life and he found himself stepping down into a small antechamber. Before him was another door and to the right of that was a neatly laid desk. To the left of the door were a pair of high-backed chairs.

Turning the brass handle of the second door, his breath taken away as he stepped into the vast room.

It was immense with a desk standing in the center. Much like the study above ground, the walls were lined with shelves of books and papers while he walked upon finely woven carpet. To the left of him were two more doors, both of them as firmly closed as the ones he had just walked through. Above him chandeliers tinkled, casting their bright glow over them. A low whistle broke the air before Billy stopped beside him.

"'E knows what he wants don't 'e? I'm takin' a closer look."

Before he could stop him, Billy was gone, striding across the spacious room and to the door in the far left corner. A moment later and there was an excited cry, "You 'ave to see this!"

Chasing his friend's footsteps, Cedo was stunned once more as he found himself standing in a bedroom that was even larger than the office. The room was dominated by a great bed, semi-opaque fabrics hanging from the four great posts that touched the high ceiling. Chandeliers hung at the four points of the bed and rich tapestries were draped over the walls, illuminating the rich tapestries that hung from the walls. One wall was covered with a mirror, while another two doors punctuated the wall beyond the bed.

"Which door do you want?" Billy asked. "Behind one door might be your future. Behind the other... death."

Cedo smiled, appreciating Billy's efforts to lift the heavy atmosphere. "I will take the right one. Might tell me my future."

Tentatively, he approached the door. Anything could lay beyond it; he was sure that the house had not yet relinquished all of its secrets. Opening the door, he felt for the small, metal plate that was prevalent throughout the subterranean bunker.

Instead, his fingers brushed against a panel of small buttons and, after a moment of indecisiveness, he pushed one. Somewhere in the darkness there was a creaking, a grinding of wheels and gears and Cedo hurriedly pressed another button, skin shivering at the sound. The button caused bright lights to flicker to life, lighting a long, narrow room.

"Billy..." Breath dashed from his body, he stepped into the room, admiring the rows of clothes that hung from tracks in the ceiling.

"'e's plannin' on stayin' down 'ere for *years*," breathed Billy.

"Not just him." Cedo's voice mirrored Billy's. Reaching for the panel of buttons, Cedo pressed one, and the tracks moved, lowering a railing of clothes to the floor. Lifting a white linen suit from it, he held it against himself, taken aback by how perfectly it was crafted to fit him. Walking further along the rail, he collected a hanger of worker's clothes and turned to Billy.

"We are going to be here as well."

Billy's eyes widened as he took the hanger from Cedo, turning them over before holding them against his body. A shiver of shock and excitement raced along Cedo's spine, the enormity of what had happened, and what was to come.

"It means he accepts you."

Billy studied the garments, blue eyes growing misty. "I don't know what to say."

"Then say nothing. At least until later. Time is of the essence and we must find this money for, without it, we will surely fail before we have begun."

"You're right." Billy returned the hanger to the rail. "Let's go take a look at the rest of this place. See if we can find somethin'."

Reaching to switch off the light, Billy pressed one of the buttons, the grating sound beginning once more, the floor rumbling beneath their feet. Jumping from the room, they turned in shock to see the floor at the far end of the closet rising. For a few moments it moved as its watchers gripped the door frame to keep their balance.

When the grinding and grating stopped, Billy gave a low whistle and stepped toward the large metal box." Now that's clever."

Cedo closed in on it. "How much...?"

"Millions an' millions an' millions of guineas." Billy whistled and knelt before it, fingers twisting the dials. "Booby trapped?"

"Most definitely."

"Impossible to break into?"

"Definitely."

Looking over his shoulder, Billy grinned, face alight with the fire of a challenge. "Better get to work then."

"Billy, you can't."

"Street scum, remember. That's what I am. An' street

scum know 'ow to get into things."

Pressing his ear to the safe, Billy set to work, leaving Cedo to anxiously watch. Back and forth went the several dials, clattering and clicking, Billy muttering to himself before he tried something else. After several minutes, there was a loud thud from deep within the safe.

Looking over the dials, Billy watched him. "It's all right , Cedo, mate. That was just one of the safety devices. 'eavy weight by the sounds of it. Probably to crush the 'ands of anyone who tries to break in."

Billy carried on working, listening attentively. After what seemed like an age there was one final, ground-shaking thud before the door swung open.

There was no explosion, no sudden imploding of the safe. Just a blissful silence. Even Billy had been stunned to silence, kneeling still before the open door. Crawling behind him, Cedo rested his chin on the blond man's shoulder. It took a second of studying the interior of the elusive box before they both burst out into riotous laughter.

For there, stacked to the roof of the metal box, were neat bricks of bank notes and bonds, jewelry and notebooks.

An hour later, Cedo assembled the house staff. Cook and her kitchen staff, Mrs. Sugden and her servants, Mr. Morris and the young men who helped him tend to the house and garden, Mr. Turnbull and the grooms. All of them looked to Billy and him with expectant eyes.

Taking a deep breath, Cedo straightened his back. "I want you all, please, to remain here. Please keep caring for the house as you always have done. Care for it, and for each other. Do what you need to. We will return, although when, we do not yet know. Nor do we know in what state or situation we will return. We do not know whether we will have Erus with us. We will try and send word when we are returning, but I cannot make any promises. Think of us often, as we will think of you. This is our home, the home that all of us share."

Fingers touched his wrist and he looked to Billy, the blond giving a quick nod. Returning his gaze to those he had lived and worked among for so long. "We must go and, in doing so, bid you farewell, at least for the moment."

Her face pale, cook stepped forward and pressed a box bound in brown paper to his hands. Her arms stretched around him, pulling him to her generous bosom, and he returned the gesture.

"Take care of yourself, Cedo. You've proved yourself to be far stronger and far braver than any of us ever thought you to be."

The words caused a lump to rise in his throat and tears to sting his eyes. It took all of his effort to thank her. As they pulled apart, each member of staff stepped forward to embrace or shake hands with him and Billy, hushed words of encouragement passing between them. Finally they were pushed toward the waiting carriage, two steamer trunks lashed to the roof, the driver giving them a nod.

Opening the door, Billy turned to him, a confident grin on his face, eyes sparkling with the adventure that lay before them. "Ready for the adventure of your life, Cedo, mate?"

Heaving himself up into the brougham, he looked down to Billy, noting his own look of expectation in the blue eyes before him. "As ready as I will ever be."

Laughing, Billy pulled himself in, crashing into one of the seats and tugging Cedo down with him. Clenching one hand into a fist, he thumped the roof of the carriage. "Let's go!"

END.

CPSIA information can be obtained at www.ICGtesting.com
Printed in the USA
LVOW111040210512

282607LV00001B/3/P